Peter Tremayne is the fiction pseudonym of a well-known authority on the ancient Celts, who utilises his knowledge of the Brehon law system and 7th-century Irish society to create a new concept in detective fiction.

Sister Fidelma made her first appearance in 1993 in short stories. This is her fourth appearance in novel form. Peter Tremayne's previous Sister Fidelma mysteries, ABSOLUTION BY MURDER, SHROUD FOR THE ARCHBISHOP and SUFFER LITTLE CHILDREN are also available from Headline and have received the following praise:

'The Sister Fidelma stories take us into a world that only an author steeped in Celtic history could recreate so vividly – and one which no other crime novelist has explored before. Make way for a unique lady detective going where no one has gone before' Peter Haining

'Definitely an Ellis Peters competitor ... the background detail is marvellous' *Evening Standard*

'I believe I have a *tendresse* for Sister Fidelma. Ingeniously plotted ... subtly paced ... written with conviction, a feel for the time, and a chill air of period authenticity. A series to cultivate' Jack Adrian

'A triumph! Tremayne uses many real characters and events as background ... bringing the ancient world to life ... The novels are admirable' *Mystery Scene*

'A fast-moving whodunnit thriller ... Unputdownable' *Irish Democrat*

'Sister Fidelma ... promises to be one of the most intriguing new characters in 1990s detective fiction' *Book & Magazine Collector*

The Subtle Serpent

A Sister Fidelma Mystery

Peter Tremayne

HEADLINE

First published in 1996
by HEADLINE BOOK PUBLISHING

First published in paperback in 1996
by HEADLINE BOOK PUBLISHING

10 9 8 7 6 5

ISBN 0 7472 5286 6

Printed and bound in Great Britain

HEADLINE BOOK PUBLISHING
A division of Hodder Headline PLC
338 Euston Road
London NW1 3BH

For Penny and David Durell of Beál na Carraige, Beara, West Cork, in appreciation of their warm and generous hospitality and Penny's advice.

'Now the serpent was more subtle than any beast of the field which the Lord God had made.'

Genesis 3:1

HISTORICAL NOTE

The *Annála Ulaidh*, the Annals of Ulster, are one of the great chronicles of Ireland, compiled in 1498, from earlier sources, by Cathal Mac Magnusa, the archdeacon of Clogher. Other scribes continued the annals down to the Seventeenth Century when the chronicle was used as one of the prime sources for the compilation of the *Annála Ríoghachta Éireann*, now better known as the 'Annals of the Four Masters', compiled between 1632–1636 by a number of historians led by Micheál Ó Cléirigh.

Against the year AD 666, for the month of January, there is an entry which starts: 'A mortality in Ireland. The battle of Áine between the Arada and the Uí Fidgenti . . .'

This is the story of the events leading up to that conflict at Cnoc Áine, now called Knockainey, two miles west of Hospital, Co. Limerick, and of Fidelma's role in them.

Previous stories have demonstrated some of the differences between the Seventh Century Irish Church, which is now generally called the Celtic Church, and Rome. Much of its liturgy and philosophies were different. It has already been made clear that the concept of celibacy among the religious was not a popular one at this time either in the 'Celtic Church' or in the Roman Church. It must be remembered that in Fidelma's era many religious houses frequently contained both sexes and they often married, raising their children in the service of the Faith. Even abbots and bishops could and did marry at this period. The appreciation of this fact is essential to an understanding of Fidelma's world.

Allowing that most readers will find Seventh Century Ireland a pretty unfamiliar place, I have provided a sketch map of the kingdom of Muman. I have maintained this name rather than the anachronistic term which was formed by adding the Norse *stadr* to Muman in the Ninth Century AD which produces the modern name of Munster. As many

Seventh Century Irish personal names may also be unfamiliar, I have, as a means of assistance, included a list of principal characters.

Lastly, readers will remember that Fidelma operates in the ancient Irish social system with its laws, the Laws of the Fénechus, more popularly known now as the Brehon Laws (from *breaitheamh* = a judge). She is a qualified advocate of the law courts, a position which was not at all unusual for women in Ireland at this time.

PRINCIPAL CHARACTERS

Sister Fidelma of Kildare, a *dálaigh* or advocate of the law courts of seventh-century Ireland

Brother Eadulf, a Saxon monk from Seaxmund's Ham, in the land of the South Folk

Ross, captain of a coastal *barc* or sailing vessel

Odar, his helmsman

At the Abbey of The Salmon of the Three Wells

Abbess Draigen

Sister Síomha, the *rechtaire* or steward of the abbey

Sister Brónach, the *doirseór* or doorkeeper of the abbey

Sister Lerben, a member of the community

Sister Berrach, a handicapped member of the community

Sister Comnat, the librarian

Sister Almu, assistant to the librarian

At the fortress of Dún Boí

Adnár, *bó-aire*, or local chieftain

Brother Febal, *anam-chara* or soul-friend to Adnár

Olcán, the son of Gulban the Hawk-Eyed, chieftain of the Beara

Torcán, son of Eoganán, prince of the Uí Fidgenti and guest of Adnár

Beccan, chief Brehon, or judge, of the Corco Loígde

Brother Cillín of Mullach

Máil, warrior of the Loígde

Barr, a farmer

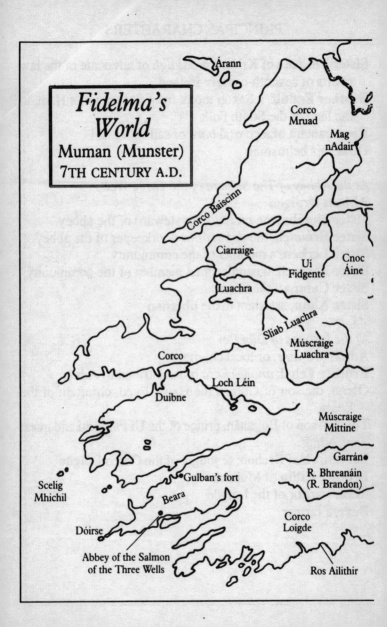

Fidelma's
World
Muman (Munster)
7TH CENTURY A.D.

Árann

Corco
Mruad

Mag
nAdair

Corco Baiscinn

Ciarraige

Uí
Fidgente

Cnoc
Áine

Luachra

Sliab Luachra

Múscraige
Luachra

Corco

Loch Léin

Duibne

Múscraige
Mittine

Garrán

Gulban's fort

R. Bhreanáin
(R. Brandon)

Scelig
Mhichil

Beara

Corco
Loígde

Dóirse

Abbey of the Salmon
of the Three Wells

Ros Ailithir

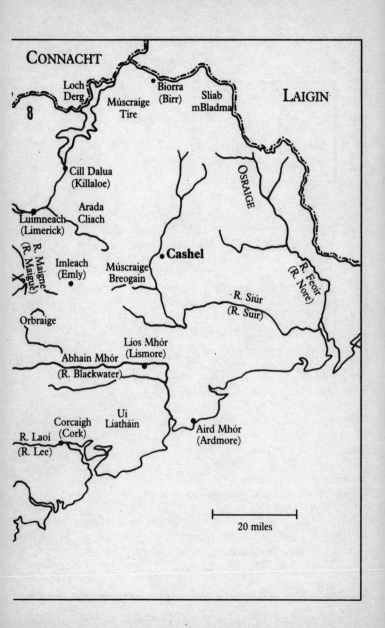

Chapter One

The gong was struck twelve times, its vibration rousing Sister Brónach from her contemplation. Then she heard the gong being struck once again; a single, clear, sharp note. She sighed as she recognised the lateness of the hour and, rising swiftly from her knees before a statue of the Christ in His Suffering, she genuflected. It was an automatic motion, hastily made without thought or meaning, before she turned and made her way from the *duirthech*, the wooden chapel of the abbey.

In the stone-flagged corridor outside the doors of the chapel, she paused as her ears detected the curious shuffling of leather-soled sandals on the stone. Round the far corner, along the gloomy passageway, which was lit by smoky candles of fat, fixed in their iron holders to the walls, came a procession of dark robed and cowled figures, walking two by two. The hooded figures of the sisters, led by the imposing, tall figure of the matriarch of their order, seemed like a line of wraiths haunting the dim corridor. The sisters of the community of The Salmon of the Three Wells, a euphemism for the Christ, shuffled along with heads bowed; no one looked up as they passed Sister Brónach, who was now standing to the side of the open door to the chapel. Not even the Abbess Draigen acknowledged her presence. The sisters proceeded, without speaking, into the chapel for the midday prayers. The last of the sisters paused only to turn and close the door behind the procession.

Sister Brónach had waited, with hands folded before her

1

and head respectfully bent, as they passed her by. Only when the chapel door thudded softly closed behind them did she raise her head. It was plain to see why Sister Brónach bore her name. Her countenance was, indeed, sorrowful. The middle-aged religieuse was never known to smile. In fact, she was never known to demonstrate any emotion, her features seemed permanently engraved in lines of doleful meditation. There was an irreverent saying among her fellow religieuses that if Brónach the Sorrowful ever smiled it would herald a 'second coming' of the Saviour.

For five years Brónach had been the *doirseór*, the door-keeper, of the community which had been founded by the Blessed Necht the Pure over three generations before. The foundation was perched on a lonely southern peninsula of the kingdom of Muman, the south-westerly of the five kingdoms of Éireann. It stood at the foot of the mountains, in a small, wooded inlet of the sea. Brónach had joined the community when she was a young, timid and unenterprising woman, thirty years ago. She had sought refuge in the community purely as a means of sanctuary from the harsh and demanding life of her isolated island village. Now, in her middle years, Sister Brónach remained as timid and un-enterprising as ever she had been; content to let her life be governed by the sounding of the gong from the small tower where the time-keeper kept watch on the community's water-clock. The community was famed throughout the kingdom for its remarkable time-keeping. On the sounding of the gong, Sister Brónach would have some task to fulfil in her office as doorkeeper of the community. The office, *doirseór*, sounded consequential but it was no more than a title for a maid of all work. Yet Sister Brónach seemed contented with her lot in life.

The gong had just sounded the hour of midday when it was Sister Brónach's task and duty to draw water from the well and take it to the Abbess Draigen's chambers. After the midday prayers and meal, the abbess liked to bathe in heated water. Therefore, instead of attending the services with the rest of her sisters, Brónach would retreat to draw the water.

Hands folded under her robes, Sister Brónach moved quickly forward, her leather sandals slapping the granite stones which paved the passage from the old wooden chapel, the *duirthech*, or oak house as such churches were always called, and into the main courtyard around which the habitations of the community were built. There had been a flurry of snow earlier that morning but it had already melted into a wet slush causing the paving of the square to be slippery. But she progressed confidently across it, passing the central bronze sundial, mounted on its polished slate plinth.

Although it was a cold, wintry day, the sky was mainly a translucent blue with a pale sun hanging high amidst wisps of straggling clouds. But here and there, along the horizon, low leaden clouds filled with snow hung in patches and Brónach could feel the chill air around the tips of her ears. She pulled her headdress tighter around her head for comfort.

At the end of the abbey courtyard stood a granite high cross, which sanctified the foundation. Brónach passed through a small opening beyond the cross and onto a tiny rocky plateau overlooking the sheltered inlet on which the religious foundation stood. On this natural rocky dais, which stood only ten feet above the stony shoreline of the inlet, from an aperture in the rugged ground, the Blessed Necht had found a gushing spring. She had sanctified the well. It had needed a benediction, for the stories told how it had previously been a spot sacred to the Druids who also drew water from this well.

Sister Brónach walked slowly to the well-head which was now encircled by a small stone wall. Over this the members of the community had constructed a mechanism for lowering a pail into the dark waters, now far below ground level, and then raising it by means of turning a handle which cranked a rope, winding it up and down. Sister Brónach could

3

remember a time when it took two or three of the sisters to raise water from the well whereas, after the mechanism was constructed, even an elderly sister could work it without great hardship.

Sister Brónach paused for a moment in silence as she stood at the well-head and gazed at the surrounding scenery. It was a curiously quiet hour of the day: a period of inexplicable silence when no birds sing, no creatures move and there is a feeling of a suspension of life, a feeling of some expectation; of waiting for something to happen. It was as if nature had suddenly decided to catch its breath. The chill winds had died away and were not even chattering among the tall granite peaks which rose behind the abbey. Sheep still wandered over their rough stone terrain like moving white boulders, while a few sinewy black cattle were gnawing at the short turf. Sister Brónach perceived the hollows of the hills were filled with the mystic blue shadows caused by the hanging clouds.

Not for the first time did Sister Brónach feel a sense of awe at her surroundings and at this mysterious hour of expectant tranquillity. She felt that the world seemed poised as if waiting for the blast of ancient horns which would summon the old gods of Ireland to appear and come striding down from the surrounding snow-peaked mountains. And the long grey granite boulders, which were scattered on the mountain sides, like men lying prone in the crystal light, would suddenly turn into the ancient warrior heroes of past ages; rise up and march behind the gods with their spears and swords and shields, to demand why the old faith and old ways had been forsaken by the children of Éire, the goddess of sovranty and fertility, whose name had been given to this primeval land.

Sister Brónach suddenly swallowed sharply and cast a swift, guilty glance around her, as if her fellow companions in Christ would hear her sacrilegious thoughts. She genuflected swiftly, as if to absolve her sin in thinking about the old, pagan gods. Yet she could not deny the truth of the feeling. Her own mother, peace be on her soul, had refused to hear the word of the Christ and remained firm in her belief in the old ways. Suanach! It was a long time since she had thought about her mother. She wished that she had not, for the thought cut like a sharp anguished blade in her memory even though it was twenty years since Suanach's death. Why had the memory come? Ah yes; she was thinking of the old gods. And this was a moment when, it seemed, the old gods and goddesses were making their presence felt. This was the hour of pagan sadness, a sorrowful echo from the very roots of the people's consciousness; a yearning for times past, a lament for the lost generations of Éire's people.

Far away, she heard the sound of the community's gong; another single stroke, from the watcher of the water-clock.

Sister Brónach started nervously.

A full *pongc*, the Irish unit of time equalling fifteen minutes, had passed since the sounding of the hour for midday prayers. The gong was sounded once to mark the passing of each *pongc*; then each hour was marked by striking the gong for the number of the hour. Every six hours, the *cadar*, or day's quarter, was also marked by an appropriate number of strikes. It was also the time when the watch was changed for no watcher was allowed more than a *cadar* at her onerous task.

Brónach compressed her lips slightly, realising how the Abbess Draigen disliked indolence, and looked round for the pail. It was not in its usual place. It was then that she noticed that the rope was already fully extended into the well. She frowned in annoyance. Someone had taken the pail, placed it on the hook and lowered it into the well but then, for some obscure reason, they had not raised it again but gone away and left the bucket in the bottom of the well. Such forgetfulness was inexcusable.

With a suppressed sigh of irritation, she bent to the handle. It was icy cold to the touch, reminding her of the coldness of the winter day. To her surprise it was hard to turn as if a heavy weight were attached to it. She renewed her efforts by pushing with all her might. It was as if the handle was obstructed in some way. With difficulty, she began to turn the mechanism, winding the rope slowly, so very slowly, upward.

She paused after a while and glanced around hoping that one of her companions was nearby in order that she could request assistance in raising the pail. Never had a pail of water weighed so much as this. Was she ailing? Perhaps she was weakening in some way? No; she surely felt well and as strong as ever she had. She caught a glimpse of the distant, brooding mountains, and shivered. The shiver was not from the cold but from the chill of the superstitious fear that caught at her thoughts. Was God punishing her for heretical contemplation of the old religion?

She glanced anxiously upwards before bending to her task again with a muttered prayer of contrition.

'Sister Brónach!'

An attractive, youthful sister was striding from the community's buildings towards the well.

Sister Brónach groaned inwardly as she recognised the domineering Sister Síomha, who was the *rechtaire*, the steward, of the community and her immediate superior. Unfortunately, Sister Síomha's manner did not match the wide-eyed innocence of her becoming features. Síomha, for all her youth, had the well-founded reputation in the community of being a hard task-master.

Sister Brónach paused again and leaned her weight against the handle to secure it. She returned the disapproving expression of the newcomer with a bland countenance. Sister Síomha halted and gazed at her with a sniff of censure.

'You are late gathering the water for our abbess, Sister Brónach,' chided the younger sister. 'She has even had to send me to find you and remind you of the hour. *Tempori parendum.*'

Brónach's expression did not change.

'I am aware of the hour, sister,' she replied in a subdued tone. To be told that 'one must yield to time' when her life was governed continuously by the sounding of the gong of the water-clock was irritating even to her timorous personality. Making such a comment was as near to rebellion as Sister Brónach could get. 'However, I am having trouble raising the pail. Something appears to be restricting it.'

Sister Síomha sniffed again as if she believed that Sister Brónach was trying to find an excuse for her tardiness.

'Nonsense. I used the well earlier this morning. There was nothing wrong with the mechanism. It is easy enough to raise the pail.'

She moved forward, her body language pushing the elder sister aside without making contact. Her delicate yet strong hands gripped the bar of the handle and pushed. An expression of astonishment passed momentarily over her face as she encountered the obstruction.

'You are right,' she conceded wonderingly. 'Perhaps both of us can work it. Come, push when I say.'

Together they put their weight into the task. Slowly, with much exertion, they commenced to turn the handle, pausing every so often to rest a moment. Clouds of their exerted breaths drifted from their mouths to vanish in the crystal cold air. The makers of the mechanism had constructed a brake so that when the rope was raised fully, the brake could be applied in order that a single person could then take the filled pail from the hook without fear that the weight would send the bucket crashing back into the well. Both sisters strained and pulled until the rope reached the maximum point of raising and Sister Síomha put on the brake.

As she stood back, Sister Síomha saw a curious expression on the usually doleful countenance of her companion. Never had she seen such a look of wide-eyed terror as Sister Brónach displayed as she stood gazing towards the well-head behind Síomha. Indeed, never had she seen an expression other th one of mournful obedience on the usually graven features of the middle-aged sister. Sister Síomha turned slowly wondering what Brónach was staring at in such a horror-struck fashion.

What she saw made her raise a hand to her mouth as if to suppress a cry of fear.

Hanging by one ankle, which was secured to the rope on which the pail was usually suspended, was a naked female body. It was still glistening white from its immersion in the icy water of the deep well. The body was hanging head downwards so that the upper part of the torso, the head and shoulders, were beyond their view being hidden in the well-head. But it was obvious from the pale, dead flesh of those parts of the body they could see, flesh smeared with cloying red mud, apparently not washed off in its immersion in the well water, and covered with innumerable scratch-like wounds, that it was a corpse.

Sister Síomha genuflected slowly.

'God between us and all evil!' she whispered. Then she made a move towards it. 'Quickly, Sister Brónach, help me cut down this poor unfortunate.'

Sister Síomha moved to the well-head and peered down, hands reaching forward to swing the body out of the well. Then, with a sharp cry which she could not stifle, she turned away, her face becoming a mask of shocked surprise.

Curious, Sister Brónach moved forward and peered into the well-head. In the semi-gloom of the well she saw that where the head of the body should have been was nothing. The body had been decapitated. What remained of the neck and shoulders were stained dark with blood.

She turned away suddenly and retched, trying to subdue her compulsion to nausea.

After a moment or so, Sister Brónach realised that Síomha was apparently too stunned to make any further decisions. Steeling herself, Brónach reached forward, quelling her revulsion, and attempted to pull the body towards the edge of the well. But the task was too great for her to manage on her own.

She glanced swiftly to Sister Síomha.

'You will have to help me, sister. If you grip the body, I will cut the rope that holds the unfortunate,' she instructed gently.

Swallowing hard, Sister Síomha sought to regain her composure, nodded briefly and unwillingly grasped the cold, wet flesh around the waist. She could not help the expression of repugnance as the chill, lifeless flesh touched her own.

Using her small knife, such as all the sisters carried, Sister Brónach cut the bonds which fastened the ankle of the corpse to the well rope. Then she helped Sister Síomha haul the headless body over the side of the well's small surrounding wall and onto the ground. The two religieuses stood for several moments staring down at the corpse, unsure of what next to do.

'A prayer for the dead, sister,' muttered Brónach uneasily. Together they intoned a prayer, the words meaningless as they vocalised the ritual. At the end of it there was a silence for some minutes.

'Who could do such a thing?' whispered Sister Síomha, after a moment or two.

'There is much evil about in the world,' replied Sister Brónach, more philosophically. 'But a more pertinent question would be – who is this poor unfortunate? The body is that of a young woman; why, she can be no more than a girl.'

Sister Brónach succeeded in dragging her eyes away from the bloodied, mangled flesh around where the head should have been. The sight of the gory mess fascinated yet appalled and sickened her. The body was plainly that of a young and previously healthy woman, perhaps scarcely out of puberty. The only other disfigurement, apart from the missing head, was a wound in the chest. There was a bluish bruise on the flesh above the heart and, looking closer, the cutting wound marked where a sharp blade point, or some such implement, had entered the heart. But the wound had long since ceased to bleed.

Sister Brónach forced herself to bend down and reached for one of the arms of the corpse to place them across the body before the stiffening of the flesh made such a task impossible. She suddenly dropped the arm and let out a loud gasp of breath almost as if she had received a blow in the solar plexus.

Startled, Sister Síomha followed the direction of Brónach's outstretched hand, now pointing to the left arm of the corpse. Something was tied around the arm which had been hidden from them by the position of the corpse. It was a length of wood, no more than a stick with notches carved on it. Sister Brónach knew Ogham, the ancient form of Irish writing, when she saw it, though she did not understand the meaning of the characters. Ogham was no longer in general use throughout the five kingdoms for the Latin alphabet was now being adopted as the form of characters in which Irish was written.

In bending forward to examine the wooden stick, however, her eyes caught sight of something clutched in the other hand of the corpse. A small, worn leather thong was wound around the right wrist and travelled into the clenched fist. Sister Brónach had steeled herself again to her task, kneeling beside the body and taking up the small white hands. She could not prise apart the fingers; the stiffening of death had already locked the hand permanently into a fist. Nevertheless, the fingers were splayed just wide enough for her to see that the leather thong was attached to a small metal crucifix and this was what the lifeless right hand was clutching so tightly.

Sister Brónach let out a low groan and glanced across her shoulder to where Sister Síomha was bending, with a fixed expression, to see what had been discovered.

'What can it mean, sister?' Sister Síomha's voice was taut, almost harsh.

10

Sister Brónach's face was grave. She was now fully in control of her features again.

She breathed deeply before replying in a measured tone as she stared down at the poorly wrought crucifix of burnished copper. Obviously no person of rank and wealth would have such a cheap object as this.

'It means that we should now summon Abbess Draigen, good sister. Whoever this poor headless girl was, I believe that she was one of our own. She was a sister of the Faith.'

Far off, in the tiny tower overlooking their community, they could hear the striking of the gong to mark the passing of another time period. The clouds were suddenly thickening and spreading across the sky. Cold flakes of snow were drifting across the mountains again.

Chapter Two

The *Foracha*, the coastal *barc* of Ross of Ros Ailithir, was making a swift passage parallel to the southern coast of the Irish kingdom of Muman. Her sails were full with an icy, cold, easterly wind almost laying the vessel over and whistling among the taut ropes of the rigging, playing on the tightly stretched cordage like harp strings. The day appeared fine, apart from the blustery sea winds swooping down from the distant coastline. A host of sea birds were circling the little ship, beating their wings against the squalls to remain in position, the gulls crying with their curious plaintive wail. Here and there, some hardy cormorants speared into the waves, emerging with their prey, oblivious to the jealous cries of the gulls and storm petrels. And among the sea birds were the species after which the *Foracha* received her name – the guillemots, with their dark brown upper parts and pure white underparts, moving in tight formations to inspect the vessel before wheeling back to their densely-packed colonies on the precipitous cliff ledges.

Ross, the captain of the vessel, stood by the steersman at the tiller with feet spaced apart, balancing to the roll as the wind thrust the waves to rush against the ship, heeling her to starboard so that the little *barc* would roll slowly, slowly until it seemed that she was heading for disaster. But then her bow would rise over the wave and plunge downwards, setting her back to the port side. In spite of the rolling motion of the ship, Ross stood without the necessity to clutch any support, forty years of sea-going was enough for him to anticipate every pitch and roll with an automatic adjustment of his weight without moving from the spot. On land, Ross was moody and irritable, but at sea he was in his element and fully alive to all its moods. He became a flesh and blood extension to his swift sailing *barc* and his deep green eyes, reflecting the changing humours of the sea, watched his half-a-dozen crewmen with a cautious approval as they went about their tasks.

His bright eyes never missed a thing, either on sea or in the sky above it. He had already perceived that some of the birds wheeling overhead were rarely to be seen in winter and had ascribed their presence to the mild autumnal weather that had only recently given way to the winter coldness.

Ross was a short, stocky man with greying, close-cropped hair, and his skin was tanned by the sea winds almost to the colour of nut. He was a man with a dour humour and always ready with a loud bellow when he was displeased.

A tall sailor, caressing the tiller in his gnarled hands, suddenly narrowed his eyes and glanced across to where Ross was standing.

'Captain . . .' he began.

'I see her, Odar,' returned Ross before he had even finished. 'I've been watching her this last half hour.'

Odar, the steersman, swallowed as he regarded his captain with surprise. The object of their conversation was an ocean-going ship with tall masts which was now a mile or so distant. It had, as Ross had indicated, been visible for some time to the smaller *barc*. But it was only in these last few minutes that the steersman had become aware that something was not right about the ship. It was under full sail and was riding very high out of the water. Not much ballast in her, Odar, the steersman had thought. But the main curiosity was that its course was erratic. In fact, twice it had changed course in such an unconventional and capricious manner that the steersman had believed that it was going to capsize. He had also noticed that the topsail of the ship seemed badly fixed and was swinging in all manner of directions. It was then that he had decided to bring the matter to the attention of his captain.

Ross, however, was making no idle boast when he said that he had been watching the ship for half-an-hour. Almost from the first time that he had noticed the other ship he was aware that it was either sailed by poor seamen or there was something wrong on board. The sails filled and deflated as each unpredictable wind caught them with no one on board seeming to correct the ship's heading.

'The way she is heading, captain,' muttered Odar, 'she'll be piling up on the rocks soon.'

Ross did not reply for he had already made the same deduction. He knew that a mile or so ahead were some semi-submerged rocks, their black granite rising among streams of sea foam which poured down the sides as the seas broke over them with a noise of thunder. Moreover, Ross knew that around the granite bastions was a line of reefs under water over which a small draught vessel such as his *barc* could easily pass but that the sea-going ship to his port had no chance.

Ross gave a low sigh.

'Stand by to turn towards her, Odar,' he grunted to the steersman and then he yelled to his crew. 'Ready to loose the main sail!'

With deft precision, the *Foracha* swung from its course to a new tack with the wind full at her back so that it fairly flew across the waves towards the large ship. It cut the distance with great rapidity until the *barc* was but a cable's distance away and then Ross moved forward to the rail, cupping his hands to his mouth.

'*Hóigh!*' he yelled. '*Hóigh!*'

There was no responding cry from the now towering, dark vessel.

Suddenly, without warning, the fickle wind changed

direction. The tall, dark bow of the sea-going ship was turned directly towards them, the sails filled and it was bearing down on them like an infuriated sea monster.

Ross yelled to the steersman: 'Hard to starboard!'

It was all he could do as he helplessly watched the larger vessel bearing remorselessly down.

With agonising slowness the bows of the *Foracha* dragged unwillingly over and the great ship went scraping along the portside of the vessel, banging against the little ship so that she heeled and wallowed and was left bobbing in the wake of the passing vessel.

Ross stood shaking angrily as he gazed at the stern of the vessel. The wind had suddenly died away and the larger ship's sails had deflated as it slid slowly to a halt.

'May the captain of that vessel never see the cuckoo nor the corncrake again! May the sea-cat get him! May he die roaring! May he fester in his grave!'

The curses poured out of Ross as he stood enraged, shaking a fist at the ship.

'A death without a priest to him in a town without clergy...'

'Captain!' The voice that interrupted him in full flow was feminine, quiet but authoritative. 'I think God has heard enough curses for the moment and knows you to be upset. What is the cause of this profanity?'

Ross wheeled round. He had forgotten all about his passenger who had, until this moment, been resting below in the *Foracha*'s main cabin.

A tall religieuse now stood on the stern deck by Odar, the steersman, regarding him with a slight frown of disapproval. She was a young woman, tall but with a well-proportioned figure, a fact not concealed even by the sombreness of her dress nor even the beaver-fur edged woollen cloak that almost enshrouded her. Rebellious strands of red hair streaked from beneath her headdress, whipping in the sea-breeze. Her pale-skinned features were attractive and her eyes were bright but it was difficult to discern whether they were blue or green, so changeable with emotion were they.

Ross gestured defensively towards the other ship.

'I regret that I have offended you, Sister Fidelma,' he muttered. 'But that ship nearly sank us.'

Ross knew that his passenger was not simply a religieuse but was sister to Colgú, king of Muman. She was, as he knew from past experience, a *dálaigh*, an advocate of the law courts of the five kingdoms of Éireann, whose degree was that of *anruth* only one grade below the highest qualification which the universities and ecclesiastical colleges could bestow.

'You have not offended me, Ross,' replied Fidelma with a grim little smile. 'Though your cursing might have offended God. I find cursing is often a waste of energy when something more positive might be done.'

Ross nodded reluctantly. He always felt uncomfortable with women. That was why he had chosen a life at sea. He had tried marriage once but that had ended with his wife deserting him and the necessity of having to care for a daughter. Even his daughter, who was now about Sister Fidelma's own age, had not made him feel any easier dealing with the opposite sex. Moreover, he felt particularly uncomfortable with this young woman whose quiet, authoritative demeanour made him feel sometimes like a child whose behaviour was constantly under judgment. The worst thing, he realised, was that the religieuse was right. Cursing the unknown captain was of no help to anyone.

'What is the cause of this?' pressed Fidelma.

Ross swiftly explained, gesturing to where the great sea-going vessel was now becalmed in this brief period of contrary winds.

Fidelma examined the ship with curiosity.

'There does not seem to be any sign of movement aboard her, Ross,' she pointed out. 'Did I hear you hail her?'

'I did so,' replied Ross, 'but received no answer.'

In fact, Ross himself had only just come to the conclusion that anyone on board the ship could not have failed to see his *barc* or return his hail. He turned to Odar. 'See if you can take us alongside,' he grunted.

The steersman nodded and slowly brought the little *barc*'s bows around, praying that the winds would continue to moderate until he was in position. Odar was a taciturn man whose skill was a by-word along the coasts of Muman. It was a short while before they bumped hulls against the taller vessel and Ross's men grabbed for the ropes that were hanging down her sides.

Sister Fidelma leant against the far rail of the *Foracha*, out of the way, gazing up at the taller ship with dispassionate interest.

'A Gaulish merchant ship, by the cut of her,' she called to Ross. 'Isn't the tops'l set dangerously?'

Ross cast her a glance of reluctant approval. He had ceased to be surprised by the knowledge that the young advocate displayed. This was the second time that he had acted as her transport and he was now used to the fact that she possessed knowledge beyond her years.

'She's from Gaul, right enough,' he agreed. 'The heavy timbers and rigging are peculiar to the ports of Morbihan. And you are right; that tops'l isn't properly secured at all.'

He glanced up anxiously at the sky.

'Forgive me, sister. We must get aboard and see what is amiss before the wind comes up again.'

Fidelma made a gesture of acquiescence with her hand.

Ross told Odar to leave the helm to another crewman and accompany him with a couple of his men. They swung easily over the side and scaled the ropes, disappearing up on deck. Fidelma stayed on the deck of the *barc* waiting. She could hear their voices calling up on the deck of the bigger vessel. Then she saw Ross's crewmen speeding aloft to lower the sails of the ship obviously in case the wind sprung up again. It was not long before Ross appeared at the side of the ship and swung himself over, dropping cat-like to the deck of the *Foracha*. Fidelma saw that there was a bewildered expression on his face.

'What is it, Ross?' she demanded. 'Is there some sickness aboard?'

Ross took a step towards her. As well as his expression of perplexity, did she detect a lurking fear in his eyes?

'Sister, would you mind coming up on the Gaulish ship? I need you to examine it.'

Fidelma frowned slightly.

'I am no seaman, Ross. Why would I need to examine it? Is there illness on board?' she repeated.

'No, sister,' Ross hesitated a moment. He seemed very uneasy. 'In fact ... there is no one on board.'

Fidelma blinked, the only expression of her surprise. Silently, she followed Ross to the side of the ship.

'Let me go up first, sister, and then I will be able to haul you up on this line.'

He indicated a rope in which he tied a loop, as he was speaking.

'Just put your foot in the loop and hold on when I say.'

He turned and scrambled up the line to the deck of the merchant ship. Fidelma was hauled up the short distance without mishap. Indeed, there was no one on the deck of the ship apart from Ross and his crewmen who had now secured the sails. One of Ross's men was stationed at the tiller to keep the ship under control. Fidelma looked about curiously at the deserted but orderly and well scrubbed decks.

'Are you sure there is no one on board?' she asked with faint incredulity in her voice.

Ross shook his head.

'My men have looked everywhere, sister. What is the explanation of this mystery?'

'I do not have sufficient information to make even a guess, my friend,' replied Fidelma, continuing to survey the clean, tidy appearance of the ship. Even the ropes seemed neatly coiled. 'Is there nothing out of place? No sign of an enforced abandonment of the ship?'

Again Ross shook his head.

'There is a small boat still secure at the amidships,' he indicated. 'From the first moment I saw her, I saw that the ship was riding high out of the water so there is no sign of any danger of her sinking. She is not holed, so far as I can make out. No, there is no indication that she was abandoned from fear of sinking. And all the sails were set straight apart from the tops'l. So what happened to the crew?'

'What about that tops'l?' Fidelma asked. 'It was badly secured and could have been ripped off in a heavy wind.'

'But no cause to abandon ship,' Ross replied.

Fidelma glanced up at the mast where the topsail had now been stowed. She frowned and called Odar who had taken in the sails.

'What is that cloth up there, there on the rigging twenty feet above us?' she asked.

Odar glanced at Ross quickly before replying.

'I do not know, sister. Do you want me to fetch it?'

It was Ross who instructed him.

'Up you go, Odar.'

The man leapt up the rigging with practised ease and was down in a moment holding out a strip of torn material.

'A nail in the mast had caught it, sister,' he said.

Fidelma saw that it was simply a piece of linen. A torn strip of material that could have come from a shirt. What interested her was that part of it was stained with blood and it was a comparatively fresh stain for it was not fully dried brown but still retained a distinctness of colour.

Fidelma looked thoughtfully upwards for a moment, walking to the base of the rigging and peering towards the furled topsail. Then, as she went to turn away, her eye caught something else. The smeared dried blood imprint of what was clearly a palm on the railing. She stared down at it thoughtfully, noting that whoever had made that imprint must have been holding the rail from the seaward side of it. She sighed quietly and placed the torn piece of linen in her *marsupium*, the large purse which she always carried on her waist belt.

'Take me to the captain's cabin,' instructed Fidelma, seeing there was nothing to be learnt above decks.

Ross turned aft to the main cabin underneath the raised stern deck. In fact, there were two cabins there. Both were neatly arranged. The bunks were tidy and in one of the cabins, plates and cups were set in place on the table, slightly jumbled. Ross, seeing her glance, explained that they would be jumbled by the erratic motion of the vessel as it swung without a helmsman before the wind.

'It is a wonder that it has not already crashed on the rocks before now,' he added. 'God knows how long it has been blown across the seas without a hand to guide it. And it is under full sail, so a hefty wind could have easily capsized it with no one to shorten or reef the sails.'

Fidelma compressed her lips thoughtfully for a moment.

'It is almost as if the crew has simply vanished,' Ross added. 'As if they were spirited away...'

Fidelma arched a cynical eyebrow.

'Such things do not happen in the real world, Ross. There is a logical explanation for all things. Show me the rest of the ship.'

Ross led the way from the cabin.

Below decks, the soft, pungent salt tang of the sea air gave place to a more oppressive odour which evolved from years of men living and eating together in a confined space, for the space between decks was so narrow that Fidelma had to bend to prevent her head knocking against the beams. The stale stench of sweat, the bitter sweet smell of urine, not dispersed by even salt water scrubbing, permeated the area where the crew had been confined while not performing their tasks above deck. The only thing to be said about it was that it was warmer down here than up on the cold wind-swept decks.

However, the crews' quarters were fairly tidy although not as neat as the cabins that were presumably used by the officers of the ship. Still, there was no sign of disorder or hasty departure. The stores were stowed meticulously.

From the crew's quarters, Ross led the way into the central hold of the ship. Another smell caught Fidelma's senses, it being a rapid change of sensual stimulus from the stale bitter odour of the crew's quarters. Fidelma halted, frowning, trying to place the perfume that assailed her nostrils. A combining of several spices, she thought, but something else dominated it. An aroma of stale wine. She peered around in the gloom of the hold. It appeared to be empty.

Ross was fiddling with some tinder and flint and struck a spark to light an oil lamp so that they could see the interior better. He exhaled softly.

'As I said, the ship was riding high out of the water which made her doubly unwieldy before the weather. I expected that we would find an empty hold.'

'Why would there be no cargo on board?' Fidelma demanded as she peered round.

Ross was clearly puzzled.

'I have no idea, sister.'

'This merchant ship is Gaulish, you say?'

The seaman nodded.

'Could the ship have sailed from Gaul without a cargo?'

'Ah,' Ross saw her point immediately. 'No, it would have sailed with a cargo. And likewise it would have picked up a cargo in an Irish port for the return journey.'

'So we have no idea when the crew deserted her? She might have been on her way to Ireland or on her way back to Gaul? And it could well be that her cargo was removed when her crew deserted her?'

Ross scratched his nose reflectively.

'They are good questions but we have no answers.'

Fidelma took a few paces into the empty hold and began to study it in the gloom.

'What does a ship like this usually carry?'

'Wine, spices and other things not so easily come by in our country, sister. See, those are racks for the wine kegs but they are all empty.'

She followed his outstretched hand. There was, together with the empty racks, a certain amount of debris, of pieces of broken wood and, lying on its side, was a iron-shod cartwheel, with one of the spokes broken. There was something else which caused her to frown a little. It was a large cylinder of wood around which was tightly wound a coarse thick thread. The cylinder was two feet in length and some six inches in diameter. She bent down and touched the thread and her eyes widened a little. It was a skein of animal gut.

'What is this, Ross?' she asked.

The sailor bent, examined it and shrugged.

'I have no idea. It has no use aboard a ship. And it is not a means of fastening anything. The skein is too pliable, it would stretch if any tension was placed on it.'

Fidelma, still on her knees, had become distracted by something else that she had observed. She was examining patches of brown red clay which seemed to lie on the wooden decking of the hold.

'What is it, sister?' demanded Ross, reaching forward and holding the lamp high.

Fidelma scooped some of it up on her fingers and stared down at it.

'Nothing, I suppose. Just red clay. I presume it was probably trodden from the shore by those who filled the hold. But there seems a great deal of it about this place.'

She rose to her feet and moved across the bare storage area to a hatchway on the far side towards the bows. Suddenly she paused and turned back to Ross.

'There is no way anyone would hide under this deck, is there?' she asked, pointing to the flooring.

Ross grimaced wryly in the gloom.

'Not unless they were a sea rat, sister. There is only the bilge under here.'

'Nonetheless, I think it would be well if every place aboard this vessel were searched.'

'I'll see to it directly,' agreed Ross, accepting her effortless authority without complaint.

'Give me the lamp and I'll continue on.' Fidelma took the lamp from his hand and moved through the hatch into the for'ard area of the ship while Ross, glancing about nervously, for he had all the superstition of a seaman, began calling for one of his crewmen.

Fidelma, holding the lamp before her, found a small flight of steps which passed a cable tier where the anchor of the large vessel was stored. At the top of the stairs were two more cabins, both were empty. They were also tidy. It was then that Fidelma realised what was lacking. Everything was tidy; too tidy for there were no signs of any personal possessions such as must have belonged to the captain, his crew or any person who might have taken passage on the ship. There were no clothes, no shaving tackle, nothing save a pristine ship.

She turned, moved up a short companionway to the deck to seek out Ross. As her hand ran along the polished rail she felt a change in texture against her palm. Before she could investigate she heard someone moving across the deck and calling her name. She continued up into daylight.

Ross was standing near the companionway entrance with a glum face. He saw her at the top of the companionway and came forward.

'Nothing in the bilge, sister, except rats and filth as one would expect. No bodies, that's for sure,' he reported grimly. 'Alive or dead.'

Fidelma was staring down at her palm. It was discoloured with a faint brown texture. She realised what it was immediately. She showed her palm to Ross.

'Dried blood. Split not all that long ago. That's the second patch of blood on this vessel. Come with me.' Fidelma retraced her steps down towards the cabins with Ross close behind. 'Perhaps we should be looking for a body in the cabins below?'

She paused on the stairway and held up her lamp. Blood had certainly been smeared along the rail and there was more dried blood on the steps and some which had splashed against the side walls. It was older than the blood on the linen cloth and on the handrail of the ship.

'There is no sign of blood on the deck,' observed Ross. 'Whoever was hurt must have been hurt on these stairs and moved downwards.'

Fidelma pursed her lips thoughtfully.

'Or else was hurt below and came up here to be met by someone who bound the wound or otherwise prevented the blood from falling to the deck. Still, let us see where the trail leads.'

At the foot of the companionway, Fidelma bent down to examine the decking by the light of the lantern. Her eyes suddenly narrowed and she smothered an exclamation.

'There are more signs of dried blood down here.'

'I do not like this, sister,' muttered Ross, anxiously casting a glance around. 'Perhaps something evil haunts this vessel?'

Fidelma straightened up.

'The only evil here, if evil it be, is human evil,' she chided him.

'A human agency could not spirit away an entire crew and a ship's cargo,' protested Ross.

Fidelma smiled thinly.

'Indeed, they could. And they did not do a perfect job of it for they have left bloodstains which tell us that it was, indeed, a human agency at work. Spirits, evil or otherwise, do not have to shed blood when they wish to destroy humankind.'

She turned, still holding her lantern up, to examine the two cabins adjoining the foot of the companionway.

Either the wounded person, for she presumed the amount

24

of blood had come from someone who had been severely injured, had been gashed with a knife or a sharp instrument at the foot of the companionway or in one of the cabins. She turned into the first one, with Ross unwillingly trailing in her wake.

She paused on the threshold and stood staring around trying to find some clue to the mystery.

'Captain!'

One of Ross's men came clambering down behind them.

'Captain, I've been sent by Odar to tell you that the wind is getting up again and the tide is bearing us towards the rocks.'

Ross opened his mouth to curse but, as his eye caught Fidelma's, he contented himself with a grunt.

'Very well. Get a line on the bow of this vessel and tell Odar to stand by to steer her. I shall tow her into a safe anchorage.'

The man scampered off and Ross turned back to Fidelma.

'Best come off back to the *barc*, sister. It will not be easy to steer this vessel to shore. It will be safer on my ship.'

Fidelma reluctantly turned after him and as she did so her eyes caught something which she had not perceived before. The open cabin door had shielded it from her as she had stood in the cabin. Now, as she turned to go, she saw something unusual hanging from a peg behind the door. Unusual because it was a *tiag liubhair*, a leather book satchel. Fidelma was astonished to see such an item in the cabin of a ship. It was true that the Irish kept their books, not on shelves, but in satchels hung on pegs or racks around the walls of their libraries, each satchel containing one or more manuscript volumes. And such satchels were also generally employed to carry books from place to place. It was always necessary for a missionary priest to have Gospels, offices and other books and so such satchels were also designed to transport them on their missions. The *tiag liubhair* which hung behind the cabin door was one that was commonly slung from the shoulder by a strap.

Fidelma was unaware of Ross now pausing impatiently at the foot of the companionway.

She unhooked the satchel and reached in. Inside there was a small vellum volume.

Suddenly her heart was racing, her mouth dry, and she stood rooted to the spot. The blood pounded in her ears. For a moment or two she thought she was going to pass out. The volume was a small, innocuous looking manuscript book, its vellum leaves bound in heavy calf-leather and embossed with beautiful patterned whirls and circles. Fidelma had recognised that it would be a Missal even before she turned to the title page. She knew also what would be inscribed on that page.

It was now over twelve months since Sister Fidelma had last held this book in her hands. Over twelve months ago, on a warm Roman summer evening, in the herb-scented garden of the Lateran Palace, she had stood holding this little book. It had been the evening before she had left Rome to return home to Ireland. She had handed the book to her friend and companion in adventure, Brother Eadulf of Seaxmund's Ham, from the Saxon land of the South Folk. Brother Eadulf, who had helped her solve the mystery of Abbess Etain's murder at Whitby and later of the murder of Wighard, the archbishop-elect of Canterbury in Rome.

The book which she now held in her hands, in this mysterious abandoned ship, had been her farewell gift to her closest friend and companion. A gift that had meant so much to them in that emotional parting.

Fidelma felt the cabin beginning to rock and turn around her. She tried to still her racing thoughts, to rationalise the awesome dread which she felt choking her lungs. She staggered dizzily backwards and collapsed abruptly onto the bunk.

Chapter Three

'Sister Fidelma! Are you all right?'

Ross's anxious face was peering close to Fidelma's as she opened her eyes. She blinked. She had not really passed out only ... she blinked again and silently rebuked herself for showing weakness. However, the shock was real enough. What was this book, her parting gift to Brother Eadulf in Rome, now doing in the cabin of a deserted Gaulish merchant ship off the coast of Muman? She knew that Eadulf would not part with it so lightly. And if not, then he had been in this cabin. He had been a passenger on this merchant ship.

'Sister Fidelma!'

Ross's voice rose in agitation.

'I am sorry,' Fidelma replied slowly and cautiously stood up. Ross leaned forward to help her.

'Did you feel giddy?' queried the sailor.

She shook her head. She again rebuked herself sternly for such a display of emotion. Yet to deny the feeling would surely be a greater betrayal of herself? She had been fighting back her emotions ever since she had left Eadulf on the quay in Rome. He had been forced to stay in Rome as tutor to the Theodore of Tarsus, the newly appointed archbishop of Canterbury, while she had to return to her own land.

However, the year that had passed had been filled with memories of Eadulf of Seaxmund's Ham and feelings of loneliness and longing, as if of a home sickness. She was home. She was in her own land among her own people again.

Yet she missed Eadulf. She missed their arguments, the way she could tease Eadulf over their conflicting opinions and philosophies; the way he would always rise good-naturedly to the bait. Their arguments would rage but there was no enmity between them.

Eadulf had been trained in Ireland, at both Durrow and at Tuaim Brecain, before accepting the rulings of Rome on matters of the Faith and rejecting the Rule of Colmcille.

Eadulf of Seaxmund's Ham had been the only man of her own age in whose company she had felt really at ease and able to express herself without hiding behind her rank and role in life, without being forced to adopt a persona much like an actor playing a part.

Now she began to realise that her feeling for Eadulf was stronger than mere friendship.

To discover the gift that she had given him abandoned on a deserted vessel off the coast of Ireland sent a riot of panic-stricken thoughts through her mind.

'Ross, there is a mystery to this ship.'

Ross grimaced wryly.

'I thought that we had already agreed on that matter.'

Fidelma thrust out the Missal which she still held in her hand.

'This belonged to a friend of mine whom I left in Rome over a year ago. A close friend.'

Ross looked at it and scratched his head.

'A coincidence?' he offered hazily.

'A coincidence, indeed,' Fidelma agreed solemnly. 'What could have happened to the people on this ship? I must find out. I must find out what happened to my friend.'

Ross look awkward.

'We must get back aboard the *barc*, sister. The wind is coming up again.'

'You intend to tow this ship to shore?'

'I do.'

'Then I will make a closer search of her when we are in sheltered waters. What point are you making for?'

Ross rubbed his chin.

'Why, the nearest harbour is the very place I was taking you to, sister. To the community of The Salmon of the Three Wells.'

Fidelma let out a low breath. Her discovery had caused her to momentarily forget why she was in passage with Ross in the first place. Yesterday morning the abbot of Ros Ailithir, with whom she had been staying, had received a message from the abbess of The Salmon of the Three Wells, a small community of religieuses perched at the end of one of the far western peninsulas of Muman. An unidentified body had been discovered there and it was feared that it might be that of a female member of the Faith, though there was little means of recognition. The head of the body was missing. The abbess sought the assistance of a Brehon, an officer of the law courts of the five kingdoms, to help her solve the mystery of the identity of the corpse and discover who was responsible for its death.

The community came under the jurisdiction of the Abbot Brocc of Ros Ailithir and he had asked Fidelma if she were willing to undertake the investigation. The community of The Salmon of the Three Wells was but a day's sailing along the rugged coastline and therefore Fidelma had sought passage in the *barc* of Ross.

The discovery of the deserted Gaulish merchant ship and the book satchel, containing her parting gift to Brother Eadulf, had caused all thoughts of the reason for her journey to be driven momentarily from her mind.

'Sister,' insisted Ross, in agitation, 'we must return to the *barc*.'

Unwillingly, she agreed, replacing the Missal back into the leather satchel and swinging it over her shoulder.

Ross's men had fastened lines from the bow of the Gaulish ship to the stern of their smaller vessel and two men were left aboard her, the steersman, Odar, and another man, while Ross and Fidelma accompanied the others to the deck of the *Foracha*.

Fidelma's mind was preoccupied as Ross issued instructions to ease his ship away from the bigger vessel and turn before the wind. Soon the tow lines grew taut and the smaller craft began to make way with the larger ship, clawing through the choppy seas, after her. The wind was up again and there was no doubt that had Ross not intervened then the Gaulish ship would have already foundered on the hidden rocks and reefs that lay nearby.

Ross kept an anxious eye on the straining ropes and the wallowing vessel behind them. Odar was an expert steersman and skilfully kept the bigger ship on course. Ross then turned to judge his course for the coast. He was heading for one of the great bays between two south-westerly thrusting granite peninsulas, towards a large peninsula along which tall mountains ran, dominated by one distant high round dome that overpowered all other peaks. Before this peninsula rose the squat, bulbous shape of a large island and Ross ordered his helmsman to guide the *barc* towards the inlet between this island and the coast of the peninsula.

Fidelma had perched herself, with folded arms, against the stern rail, her head bowed in thought, oblivious to the approaching coast and its spectacular scenery. She also seemed oblivious to the pitch and toss of the *barc* as it was propelled before the winds tugging its prize after it.

'We'll soon be in sheltered waters,' Ross informed her, feeling sympathy for the young religieuse for the distress which her discovery had caused showed plainly on her features.

'Could it have been slavers?' she suddenly asked him without preamble.

Ross thought a moment. It was known that raiders, seeking slaves, often penetrated Irish waters, sometimes attacking coastal villages or fishing boats and carrying off inhabitants to be sold in the slave markets of the Saxon kingdoms or even further afield in Iberia, Frankia and Germania.

'Perhaps slavers might have attacked the merchant ship and carried everyone off?' Fidelma pressed as he hesitated.

Ross made a negative gesture of his head.

'Forgive me, sister, but I do not think so. If, as you say, a slaver had captured the merchant ship, then why not simply put a prize crew on board her and sail her back to their home port? Why remove the crew and, what is more curious, why remove the cargo leaving the ship behind? They would get as much, if not more money, for the ship as for its crew and cargo.'

Fidelma saw that Ross's logic was right. Indeed, why leave the ship so neat and comparatively tidy? She sighed deeply as no immediate answers came to the innumerable questions which hammered in her mind.

She tried to stop wasting emotional energy asking questions which were impossible to answer. Her mentor, Brehon Morann of Tara, had taught her that it was no use worrying about answers to problems unless she knew the questions that should be asked. Yet even when she tried to clear her mind and seek refuge in the art of the *dercad*, the act of meditation, by which countless generations of Irish mystics had achieved the calming of extraneous thought and mental irritations, she found the task impossible.

She decided to focus on the approaching coastal scenery. They had now entered the mouth of the great bay and moved close to the southern shore of the mountainous peninsula. The cold winds and choppy seas began to ease as they entered into these more sheltered waters. And when Ross's course placed the southern tip of the bulbous island to their eastern flank, the weather became much calmer as the land protected them from the main brunt of the winds. There were few clouds in the sky which was a soft blue with the pale yellow orb of the sun hanging high above casting no warmth at all. The scenery seemed painted in limpid pastel shades.

'A short way ahead lies a large inlet,' Ross announced. 'That is where the abbey of the community of The Salmon of the Three Wells is. I'll anchor in there, in the quiet waters.'

Fidelma, in spite of her preoccupied thoughts, was not entirely oblivious to the serene beauty of the inlet which was circled by an oak forest which rose in ridges all around and was fringed with varied evergreens. Even while her mind was agitated by the worry of what had happened to Brother Eadulf, the tranquil aura of the area registered with her. It would be spectacular in summer with the multi-coloured flowers and all the trees bursting in varied shades of green. Behind the inlet, the mountains rose, their bald peaks dusted with snow and their slopes studded with granite boulders. A rushing stream emptied into the inlet at one point where, on a headland, a small circular fortress stood. Even looking at its sparkling crystal waters, Fidelma shuddered at how cold those waters must be.

'That is the fortress of Adnár, the *bó-aire* of this district,' Ross jerked his thumb towards the fortress.

A *bó-aire* was, literally, a cow-chief, a chieftain without land whose wealth was judged by the number of cows he owned. In poor areas, the cow-chief acted as a local magistrate and owed his allegiance to greater chieftains. To this greater chieftain, the *bó-aire* paid tribute for his position and rank.

Fidelma tried to force her mind back to the task which she had originally come to perform.

'The fortress of Adnár?' she repeated, phrasing it as a question to ensure that she had the name correct.

'Yes. It is called *Dún Boí* – the fortress of the cow goddess.'

'Where is the religious community?' asked Fidelma. 'The abbey of The Salmon of the Three Wells?'

Ross indicated another small headland on the other side of the rivulet, directly opposite Adnár's fortress.

'It stands among those trees on that ridge. You can just see the tower of the abbey buildings there. You can also see a small quay leading to a rocky platform on which you might be able to make out the abbey's main well.'

Fidelma followed his directions. She saw movement on the quay.

'Captain!' the helmsman called softly to Ross. 'Captain, there are boats coming out – one from the fortress and one from the abbey.'

Ross turned to confirm the fact for himself and called on his crew to start furling the sails of the *Foracha* before dropping the anchor. He turned to signal Odar, on the Gaulish vessel, to release his anchor also so that the ships would not collide. There was a cracking of the great sheets as they were hauled down, the splash as the anchors hit the still waters and the startled cry of seabirds surprised by the unexpected sharpness of the sound. Then – silence.

For a moment or so Fidelma stood still, aware of that sudden silence in the sheltered inlet. Aware of the beauty of the place with the blues, greens, browns and greys of the mountains rising behind, and the sky creating a light blue on the waters around her, reflecting and shimmering in the early afternoon light, giving the impression of a mirror, so still and clear was its surface. Around the end of the inlet was a grey green belt of seaweed abandoned by the tides, the white and grey of rocks and the trees lining the banks, their varying greens and browns coloured by occasional bursts of groundsel and the white flowers of shepherd's purse. Here and there were strawberry trees. The silence magnified the slightest sound ... such as the lazy flap of a grey heron's wings as it circled the boats with its long sinuous neck seemingly arched in curiosity before turning indolently and unconcerned in the sky and heading further along the coast for a quieter fishing ground. And now she could hear the rhythmic slap of oars of the approaching boats on the still waters.

She sighed deeply. Such peace was a cloak, a disguise to reality. There was work to do.

'I'll go back aboard the merchant ship and make a more detailed examination, Ross,' she announced.

Ross gazed at her with anxious eyes.

'With respect, I would wait awhile, sister,' he suggested.

A frown of annoyance crossed her features.

'I do not understand...'

Ross cut her short by gesturing with his head towards the approaching two craft.

'I doubt that they are coming to visit me, sister.'

Fidelma wavered, still not understanding.

'One boat carries the *bó-aire* from his fortress while the other carries the Abbess Draigen.'

Fidelma raised her eyebrows in quiet surprise and gave the occupants of the approaching boats a more careful attention. One of the boats was being rowed by two religieuses with a third sitting upright in the stern. She appeared a tall, handsome-faced woman, even taller than Fidelma herself, muffled in a robe of fox fur. The other boat, racing towards them from the fortress, was rowed by two sturdy warriors and in the stern of that boat sat a tall, black-haired man, wrapped in a badger fur cloak and his silver chain of office proclaimed him to be someone of position. He kept glancing anxiously towards the other boat and, with barks of command, which could be discerned even from this distance, was urging his men to greater efforts as if wishing to reach the *barc* of Ross first.

'They look as though they are engaged in some race,' observed Fidelma dryly.

Ross's voice was humourless.

'I think their race, as you put it, is to reach you first. Whatever the purpose, I do not think there is a spirit of friendship between them,' he replied.

It was the boat from the abbey which reached the side of the *barc* first and the handsome religieuse scrambled up with surprising agility, reaching the deck just as the second boat came alongside and the tall man, with his shock of black hair, came springing onto the deck after her.

The woman, whom Ross had identified as the abbess of the community, was straight-backed as well as tall. Her cloak was flung back to reveal her homespun robes. The red-gold craftsmanship of her crucifix showed that she had not quite decided to relinquish riches for a vow of poverty and obedience, as it was of ornate workmanship and studded with semi-precious gems. Her face was autocratic with red lips and high cheekbones. She was in her mid-thirties and her face spoke of a beauty strangely intermixed with a coarseness of expression. Her eyes were dark and flashed with a hidden fire which was clearly anger as she glanced over her shoulder towards the black-bearded man, hurrying behind her.

She spied Ross at once. It was evident that she had met him before. Fidelma knew that Ross was a frequent trader along the coast of Muman and would obviously have done business with the religious community here.

'Ah, Ross. I recognised your ship the moment it entered the inlet,' her voice did not carry any warmth of greeting. 'I trust that you have come directly from Abbot Brocc of Ros Ailithir? I anticipate that you have brought me the Brehon in answer to my request?'

Before Ross could respond, the tall, black-haired chieftain joined her, puffing slightly in his exertion. He was into his forties, a handsome-faced man with pleasing features whose eyes bore a striking resemblance to the flashing dark eyes of the abbess. Fidelma noticed that he wore a pleasant, though anxious smile as he came up to Ross.

'Where is the Brehon? Where is he, Ross? I must see him first.'

The abbess turned swiftly on her apparently unwelcome companion with a look of unbridled animosity.

'You have no authority here, Adnár,' she snapped,

confirming Ross's identification of the man as the local chieftain.

Adnár coloured furiously.

'I have every authority to be here. Am I not *bó-aire* of this district? My word...'

'Your word is dictated by Gulban, chieftain of the Beara,' sneered the woman. 'If he says nothing then you say nothing. I have asked Abbot Brocc of Ros Ailithir to send a Brehon who is answerable only to the king of Cashel to whom your chieftain, Gulban, has to give account.' She turned back to Ross. 'Where is he, Ross? Where is the Brehon sent by the Abbot Brocc?'

Ross glanced towards Fidelma and gave a curious apologetic shrug as if he were trying to absolve himself from any responsibility for the visitors.

The gesture drew the attention of the newcomers to Fidelma. For the first time the austere-faced abbess seemed to catch sight of her and frowned.

'And who are you, sister?' she snapped imperiously. 'Have you come to join our community here?'

Fidelma managed a faint smile.

'I believe that I am the person you seek, mother abbess,' she replied evenly. 'I have been sent by the Abbot Brocc of Ros Ailithir in answer to your request.'

For a moment a look of utter astonishment sat on the abbess's face.

The sound of raucous laughter distracted everyone for a moment. Adnár was shaking with mirth.

'You ask for a Brehon and Brocc sends this slip of a girl! Ha! Your precious abbot does not think so highly of you after all!'

The abbess did her best to control the fury that blazed in her eyes and she stared, tight-mouthed, at Fidelma.

'Is this some kind of amusement for Abbot Brocc?' she asked coldly. 'Am I to be insulted thus?'

Fidelma shook her head tiredly.

'I do not think my cousin,' Fidelma paused for a fraction of a second, allowing the pause to emphasise the word, 'I do not think my cousin, the abbot, is given to amusing himself in such a manner.'

The abbess's expression began to twist into a sneer but Ross, feeling it time to intervene as captain of the ship, stepped quickly forward.

'Allow me, abbess, to introduce Sister Fidelma who is an advocate of the courts. She holds the qualification of *anruth*.'

The abbess's eyes widened imperceptibly while Adnár abruptly ceased to chuckle. The qualification of *anruth* was only one degree below the highest that the universities and ecclesiastical colleges of Ireland could bestow.

There was a pause before the abbess asked slowly: 'What did you say your name is?'

'I am Fidelma, currently of the community of Kildare.'

The abbess's flashing eyes narrowed again.

'Of Kildare? Kildare is in the kingdom of Laigin. Yet you say that you are related to Abbot Brocc of Ros Ailithir. What does this mean?'

Fidelma savoured the moment.

'My brother is Colgú, king of Cashel.' Fidelma could not help her eyes flickering in the direction of Adnár to gauge his reaction. She was rewarded by his open mouth and staring eyes. He looked, for a moment, like a fish as it is taken from the water. 'I serve the Faith, which is not encompassed by the boundaries of earthly kingdoms.'

The abbess gave a soft sigh before holding out her hand to Fidelma. Her imperiousness seemed to have evaporated a little. Her face was moulded into an expression of contrite apology. Whether it was genuine or not, Fidelma could not be sure.

'Let me bid you welcome to our community, sister. I am Abbess Draigen, superior of the foundation of The Salmon of the Three Wells.' She waved a hand towards the shore as if to indicate her community. 'I am sorry for my churlish greeting. These are trying times. I had expected that Brocc would have sent someone with some practical expertise in, in . . .'

Fidelma smiled gently as she hesitated.

'In the solution of crimes of violence? In the solution of mysteries? Have no fear on that matter, mother abbess. There is a proverb – *usus le plura doceit*. Experience teaches many things. I have acquired some aptitude for the task you have in mind by my experiences as an advocate of the courts.'

There was a grunt as Adnár came forward. He tried hard to resume his confident posture but his eyes fell momentarily before Fidelma's twinkling green ones. His head hung a little in his obvious embarrassment.

'Welcome, sister. I am Adnár.'

Fidelma examined him closely. She was not sure that she liked what she saw. The man was handsome, true enough, but she was always uneasy when she was confronted by good-looking, confident men.

'Yes. I have heard. You are the *bó-aire* of this territory,' Fidelma's voice was icy. In fact, she enjoyed the man's apparent discomfiture, mentally rebuking herself for her enjoyment of another's chagrin. It was against the teaching of the Faith but she was only human.

'I did not mean, that is, I . . .' began Adnár.

'Yet you wanted to see me?' Fidelma pressed innocently.

Adnár glanced in annoyance at Abbess Draigen. He seemed to have the need to choose his words carefully when he addressed Fidelma.

'Sister, I am *bó-aire* here. I am magistrate and judge of the courts under the jurisdiction of my chieftain, Gulban. There is no need for anyone in this territory to require outside assistance in the matter of law. However, this is not the time nor place to discuss such a matter. There you see my fortress,' he waved his hand. 'I would bid you welcome to feast with me this night.'

Abbess Draigen smothered an exclamation of protest by coughing.

'You are expected at the abbey this evening, Sister Fidelma, in order that I can explain more fully why you were sent for,' she said hastily.

Fidelma gazed from the abbess to the chieftain and then firmly shook her head.

'It is true that my first duty does lie at the abbey, Adnár,' she told the chieftain. 'However, I will come tomorrow morning and break my fast with you.'

Adnár flushed, glancing in annoyance towards the abbess whose features had formed into a smile of satisfaction. He nodded curtly to Fidelma.

'I shall look forward to it, sister,' he spoke reluctantly. He was about to move away but he hesitated and stared across to the Gaulish merchant ship as if becoming aware of it for the first time. 'You keep odd company, Ross. What ails this ship that its captain asks you to tow him into this harbour?'

Ross shifted his weight.

'I am not sure that I understand your meaning by odd company?'

'You keep company with a Gaulish ship. I saw your tow rope as you entered our harbour. What is wrong with the captain? Can he not sail himself? No matter, I will row across and have a word with him.'

'You will not find him aboard,' replied Ross.

'Not on board?'

'That is so,' Fidelma confirmed. 'The ship was discovered abandoned off the coast here.'

Once more an expression of astonishment crossed Adnár's face.

'Then we will have two matters to discuss when you come tomorrow.' With a brief nod to the abbess and to Ross, he went quickly over the side to his boat. They heard his men slap their oars into the water and watched silently as the boat pulled away back to the shore.

'An irritating man, that one,' sighed the abbess. 'Still, you have made the right decision, sister. Let me row you across to the abbey and I will explain everything.'

Her handsome face showed surprise when Fidelma shook her head.

'I will come to the abbey this evening for the evening meal, mother abbess. There are other matters that I must attend to before that.'

'Other matters?'

There was a dangerously querulous note to Abbess Draigen's voice.

'I will come ashore this evening,' Fidelma repeated but did not enlighten her further.

'Very well,' Abbess Draigen sniffed sourly. 'You will hear our bell ring for the evening Angelus. We sit down to eat following the prayers. A gong sounds twice for the meat to commence.'

She left, without another word, climbed over the side of the *barc* and clambered down into her boat.

Ross grimaced, leaning on the rail and watching the sisters rowing their abbess back across the inlet.

'Well, sister, I do not think that you have evoked much affection either in the heart of the abbess or that of the *bó-aire*.'

'It is not my task to evoke affection, Ross,' replied Fidelma softly. 'Now let us return to the Gaulish merchant ship.'

Fidelma, together with Ross, spent two hours searching the Gaulish ship once again from top to bottom without discovering any further indication of what had happened to her crew and her cargo. Apart from the dried blood stains, there was nothing to suggest why the crew and cargo of the vessel had simply vanished. Only Odar, the steersman, had come up with a further piece of information. He had approached Fidelma and Ross almost as soon as they had come aboard the Gaulish vessel.

'Begging your pardon, captain, but there is something you might like to see . . .' he began, hesitantly.

'Well?' Ross's voice was not exactly an encouragement to continue but Odar did so.

'I heard you and the sister here,' he gestured to Fidelma, 'remarking about how neat and tidy everything is aboard this ship. Well, there are two things out of place.'

Fidelma was interested at once.

'Explain, Odar,' she invited.

'The mooring ropes, sister. Both fore and aft. The mooring ropes have been cut.'

Ross immediately led the way to the nearest oak bollard at the bow of the ship.

'I left the ropes hanging in place so that you might see them for yourself,' Odar explained. 'I only noticed them myself when we were making fast a short while ago.'

Ross bent to where the strong flax cordage was fastened to the bollard and began to haul up the loose end which dangled down the side of the ship. It finished after about twenty feet or so, its end frayed into numerous strands. Fidelma took it from Ross's hands and examined it carefully. The end had certainly been cut; hacked at by an axe judging from the way the pieces of flaxen rope had frayed. The thickness of the ship's rope would confirm that only an axe could have cut it.

'And what of the other mooring line?' she asked Odar. 'Is it the same as this?'

'Yes, but you may see for yourself, sister,' the sailor replied.

Fidelma thanked him for bringing the matter to her attention and went to perch herself on the taffrail. She stared moodily into the middle distance. Ross, by her side, examined her with a bewildered expression. He knew when it was best to remain silent.

Finally, Fidelma let out a sigh.

'Let us sum up what we know,' she began.

'Which is not much,' interposed Ross.

'Nevertheless ... first, we know that this is a merchant ship from Gaul.'

Ross nodded emphatically.

'True. It is about the only thing that we can be certain of. I can swear that her construction is in keeping with the methods of the ship-builders of Morbihan.'

'Which then presumes that she might have sailed from a port in that area?'

'True again,' Ross agreed. 'Merchant ships, like her, often trade along our coast.'

'They bring mostly wine and barter for goods from our merchants?'

'That is so.'

'The fact that there was no cargo on board might suggest that this ship had already delivered her cargo to an Irish port?'

Ross rubbed his chin.

'Perhaps.'

'I'll grant you your "perhaps". However, if she had a cargo when it was removed, and we presume that it was removed at sea, then to remove kegs of wine would be a difficult task. Would it not be a simpler supposition that she had already unloaded the casks of wine in an Irish port and was then returning to Gaul either without a cargo or with a cargo more easily removed at sea?'

'There is a logic in that suggestion,' Ross admitted.

'Then I think we are progressing,' Fidelma said triumphantly. 'Now, let us reflect on what else we know. There is blood in this ship. Some of the blood was below deck. There was also some blood of more recent shedding on a strip of linen found caught in the rigging and smeared on the handrail below the rigging. That blood, though dried, is not old and was probably spilt within the last twelve to twenty-four hours. The blood could belong to a crew member or ...' she paused and tried not to think of Eadulf, 'or to a passenger.'

'Why not to one of the raiders?' demanded Ross. 'One of those who removed the cargo or the crew?'

Fidelma reflected on the point and then conceded the possibility.

'Why not? And, of course, who is to say that there was a raider or raiders? Perhaps the crew themselves took the cargo and left their vessel.' She held up her hand as Ross started to point out the objections to such an idea. 'Very well. The main point is that the blood seems to have been spilt during the time of the crew's disappearance; at the moment when whatever happened on board the ship took place.'

Ross waited while she reviewed the matter silently.

'The ship's fore and aft mooring ropes were severed, as if by an axe. From that we learn that she must have been moored against something, not merely anchored in a harbour for the anchor is still in place but the mooring ropes are cut. Why? Why not simply untie the mooring ropes? Was someone on board in a hurry to depart from somewhere? Or was the ship tied to another vessel and then cut adrift?'

Ross glanced admiringly at Fidelma as she conjured possibilities.

'How long was she under view until we boarded her?' she asked him abruptly.

'I had noticed her about half an hour before Odar drew attention to her dangerous course. We took a further half an hour to close up and board her.'

'This means that the ship might have been close to this shore when whatever took place. Do you agree?'

'Why so?'

'The ship could only have been attacked within the last twelve to twenty-four hours before we sighted her.' She suddenly straightened. 'You know this coast well, don't you, Ross?'

'I know it,' he admitted, without boasting. 'I have sailed these waters for forty years.'

'Can you judge by the winds and tides what place this ship

might have sailed from to the spot when you first sighted her?'

Ross looked at Fidelma's excited features. He did not want to disappoint her.

'It is difficult, even knowing the tides. The blustery winds are changeable and inconsistent.'

Fidelma's mouth drooped in disappointment.

Seeing her dissatisfaction, he added hastily: 'But I can, perhaps, calculate a good guess. I think it is safe to say that there are two probable places. The mouth of this bay or further around at the southern end of this peninsula. The tides from those points would certainly carry the ship in the direction of the spot we first saw her at.'

'That gives us a wide area of territory to search.' Fidelma was still not satisfied.

'This friend to whom that book satchel belongs . . .' Ross changed the subject, then hesitated. 'This friend . . . was he a good friend?'

'Yes.'

Ross caught the emotional tightness in her voice as she uttered the single syllable. He waited a moment and then said softly:

'I have a daughter of your age, sister. Oh, she is on shore and married. Her mother lives with someone else. I do not pretend to have an understanding of women. One thing I know, my daughter's husband was lost at sea. That same look of hurt and anguish in her eyes on the morning the news came to Ros Ailithir, I now see in your eyes.'

Fidelma drew herself up defensively with a snort of irritation.

'Brother Eadulf is simply a friend of mine, that is all. If he is in trouble, I will do what I can to help him.'

Ross nodded imperturbably.

'Just so,' he said quietly. She knew he was not fooled at all by her protest.

'And at the moment,' Fidelma continued, 'I have other

things to do. My duty is now to the Abbess Draigen. I may be several days at the abbey here before I can spend time searching. And what will I be searching for?'

'Of course, your duty comes first,' Ross assured her. 'However, if it would help you, sister, while you are ashore at the abbey, I could take my *barc* and sail to the points I have indicated to see if there is any sign of a solution to this mystery. I will leave Odar and another man to keep an eye on this vessel and you may call on them should you need to.'

Fidelma's face flushed. Then, with an abrupt movement, she bent forward and kissed the old seaman on the cheek.

'Bless you, Ross,' her voice had a catch which she could not disguise.

Ross smiled awkwardly.

'It is nothing. We'll sail on the early morning tide and return within a day or two, no longer. If we find anything...'

'Come and tell me first.'

'Even as you say,' agreed the sailor.

Across the darkening waters of the inlet they heard the sounding of a bell.

'Time for me to go to the abbey.' Fidelma moved forward to the rail of the ship. She paused and glanced quickly across her shoulder at Ross. 'God watch over your voyage, Ross.' Her expression was serious. 'I do fear that there is some evil human agency at work here. I would not want to lose you.'

Chapter Four

'And now, sister, I presume that you would like to inspect the corpse?'

Sister Fidelma started in surprise at Abbess Draigen's suggestion. They were emerging from the abbey's refectory in which most of the community of The Salmon of the Three Wells had taken the evening meal together.

Night had already settled over the tiny community and the buildings were shrouded in gloom although lamps had been lit in strategic places among the buildings to aid the sisters. It was another cold night and already a frost lay white over the ground, almost like a covering of snow. The wood fires were smoking among the abbey buildings. So far as Fidelma had been able to discern, there were a dozen buildings centred around a granite paved courtyard, in which a high cross had been erected. On one side of the courtyard was a cloister which fronted a tall wooden building, the *duirthech* or oak house, which was the abbey chapel. In fact, the majority of the buildings were wooden constructions, mainly built of oak timbers. The surrounding countryside was replete with oaks. There were also a few buildings of stone. Fidelma presumed these to be store rooms. Dominating all these buildings, and situated at one end of the *duirthech*, was a squat tower with stone foundations but wooden upper floors.

The abbey of The Salmon of the Three Wells was not unusual from many that Fidelma had seen in the length and breadth of the five kingdoms. There were, however, no outer

46

walls such as at the main abbey complexes like Ros Ailithir. She had gathered, during the meal at which some conversation was allowed, unlike other houses where a *lector* usually intoned passages from the Gospels, that only fifty sisters constituted the community. Under the direction of the Abbess Draigen, one of the main devotions of the community was the keeping of a water-clock and the recording of the passing of time. The abbey, it seemed, was also proud of its library and some of the sisters spent their time in copying books for other communities. It was a quiet backwater, engaged in no more controversial work than study and contemplation.

'Well, sister,' inquired the abbess again, 'do you want to see the corpse?'

'I do,' Fidelma agreed. 'Though I am surprised that you have not yet buried it. How many days is it since it was discovered?'

The abbess turned from the door of the refectory and led the way across the courtyard towards the wooden chapel.

'Six days have passed since the unfortunate was taken out of our well. Had you been longer in your arrival then we would, of course, have had to bury the corpse. However, as it is winter, the weather has been cold enough to retain the body for a while and we have a cold place for food storage under the chapel, a *subterraneus*, where we have placed the body. There are reputed to be several caves under the abbey buildings. But, even in these conditions, we could not have kept it forever. We have arranged to bury the body in our abbey cemetery tomorrow morning.'

'Have you discovered the identity of the unfortunate?'

'I am hoping that you will solve that matter.'

The abbess led the way through the cloisters, along the stone-paved corridor, passing the chapel doors, to the entrance of a small building made of rough-hewn granite blocks whose walls were built in the dry stone method, simply laid one on top of another. It was an appendage built on the side of the wooden tower. This stone building, which also connected with the tower, was apparently a store room and the pungent aroma of stored herbs and spices caught at Fidelma's senses making her momentarily breathless. However, it was a pleasing, refreshing odour.

Abbess Draigen crossed to a shelf and took up a jar. She then took, from a pile, two squares of linen and soaked them with the liquid from the vessel. Fidelma inhaled the piquant odour of lavender. Solemnly, Abbess Draigen handed her the impregnated square of cloth.

'You will need this, sister,' she advised.

She led the way to a corner of the room where a flight of stone steps descended. They wound down into a cave which stretched about thirty feet in length, was twenty feet wide and whose naturally arched ceiling rose ten feet or more. Fidelma noticed what at first seemed to be some scratch marks on the entrance arch and then realised that it was the etched outlines of a bull; no, not a bull. It was more like a calf. The Abbess Draigen noticed her examination.

'This place was once used in pagan worship, so we are told. The well which Necht blessed, for instance. There are a few remains from ancient times such as this scratching of a cow or some such animal.'

Fidelma silently acknowledged the reception of this information. She noticed another series of stairs ascending into the darkness just beyond the arched entrance.

'Those lead directly up to the tower of the abbey,' explained the abbess before Fidelma could frame the obvious question. 'It is where we house our modest library and, at the top of the tower, our pride . . . a water-clock.'

They passed on into the cave itself. It was deathly cold. Fidelma reasoned that the *subterraneus* must be below sea level at this point. The cave was lit. She saw at once that the flickering light came from four tall candles at the far end.

Fidelma did not need to be told what it was that was lying under the shroud of linen on what appeared to be a table whose four corners were marked by the candles. The outline was easily recognisable except that the body seemed foreshortened. She approached cautiously. There was not much else in the cave. Some boxes were stacked against one wall and nearby were rows of *amphorae* and earthen containers, whose faint odours identified them as being used for storing wine and spirits.

In spite of the cold, Abbess Draigen was right. She did need the piece of lavender-impregnated cloth. While herbs and other scented plants had been strategically placed around the body, there was no mistaking the bitter stench that rose from the already decomposing corpse. Fidelma involuntarily caught her breath and raised the linen to her nostrils. Winter chill or not, the corpse was reeking with putrefaction.

Abbess Draigen, standing on the other side of the corpse, smiled thinly, her face half hidden by her own lavender-impregnated cloth.

'The burial service will be performed at first light tomorrow, sister, that is if you do not require the corpse further for your investigation. The sooner it is done, the better.' It was a statement rather than a question.

Fidelma did not answer but, bracing herself, she drew back the cloth from the body.

No matter how many times Fidelma encountered death, and violent death was no stranger to her, she always felt an abhorrence at the savagery of it. She always tried to look at corpses as an abstract, tried not to think of them as once living, sentient beings who had loved, laughed and enjoyed life. She compressed her lips firmly and forced herself to look down at the white rotting flesh.

'As you will see, sister,' the abbess pointed out unnecessarily, 'the head has been hacked off. Thus we have no means of identifying the unfortunate.'

Fidelma's eyes had immediately gone to the wound above the heart.

'Stabbed first,' she said, half to herself. 'The slight bruising shows that the wound was not made after death. Stabbed in the heart and then decapitated afterwards.'

Abbess Draigen watched the young *dálaigh* with an impassive expression.

Fidelma forced herself to examine the severed flesh around the neck. Then she pulled back and looked at the body as a whole.

'A young woman. Scarcely beyond the age of choice. I would hazard that she was no more than eighteen. Perhaps younger.'

Her eye caught a discolouration of the flesh around the right ankle. She frowned and examined it more closely.

'Was this where she was tied to the well rope?' she demanded.

Abbess Draigen shook her head.

'The sisters who found the corpse said it was hanging by the left ankle and tied with rope.'

Fidelma turned her attention to the left ankle and saw faint marks and indentations on it. Indeed, such marks looked more consistent with rope burn and there was no bruising, showing that the rope had undoubtedly been placed after death. She turned her attention back to the right ankle again. No, this mark had been made during life. And it did not look as though a rope or cord had made such a mark. It was a regular circle around the leg, a band of discolouration of two inches in depth. The skin had clearly been marked while it was still living flesh.

She turned her attention to the feet. The soles were padded with hardened skin and there were innumerable cuts and sores on them showing that the owner, in life, had not led a pampered existence and probably had not worn shoes much. The toenails were unkempt and several of them were cracked and broken. And curiously, under the nails, there were dirt deposits. There had been an attempt to clean the body but this dirt seemed ingrained and was curiously red in texture, like a deep red clay that permeated into the very skin of the toes themselves.

'I presume that the body has been washed since it was removed from the well?' Fidelma asked, glancing up.

'Of course.' The abbess seemed irritated by the question. It was the custom to wash the body of the dead while waiting burial.

Fidelma made no further comment but turned her attention to the legs and the torso. These could tell her nothing except that, in life, the girl had a well-proportioned body and limbs. She next turned her attention to the hands. Fidelma controlled her surprise for the hands did not seem to balance the image of the feet. They were soft, without callouses, the fingernails were clean and manicured. She saw that the right hand had a strange blue stain on it covering the side of the little finger and the edge of the hand. The stain also occurred on the thumb and forefinger. She examined the other hand but there was no such identical staining there. The hands were not the hands of someone accustomed to manual work. Yet this seemed to contrast totally with the feet.

'I was told that the corpse was clutching some items. Where are they?' Fidelma inquired after a while.

The abbess shifted her weight from one foot to another. 'When the sisters washed the body and prepared it, the items were removed. I have them in my chamber.'

Fidelma controlled the disapproving response that came to her tongue. What was the point of her examination if vital evidence had been removed? She checked herself and said: 'Be so good as to tell me where these items were placed on the corpse.'

Abbess Draigen sniffed dangerously. She was obviously unused to being ordered to do anything, especially by a young religieuse.

'Sister Síomha and Sister Brónach, who found the corpse, will be able to inform you of this matter.'

'I will speak with them later,' Fidelma replied patiently. 'As of this moment, I would like to know where the items were found.'

The abbess's mouth tightened and then she relaxed a little yet her voice was stiff.

'There was a copper crucifix, with a leather thong, poorly made, gripped in the right hand of the corpse. The thong was wrapped around the wrist.'

'Did it seem to have been placed there?'

'No; the fingers of the hand were clasped tightly around it. In fact, the sisters had to break the bones of two fingers to extract it.'

Fidelma forced herself to examine the hand in order to verify it.

'And apart from the breaking of the fingers, when the body was washed, was any particular attention given to the hands? Were they specifically manicured?'

'I do not know. The body was washed and cleaned in accordance with custom.'

'Can you speculate on the blue stain?'

'Not I.'

'And what was the other item which was found?'

'There was a wooden wand inscribed in Ogham on the left arm,' continued the abbess. 'This was tied on to the forearm and more easily removed.'

'Tied on? And you have this still? You have it together with the binding?' pressed Fidelma.

'Of course,' replied the abbess.

Fidelma stood back and surveyed the corpse.

Now came the most distasteful part of the task.

'I need help to turn the corpse over, Abbess Draigen,' she said. 'Would you assist me?'

'Is it necessary?' demanded the abbess.

'It is. You may send for another sister, if you so wish.'

The abbess shook her head. Sniffing at her piece of cloth to inhale the odour of lavender, before thrusting it into her sleeves, the abbess moved forward and helped Fidelma manipulate the corpse, firstly moving it on to its side and then over so that the back was exposed. The blemishes were immediately apparent. The marks of recent welts criss-crossed the white flesh as if this body had been scourged before death. In life, some of those abrasions had broken the skin and caused bleeding.

Fidelma breathed in deeply and promptly regretted doing so for the stench of decay caused her to retch and cough, scrabbling for her lavender cloth.

'Have you seen enough?' demanded the abbess, coldly.

Fidelma nodded between coughs.

Together, they returned the corpse to its former position.

'I presume that you now want to see the items found on the corpse?' asked the abbess, as she conducted Fidelma from the cave into the main store room.

'What I want first, mother abbess,' Fidelma replied carefully, 'is to wash.'

Abbess Draigen's lips thinned, almost in a malicious expression.

'Naturally. Then come this way, sister. Our guests' hostel has a bath-tub and it is the hour when our sisters usually bathe so the water will be heated.'

Fidelma had already been shown the *tech-óired*, the guests' hostel of the abbey, where she would be staying during the time she was with the community. It was a long, low wooden building divided into half a dozen rooms with a central room for a bathing chamber. Here there was a bronze container in which water was heated by a wood fire and then poured into a wooden *dabach* or bath-tub.

The abbey apparently followed the general fashion of bathing in the five kingdoms. People usually had a full bath every evening, the *fothrucud* which took place after the evening meal, while first thing in the morning people washed their face, hands and feet, which process was called the *indlut*. Daily bathing was more than just a custom among the people of the five kingdoms, it had grown almost into a religious ritual. Every hostel in the five kingdoms had its bath-house.

The abbess left Fidelma at the door of the guests' hostel and agreed to meet her an hour later in her own chamber. There was no one else staying in the *tech-óired* and so Fidelma had the place to herself. She was about to move into her own chamber when she heard sounds coming from the central bathing room.

Frowning, she moved along the darkened corridor and pushed open the door.

A middle-aged sister was straightening up after stoking the fire beneath the bronze container in which water was already steaming. She caught sight of Fidelma and hastily dropped her eyes, folding her hands under her robes and bowing her head obsequiously.

'*Bene vobis*,' she greeted softly.

Fidelma entered the room.

'*Deus vobiscum*,' she replied, returning the Latin formula. 'I did not realise there were other guests here.'

'Oh, there are not. I am the *doirseór* of the abbey but I also look after the guests' hostel. I have been preparing your bath.'

Fidelma's eyes widened slightly.

'It is kind of you, sister.'

'It is my duty,' replied the middle-aged religieuse without raising her eyes.

Fidelma gave a glancing examination to the scrupulously clean bathing chamber, the wooden tub standing ready almost filled with hot water, the room heated by the warmth of the fire. Pleasant smelling herbs permeated the atmosphere of the room. A linen cloth was laid ready with a tablet of *sléic*, a fragrant soap. Nearby was a mirror and a comb together with cloths for drying the body. Everything was neat and orderly. Fidelma smiled.

'You do your duty well, sister. What is your name?'

'I am Sister Brónach,' replied the other.

'Brónach? You were one of the two sisters who found the corpse.'

The religieuse shivered slightly. Her eyes did not meet Fidelma's.

'It is true, sister. I and Sister Síomha found the body.' She genuflected quickly.

'Then it will save me some time, sister, if, while I bathe, you tell me of that event.'

'While you bathe, sister?' There was a tone of disapproval in the other's voice.

Fidelma was curious.

'Do you object?'

'I . . . ? No.'

The woman turned and, with surprising strength, lifted the heated water in the bronze container from the fire and tipped it into the wooden *dabach*, already partly filled with steaming water.

'Your bath is ready now, sister.'

'Very well. I have clean garments with me and my own *ciorbholg*.' The *ciorbholg* was, literally a comb-bag, which was indispensable to all women in Ireland for in this little bag they carried not only combs but articles for their toilet. The old laws of the *Book of Acaill* even laid down that, in certain cases of a quarrel, a woman could be exempted from liability if she showed her 'comb-bag' and distaff, the cleft stick three feet in length from which wool or flax was wound. These were the symbols of womanhood.

Fidelma went to get a change of clothing from her bag. She was fastidious about personal cleanliness and like to keep her clothing washed regularly. There had been few opportunities to wash or change clothing on Ross's small ship and so she now took the occasion to change. When she returned, Sister Brónach was heating more water on the fire.

'If you hand me your dirty clothes, sister,' she greeted as Fidelma reentered the room, 'I will launder them while you bathe. They can be hung before the fire to dry.'

Fidelma thanked her but again she could not make eye contact with the doleful religieuse. She removed her clothes, shivering in the cold in spite of the fire, and swiftly slid into the luxuriously warm waters of the bath tub, letting out a deep sigh of contentment.

She reached for the *sléic* and began to work it into a lather against her body while Sister Brónach gathered her discarded dirty clothes and placed them into the bronze container.

'So,' Fidelma began, as she luxuriated in the foam of the perfumed soap, 'you were saying that you and Sister Síomha found the body?'

'That is so, sister.'

'And who is Sister Síomha?'

'She is the steward of the abbey, the *rechtaire* or, as some of the largest abbeys in this land call it by the Latin term, the *dispensator.*'

'Tell me when and how you found the body?'

'The sisters were at midday prayers and the gong sounded the start of the third *cadar* of the day.'

The third quarter of the day began at noon.

'My task at that time was to ensure the abbess's personal bath-tub was filled ready. She prefers to bathe at that time. The water is drawn from the main well.'

Fidelma lay back in the tub.

'Main well?' she frowned slightly. 'There is more than one well here?'

Brónach nodded gloomily.

'Are we not the community of *Eo na dTrí dTobar*?' she asked.

'The Salmon of the Three Wells,' repeated Fidelma,

inquisitively. 'Yet this is but a metaphor by which the Christ is named.'

'Even so, sister, there are three wells at this spot. The holy well of the Blessed Necht, who founded this community, and two smaller springs that lie in the woods behind the abbey. At the moment, all water is brought from the springs in the wood, for the Abbess Draigen has not fully performed the purification rituals for the main well.'

Fidelma was at least happy to learn that, for she had a horror of drinking water in which the headless corpse had reposed.

'So you went out to draw water from the well?'

'I did but could not easily work the winding mechanism. It was hard to turn. Later I realised that it was the weight of the body. As I was trying my best to wind up the pail of water, Sister Síomha came out to rebuke me for my tardiness. I do not think that she believed that I was having difficulty.'

'Why was that?' asked Fidelma from the tub.

The middle-aged nun ceased stirring the cauldron with Fidelma's clothes in it and reflected.

'She said that she had recently drawn water from the well and there was nothing wrong with the mechanism.'

'Had anyone else used the well that morning – either before Sister Síomha or before the time that you went to draw water there?'

'No, I do not think so. There was no need to draw fresh water until midday.'

'Go on.'

'Well, we both hauled away at the mechanism until the corpse appeared.'

'You were both shocked, of course?'

'Of course. The thing was without a head. We were afraid.'

'Did you notice anything else about the corpse?'

'The crucifix? Yes. And, of course, the aspen wand.'

'The aspen wand?'

'Tied on the left forearm was a stick of aspen wood on which Ogham characters were cut.'

'And what did you make of it?'

'Make of it?'

'What did the characters say? You clearly recognised what it was.'

Brónach shrugged eloquently.

'Alas, I can recognise Ogham characters when I see them written, sister, but I have no knowledge of their meaning.'

'Did Sister Síomha read it?'

Brónach shook her head and lifted the bronze vessel from the fire, removing the items of clothing with a stick and putting them into a tub of cold water.

'So neither of you were able to read the Ogham or recognise its purpose?'

'I told the abbess at the time that I thought it was some pagan symbol. Didn't the old ones tie twigs on a corpse to protect against the vengeful souls of the dead?'

Fidelma stared carefully at the middle-aged sister but she had her back turned as she bent to her task beating the clothes to take the water out of them.

'I have not heard that, Sister Brónach. What was the abbess's response to your idea?'

'Abbess Draigen keeps her own counsel.'

Was there an angry tone to her voice?

Fidelma rose from the tub and reached for the drying cloth before scrambling out. She rubbed herself energetically, rejoicing in the invigoration of her limbs. She felt fresh and relaxed as she put on her clean clothing. Since her return from Rome she had indulged herself by using undershirts of white *sída* or silk, which she had brought back with her. She noticed Sister Brónach casting a look at the garments, an almost envious look which was the first emotion Fidelma had witnessed on her generally mournful countenance. On top of her underwear, Fidelma drew on her brown *inar* or tunic which came down nearly to her feet and was tied with a tasselled cord at her waist. She slipped her feet into her well-shaped, narrow-toed leather shoes, *cuaran*, which were seamed down along the instep and were fitted without the necessity of thongs to fasten them.

She turned to the mirror and completed her toilet by setting her long, rebellious red hair in place.

She was aware that Sister Brónach had fallen silent now, as she finished laundering Fidelma's dirty clothes.

Fidelma rewarded her with a smile.

'There now, sister. I feel human again.'

Sister Brónach was contented to nod without any comment.

'Is there anything else to tell me?' Fidelma pressed. 'For example, what happened after you and Sister Síomha pulled the body from the well?'

Sister Brónach kept her head lowered.

'We said a prayer for the dead and then I went to fetch the abbess while Sister Síomha stayed with the body.'

'And you returned directly with Abbess Draigen?'

'As soon as I had found her.'

'And the Abbess Draigen took charge?'

'Surely so.'

Fidelma picked up her bag, turning for the door but then pausing a moment by it to glance back.

'I am grateful to you, Sister Brónach. You keep your guests' hostel well.'

Sister Brónach did not raise her eyes.

'It is my duty,' she said shortly.

'Yet for duty to have meaning you must be content in its performance,' Fidelma replied. 'My mentor, the Brehon Morann of Tara, once said – when duty is but law then enjoyment ends for the greater duty is the duty of being happy. Good night, Sister Brónach.'

In the Abbess Draigen's chamber, the abbess regarded the flushed-faced Fidelma – her flesh still tingling after the warmth of her bath – with begrudging approval. The abbess was seated at her table on which a leather-bound Gospel was open at a page she had been contemplating.

'Sit down, sister,' she instructed. 'Will you join me in a glass of mulled wine to keep out the evening chill?'

Fidelma hesitated only a moment.

'Thank you, mother abbess,' she said. As she had been conducted across the abbey courtyard by a young novice, who introduced herself as Sister Lerben, personal attendant to the abbess, she had felt a soft flurry of snow and knew that the evening would become more icy.

The abbess rose and went to a jug standing on a shelf. An iron bar was already heating in the fire and the abbess, wrapping a leather cloth around it, drew it out of the fire and plunged its red hot point in the jug. She then poured the warm liquid into two pottery goblets and handed one to Fidelma.

'Now, sister,' she said, as each had taken some appreciative sips at the liquid, 'I have those objects which you wanted to see.'

She took something wrapped in cloth and placed it on the table, then sat opposite and began to sip her wine again while watching Fidelma above the rim.

Fidelma set down her goblet and unwrapped the cloth. It revealed a small copper crucifix and its leather thong.

She stared at the burnished object for a long time before she suddenly remembered her mulled wine and took a hurried sip at it.

'Well, sister,' asked the abbess, 'and what do you make of it?'

'Little of the crucifix,' Fidelma replied. 'It is common enough. Poor craftsmanship and the sort that many of the sisterhood have access to. It could well be of local craftsmanship. It is a crucifix that an average religieuse might possess. If this belonged to the girl whose body you found then it denotes that she was an anchoress.'

'In that, I concur. Most of our community have similarly worked copper crucifixes. We have an abundance of copper in this area and local craftsmen produced many such as that. The girl does not appear to be local, though. A farmer from nearby thought it might have been his missing daughter. He came to see the body but that turned out not to be the case. His daughter had a scar which the body did not possess.'

Fidelma raised her head from contemplation of the crucifix.

'Oh? When was this farmer come here?'

'He came to the abbey on the day after we found the body. He was named Barr.'

'How did he know the body had been found?'

'News travels rapidly in this part of the world. Anyway, Barr spent a long time examining the body, he obviously wanted to make sure. The corpse may be that of a religieuse from some other district.'

Indeed, thought Fidelma, it would fit in with the condition of the corpse's hands if she was a member of a religious house. The women who did not labour in the fields, indeed the men also, prided themselves on having well manicured hands. Fingernails were always kept carefully cut and rounded and it was considered shameful for either men or women to have unkempt nails. One of the great terms of abuse was to call someone *créchtingnech* or 'ragged nails'.

Yet it did not fit with the coarsely-kept feet, the mark of an ankle manacle, and the signs of scourging on the girl's back.

The abbess had picked up another piece of cloth and laid it carefully on the table.

'This is the aspen wand which was found tied on the left forearm,' she announced, carefully throwing back the cloth.

Fidelma was gazing at a wand of aspen some eighteen inches in length. The first thing that she noticed was that it was notched in regular measurements and then, to one side, was a line of Ogham, the ancient Irish form of writing. The characters were more newly cut than the measurements on the other side of the stick. She looked closely at them, her lips forming the words.

'Bury her well. The Mórrígú has awakened!'

Her face whitened. She sat up stiffly and found the abbess's eye quizzically regarding her.

'You recognise what that is?' Abbess Draigen asked softly.

Fidelma nodded slowly: 'It is a *fé*.'

A *fé*, or rod of aspen, usually with an Ogham inscription, was the measurement by which corpses and graves were calibrated. The *fé* was the tool of a mortician and was regarded with utmost horror so that no one, on any consideration, would take it in their hand or touch it, except, of course, the person whose business it was to measure corpses and graves. A *fé* had been the symbol of death and ill-luck since the days of the old gods. Still, the worst imprecation that could be uttered at any person was 'may the *fé* be soon measuring you'.

There was a silence as Fidelma sat for a long time staring down at the aspen wood.

It was only when she heard a soft but exasperated sigh that she stirred herself and raised her eyes to meet those of the Abbess Draigen.

It was clear that the abbess knew well what the rod symbolised for her face was troubled.

'You see, now, Fidelma of Kildare, why I could not allow the local *bó-aire* to assume his magisterial powers on this matter? You see now why I sent a message to Abbot Brocc to dispatch a *dálaigh* of the Brehon courts who was answerable to none save the king of Cashel?'

Fidelma returned her gaze with serious eyes.

'I understand, mother abbess,' she said quitely. 'There is much evil here. Much evil.'

It took Fidelma some time to fall asleep. Snow was falling

heavily now but it was not the chill air permeating her cell which caused her to have difficulty in sleeping. Neither was it the conundrum of the headless body that stirred her thoughts and kept her awake as she tried to quell the anxiety that they produced. Twice she took the small Missal from her side table and turned it over and over in her hands, peering at it as if it would produce an answer to her questions.

What had happened to Eadulf of Seaxmund's Ham?

Twelve months ago or more she had parted from Eadulf on the wooden quay near the Bridge of Probi in Rome and had handed him this little Mass Book as a gift. There was her inscription on its first page.

Twice she and Eadulf had been thrown together to investigate deaths of members of their respective churches and found that, while opposite in character, they found mutual attraction and complementary talents in their pursuit of solutions to the problems they had been set. Then the time came for them to go their different ways. She had to return to her homeland and he had been appointed *scriptor* and advisor to Theodore, of Tarsus, the newly appointed archbishop of Canterbury, Rome's chief apostle to the Saxon kingdoms. Theodore, being a Greek, and only a recent convert to the Church of Rome, required someone to instruct him in the ways of his new spiritual charges. Even though Fidelma had thought, at the time, that she would never see Eadulf again, she had found her thoughts gravitating more and more to memories of the Saxon monk. She had been experiencing feelings of isolation and had only recently come to admit to herself that she missed the companionship of Eadulf.

Now she was faced with a mystery that was more aggravating to her mind than any of the riddles she had been called to solve before.

Why was this small Missal, her parting gift to Eadulf in Rome, on a deserted Gaulish merchant ship, an entire world away, off the coast of south-west Ireland? Had Eadulf been a passenger on that vessel? If so, where was he? If he had not, who had possessed the book? And why would Eadulf have parted company with her gift?

Eventually, despite the throbbing questions in her head, sleep caught her unawares.

Chapter Five

Fidelma was awakened by Sister Brónach while it was still dark although there was that tell-tale texture to the sky which foretold the imminent arrival of dawn. A bowl of warm water was placed for her toilet and a candle was left burning so that she could accomplish this task in comfort. It was intensely cold at this early hour. She had barely finished dressing when a slow chiming bell began to sound. Fidelma recognised it as the traditional 'death-bell' which custom decreed should be rung to mark the passing of a Christian soul. A moment later Sister Brónach returned, head bowed, eyes floor-ward.

'It is time for the observance, sister,' she whispered.

Fidelma acknowledged and followed her out of the guests' hostel, to the *duirthech* where the entire community appeared to have gathered. To her surprise, the snow of the previous evening had not lain around the abbey buildings, though a glance showed that a thin layer of snow covered the surrounding woods and hills beyond. There was an eerie white glow to the early morning.

Inside the wooden chapel building, it was so cold that someone had lit a fire which blazed in a brazier standing at the back. The damp and cold struck up from the stone flags of the floor of the *duirthech*. The Abbess Draigen was kneeling behind the altar on which a large, and rather magnificent, tall gold cross stood, almost dominating the chapel. Before the altar, in front of the congregation, stood the *fuat*, the funeral bier, on which the body of the unknown girl had been laid.

65

Fidelma took her place on the end bench next to Sister Brónach. She was thankful for the warmth from the nearby brazier. She looked round, appreciatively taking in the opulence of the furnishings of the wooden chapel. As well as the richness of the altar cross, the walls were hung with numerous icons with gold fixtures conspicuous everywhere. She presumed that the obsequies had been observed since last night. The corpse was now wrapped in a *racholl*, a white linen shroud. At each corner of the bier a candle fluttered in the slight morning breeze.

The Abbess Draigen stood up and slowly began to clap her hands in the traditional *lámh-comairt* which signified the lamentation for the dead. Then the sisters began to start a soft wailing cry – the *caoine*, the sorrowing. It was a chilling sound in the half light of early morning and caused Fidelma's neck to tingle although she had heard it so many times before. The lament to the dead was a custom which went back to the time before the new Faith had displaced that of the old gods and goddesses.

After ten minutes the *caoine* stopped.

Abbess Draigen stepped forward. At this point in the ritual it was customary for the *amra*, or elegy, to be given.

It was then that there came a strange noise, seeming to well up from beneath the stone floor of the chapel. It was not particularly loud. It was an odd scraping sound, a deep, hollow scuffling sound as when two wooden boats bump against one another, bobbing on the waves of the sea. The members of the community peered fearfully at one another.

Abbess Draigen raised a slim hand for silence.

'Sisters, you forget yourselves,' she admonished.

Then she bent her head to continue the service.

'Sisters, we are mourning one who is unknown to us and therefore no elegy can mark her passing. A unknown soul has sped to God's holy embrace. Yet she is known to God and that is enough. That the hand that cut short this life is also known to God may also be accepted. We lament the passing of this soul but rejoice in the knowledge that it has passed to God's good keeping.'

Six of the sisters of the community moved forward, at a signal from the abbess, and lifted the bier to their shoulders and then, led by the abbess, they moved out of the chapel followed by the rest of the community, forming a double line in the wake of the bier.

Fidelma held back to follow at the rear of this column and, as she did so, she saw that another of the religieuses was also holding back for the same purpose. She noticed this as Sister Brónach seemed to remain in her place for the specific purpose of walking with the other anchoress. At first, Fidelma thought the woman was extremely short in height but then she realised that the anchoress clutched a stick and moved in a curious waddling posture. It was clear that her legs were deformed although her upper body was well shaped. With sadness, Fidelma saw that she was young, with a broad, perhaps rather plain face, and watery blue eyes. She swung from side to side, heaving herself forward with the aid of her blackthorn stick, keeping well up with the procession. Fidelma felt a compassion for the misfortune of the young sister and wondered what mischance had caused her debility.

The sky had already lightened and it was now bright enough for the procession to wind its way through the buildings towards the forest that grew around the abbey. One of the sisters, with a soft soprano voice, began to intone in Latin, the chorus being taken up by the other sisters:

> *Cantemus in omni die*
> *concinentes uarie,*
> *conclamantes Deo dignum*
> *hymnum sanctae Mariae*

Fidelma whispered the translation to herself as they

proceeded onwards: 'Let us sing each day, chanting together in varied harmonies, declaiming to God a worthy hymn for holy Mary'.

They paused in a little clearing where, it seemed, a burial place for the community had been prepared, judging by the memorial stones and crosses that stood in abundance. A light dusting of flaky snow covered the ground. The abbess had conducted the bier to an isolated corner of the cemetery. Here the sisters, carrying the bier expertly, as if they had much practice, took the body from it and lowered it into the grave which had apparently been dug the day before in readiness.

Fidelma was prepared for what came next. It was an ancient custom. The wooden bier on which the body had been carried was smashed into little pieces by two sisters wielding hammers. According to ancient superstition, which the Faith had not yet destroyed, the bier must be broken for, if this was not done, the evil spirits might use it to carry off the corpse in their night excursions. If the bier was destroyed the evil spirits had to let the corpse rest.

An extremely young sister of pleasing appearance, approached carrying a huge bunch of green bushy branches. Fidelma recognised her as Sister Lerben, the young novice who had conducted her to the abbess' chamber on the previous evening. The others formed a line before her at the graveside and as they passed the youthful-looking Sister Lerben, each took a small branch before pausing at the open grave and dropping it in. Fidelma and the disabled religieuse, helped by Sister Brónach, were standing last in line. With a gentle smile, Fidelma signalled Sister Brónach and the disabled sister to precede her before taking one of the remaining branches from Sister Lerben to deposit it in the grave and returning to her place. The birch branch was called *ses sofais* which not only gave the body a covering before the earth was shovelled in but was traditionally thought to protect the corpse from any malignant force.

Abbess Draigen moved forward to deposit the last piece of birch in the open grave. As two sisters began to fill the grave with earth, the abbess began to intone the words of the *Biait*, the Irish name for Psalm 118, the word 'blessed' being taken from the first line which was considered the most powerful invocation for efficacy of the suffering soul. Yet Abbess Draigen did not recite the *Biait* in its entirety but was selective in her rendering.

'I call upon the Lord in my distress; the Lord answered me, and set me free.

'The Lord is on my side; I will not fear; what can man do to me?

'The Lord is on my side and helps me against my enemies,

'It is better to find refuge with the Lord than to trust men;

'It is better to find sanctuary with the Lord than to trust princes.'

Fidelma frowned at the vehemence of the abbess's enunciation as if the words had some deeper significance for her.

Then the task was over. The poor headless corpse had been interred and the appropriate prayers and blessings had been said in accordance with the rituals of the Faith.

The sun was now well up and Fidelma could feel the faint warmth of its early morning, winter rays on her face. The woods had burst into life now, the tuneful sounds of birdsong and the soft whispering of the leaves and branches, shaking off their snow covering in the morning breeze, changed the solemnity of the proceedings to a joyous serenity.

She was aware that the sisters of the community were wending their way slowly back towards the abbey buildings. Fidelma saw the disabled religieuse, behind the others, propelling her way along the path with her stick, accompanied by Sister Brónach. A hollow cough distracted her attention and she turned to find the abbess approaching and with her was a young sister who had stood at the right hand of the abbess throughout the proceedings.

'Good morning, sister,' the abbess greeted.

Fidelma returned the salutation.

'What was the strange noise in the chapel?' she asked immediately. 'The community seem quite disturbed by it.'

Abbess Draigen grimaced disdainfully.

'They should know better. I have shown you our *subterraneus*.'

'Yes, but any noise from that would not be heard in the chapel, surely? It does not extend under the *duirthech*.'

'True enough. Yet, as I told you, there are supposed to be several caves over which the abbey was raised and we have been unable to find entrances to them apart from our store cave. Doubtless there is a cave under the chapel which probably floods and produced the sound we heard.'

Fidelma conceded this was possible.

'So you have heard this before?'

Abbess Draigen seemed suddenly impatient.

'Several times during winter months. It is an irrelevant matter.' It was clear that she was weary of the subject. She turned slightly to her companion. 'This is Sister Síomha, my steward, who discovered the corpse with Sister Brónach.'

Fidelma examined the attractive features of Sister Síomha with some surprise. They were the features of a young, angelic girl, not the experienced eyes of someone who looked like a *rechtaire*, the steward of a community. Fidelma tried to overcome her surprise with a belated smile but she found there was no answering warmth from the young steward of the abbey.

'I have duties to see to, sister, so perhaps you would be good enough to ask me your questions immediately.' The tone was abrupt, almost testy. It was so unlike the tone Fidelma had been expecting from the sweet-looking girl that she blinked and was unable to answer for a moment.

'That I cannot do,' she replied stolidly.

She was rewarded by seeing a disconcerted expression pass over Sister Síomha's face.

Fidelma turned to follow the other sisters.

'I beg your pardon, sister?' Síomha's voice had risen slightly in a querulous tone as she took a hesitant step after her.

Fidelma glanced over her shoulder.

'I will be able to see you at noon today. You may come to the guests' hostel to find me.' Fidelma proceeded on her way before Sister Síomha could respond.

A moment or so later the abbess, who had hurried after her, fell in step. She was slightly breathless.

'I do not understand, sister,' she said, her brows were drawn together. 'I thought last night that you expressed a desire to speak with my house steward.'

'And so I do, mother abbess,' Fidelma said. 'But, as you'll recall, I also promised to break my fast with Adnár this morning. The sun has already risen and I must find a way of crossing to his fortress.'

Draigen looked disapproving.

'I do not think your visit to Adnár is necessary. The man has no jurisdiction over this matter and God is to be thanked for that.'

'Why so, mother abbess?' queried Fidelma.

'Because he is a mean, spiteful man, capable of great slanders.'

'Meaning slanders directed at yourself?'

Abbess Draigen shrugged.

'I not know, nor do I care. It concerns me little what Adnár has to tittle-tattle about. But I think that he is keen to impart some gossip to you.'

'Is that why he tried to race your boat to Ross's ship when it arrived here?'

'Why else? He is certainly piqued that he, as *bó-aire*, and therefore magistrate, has not been put in charge of this matter. He would like to have some power over this community.'

'Why so?'

Abbess Draigen pursed her lips angrily.

'Because the man is vain, that is why. He loves his little brief authority.'

Fidelma abruptly halted and examined the features of the abbess closely.

'Adnár is chieftain of this territory. His fortress stands just across the inlet and therefore this abbey must pay dues to him. Yet I detect some great animosity between this abbey and Adnár.'

Fidelma was careful not to personalise things.

Abbess Draigen flushed.

'I can have no control over your thoughts, sister, or your interpretation of what you see about you.' She began to turn away and then paused. 'If you have it in mind to break your fast with Adnár this morning, then it will be a long walk around the shoreline to the headland on which Adnár's fortress is set. However, you will find a small boat tied to our quay. You may use it, if you will, for it takes ten minutes to row across the inlet from this point.'

Fidelma was about to thank her but the abbess was already walking away.

The abbess was right. It was a short and pleasant crossing in front of the mouth of the small river, emptying into the inlet between the headland on which the abbey had been built and the bald promontory of rock on which the circular stone fortress of Adnár stood. What was it that Ross had called it? The fortress of the cow-goddess – Dún Boí. Fidelma had to admire the foresight of the builders of the fort for the promontory it stood on commanded not only the open gateway to the sea but the entire inlet, which was several miles across. The forests had been cleared from the promontory so that the lookouts' view across the inlet was totally unimpeded and from the wooden buildings which rose beyond its grey granite walls, the woods cut down had been put to good use in the construction of the fortress itself.

As Fidelma rowed across the shallow bay which separated the abbey from the fortress, she heard a shout from a dark silhouette on the fortress wall. She gave a half glance over her shoulder and saw another figure running. Her coming had obviously been spotted and the news was being relayed to Adnár.

Indeed, by the time Fidelma worked her small craft alongside the wooden jetty below the fortress, Adnár himself was standing with a couple of his warriors to welcome her ashore. He bent forward, smiling and was courtesy itself as he helped her from the boat.

'Welcome, sister. The journey was not arduous?'

Fidelma found herself returning his smile.

'Not arduous at all. It is but a short distance,' she added, pointing out the obvious.

'I thought I heard a service bell tolling earlier?' The comment was put more in the form of a question.

'Indeed, you did,' Fidelma confirmed. 'It was the burial service for the corpse that was found.'

Adnár looked startled.

'Does that mean that you have discovered the identity of the corpse?'

Fidelma shook her head. For an odd moment she wondered whether she had detected a note of anxiety in the chieftain's voice.

'The abbess decided that the corpse should be buried without a name. If she had delayed any longer then the matter would have become a danger to the health of the community.'

'A danger?' Adnár seemed preoccupied with his own thoughts for a while and then he realised what she meant. 'Ah, I see. So you have come to no conclusions on the matter as yet?'

'None.'

Adnár turned and motioned with his hand up the short pathway which led from the jetty to a wooden gate in the grey walls of the fortress.

'Let me show you the way, sister. I am pleased that you have come. I was not sure whether you would or not.'

Fidelma frowned slightly.

'I told you that I would break my fast with you this morning. What I say I will do, I do.'

The tall, black-haired chieftain spread his hands apologetically as he stood aside to allow her through the gate first.

'I meant no insult, sister. It is just that the Abbess Draigen has no love for me.'

'That I could witness for myself yesterday,' Fidelma replied.

Adnár turned up a short flight of stone steps to a large wooden building made from great oak timbers. The double doors were ornately carved. She noticed that the two warriors who had been surreptitiously accompanying them now took a stand at the bottom of the steps as Adnár pushed open the doors.

Fidelma gave a quick intake of breath at the scene which greeted her. The feasting hall of Adnár was warm, a large fire roared in a great hearth. The whole room was richly decorated and far beyond the standard which she would have expected of a simple *bó-aire*, a cow chieftain of no landed property. The building was mainly of oak but the walls were inset with panels of polished yew. Burnished bronze and silver shields hung around the walls between rich foreign tapestries. There were even some book satchels hung on the walls and a lectern for reading them. Animal skins, such as otter, deer and bear, were strewn across the floor. A circular table had already been set for the meal, piled with fruits and cold meats and cheeses and jugs of water and wine.

'You keep a fine house, Adnár,' Fidelma commented, gazing at the munificence of the table's contents.

'He keeps it only when he knows that special guests will grace the table, sister.'

Fidelma turned sharply at the sound of the pleasant tenor, male voice.

A thin-faced young man had entered the room. Fidelma found herself taking an instant dislike to the man. He was clean shaven, but the stubble grew almost blue against his thin jowls. In fact, his whole body was thin, the nose angular, the lips red but little more than a slit, and his eyes were large black orbs which never seemed to stay still for longer than a few seconds. They darted constantly, giving the man a furtive expression. Over his saffron shirt he wore a sleeveless sheepskin jerkin, belted around the middle. A red-gold necklace adorned his neck. Fidelma saw that he also carried a bejewelled dagger in a leather sheath at his side. Only men and women of high rank were allowed to carry a dagger into a feasting hall where no greater weapons were ever allowed.

The young man was not much older than the 'age of choice', his maturity. Fidelma placed him at no more than eighteen years of age – perhaps nineteen at the most.

Adnár moved forward a pace.

'Sister Fidelma, allow me to present Olcán, son of Gulban the Hawk-Eye, prince and ruler of the Beara, whose territory you are now in.'

The hand that the young man extended was damp and limp. Fidelma felt a slight shudder go through her body as they touched hands in greeting. It was like touching the flesh of a corpse.

Fidelma knew that she was wrong to take a dislike to Olcán simply on account of his appearance. What was the line from Juvenal? *Fronti nulla fides.* No reliance can be placed on appearance. She, above all people, should be warned against hasty judgments made solely on what the eye perceived.

'Welcome, sister. Welcome. Adnár has told me that you had arrived and why.'

She had never met Olcán before but she knew that his

father Gulban claimed descent back to the great king of
Muman, Ailill Olum, who had ruled three or four centuries
before and from whom her own family had descended. From
this descent her own brother now sat on the throne of Cashel.
Yet, she also knew that Gulban was chieftain of only one sept
of the greater clan of the Loígde.

'I had no idea that you resided here, Olcán,' she said.

The young man shook his head swiftly.

'I do not. I am only a guest enjoying the hospitality of
Adnár. I am here to fish and to hunt.'

He half turned as a hollow cough sounded in the shadows.

Behind him, a broad-shouldered, good-looking man in a
religieux robe came forward. He was about forty, perhaps
even in his mid-forties. Fidelma took in his pleasant features.
His red gold hair, whose lights shone like burnished metal in
the sun that permeated the windows, was cut in the tonsure
of St John, the front half of his head shaven back to a line
from ear to ear. His eyes were wide and blue, the nose slightly
prominent but the lips were red and humorous. Yet his
appearance was made slightly sinister by the fact that the
religieux had stained his eyelids black with berry juice. It was
an old custom of some religieux; a custom, so it was said,
which dated back to the time of the Druids. Many Irish
missionaries going abroad often adopted the style.

Again it was Adnár who moved quickly forward to make
introductions.

'This is Brother Febal, sister,' he announced. 'He is
my *anam-chara* and tends to the spiritual needs of my
community.'

It was the custom in the church to have a 'soul-friend' in
whom to confide one's spiritual problems and confusion. The
custom, Fidelma knew, differed in the Church of Rome
where people were encouraged to confess their sins to a
priest. But in the five kingdoms the *anam-chara* was more a
confidant and a spiritual guide than one who simply allotted
punishment for spiritual transgressions. The handsome

religieux smiled warmly and his handshake was firm and sure. Yet there was something Fidelma found she did not trust about the man. Something that conjured up ladies' bedchambers and softly turning door handles. She tried to shake the thought from her mind.

Olcán seemed to have taken over as host in Adnár's feasting hall and waved Fidelma to take a seat near him while Adnár and Brother Febal sat opposite them at the round table. As soon as they were seated, a youthful attendant hurried forward to pour wine for them.

'Is your brother, Colgú, well?' asked Olcán. 'How goes it with our new king?'

'He was well when I last saw him at Ros Ailithir,' replied Fidelma cautiously. 'He returned to Cashel just before I came away.'

'Ah, Ros Ailithir!' Olcán cast her an appraising look. 'All Muman thrilled to the news of how you solved the mystery of the murder of the Venerable Dacán there.'

Fidelma stirred with embarrassment. She did not like her work to be considered anything out of the ordinary.

'It was a puzzle to be solved. And it is my task as an advocate of the courts to probe conundrums and perceive the truth. However, you said *all* Muman thrilled at my solution. I doubt this could be true among your people, the Loígde? Salbach, your former chieftain, did not come well out of that situation.'

'Salbach was an ambitious fool.' Olcán pursed his lips sourly at her response. 'My father, Gúlban, had often clashed with him when attending the clan assembly. Salbach was not welcome in this land.'

'Yet the people of Beara are a sept of the Loígde,' Fidelma pointed out.

'Our first allegiance is to Gulban and his allegiance is then to the chieftain who sits at Cuan Dóir. Anyway, Salbach is no longer chieftain but Bran Finn Mael Ochtraighe. Personally, I have no interest in politics. For this, my father and I are—'

he grinned, 'are estranged. My view is that life is to be enjoyed and what better means than hunting...?' He was about to go further but hesitated and then ended: 'However, you did well in ridding our people of an ambitious incompetent.'

'As I have said, I performed no more than my duty as an advocate.'

'A task that not everyone is as adept at. You have earned a reputation of being very accomplished. Adnár tells me that it is just such a mystery as brings you hither. Is this true?'

He passed her a plate of cold meats which she declined, preferring to help herself to a bowl of oats and nuts with fresh apples to follow.

'That is so,' Adnár intervened quickly.

Brother Febal had appeared uninterested in the opening conversation and was devoting himself, head down, to concentrating on his meal.

'I have come at the request of the Abbess Draigen,' confirmed Fidelma. 'She asked the Abbot Brocc to send a *dálaigh* to her abbey.'

'Ah,' Olcán sighed deeply, apparently studying the dregs in his wine goblet as if interested by them. Then he raised his gaze to Fidelma. 'I am told that the abbess has something of a reputation in this land. She is not regarded as, how can I say it?, "spiritually advanced"? Isn't that so, Brother Febal?'

Febal raised his head quickly from his plate. He hesitated and swung his blue eyes to Fidelma, staring at her for a moment, before dropping his gaze back on his plate.

'It is as you say, my prince. The Abbess Draigen is said to have unnatural tendencies.'

Fidelma leaned forward, her eyes narrowed as she concentrated on Brother Febal.

'Perhaps you would be good enough to be more explicit, brother?'

Brother Febal jerked his head up again, his expression startled, and glanced nervously to Olcán and Adnár. Then he reset his features almost woodenly.

'*Sua cuique sunt vitia*,' he intoned.

'Indeed, we all have our own vices,' agreed Fidelma, 'but perhaps you will tell us what you discern are the vices of the abbess?'

'I think that we all know what Brother Febal means,' Adnár interrupted petulantly, as if annoyed at Fidelma's lack of understanding. 'I think that if a young female corpse were found in the abbey, and I were conducting an investigation, then I would look no further than the abbey for a suspect and, for a motive, no further than base and perverted passion.'

Sister Fidelma sat back and regarded Adnár curiously.

'And is this what you have invited me here to tell me?'

Adnár inclined his head in a brief gesture of affirmation.

'Originally, I invited you here to register my protest that the Church has sent one of its own to deal with the matter at the request of the chief suspect. I thought you had come here to help exonerate the abbess.'

'And now you have changed your mind?' Fidelma caught the careful phraseology of the *bó-aire*.

Adnár cast an uncomfortable look at Olcán.

'Olcán assures me that he knows of your reputation; that you have been trusted by the High King himself as well as kings and princes in other lands. I am therefore content to leave this matter in your hands, sister, knowing that you will not exonerate where blame is due.'

Fidelma was studying the man, trying to keep her surprise to herself. That an accusation of this kind should be brought against the leader of a religious community was a matter of gravity.

'Let me get this clear, Adnár,' she said slowly. 'You are openly claiming that the Abbess Draigen was responsible for the death of this young girl and the motive was to hide her own sexual partiality?'

Adnár was about to reply when Olcán interrupted.

'No, I do not think that Adnár is making an official charge. He is pointing out an obvious course of inquiry. It appears common knowledge in these parts that the Abbess Draigen has a predilection for attractive young religieuses and encourages them to her abbey. That is no more than common gossip. Now we have a young female corpse found at the abbey. I think Adnár is advising you that it would be well to examine whether anything amiss has happened within the abbey walls.'

Fidelma was examining the young man while he was speaking. He appeared to speak with straightforward conviction and honesty but was intelligent enough to lead Adnár out of a dangerous path whereby he could stand answerable before the law for spreading dangerous stories about the abbess. Brother Febal did not appear to concern himself with the matter, continuing to pick at the food on the table. Olcán seemed merely anxious that she should know the full extent of the situation.

She sighed deeply.

'Very well. This conversation will not go beyond these walls,' she agreed at last. 'In return, I will undertake to investigate closely any information that may lead to the culprit, however unpalatable it is for anyone of position and rank.'

Olcán sat back in relief.

'That is all Adnár is concerned with, is that not so?'

The chieftain gestured affirmatively.

'I am sure that you will find many people hereabouts to support our views of the Abbess Draigen. Brother Febal speaks as a churchman. He is extremely concerned at the stories which he hears about the abbess and is jealous for the good reputation of the Faith.'

Fidelma looked sharply at the religieux.

'There are many stories?'

'Several,' agreed Brother Febal.

'And have any of them been proved?'

Brother Febal shrugged indifferently.

'There are several stories,' he repeated. '*Valeat quatum valere potest.*'

He added the standard phrase when a person passes on information which has not been proved, meaning 'take it for what it's worth'.

Fidelma sniffed suspiciously.

'Very well. But, if your accusation is correct, you would have to accept that many people in the abbey are in collusion with the abbess. To take this to a logical conclusion, someone else would have known if the abbess was having an affair with the murdered girl. If the corpse was a member of the abbey community, surely someone would know and, if so, there is the collusion. If not, the girl would either have been a local, in which case why has her disappearance not been reported to you, Adnár, as *bó-aire*? Or, she must have been a stranger, presumably staying at the abbey. Again, the community at the abbey would have known this.'

Brother Febal's eyes darted quickly to Fidelma.

'We see a sample of your deductive powers, sister,' he said in a warm tone. 'All my lords ask is that you use your talent fairly in finding the culprit. *Res in cardine est.*'

Fidelma had begun to feel very irritated at what she saw was the patronising tone of the brother. She was also irked by his questionable Latin tags. To say that 'the matter is on a door hinge' was to imply that Fidelma would work out the truth soon enough. But he had prefaced his remark with a deliberate insult and she decided to take issue with Brother Febal's suggestion that she would not undertake the investigation fairly.

'The validity of my oath as an advocate of the courts of the five kingdoms has never been questioned before,' she replied waspishly.

Olcán immediately reached forward and laid a consoling hand on her arm.

'My dear sister, I think Brother Febal badly phrased his words. I believe that he merely wishes to express concern at this matter. Indeed, Adnár and I are very concerned. After all, the murder happened in the territory of Adnár, so you will agree that it is right for him, as magistrate, to show disquietude. Adnár's allegiance is to my father, Gulban, whose interests I am forced to represent. Therefore, I also share his apprehension.'

Fidelma sighed inwardly. She knew that sometimes she could give way too easily to her prickly ire.

'Of course,' she responded, forcing herself to smile briefly. 'Yet I am merely jealous of my reputation when it comes to judgments and the law.'

'We are happy to leave the matter in your capable hands,' Olcán agreed. 'I am sure Brother Febal regrets if his words were ill-chosen . . . ?'

Brother Febal smiled ingratiatingly.

'*Peccavi*,' he said, placing his hand on his heart, expressing in Latin that he had sinned. Fidelma did not bother to answer him.

Olcán glossed the awkward moment.

'Now, let us to other matters. Is this your first visit to this land of Beara?'

Fidelma confessed it was, for she had never been to the peninsula before.

'It is a beautiful place, even in the throes of winter. It is a land of the primal beginnings of our people,' enthused Olcán. 'Did you know that this is the shore where the sons of Míl, the first of the Gaels, landed? Where Amairgen the Druid promised the three goddesses of the Dé Danaan, Banba, Fodhla and Éire, that the country would forever bear their names?'

Fidelma was suddenly amused at the young man's enthusiasm for his native territory.

'Perhaps when I am finished here I shall be able to see something more of this land of yours,' she replied solemnly.

'Then I will be delighted to accompany you,' offered Olcán. 'Why, from the side of the mountain behind us, I can point out the distant island where the god of death, Donn, gathered the souls of the departed to transport them in his great black ship to the west, to the Otherworld. Adnár also has much knowledge of the local history. Isn't that so, Adnár?'

The chieftain bowed his head in stiff acknowledgment.

'As Olcán says, should you wish to see the ancient sites of this land, we would be pleased to offer you our company as guides.'

'I shall look forward to that,' agreed Fidelma, for she did have a great fascination for the ancient legends of her land. 'But now I should be returning to the abbey to continue my investigation.'

She rose from the table and they reluctantly rose with her.

Olcán placed his hand familiarly under Fidelma's elbow and guided her from the feasting hall. Brother Febal seemed content to reseat himself and continue his meal without a gesture of farewell while Adnár quickly followed them.

'It has been good to meet with you, Fidelma,' Olcán said, as they came out on to the steps, pausing for a moment. 'It is sad, however, that this meeting has been precipitated by such a terrible event.' The view of the inlet was lit by the pale light of the sun. Olcán glanced across to where the Gaulish merchant vessel was anchored, the solitary ship in the bay. 'Is that the ship in which you came from Ros Ailithir?' he asked, regarding its alien lines with sudden interest.

Fidelma quickly sketched the mystery.

Then Adnár broke in.

'I shall be sending my men aboard the Gaulish ship this afternoon,' he said decisively.

Fidelma turned to him in some astonishment.

'For what purpose?'

Adnár gave a complacent smile.

'Surely you are acquainted with the salvage laws?'

His tone immediately drew Fidelma's indignation.

'If your purpose is sarcasm, Adnár, I would advise against it. It never wins an argument against logic,' she replied coldly. 'I know the salvage laws and still ask you on what grounds you plan to send your men to claim the Gaulish ship?'

Olcán smiled wryly at Adnár's red-cheeked mortification. Resentfully the *bó-aire*'s mouth narrowed.

'I am advised on the texts of the *Mur-Bretha*, sister. I have to know such things as I am magistrate of a stretch of this shoreline. Any salvage thrown up on this sea shore belongs to me . . .'

Olcán turned to Fidelma with an apologetic smile.

'Surely, he is right, sister? But in so far as the object of salvage is valued to five *séts* or cows. If it is worth more, then the excess has to be divided, one third to the *bó-aire*, a third to the ruler of this territory, my father, and a third to the heads of the major clans in this area.'

Fidelma regarded the triumphant features of Adnár and turned back to Olcán with a grave expression.

'You neglected to add, in your reading of the sea laws, that your father would also have to give one-fourth of his share to the provincial king, my brother, and the provincial king would then have to give one fourth of that share to the High King. That is the strict law of salvage.'

Olcán chuckled loudly in appreciation of Fidelma's knowledge of the law of salvage.

'By my soul, you live up to your reputation, Sister Fidelma.'

If the truth were known, Fidelma had only recently read the texts of the *Mur-Bretha* while investigating the problem at Ros Ailithir. At the time, she had found that she was woefully deficient in her knowledge of the laws appertaining to the sea. Only her recent study had now made her so perspicuous on the matter.

'So you will also know,' Adnár added, almost slyly, in his

confidence, 'as *bó-aire* I have to impose a fine on Ross for not immediately sending out a notice to me and the chieftains of this district that he has brought this ship as salvage into this port. That also is the law.'

Fidelma looked at Adnár's grinning face but remained solemn. She slowly shook her head and saw his expression change into one of disconcertion.

'You need to study your laws on the *frith-fairrgi*, or "finds of the sea", more closely.'

'Why so?' Adnár demanded, his tone losing its former confidence at her calm assurance.

'Because if you had studied the text carefully, you would see that if a man brings in a valuable article floating on the sea, which includes a ship as well as mere flotsam and jetsam, and he has salvaged that article beyond the distance of nine waves from the shore, then he has a right to it and no other person can lay claim to it, not even the High King. The ship, therefore, belongs to Ross and no other. Only if the salvage was made within the distance of nine waves from this shore do you have any claim on it.'

The length of nine waves was considered to be the length of a measure called a *forrach* and each *forrach* was one hundred and forty-four feet. So Ross's encounter with the Gaulish ship had been well out of territorial waters and on the high seas.

The distance of nine waves had a symbolism going back to pagan times. Even now, among those who purported to believe in the new Faith of the Christ, the magical symbol of the nine waves was entirely accepted. Two years previously, when the awesome Yellow Plague was devastating the five kingdoms of Ireland, Colmán, the chief professor of the Blessed Finbarr's college at Cork, had fled with his pupils to an island so as to place nine waves between him and the Irish mainland. He had claimed 'pestilence does not make its way farther than nine waves'.

Adnár stared at Fidelma aghast.

'Do you jest with me?' he demanded, almost through clenched teeth.

Olcán saw Fidelma's brows drawing together and disarmed her with a hearty laugh.

'Of course she does not, Adnár. No officer of the courts will ever jest about the law. You, my dear *bó-aire*, have been misinformed about the law.'

Adnár turned his outraged gaze to the young prince.

'But . . .' he began to protest but was silenced with a quick, angry glance from Olcán.

'Enough! The matter wearies me as I am sure it does Sister Fidelma.' He smiled pleasantly at her. 'We must let her return to the abbey now. You will bear in mind the advice from Adnár and Brother Febal? Yes, I am sure you will,' he went on before she could answer. 'However, if there is anything you wish while you are staying in our land of Beara you have but to ask. I believe I speak for my father, Gulban, as well as myself.'

'That is good to know, Olcán,' Fidelma answered gravely. 'And now, I will give my attention to the more pressing problem. I thank you for your hospitality, Adnár . . . and your advice.'

She was aware of them watching her from the walls of the fortress as she made her way to the wooden jetty and was helped into the boat by a silent warrior. She saw them still watching as she bent into the rhythm of the oars, speeding the little craft back over the bay towards the abbey. She felt uneasy. There was something which troubled her about her visit to Adnár's fortress.

Adnár and Olcán were pleasant enough company. But she could not quite understand her antipathy towards them. Olcán's physical appearance was rather loathsome but he was not unfriendly. Adnár had tried to score a point over the salvage of the Gaulish ship. She should not blame him for that. It was the almost unreasonable aversion to them, which was not borne out by an analysis of logic, that worried her more. There was something she really distrusted and felt herself immediately bristle against. Perhaps she resented their combined spreading of stories about Draigen. It would not take long to discover whether the stories about the abbess were true. And if they were true, did they immediately presuppose some guilt on the part of the abbey's community? For, if guilt there was, then the entire community could not be lacking in some knowledge of it.

She manoeuvred the craft alongside the wooden landing stage of the abbey and once again asked herself if there could be any truth in the accusations?

As she secured the craft and climbed ashore, she heard a gong sounding.

Chapter Six

When Sister Síomha had not shown up at the guests' hostel half-an-hour after the noon hour, the time when Fidelma had requested her presence, Fidelma decided to go in search of the steward of the community. She checked the time as she passed the ornate bronze sundial which stood in the centre of the courtyard with its ostentatious Latin inscription: '*Horas non numero nisi serenas* – I do not count the hours unless they are bright.' The day was cold but, certainly, it was bright and clear. The snow clouds that had passed in the night were long gone.

It was the pretty young Sister Lerben who was able to direct Fidelma to the tower which rose behind the wooden church. Fidelma had discovered that Sister Lerben was more personal servant than simple attendant to the abbess. Lerben told Fidelma that she would find Sister Síomha in the tower attending to the water-clock. The tower was a large construction standing immediately next to the stone store room which Fidelma had entered on the previous evening. The tower's foundations were of stone and then its upper storeys were built of wood, rising to a height of thirty-five feet. Fidelma could see, on the flat top of the tower, the main bell by which the community was summoned to prayer.

Ascending the wooden stairs within the squat stone foundations, Fidelma felt an increasing annoyance at the arrogance of the steward who had ignored her summons. If a *dálaigh* demanded the presence of a witness, then the witness had to obey on pain of a fine. Fidelma determined that she would ensure the conceited Sister Síomha learned this lesson.

The square tower was built in a series of chambers placed one on top of the other with floors of birch planking supported by heavy oak beams from which steps led from one chamber to another. Each chamber had four small windows which commanded views on all four sides but these made the rooms gloomy rather than bringing light into them. The tower itself, or at least the first two floors of it, were filled by the community's *Tech-screptra*, the 'house of manuscripts' or library. Wooden fames crossed the room on which rows of pegs hung and from each peg was suspended a *tiag liubhar* or book satchel.

Fidelma paused amazed at the collection of books which the abbey of The Salmon of the Three Wells had in its possession. There must have been fully fifty or more hanging from the pegs on the first two floors. She carefully examined several of them finding, among them, to her further surprise, copies of the works of the eminent Irish scholar Longarad of Sliabh Marga. Another book satchel contained the works of Dallán Forgaill of Connacht, who had presided at the Great Bardic Assemblies of his day, and who had been murdered seventy years ago. Suspicion was laid at the door of Guaire the Hospitable, king of Connacht, but nothing was ever proved. It was one of the great mysteries which Fidelma often found herself contemplating and wishing that she had lived in those times so that she could solve the riddle of Dallán's death.

She looked in a third book satchel and found a copy of *Teagasc Rí*, The Instruction of the King. The author of this work was the High King Cormac Mac Art, who had died at Tara in AD 254. Although he had not been of the Faith he was famed as one of the wisest and most beneficent of monarchs. He had composed the book of instructions on the conduct of life, health, marriage and manners. Fidelma smiled as she remembered her first day under instruction of her mentor, the Brehon Morann of Tara. She had been shy and almost afraid to speak. Morann had quoted from Cormac's book: 'If you be too talkative, you will not be heeded: if you be too silent, you will not be regarded.'

A frown crossed her face as she examined the vellum leaves of the book. Many of them were stained with a reddish mud. How could any good librarian allow such a treasure to be so defaced? She made a mental note to speak of the condition of the book to the librarian and thrust it back into its satchel, rebuking herself from being waylaid from her purpose in coming to the tower.

Reluctantly, she drew herself away from the library and climbed to the third floor. Here was a room set out for the scribes and copyists of the community. It was empty now but there were writing tables ready with piles of quills of geese, swans, and crows ready to be sharpened. Writing boards with vellum, the stretched skins of sheep, goat and calves, stood ready. Pots of ink made from carbon, black and durable.

Fidelma glanced around and presumed that the scriptors who occupied the copying room were at their midday meal following the noon Angelus. The pale sun infiltrated into the room from the southern and western windows, illuminating it in a sharp beam of translucent light, making it seem warm and comfortable in spite of the chill air. It was a spacious and secure place to work in, she reflected. From here the view was breathtaking. To the south and west, through the windows, she could see the shimmering sea and encompassing headlands around the inlet. The Gaulish ship still rode at anchor. The sails were furled but she could see no sign of Odar and his men on board. She presumed they were resting or at their noonday meal. The water sparkled around the vessel reflecting the pastel colour of the clear sky. Looking due west she could see the fortress of Adnár and turning to the north and east, she could see the forests and the rising snow-capped peaks of the mountains behind the abbey, peaks which ran along the peninsula like the ridged back of a lizard.

She moved across to the northern window and peered out. Below her the buildings of the abbey stretched around the large clearing on the low-lying headland. The place seemed deserted now, confirming her belief that the sisters were eating their midday meal in the refectory. The abbey of The Salmon of the Three Wells was certainly situated in a most beautiful spot. The high cross stood tall and white in the sun. Immediately below was the courtyard, with its central sundial. There were numerous unconnected buildings forming the sides of the courtyard with the large wooden church, the *duirthech*, which ran along the southern side of the paved yard. Behind the main buildings fronting the courtyard were several other structures of wood, and a few of stone, in which the community lived and worked.

Fidelma was about to turn back into the room when she caught a slight movement on a track about half a mile distant from the abbey. It was a track that seemed to wend its way down from the mountains and disappear behind the tree line, heading, presumably, in the direction of Adnár's fortress. A dozen riders were cautiously guiding their horses along this road. Fidelma screwed her eyes to sharpen the vision. Behind the horsemen, more men were trotting on foot. She felt sorry for them as she saw they were hard pressed to keep up with the riders on the sloping, rocky ground.

She could make out nothing, except that the foremost riders were richly accoutred. The sun splashed on the vivid colours of their dress and sparkled and blazed on the burnished shields of several of the mounted men. At the head of the column, one of the riders carried a banner on a long pole. A stream of silk, with some emblem which she could not discern, snapped and twisted in the breeze. She frowned at some strange shape on one of the riders' shoulders. From this distance, her first glance made it initially seem as if he had two heads. No! She could now and then see a movement from the shape and realised that perched on this rider's shoulder was a large hawk. The line of riders, with those following on foot, eventually passed down below the tree line and out of her vision.

Fidelma stood a few moments wondering if she would catch sight of them again but the thick surrounding oak forest hid them from view now that they were down off the high ground. She wondered who they were and then gave a mental shrug. It was no use wasting time wondering when she did not have the ability to resolve the answer.

She turned away from the window and made her way to the steps that led to the fourth and highest room of the tower.

She entered through the trap door into this upper room without pausing to knock or otherwise announce her presence.

Sister Síomha was bending over a large bronze basin which stood on a stone fireplace and was steaming gently. The *rechtaire* of the community glanced up with an angry frown and then let her expression change a little when she recognised Fidelma.

'I was wondering when you would come,' the steward of the community greeted her in an irritable tone.

For once, Fidelma found herself without words. Her eyes involuntarily widened.

Sister Síomha paused to adjust a small copper bowl which was floating on top of the steaming bronze basin before straightening up and turning to face Fidelma.

Once more Fidelma found the angelic heart-shaped face difficult to equate with the attitude and office of *rechtaire*. Fidelma examined her carefully, registering that the eyes were large and of an amber colour. The lips were full and here and there a strand of brown hair poked from under her head dress. A disarming splash of freckles daubed her face. The young sister gave an impression of wide-eyed innocence. Yet something sparkled deep within those amber eyes, an expression that Fidelma had difficulty in interpreting. It was a restless, angry fire.

Fidelma drew her brows together and tried to recover her feeling of annoyance.

'We agreed to meet at the guests' hostel at noon,' she began but to her surprise the young sister shook her head firmly.

'We did not agree,' she replied in an abrupt tone. 'You told me to be there at noon and then walked away before I could answer.'

Fidelma was taken aback. It was certainly one interpretation of the exchange. However, one had to bear in mind the young girl's initial haughty presumption that had made Fidelma react in order to curb her insolence and disrespect for Fidelma's office. Obviously, no lesson had been learned and now Fidelma had been placed on a wrong footing.

'You realise, Sister Síomha, that I am an attorney of the court and have certain rights? I summoned you before me as a witness and failure to obey my summons results in your liability to a fine.'

Sister Síomha sneered arrogantly.

'I have no concern for your law. I am steward of this community and my responsibilities here require my attention. My first duty is to my abbess and to the Rule of this community.'

Fidelma swallowed sharply.

She was unsure whether the younger sister was innocently obstructive or merely wilful.

'Then you have much to learn,' Fidelma finally replied with bite. 'You will pay me such fine as I judge worthy and, to ensure your compliance, this will be done before the Abbess Draigen. In the meantime, you will tell me how you came to be with Sister Brónach when the corpse was drawn from the well.'

Sister Síomha opened her mouth as if to dispute with Fidelma but she changed her mind. Instead, she moved to a chair and slumped in it. There was no indication in the movement of her body that her carriage was that of a religieuse. There was no calm poise, no modest folding of her hands, no contemplative submission. Her body spoke of aggression and arrogance.

It was the only seat in the room and there was nothing for Fidelma to do but to stand before the seated girl. Fidelma quickly cast a glance around. The room, like the others before, had four open windows but these were larger than those on the lower floors. There was a stack of small logs and twigs on one side of this room. On the other side was the stone fireplace whose smoke escaped through the western aperture, though, with the changing breeze, sometimes the smoke blew back into the room causing a pungent odour of woodsmoke. A small table, with writing tablets and a few *graib*, or metal writing stylus, on it, was the only other furniture in the room. However, before the north window, there stood a large copper gong and a stick.

A ladder in another corner gave access to the flat roof of the tower on which, she knew, stood the structure from which hung a large bronze bell. At the appropriate time of service and prayer, a sister would climb up to ring it.

All this, Fidelma took in during her brief glance. Then she turned her gaze back to the discourteously seated Sister Síomha.

'You have not replied to my question,' Fidelma said quietly.

'Sister Brónach undoubtedly told you what happened,' she answered stubbornly.

Fidelma's expression held a dangerous fire.

'And now you will tell me.'

The steward repressed a sigh. She made her voice wooden, like a child repeating a well-known lesson.

'It was Sister Brónach's task to draw water from the well. When the Abbess Draigen returned from the midday prayers in the church, Sister Brónach usually had the water waiting for her in her chamber. That day there was no sign of the water or of Sister Brónach. I was with the abbess who asked me, as steward, to go in search of Brónach...'

'Sister Brónach holds the title of doorkeeper of this abbey, doesn't she?' interrupted Fidelma, knowing full well the answer but seeking a means to disrupt the wooden delivery.

Síomha looked disconcerted for a moment and then gave a little motion of her head which implied confirmation.

'She has been here many years. She is older than most people in the community, except our librarian who is the eldest. She bears the title, in respect of her age, rather than her ability.'

'You do not like her, do you?' Fidelma observed sharply.

'Like?' The young girl seemed surprised by the question. 'Didn't Aesop write that there can be little liking where there is no likeness? There is no affinity between Sister Brónach and myself.'

'One does not have to be a soul friend to find affection for another.'

'Pity is no basis for affection,' replied the girl. 'That would be the only emotion I could summon towards Sister Brónach.'

Fidelma realised that Sister Síomha was not without intelligence for all her vanity. She had a verbal dexterity which would conceal her innermost thoughts. But, at least, Fidelma had stopped her wooden-voiced obstruction. Much could be discerned when the voice was more animated. She decided to try another tack.

'I am under the impression that there are not many in this community with whom you have a friendship. Is that not so?'

She had picked this idea up from Sister Brónach but was surprised when Síomha did not deny it.

'As steward it is not my job to please everyone. I have to make many decisions. Not all my decisions please the community. But I am *rechtaire* and I hold a responsible position.'

'But your decisions are made with the approval of the Abbess Draigen, of course?'

'The abbess trusts me implicitly.' There was a boastful note in the girl's voice.

'I see. Well, let us continue with the discovery of the body. So, at the mother abbess's request, you went in search of Sister Brónach?'

'She was at the well but having difficulty in drawing the rope up. I thought that she was trying to hide her tardiness.'

'Ah yes. Why was that?'

'I had drawn water but an hour or two before and there had been no difficulty.'

Fidelma leant forward quickly. 'Do you recall at precisely what hour you had drawn water from that well?'

Sister Síomha placed her head to one side, appearing to reflect on the question.

'No more than two hours before.'

'And there was, of course, no sign of anything amiss at that time?'

'If there had been,' Sister Síomha replied with heavy irony, 'I would have said something.'

'Of course you would. But let me be clear, there was nothing unusual around the well? No sign of any disturbance, no stains of blood in the snow?'

'None.'

'Was anyone else with you?'

'Why should there be?'

'No matter. I merely wanted to ensure that we could narrow the time when the body was placed in the well. It would appear that the body was placed in the well a short time before it was found. That would mean, whoever placed it in the well did so in full daylight with the prospect of being seen by anyone from the abbey. Do you not find that strange?'

'I could not say.'

'Very well. Continue.'

'We hauled the rope up, it took some effort and time. Then we found the corpse tied to it. We cut it down and sent for the abbess.'

The details fitted with those given by Sister Brónach.

'Did you recognise the corpse?'

'No. Why should I?' Her voice was sharp.

'Has anyone gone missing from this community?'

The large amber eyes widened perceptibly. For a moment Fidelma was sure that a glint of fear flitted in their unfathomable depths.

'Someone did disappear, who was it?' Fidelma demanded quickly, hoping to take advantage of the almost imperceptible reaction.

Sister Síomha blinked and then was back in control again.

'I have no idea what you are talking about,' she replied. 'No one has *disappeared*,' Fidelma just managed to catch the soft inflection, 'from our community. If you are trying to imply that the body was one of our sisters, then you are mistaken.'

'Think again and remember the penalties for not telling the truth to an officer of the court.'

Sister Síomha rose to her feet with an expression of anger.

'I have no need to lie. Of what do you accuse me?' she demanded.

'I accuse you of nothing ... so far,' replied Fidelma, unperturbed by the display of defiance. 'So, you state that no one had disappeared from the community? All your sisters are accounted for?'

'Yes.'

Fidelma could not help but notice the slight hesitation before Sister Síomha's reply. It was, however, no use pressing the steward. She continued:

'When you sent for the abbess, did she give an that she recognised the corpse?'

The steward stared at her for a moment fathom out the motives behind the question

'Why should the abbess recognise the corpse? Anyway, it was without a head.'

'So the Abbess Draigen was surprised and horrified by the sight of the corpse?'

'As, indeed, we all were.'

'And you have no idea of who this corpse was?'

'On my soul!' snapped the girl. 'I have said as much. I find your questions highly objectionable and I shall report this matter to Abbess Draigen.'

Fidelma smiled tightly.

'Ah yes: Abbess Draigen. What is your relationship with Abbess Draigen?'

The glare of the steward faltered.

'I am not sure what you mean.' Her voice was cold and there was a threatening tone in it.

'I thought my words were clear enough.'

'I enjoy the abbess's trust.'

'How long have you been *rechtaire* here?'

'A full year now.'

'When did you join the community?'

'Two years ago.'

'Isn't that a short time to be in a community and yet be trusted with its second most important office in the abbey – that of *rechtaire*?'

'Abbess Draigen gave me her confidence.'

'That is not what I asked.'

'I am proficient at my work. Surely if someone has an aptitude for a task then it matters not how young they are?'

'Yet, by any standards, it is a remarkably short period from the time that you entered the service of the Faith to the time you were appointed to this position.'

'I know of no comparison to make a judgment.'

'Were you in any other religious community before coming here?'

Sister Síomha shook her head.

'So at what age did you enter here?'

'The age of eighteen.'

'Then you are no more than twenty?'

'I stand a month from my twenty-first birthday,' replied the girl defensively.

'Then, truly, the Abbess Draigen must trust you implicitly. Aptitude for your tasks or not, you are young to hold the position of *rechtaire*,' Fidelma said solemnly and before Sister Síomha could respond, she added: 'And you, in turn, trust Abbess Draigen, of course?'

The girl frowned, unable to follow the trend of Fidelma's questioning.

'Of course, I do. She is my abbess and the superior of this community.'

'And you like her?'

'She is a wise and firm counsellor.'

'You have nothing to say against her?'

'What is there to say?' Sister Síomha snapped. 'Again I find that I do not like your questions.'

The girl regarded Fidelma with an expression of suspicion mixed with irritation.

'Questions are not something you like or dislike. They are to be answered when a *dálaigh* of the Brehon Court asks them.' Once again Fidelma decided to counter the girl's challenge to her authority with a waspish reply.

Sister Síomha blinked rapidly. Fidelma judged that she was unused to anyone challenging her.

'I . . . I have no idea why you are asking me these questions but you seem to be implying criticism of myself and now of the abbess.'

'Why could you be criticised?'

'Are you trying to be clever with me?'

'Clever?' Fidelma allowed surprise to register on her features. 'I make no attempt to be clever. I am simply asking questions to gain a picture of what has happened in this place. Does that worry you so much?'

'It worries me not at all. The sooner this mystery is

resolved, then the sooner we can return to our normal routine.'

Sister Fidelma gave an inward sigh. She had tried to bludgeon the arrogance out of Sister Síomha and had failed.

'Very well. I believe that you are a discerning and intelligent person, Sister Síomha. You are telling me that the headless corpse was a stranger to this community. From where do you think it came?'

Sister Síomha simply shrugged.

'Isn't that your task to discover?' she said sarcastically.

'And I am doing my best to achieve that discovery. However, you have assured me that it was no member of your community. If so, could it be a member of any local community?'

'It was headless. I have told you before that I did not recognise it.'

'But it might have been a member of a local community. Perhaps the girl belonged to Adnár's community across the bay here?'

'No!' the reply was so sharp and immediate that Fidelma was surprised. She raised her eyebrows in interrogation.

'Why so? Do you know Adnár's community so well?'

'No ... no; it's just that I do not think...'

'Ah,' Fidelma smiled. 'If you only *think* it is or is not, then you do not know. Isn't that right? In which case you are guessing, Sister Síomha. If you are guessing in this instance, have you been guessing in your answers to my previous questions?'

Sister Síomha looked outraged.

'How dare you suggest...!'

'Indignation is no response,' replied Fidelma complacently. 'And arrogance is no answer to...'

There was a timid knocking. Sister Brónach entered through the trapdoor.

'What is it?' Sister Síomha snapped at her.

The middle-aged sister blinked at the curtness of the greeting.

'It is the mother abbess, sister. She requires your presence immediately.'

Sister Síomha let her breath exhale slowly.

'And how am I to leave the water-clock?' she demanded, with a gesture to the bowl which stood behind her, her tone bitterly sarcastic.

'I am to take charge of it,' Sister Brónach replied calmly.

Sister Síomha rose to her feet and stared at Fidelma for a moment.

'I presume that I have your permission to go now? I have told you all I know of this matter.'

Fidelma inclined her head without saying anything and the young steward of the community stomped in obvious temper from the room. For once Fidelma rebuked herself for having allowed the temperament of a person to set the tone of her questioning. She had hoped that her sharpness, her bludgeoning style of interrogation would have deflated Sister Síomha's arrogance. But she had not succeeded.

Sister Brónach broke the silence.

'She is annoyed,' she observed softly as she moved to the fireplace and checked the basin of steaming water.

Even as she did so, the floating copper bowl sank abruptly, and Sister Brónach immediately turned to a large gong which stood by the open window. She took a stick and struck it firmly so that the sound seemed to resound across the grounds of the abbey. Then she quickly moved to remove the bowl from the water, deftly using a pair of long wooden tongs which were eighteen inches in overall length so that her hands did not have to contact the water. She removed the bowl and emptied it so that she could refloat it on top of the water.

Fidelma found herself intrigued by the operation, and dismissed Sister Síomha momentarily from her mind. She had seen one or two water-clocks at work before.

101

'Tell me of your system here, Sister Brónach,' she invited, genuinely interested.

Sister Brónach cast an uncertain glance at Fidelma, as if wondering whether there was some hidden purpose to her question. Deciding there was not, or if there was she could not appreciate it, she pointed to the mechanism.

'Someone is obliged to constantly watch the clock, or the clepsydra, as we call it.'

'That I can understand. Explain the mechanism to me.'

'This basin,' Sister Brónach pointed to a large bronze bowl which stood on the fire, 'is filled with water. The water is kept constantly heated and then on it is placed the empty small copper dish, which has a very small hole in its base.'

'I see it.'

'The hot water percolates through the hole in the bottom of the copper dish and gradually fills it and so it eventually sinks to the bottom. When that happens, a period of time of fifteen minutes has passed. We call it a *pongc*. When the dish sinks to the bottom of the basin, the watcher must strike a gong. There are four *pongc* in the *uair* and six *uair* make a *cadar*. When the fourth *pongc* is sounded, the striker of the gong pauses and then strikes the number of the *uair*; when the sixth *uair* is sounded, the striker must pause and then strike the number of the *cadar*, of the quarter of the day. It is a very simple method really.'

As Sister Brónach warmed to her explanation, she seemed to come alive for the first time in Fidelma's brief encounters with her.

Fidelma paused for a moment in thought, seeing a path to extend her knowledge.

'And this water-clock was the method by which you were sure of the hour in which you found the body?'

Sister Brónach nodded absently, as she checked the heat of the water and stoked the fire underneath the big basin.

'It is a tedious business then, tending this water-clock?'

'Tedious enough,' agreed the sister.

'It was therefore surprising to find the *rechtaire* of the community, the house steward, fulfilling this task,' Fidelma commented pointedly.

Brónach replied with a shake of her head.

'Not so; our community prides itself on the accuracy of our clepsydra. Each member of the community, when they join us, agrees to take her turn in keeping the watch. It is written into our Rule. Sister Síomha has been keen that this rule be applied. Why, during these last few weeks, for example, she has insisted on taking most of the night watches herself – that is from midnight until the time of the morning Angelus. Even the mother abbess herself sometimes takes her turn, like everyone else. No one is allowed to keep watch above one *cadar*, that is a six hour period.'

Fidelma suddenly frowned.

'If Sister Síomha takes this night watch, what was she doing here just now, after noon?'

'I did not say that she takes every night watch. It would not be allowed for every sister must do her turn. She takes most of them and she is a very meticulous person.'

'And was Sister Síomha taking the night watch on the night before the body was discovered?'

'Yes. I believe she was.'

'It is a long time to be here, just watching, waiting for the bowl to sink and then remembering how many times to strike a gong,' Fidelma observed.

'Not if one is a contemplative,' replied Sister Brónach. 'There is nothing more relaxing than to take the period of the first *cadar*, that is from midnight until the morning Angelus at the sixth hour. That is the time I like best. That is probably why Sister Síomha also likes to take most of these night watches. One is here, alone with one's thoughts.'

'But thoughts can run away with one's mind,' persisted Fidelma. 'You could forget the period that has passed by and how many times you must strike the gong.'

Sister Brónach picked up a tablet, a wooden-framed

construction in which was a layer of soft clay. There was a
stylus nearby. She made a mark with the stylus and then
handed it to Fidelma.

'Sometimes it does happen,' she confessed. 'But there are
rituals to be observed. Each time we sound the gong, we have
to record the *pongc*, the *uair* and the *cadar*.'

'But mistakes happen?'

'Oh yes. In fact the night you were speaking of, the night
before we found the corpse, even Sister Síomha had made a
miscalculation.'

'A miscalculation?'

'It is a very exacting task being a time keeper, but if we
forget the number of times to strike, we merely have to
look at the record and when the tablet is filled, we simply
scrape it smooth again and start all over again. Síomha
must have misjudged several time periods for when I took
over from her that morning, the clay tablet was smudged
and inaccurate.'

Fidelma peered carefully at the clay tablet. She was not so
much concerned with the figures that were enumerated there
but with the texture of the clay. It was a curious red colour
and seemed familiar to her.

'Is this local clay?' she asked.

Sister Brónach nodded.

'What makes it so strangely red in colour?'

'Oh, that. We are not far from the copper mines and the
soil around here often produces this distinctive clay. The
copper mixes with natural clay and water to produce that
fascinating red effect. We find the clay very good for writing
tablets. It keeps its soft surface longer than normal clay, so
that we do not have to waste other writing materials. It is
perfect for keeping the enumeration of the clepsydra.'

'Copper,' breathed Fidelma reflectively. 'Copper mines.'

She let a finger trail over the surface of the smooth damp
clay and then, with an abrupt motion, dug her fingernail into
it and lifted a fragment out.

'Careful, sister,' protested Sister Brónach, 'do not damage the enumeration.'

Sister Brónach looked slightly outraged as she gently removed the writing tablet from Fidelma's hand and carefully erased the disturbance to its smooth surface.

'I am sorry,' Fidelma smiled absently. She was examining the reddish material on her fingertips with fascination.

Chapter Seven

Sister Fidelma left the tower through the library rooms and began to cross the abbey courtyard. She was half-way across when she became aware of the short figure of a heavy-set religieuse waddling towards her with the aid of a stick. She recognised that it was the disabled religieuse whom she had seen at the funeral with Sister Brónach and it was clear that she was attempting to intercept Fidelma. Fidelma halted and allowed the sister to catch up. Once again, Fidelma felt compassion as she surveyed the girl's broad, rather plain face with pale, watery eyes. But it was a young, intelligent face. When the sister spoke, Fidelma heard that she had a nervous stammer as a further handicap. The girl twisted her lips and made faces as she tried to get her words out, as if it were some painful exercise.

'Sis... Sister Fidelma? Sis... Sis... Lerben is loo... looking for you... The mo... mo... mother abbess... requests your pres... presence immediately in her cha... chamber.'

Fidelma tried not to alter her expression but she felt a grim satisfaction. She had estimated that Sister Síomha would have immediately complained about her to the Abbess Draigen. It was obvious what the abbess wanted to see Fidelma about.

'Very well. Will you show me the way? I have forgotten where the abbess's chamber is, Sister...?'

She raised her eyebrows in interrogation.

'I am Sis... Sis... Sister Berrach,' replied the girl.

106

'Very well, Sister Berrach. If you will lead the way?'

The young religieuse nodded her head rapidly several times before turning to lead the way. Her body swayed from side to side on her short, deformed legs, across the courtyard to the group of stone buildings in which the Abbess Draigen had her chambers. She paused before a heavy oak door and tapped timidly with the tip of her staff. Then she swung it open.

'Sis... Sis... Sister Fidelma, mo... mother abbess,' gasped the girl and turned, with relief on her face, as if thankful to escape, and disappeared.

Fidelma entered and closed the door behind her.

Abbess Draigen was seated alone in her chamber at her dark oak work table. The room was gloomy, for the windows did not provide much light. Even though it was just after noon, there was a lighted tallow candle on the table by which she was reading. The expression she raised to Fidelma, lit by the flickering candle, was unfriendly and set in pinched lines.

'It has been reported that you have been extremely discourteous to my *rechtaire*. A house steward is deserving of respect. Surely I do not have to remind you of this?'

Fidelma moved forward and took a seat opposite the abbess. For a moment, Abbess Draigen's features took on a look of astonishment and then outrage.

'Sister, you forget yourself. I did not ask you to be seated.'

Fidelma was usually respectful of rules and fairly easy-going but when she felt it in her interests to throw her weight around to achieve an advantage then she was not above doing so.

'Abbess Draigen, I am in no mood for formalities. Need I remind you that I hold the degree of *anruth* and may sit in the presence of provincial kings, indeed – I may dispute on their level? I may even be invited to sit in the presence of the High King himself, if he so wishes. I am not here to engage in rituals of etiquette. I am here to investigate a case of unlawful killing.'

If Abbess Draigen had been expecting to exert her authority over Fidelma she was thwarted in her aim. The cold response seemed to impede her power of speech. She simply stared at Fidelma, with hostility showing in her expression.

Fidelma felt a pang of regret for her behaviour. She knew that she was behaving disrespectfully, although within her rights as a *dálaigh*, but there was much on her mind and she felt she had little time for meticulous observance of the conventions. She decided to unbend a little and leant forward with a look that she meant as friendly.

'Abbess Draigen, I must be blunt for time precludes any other course. I was abrupt with Sister Síomha because I had to cut through her vanity to find answers to my questions. She is very young to hold the position of a house steward. Perhaps, too young?'

Abbess Draigen remained silent for a moment and then she retorted icily: 'Do you question my choice of a house steward?'

'You are best suited to make your own decisions, mother abbess,' replied Fidelma. 'I observe merely that Sister Síomha is very young and inexperienced in the ways of the world. Her inexperience leads to her arrogance. Surely, you have other members of your community who are equally capable to take on the position of *rechtaire* of the community? Sister Brónach for example?'

Abbess Draigen's eyes narrowed.

'Sister Brónach She is introverted and lacks ability. My choice was made carefully. You may be a *dálaigh* of the courts but I am abbess here and I make the decisions.'

Fidelma spread her hands.

'I would not dream of interfering. But I speak as I find. It was my response to Sister Síomha's conceit and her insolence towards me that made me act as I did.'

Abbess Draigen sniffed.

'You seemed to imply that Sister Síomha was somehow connected with the corpse. I hardly think that was merely a reaction to someone's personality.'

Fidelma smiled quickly. Sister Síomha was not unintelligent and had doubtless given Draigen a full report.

'There were some answers that I was not happy with, abbess,' she confided. 'And since we are speaking of this matter, I would like to ask some questions of you.'

Abbess Draigen's mouth tightened.

'I have not finished with the matter of the complaints of Sister Síomha.'

'We will return to that matter in a moment,' Fidelma assured her with a dismissive wave of her hand. 'How long have you been abbess here?'

It was such an abrupt change of questioning that the abbess jerked her head back in surprise and studied Fidelma's face carefully. Seeing her calm resolution, the abbess sat back on her chair.

'I have been abbess of this community for six years. Previously to that I, too, was *rechtaire* here.'

'For how long?'

'Four years.'

'And before that?'

'I was of the community here for over ten years.'

'So you have been here twenty years in all? Are you from this part of the country?'

'I do not see what this has to do with the matter you are investigating?'

'It is just to give me some background,' cajoled Fidelma. 'Are you from this area?'

'I am. My father was an *óc-aire*; a free clansman of this area who owned his own land but which was not adequate enough to render him self-sufficient.'

'So you joined this community?'

Abbess Draigen's eyes flashed.

'I did not have to, if that is what you imply! I was free to do what I wanted in life.'

'I made no such comment.'

'My father was a proud man. They called him Adnár Mhór – Adnár the Great.'

Abbess Draigen's mouth snapped shut as if she realised that she had said too much.

'Adnár?' Fidelma moved forward in her seat and gazed closely at Draigen. Now she realised what she saw in the face of the abbess and her neighbour the *bó-aire*.

'Is Adnár of Dún Boí your brother?'

Abbess Draigen did not deny it.

'You do not get on with your brother.'

It was an observation but Abbess Draigen did not hide her look of distaste.

'My brother is nothing that his name implies,' she said tightly.

Fidelma smiled softly. The meaning of the name Adnár was one who was very modest.

'Since you observe the meaning of names, I presume that you were the staff of your family?'

Draigen's mouth quirked into a smile. Her name meant 'blackthorn' and she conceded Fidelma was a worthy opponent with word games.

'My brother Adnár left my father just when my father needed help to work his land. My mother had died and the strength had gone out of my father ... the very will to pit his wits against the soil and sustain a living. Adnár went off to serve the chieftain of Beara – Gulban the Hawk-Eyed – who was raiding against the northern clans. When Adnár returned with cattle, as his reward for his services, my father was already dead. I had joined this community and my father's land had been sold and donated to the abbey. That is why my brother became a *bó-aire* – a cattle chief, a chieftain without land but with wealth which he increases by his service to Gulban.'

The vehemence with which she spoke was such to give Fidelma an indication that the story had never been told before and that Draigen was using Fidelma to release her anger against her brother.

'I see no reason in this story why you and Adnár should hate each other so violently, unless there was an argument over the disposal of your father's land?'

Draigen did not deny her ill-feelings for her brother.

'Hate? Hate is, perhaps, too strong a word. I despise Adnár. My father and mother should have lived out an old age on their land, watching their son rewarding them for his good health and secure upbringing by continuing to farm what they had wrenched from nature. They died too early. My father died doing work he was no longer fit to do. But enmity did start when Adnár demanded our father's land on his return.'

'So you blame your brother for your father's death? But he blames you for the loss of, what he considers, his land?'

'His claim was ruled on by a Brehon. It was judged that Adnár could not support his claim.'

'But you blame him for the death of your father. Is that logical?'

'Logic? That dreary prison cell for human feeling?'

Fidelma shook her head.

'Logic is the mechanics of making the truth prevail. Without it we would live in an irrational world.'

'I can live comfortably with my feelings towards my brother,' advised Draigen.

'Ah ... *facilis descensus Averno,*' sighed Fidelma.

'I do not need to have Virgil's *Aeneid* quoted at me, sister. I do not need to be cautioned that the descent to hell is easy. Preach your Latin to my brother.'

'I am sorry,' Fidelma conceded. 'The words simply sprang into my mind. I am sorry for you, Draigen. Hate is such a waste of emotional strength. But tell me, you have given your reasons for hating ... despising,' she corrected herself as she saw Draigen's expression, 'despising your brother, but why should he hate you so much?'

She wondered whether to tell Draigen of Adnár's claim that his sister had relationships with the younger members of her community; that he went so far as to claim that Draigen might well have been responsible for the murder of a former lover to hide the affair. She wondered how a brother could hold his sister in such bitter hostility as to make such an accusation. Surely not simply over a land dispute?

'I do not care about his hate. He and his so-called soul-friend may slowly rot of disease. I pray for the sorrow of my brother's house!'

'So you know Brother Febal?'

'Know him?' Abbess Draigen laughed hollowly. 'Know him? He was my husband.'

For the second time in a short period, Fidelma was shocked. That Adnár was Draigen's brother was a matter of surprise. That Febal turned out to be her former husband was almost absurd. There was some deeper mystery here that she could not quite understand.

Abbess Draigen had suddenly drawn herself together and said coldly: 'I think that is enough prying into my personal life, sister. As you so succinctly put it, you are here to investigate a murder. In doing so, you seem to display a talent to vex people, including my house steward as well as myself. Perhaps you would now confine yourself to your investigation.'

Fidelma hesitated, not wishing to make the situation any worse. Then she decided that she had to continue the road her investigation was taking her.

'I thought, Abbess Draigen, that I was confining myself to the investigation. You may wish to know that both your brother and Febal suggest that you might be implicated in the murder of the girl found in your well.'

The abbess's eyes glinted with anger.

'Yes? For what reason?'

'They suggested that you had a reputation.'

'A reputation?'

'Of a sexual nature. It was suggested that the crime might have been committed to cover such misdemeanours.'

There was no disguising the look of repulsion on Abbess Draigen's face.

'I might have expected this from my brother and his lickspittle. Their souls to the devil! May they die the death of kittens!'

Fidelma sighed deeply. The curse of the death of kittens was to wish someone would die of drowning.

'Mother abbess, it ill behoves one of your position to utter such curses. I need to ask you again, why it is your brother and Brother Febal should level such charges against you, or spread such rumours? Your attitude indicates to me that they are without foundation.'

'Ask Adnár and his lickspittle, Febal, if you must know. I am sure that they will invent a suitable story.'

'Mother abbess, ever since I arrived here, I have found much arrogance and deception. Also, there is great hatred and threatening evil here. If there is anything I should know further about the background to this matter, I urge you to tell me now. I shall find out, eventually. Be sure of that.'

Abbess Draigen's face was graven.

'And I can assure you, Sister Fidelma, that the finding of an unidentified corpse at this abbey has nothing to do with the mutual dislike that exists between my brother, myself, and my former husband Brother Febal.'

Fidelma tried to read beyond Draigen's wooden expression but gathered nothing.

'I must ask these questions,' she said, slowly rising to her feet. 'If I do not then I shall be failing in my task.'

Draigen followed her with her eyes.

'You may do what you think you must, sister. I can now

113

see the purpose of your questions to Sister Síomha which touched on me. I can assure you that I am not guilty of any crime. If I were, surely I would not have sent to Brocc, the abbot of Ros Ailithir, requesting an advocate of the courts to come here to investigate.'

'I follow your reasoning, mother abbess. Yet others have been subtle in seeking to evade suspicion in ways that you might not credit.'

Draigen snorted in disgust.

'Then you must do as you think fit. Neither I nor Sister Síomha have anything to fear from the truth.'

Sister Fidelma was halfway to the door when the abbess's last sentence halted her. She swung round and faced Abbess Draigen.

'Since you mention it, I have seen fear in Sister Síomha's eyes. I asked her if she recognised the headless corpse...'

She held up a hand to silence Draigen's immediate protest.

'One may still recognise a corpse even when its head is missing.'

'I am sure that Sister Síomha did not.'

'So she told me. But why would she fear that question?'

Abbess Draigen shrugged eloquently.

'That is not a matter for me.'

'Of course not. Her fear increased when I asked her whether all the sisters of this community were accounted for.'

Abbess Draigen gave another of her dry chuckles.

'You think that the headless corpse was one of our own sisters? Come, Sister Fidelma, you must have more talent in your art than to consider that we would not know if one of our own sisters had been murdered, decapitated and thrown down our drinking well!'

'It would be logical to presume so. Though members of a religious community would hardly be able to recognise a naked body without a head as someone they are used to seeing and recognising by face only.'

'This is true. But no one here is unaccounted for,' confirmed the Abbess Draigen.

'So every member of the community is within the confines of the abbey?'

Abbess Draigen hesitated.

'No. I did not say that. I said that every member of the community is accounted for.'

Fidelma felt a sudden surge of adrenalin.

'I have yet to reason that subtle alteration in emphasis.'

'Often members of our community go on missions, on journeys to other abbeys.'

'Ah,' Fidelma tensed. 'So there are members of your community away at the moment?'

'Only two members.'

'Why was I not told this?'

'It was not the question which you asked, sister,' replied the abbess.

Fidelma's lips compressed.

'There is hardship enough in this matter without games of mind reading and semantics. Explain who is away from the abbey at this time and why.'

Abbess Draigen blinked at the sharpness in Fidelma's voice.

'Sister Comnat and Sister Almu are away at this time. They are on a mission to the abbey of the Blessed Brenainn at Ard Fhearta.'

'When did they go?'

'Three weeks ago.'

'Why did they go?'

Abbess Draigen was looking irritated.

'You may not know that we, in this abbey, have some reputation for our penmanship. We copy books for other houses. Our sisters have just completed a copy of Murchú's life of the Blessed Patrick of Ard Macha. Sister Comnat was our *leabhar coimedach*, our librarian, while Almu was her assistant. They were given the task of taking the copy of t' book to Ard Fhearta.'

'Why didn't Sister Síomha tell me this?' snapped Fidelma.
'Presumably because . . .'
'I am tired of hearing presumptions, Abbess Draigen,' she interrupted. 'Summon Sister Síomha now.'

The Abbess Draigen paused for a moment as if to control her response to Fidelma's anger and then, clenching her jaw tight, she reached forward and rang a small silver bell that stood on her table. Sister Lerben entered a moment later and the abbess told her to ask the *rechtaire* to attend her immediately.

A few moments passed before there came a tap on the door and it opened. Sister Síomha entered, saw Fidelma, and her mouth broadened in a slight smile of obvious contempt.

'You rang for me, mother abbess?'

'I summoned you,' Fidelma replied harshly.

Sister Síomha looked startled, her face loosing the self-satisfied expression.

'A short time ago I asked you if every member of the community was accounted for. You replied that they were. Now I discover that two members of this community are not accounted for. Sister Comnat and Sister Almu. Why was I misled?'

Sister Síomha had flushed and glanced quickly at the abbess who seemed to incline her head slightly.

'You do not have to ask permission of the mother abbess to reply to my questions,' Fidelma said sharply.

'Every member of this community was accounted for,' replied Sister Síomha defensively. 'I did not mislead you.'

'You told me nothing of Comnat and Almu.'

'What was there to tell you? They are on a mission to Ard Fhearta.'

'They are not in the abbey.'

'Yet they are accounted for.'

Fidelma exhaled in exasperation.

'Semantics!' she jeered. 'Do you care more about morphology, with word formations and inflections, than with truth?'

'You did not...' began Sister Síomha, but this time it was Abbess Draigen who interrupted.

'We must help Sister Fidelma all we can, Sister Síomha,' she said, causing the young sister to glance at her in surprise. 'She is, after all, a *dálaigh* of the court.'

There was a slight pause.

'Very well, mother abbess,' Sister Síomha said, bowing her head in compliance.

'Now, as I understand it,' began Fidelma determinedly, 'there are two members of this community who are not in the abbey?'

'Yes.'

'And they are the only two members of your community who are unaccounted for?'

'They are not unaccounted for...' began Sister Síomha but halted at the look of thunder on Fidelma's face. 'There is no one else outside of the abbey at the moment,' she confirmed.

'I am told that they left for Ard Fhearta three weeks ago.'

'Yes.'

'Surely the journey there and back is not so long? When were they expected to return?'

It was Abbess Draigen who confessed: 'They are overdue. That is true, sister.'

'Overdue?' Fidelma arched an eyebrow disdainfully. 'And no one thought to inform me of this?'

'It has no bearing on this matter,' interposed the abbess.

'I am the arbiter of what has or has not a bearing on the matter,' replied Fidelma icily. 'Have you had any word from the sisters since they left?'

'None,' replied Sister Síomha.

'And when were they expected back?'

'They were expected back after ten days.'

'Have you informed the local *bó-aire*?' The question was

directed at Abbess Draigen. 'Whatever you may think of Adnár, he is the local magistrate.'

'He would be of no help,' Draigen said defensively. 'But nevertheless, you are right. He shall be informed that they are missing. Messengers often go between his fortress and that of Gulban which is on the road to Ard Fhearta.'

'I shall be seeing Adnár shortly to discuss the matter we have touched on, abbess. I will inform him of this matter. Tell me, what are these sisters like? A physical description, if you please.'

'Sister Comnat has been here at least thirty years. She is sixty or more years of age and has been our librarian and our chief penman for fifteen of those years. She is well skilled in her work.'

'I need a more physical description,' insisted Fidelma.

'She is short and thin,' replied Draigen. 'Her hair is grey though her eyebrows still retain the blackness of their youth and the eyes, too, are dark. She has a distinctive mark, a scar on her forehead where once a sword cut her.'

Fidelma mentally ruled out the librarian as the headless victim.

'And of Sister Almu?'

'She was chosen to accompany Sister Comnat not only because she is her assistant but because she is young and stronger. She is about eighteen. Fair-haired and blue-eyed with pleasing features. She is a little on the short side.'

Fidelma was silent for a moment.

'The headless corpse could have been eighteen years old. It gave the impression of fairness and was short in stature.'

'Are you claiming that this headless corpse is Sister Almu?' demanded the abbess in disbelief.

'It is not!' snapped Sister Síomha.

'Almu was a close friend of my steward,' Draigen explained. 'I am prepared to believe that she would recognise the body of Almu.'

Fidelma folded her arms determinedly.

'Since we like to play with semantics, mother abbess, let me be precise. I am saying that it could be Sister Almu. You say Almu is an assistant to the librarian and worked copying books?'

'Yes. Sister Almu promises to be one of our best scribes. She is highly proficient in her art.'

'There was blue staining on the fingers of the hand of the corpse. Would that not point to the corpse having worked with a pen?'

'Staining?' interrupted Sister Síomha in annoyance. 'What staining?'

'Do you tell me that you did not notice the blue stains on thumb, index finger and along the edge of the little finger where it would rest on paper? The blue-black of an ink? The sort of stain someone who practised penmanship might have?'

'But Sister Almu is with Sister Comnat at Ard Fhearta,' protested the abbess.

'She is certainly not among the community of this abbey, that much is certain,' Fidelma commented dryly. 'Are you sure that no one recognised the body?'

'How can one recognise the body without a head?' Sister Síomha demanded. 'And if it was Almu, I would know. She is a close friend of mine, as the abbess has said.'

'Perhaps you are right,' conceded Fidelma. 'But as to recognising a body without a head, why, I have just shown you one method of recognition. I will acknowledge that, in a religious community, one's first and usually only contact with the physical features of a fellow religious is with the face. But I would ask, didn't the thought ever occur that, as these sisters were overdue, there was a remote possibility that this body, which had marks of being a member of the Faith, was that of your assistant librarian?'

'Not even a slightest thought,' replied Sister Síomha stiffly. 'Neither does your suggestion make it so. You have provided no proof that the body belongs to Almu.'

'No, that is so,' Fidelma agreed. 'What I am doing at this time is putting forward some hypotheses based on the information that I am now getting. Information which,' she held Abbess Draigen's eyes a moment and then turned to Sister Síomha who now dropped her gaze, 'information which should have been given me freely, instead of this wasting of time with the sins of self-regard.'

'Why would anyone want to stab and decapitate Sister Almu and thrust her body down a well?' demanded the abbess. 'If it is the body of the sister, that is.'

'We have not been able to prove it was Almu. And we doubtless will not until we find the other part of the corpse.'

'You mean her head?' asked the abbess.

'I have been told that when the corpse was taken from the well, no one was allowed to draw water and that the community has used the other springs hereabouts?'

Abbess Draigen nodded confirmation.

'Has anyone been down the well shaft to see if the head was also placed down there?'

The abbess looked towards Sister Síomha.

'The answer is – yes,' Sister Síomha replied. 'As steward it was my duty to arrange for the purification of the well. I sent one of our strongest young girls down it.'

'And she was?'

'Sister Berrach.'

Fidelma's expression showed total astonishment.

'But Sister Berrach is...' She bit her tongue, regretting what she had been about to say.

'A cripple?' sneered Sister Síomha. 'So you have noticed her?'

'I merely observed that Sister Berrach is surely disabled. How can she be strong?'

'Berrach has been in this community since she was three years old,' said the abbess. 'She was adopted not long before I came here myself and raised by the community. Although the growth of her legs was stunted, she has developed a strength in her arms and torso that is truly surprising.'

'And did she find anything when she went down the well? Perhaps I should hear this from her own lips?'

Abbess Draigen reach forward and rang the bell on the table before her.

'Then you may ask her yourself, sister.'

Once more Sister Lerben, the attractive, young novice, opened the door almost immediately.

'Lerben,' ordered the abbess, 'fetch Sister Berrach here.'

The novice bobbed her head and disappeared. It was only a few moments later that there was a timid knock at the door and, at the abbess's response, the wary features of Sister Berrach peered around the portal.

'Come in, sister,' Draigen spoke to her almost consolingly. 'Do not be alarmed. You know Sister Fidelma? Yes, of course you do.'

'H... h... how can I se... serve?' stuttered the sister, propelling herself forward into the chamber with her heavy blackthorn stick.

'Easy enough,' Sister Síomha intervened. 'I had the responsibility of examining the well of the Blessed Necht after the headless corpse was removed. You will recall, Berrach, that I asked for your assistance in this, didn't I?'

The disabled religieuse nodded, as if eager to please.

'You asked me to go down the well, to be lowered on a rope with a lantern. I was to wash down the walls of the well and cleanse it with water that had been blessed by our mother abbess.'

She phrased her sentences like an oft repeated lesson. Fidelma noticed that her stammer vanished in the recital of this. She found herself wondering whether poor Sister Berrach was simple, a grown woman with a deformed body and the mind of a child.

'That is so,' Sister Síomha said approvingly. 'What was it like in the well?'

Sister Berrach seemed to consider for a moment and then smiled as the answer came to her.

'D... d... dark. Yes, it was very d... dark d... down there.'

'But you had a means of lighting that darkness,' Fidelma spoke encouragingly and moved forward towards the girl. She laid a friendly hand on her arm and felt its strength and sinew under the sleeve of the robe. 'You had a lantern, didn't you?'

The girl glanced up at her nervously and then returned Fidelma's smile.

'Oh yes,' she smiled. 'I was given a la... lantern and with th... th... that I c... could see well enough. But it was n... n... not really light d... d... down there.'

'Yes. I understand what you mean, Sister Berrach,' Fidelma said. 'And when you reached the bottom of the well, did you see anything that ... well ... anything that should not have been down there?'

The girl put her head on one side and thought carefully.

'S... sh... shouldn't be d... down there?' she repeated slowly.

Sister Síomha made her exasperation clear.

'The head of the corpse,' she explained bluntly.

Sister Berrach shivered violently.

'There was no... nothing else d... down there but the dark and the water. I saw n... n... nothing.'

'Very well,' Fidelma smiled. 'You may go now.'

After Sister Berrach had left the abbess sat back and studied Fidelma speculatively.

'What now, Sister Fidelma? Do you still hold to your belief that this body is that of Sister Almu?'

'I did not say it was,' countered Fidelma. 'At this stage of my investigation, I must speculate. I must hypothesise. The fact that Sister Comnat and Sister Almu are overdue in returning to this abbey may simply be a matter of coincidence. Nevertheless, I must be in possession of all the facts if I am to progress. There must be no further playing of games. When I ask questions, I shall expect appropriate answers.'

She glanced to Sister Síomha but directed her remarks to Abbess Draigen. She saw an angry look remould the features of the *rechtaire* of the community of The Salmon of the Three Wells.

'That much is clear, sister,' replied the abbess tautly. 'And perhaps now that all our bruised dignities and self-esteems have been massaged, we may return to our respective businesses?'

'Willingly,' agreed Sister Fidelma. 'But one thing more . . .'

Abbess Draigen waited with raised eyebrows.

'I am told that there are some copper mines in this vicinity?'

The question was not expected by the abbess and Draigen looked surprised.

'Copper mines?'

'Yes. Is this not so?'

'It is so. Yes; there are many such mines on this peninsula.'

'Where are they in relationship to this abbey?'

'The nearest ones are on the far side of the mountains to the south-west.'

'And to whom do they belong?'

'They are the domain of Gulban the Hawk-Eyed,' replied Draigen.

Fidelma had expected some such answer and she nodded thoughtfully.

'Thank you. I will detain you no longer.'

As she turned from the abbess's chamber she saw Sister Síomha regarding her with an intense expression. If looks could kill, Fidelma found herself thinking wryly, then she would have been dead on the spot.

Chapter Eight

In returning to Adnár's fortress that afternoon, Fidelma decided not to give any advance warning to the chieftain by crossing directly over the strip of water separating the community of The Salmon of the Three Wells from the fortress of Dún Boí, but to traverse the path through the forest, and come upon the fortress from the landward side. The journey was further, but she had been so long on shipboard that she desired a leisurely walk through the forest in order to clear her mind. The forest presented just the sort of countryside she enjoyed walking in. Its great oaks spread along the shoreline and across the skirts of the high mountain behind.

She had informed Sister Brónach of her intentions and left the abbey mid-afternoon. It was still a pleasant day, the mild sun warming to the skin when it flickered through the mainly bare branches of the trees. High up, beyond the snow-dusted forest canopy, the sky was a soft blue with strands of white, fleecy clouds straggling along in the soft winds. The ground was hard with a winter frost toughening what would otherwise have been soft mud underfoot. The sun had not yet penetrated it and the crisp leaves, shed weeks ago, crackled under her tread.

From the abbey gates a track drove through the forest around the bay but at a distance so that the sea's great inlet was mainly obscured from the gaze of any traveller taking this route. Only now and again, through the bare trees, could a glimpse of flashing blue, caused by the sun's reflection, be discerned. Not even the sounds of the sea could be heard, so good a barrier were the tall oak trees, interspersed with protesting clumps of hazel trying to survive among their mighty and ancient brothers. There were whole clumps of strawberry trees with their toothed evergreen leaves, their short trunks and twisting branches rising twenty feet and more in height.

Through the trees, now and then, Fidelma could pick up the rustle of undergrowth as a larger denizen of the forest made its cautious passage in search of food. The startled snap of twigs and branches as a deer leapt away at the sound of her approach, the swish of dried, rotting leaves as an inquisitive red squirrel tried to remember where it had left a food hoard. The sounds were numerous but identifiable to anyone attuned to the natural world.

As she walked along, Fidelma came to an adjoining road that led in the direction of the distant mountains and she saw that there were signs that horses had recently passed this way. While the ground was hard, there were traces of horses' droppings. She remembered having seen, that morning, the procession of horses, riders and running attendants, moving down from the mountain and realised that this was the point where they must have joined the road.

For some reason she found that she had abruptly started to think about Eadulf of Seaxmund's Ham again and wondered why he had sprung into her thoughts. She wondered if Ross would find any clue to the origins of the abandoned ship. It was much to ask of him. There was a whole ocean and hundreds of miles of coastline in which to hide any clue to what had happened on that vessel.

Perhaps Eadulf had not been on board at all?

No, she shook her head, deciding against the theory. He would never have given that Missal to anyone – voluntarily, that was.

But what if it had been taken from him in death? Fidelma shivered slightly and set her mouth in a thin, determined line. Then whoever had perpetrated such a deed would be brought to justice. She would make it so.

She suddenly halted.

Ahead of her a chorus of protesting bird cries made a din that drowned out most of the forest sounds. They made an odd 'caaarg-caaarg' scolding. She saw a couple of birds flitting upwards to the high bare branches of an oak, recognising the white rump and pinkish-buff plumage of jays. In a nearby clump of alders, where they had been pecking at the brown, woody cones, several little birds with conical bills and streaked plumage joined in chirping in agitation.

Something was alarming them.

Fidelma took a pace forward hesitantly.

It saved her life.

She felt the breath of the arrow pass inches by her head and heard the thump as it embedded itself into the tree behind her.

She dropped to her knees automatically, her eyes searching for better cover.

While she crouched undecided as to what to do, there was a sharp cry and two large warriors, with full beards, and polished armour, came bursting through the undergrowth and seized her arms in vice-like grips before she had time to regain her wits. One of them held a sword, which he raised as if to strike. Fidelma flinched, waiting for the blow.

'Stop!' cried a voice. 'Something is amiss!'

The warrior hesitantly lowered the weapon.

In the gloom of the woodland track, a figure mounted on horseback loomed up before them. A short bow was held loosely in one hand and the reins of his steed in the other. It seemed clear that he had been the perpetrator of her near clash with death.

Fidelma did not have time to respond to express her astonishment or protest because they then began to drag her towards the mounted figure. They halted before him. He bent forward in his saddle and examined her features carefully.

'We are misled,' he exclaimed with disgust in his voice.

Fidelma threw back her head to return his examination. The stranger was impressive. He had long red-gold hair on which a circlet of burnished copper was set with several precious stones glinting. His face was long and aquiline, with a broad forehead. The nose was more a beak, the bridge thin, the shape almost hooked. The hair grew scantily from his temples and gathered in thickness at the back of his head, flashing in red, coppery glints as it fell to his shoulders. The mouth was thin, red, rather cruel, so Fidelma felt. The eyes were wide and almost violet in hue and seemed to have little trace of a pupil, although Fidelma conceded that this must clearly be a trick of the light.

He was no more than thirty. A muscular warrior. His dress, even had he not been wearing the copper circlet of office on his head, spoke of rank. He was clad in silks and linen trimmed with fur. A sword hung from his belt whose handle she saw was also worked with semi-precious metals and stones. A quiver of arrows hung from his saddle bow and the bow, still in his hand, was of fine craftsmanship.

He continued to examine her with a frown.

'Who is this?' he demanded coldly to the men holding her.

One of the warriors chuckled dryly.

'Your quarry, my lord.'

'Must be another wench from that religious house nearby,' chimed in the other. Then, with some strange emphasis which Fidelma could not understand, he added: 'She must have disturbed the deer that we were after, my lord.'

Fidelma finally found breath.

'There was no deer within a hundred yards of me!' she cried in suppressed rage. 'Tell your men to unhand me or, by the living God, you shall hear more about it.'

The mounted man raised his eyebrows in surprise.

Both men holding her arms merely increased the bruising pressure. One of them starting laughing lewdly.

'She has spirit, this one, my lord.' Then he turned, putting his evil-smelling face next to her: 'Silence, wench! Do you know to whom you speak?'

'No,' Fidelma gritted her teeth, 'for no one has had the manners to identify him. But let me tell you to whom you speak ... I am Fidelma, *dálaigh* of the courts, and sister to Colgú, king of Cashel. Does that suffice for you to unhand me? You are already guilty of assault before the law!'

There was a silence and then the mounted man spoke sharply to the two warriors.

'Let her go at once! Release her!'

They dropped their hold immediately, almost like well-trained dogs obeying their master. Fidelma felt the blood gushing into her lowers arms and hands again.

The sounds of a horse crashing through the winter forest caused them all to turn. A second rider, bow in hand, came trotting up. Fidelma saw the flushed young features of Olcán. He drew rein and stared down, his expression was one of bewilderment as he recognised Fidelma. Then he had slid off his horse and was moving forward, hands outstretched.

'Sister Fidelma, are you hurt?'

'Small thanks to these warriors, Olcán,' she snapped, rubbing her bruised arms.

The first rider turned to his men with an angry gesture.

'Precede me back to the fortress,' he snapped, and, without a word, both men turned and moved off at a shambling trot. As they did so the tall man bowed stiffly in his saddle from the waist towards Fidelma.

'I regret this incident.'

Olcán looked from Fidelma to the man, frowning. Then he realised his manners.

'Fidelma, may I present my friend, Torcán. Torcán, this is Fidelma of Kildare.'

Fidelma's eyes narrowed as she recognised the name.

'Torcán, the son of Eoganán of the Uí Fidgenti?'

The tall man again bowed from the saddle, this time it was more of a sort of mock salute.

'You know me?'

'I know of you,' Fidelma replied curtly. 'And you are a long way from the lands of the Uí Fidgenti.'

The Uí Fidgenti occupied the lands to the north-west of the kingdom of Muman. She knew from her brother that they were one of the most restless of his peoples. Eoganán was an ambitious prince, ruthless in his desire to dominate the surrounding clans and expand his power base.

'And you are surely a long way from Kildare, Sister Fidelma,' riposted the other.

'As an advocate of the courts, it is my lot to travel far and wide to maintain justice,' replied Fidelma gravely. 'And what is the reason for your journey to this corner of the kingdom?'

Olcán intervened hurriedly.

'Torcán has been a guest of my father, Gulban of Beara and is currently enjoying, with me, the hospitality of Adnár.'

'And why was it necessary to shoot at me?'

Olcán looked shocked.

'Sister...' he began but Torcán was smiling quizzically down at Fidelma.

'Sister, it was not my intention to shoot at you,' protested Torcán. 'I was actually shooting at a deer, or so I thought. However, I concede that my men were lacking in manners, and in this regard I fear that injury to yourself lies, not in my badly aimed arrow, for which I do heartily wish to atone.'

Torcán was either short-sighted or an easy liar for Fidelma knew that there was no animal near her when the arrow was fired. Nor could any experienced hunter have mistaken her movements for that of a deer in the bare forest. Still, there was a time when confrontation did not achieve any result and therefore she would pretend that she accepted the explanation. She let her breath exhale softly.

'Very well, Torcán. I will accept your apology and not press a case in law for injury to myself in that you have placed me in fear of death. I do so accepting that it was an accident. However, the behaviour of your warriors was no accident. From them, a fine of two *séts* each will be paid for their mishandling and bruising of me and further conveying the fear of death. In this you will find that I act in accordance with the fines outlined in the *Bretha Déin Chécht*.'

Torcán was regarding her with mixed emotions, though it appeared that a reluctant admiration of her cool attitude was uppermost.

'Do you accept the fine on behalf of your warriors?' she demanded.

Torcán chuckled hollowly.

'I will pay their fine, but I will ensure that they pay me.'

'Good. The fine shall be a contribution to the funds of the abbey of The Salmon of the Three Wells to help them in their work.'

'You have my word that it will be paid. I shall instruct one of my men to come to the abbey with the fine tomorrow morning.'

'Your word is accepted. And now I shall be obliged if you will allow me to continue my way.'

'In which direction is your objective, sister?' asked Olcán.

'My journey takes me to Adnár's fortress.'

'Then let me share my saddle with you,' offered Torcán.

Fidelma declined the offer to ride behind the son of the prince of the Uí Fidgenti.

'I prefer to continue on foot.'

Torcán's mouth tightened and then he shrugged.

'Very well, sister. Perhaps we will see you at the fortress in a while.'

He turned his horse, slapped its flank with the side of the bow which he still held and sent it cantering along the forest path. Olcán stood hesitating a moment, looking as if he wished to speak further with Fidelma. Then he remounted his horse and raised a hand in farewell before turning and riding swiftly after his guest. Fidelma stood still, staring after them for a while, her face frowning in concentration. She tried to fathom out what this encounter meant; indeed, if it meant anything at all. Yet it must have some meaning. She simply could not believe that Torcán was serious in suggesting that he had mistaken her for a deer in the forest, especially a winter forest with fair visibility among the mainly bare trees and sparse undergrowth. And if it was no more than an accident, why had he allowed his men to manhandle her? It seemed logical to conclude that he was not expecting her – for as soon as she gave her name and station, he had ordered her release. Then who was it that he had been expecting along that road? A woman? A religieuse? Surely that much was certain for none could mistake her gender or her calling by the distinctive robes she wore. Why would a visitor to this area, the son of the prince of the Uí Fidgenti, want to kill a religieuse?

She suddenly felt cold.

Someone had probably already killed a religieuse; decapitated her and hung her body down the well at the abbey. Fidelma was sure that the headless corpse was that of a sister of the Faith. Her instinct and what evidence she had seen told her so. She shivered. Had she come close to following the nameless corpse into Christ's Otherworld?

She raised her head abruptly from her contemplation as her ears caught the sound of a horse cantering on the path ahead. Was Torcán returning? She stood still and peered along the path. A rider was coming rapidly towards her. Her body tensed. The rider soon emerged through the shadowy shrubbery of the forest. It was Adnár.

The handsome, black-haired chieftain swung easily down

from his horse, almost before the beast had stopped. He greeted Fidelma with a worried glance.

'Olcán told me that he and Torcán had met you on the forest road and that you were on your way to my fortress. Olcán told me that there had been an accident. Is it so?' Adnár was examining her anxiously.

'A near accident,' Fidelma corrected pedantically.

'Are you hurt?'

'No. It is nothing. Nevertheless, I was on my way to see you. Your coming has saved me the trouble of completing the journey.' She turned and pointed to a fallen tree trunk. 'Let us sit for a while.'

Adnár hitched his horse's reins to a twisted branch on the dead tree and joined Fidelma.

'You have not been entirely honest with me, Adnár,' Fidelma opened.

The chieftain's head jerked slightly in surprise.

'In what way?' he demanded defensively.

'You did not say that the Abbess Draigen was your sister by blood. Nor did Brother Febal explain that he was once married to Draigen.'

Fidelma was not prepared for the amused look which crossed the man's pleasant features. It was as if he had been expecting some other accusation. His shoulders slumped a little in relaxation.

'*That*!' he said in a dismissive tone.

'Is it not of importance to you?'

'Little enough,' admitted Adnár. 'My relationship to Draigen is not something I wish to boast of. Luckily, she has my father's red hair while I my mother's black mane.'

'Do you not think that mention of your relationship was of importance to me?'

'Look, sister, it is my misfortune and perhaps Draigen's misfortune, too, that we were born from the same womb. As for Febal, I will not answer for him.'

'Then answer for yourself. Do you really hate your sister as much as you appear to?'

'I am indifferent to her.'

'Indifferent enough to claim that she has unnatural affairs with her acolytes.'

'That much is true.'

Adnár spoke in earnest without anger. Fidelma had previously seen his irritable temper and was surprised how calm he now was, sitting there in the wood, hand clasped between his knees, gazing moodily at the ground.

'Perhaps you should tell me the story?'

'It is not relevant to your investigation.'

'Yet you claim that Draigen's sexual proclivities are relevant. How, then, am I to judge this if I am not possessed of the truth of these matters?'

Adnár made a slight movement of his shoulders as if to shrug but changed his mind.

'Did she tell you that our father, whose name I take, was an *óc-aire*, a commoner who worked his own land but had not sufficient land or chattels to render him self-sufficient? He worked all his life on a small strip of inhospitable land on a rocky mountain slope. Our mother worked with him and at harvest time, it was she who gathered what small crop we had while my father went to hire himself to the local chieftain in order to make sufficient to keep our bodies and souls together.'

He paused for a moment and then went on: 'Draigen was the youngest and I, I was two years her senior. We both had to help our parents on their small plot of land and there was no time or money to spare on educating us.'

There was a bitter tone to his voice but Fidelma made no comment.

'As a boy, I did not want to follow in my father's footsteps. I did not want to spend the rest of my life working unprofitable land simply in order to live. I had ambition. And so I would sneak along to the clan hostel every time I

heard that a warrior was passing through the territory. I
would try to persuade the warrior to tell me about soldiering,
about the warrior's code and how one trained to be a warrior.
I made my own weapons of wood and would go into the
forests and practise fighting bushes with a wooden sword. I
made a bow and arrows and became an expert shot in my own
way. I knew that this was my only path to escape the poverty
of my life.

'As soon as I was at the age of choice, on my seventeenth
birthday when no law could stop my going, I left home and
sought out our chieftain Gulban of the Beara. He was
engaged in wars against the Corco Duibhne over the
boundaries of his territory. As a bowman, I distinguished
myself, and was soon placed in command of a band of one
hundred men. At the age of nineteen Gulban appointed me a
cenn-feadhna, a captain. It was the proudest day of my life.

'The wars made me rich in cattle and when they ended, I
returned here to be appointed *bó-aire*, a cattle chieftain.
Although the land was not mine, I had a sufficient cattle herd
to be a person of influence and wealth. I am not ashamed of
my escape from poverty.'

'It is a laudable tale, Adnár. Any tale of a man or woman
transcending difficulties is commendable. But it tells me
nothing of the animosity between you and your sister nor
why you should accuse her of unnatural relationships.'

Adnár grimaced expressively.

'Draigen talks much of her loyalty to our parents. She
claims that I deserted them. She was no more loyal to them
than I was. She wanted to escape the poverty as much as I
did. When she was approaching the age of choice, she would
even try to conjure the old pagan spirits – the goddesses of
ancient times – to help her.'

Fidelma regarded him closely. But Adnár seemed lost in
his memories, not as if he were speaking for effect at all.

'What did she do?'

'There was an old woman who dwelt in the woods nearby

134

who claimed to adhere to the old ways. Her name was Suanech, as I recall. All the children were frightened of her. She claimed that she worshipped Boí, the wife of Lugh, god of all arts and crafts. Boí was known as the cow goddess, or the old woman of Beara. You see, this land was once her domain in the dark, pagan days. My fortress was named after her, Dún Boí.'

'There are many old ones who still cling to the ancient times and the old gods,' Fidelma pointed out. The Faith had only come to the five kingdoms during the last two centuries and Fidelma realised that there were still isolated pockets where the beliefs of the Ever Living Ones, the old gods and goddesses, still held sway.

'And you may find many territories where even the mountains are named after gods and goddesses,' Adnár agreed.

'So your sister was influenced by this old pagan woman?' pressed Fidelma. 'When did she come back to the True Faith and join the religieuses?'

Adnár grinned crookedly.

'Who said that she had returned to the True Faith?'

Fidelma looked at him in surprise.

'What are you saying?'

'I say nothing. I merely point the way. Since she was a young girl, especially when she went to see the old woman, she has always acted strangely.'

'You have still not presented me with evidence of any of your claims or why there is this animosity between you.'

'That old woman turned her head with her tales and with her . . .'

He stopped and shrugged.

'While I was serving in Gulban's army, my father and mother died. Draigen went to live with this old woman in the forests.'

'This made you hate her?'

He shook his head.

'No. I am not sure of the story but Draigen fell foul of the law and had to pay compensation. To do this she sold the pitiful plot of land and entered the abbey of The Salmon of the Three Wells. The loss of the land was an annoyance to me. I will not deny that. I should have inherited some of it. I laid a claim against Draigen for my share of the land but a Brehon dismissed the claim.'

'I see. This claim was the cause of the animosity?'

Adnár shrugged.

'I resented what she had done. But I had accrued wealth. I did not really need it. It was principle. No, the hate started to come from Draigen. Perhaps she hated me for making the claim. She avoided me afterwards. When I became *bó-aire* of this district, she was forced to have dealings with me but always used a third party to intermediate. Her hatred of me was keen.'

'Did Draigen give you a reason for her hatred?'

'Oh yes. She claims to blame me for the death of our father and mother. But it does not ring true to me. Perhaps it really was simply resentment that I made a legal claim against her. Anyway, whatever the primary cause, the years have served merely to increase her hatred.'

'She denies it and says that it is you who hates her. So, I ask you again, have you come to return her hate?' Fidelma realised that she was faced with two opposing testimonies without room for compromise.

'I felt hurt at first, then anger towards her. I do not think I have ever felt true hatred. Of course, there were stories from the abbey about Draigen. I heard stories of her liking for young novices. Then when I heard the story of the body of a young woman being found in the well, I feared the worst.'

'Why?'

For the first time he raised his head and gazed directly into her eyes.

'Why?' he repeated, as if he had not understood the question.

136

'Why should this make you come to the conclusion that your sister, your own sister, had murdered this girl as the result of some illicit relationship? I do not see how there is a connection. At least, not from what you have told me so far.'

Adnár looked uncomfortable for a moment or two as he gave the matter thought.

'It is true that I cannot give you a truly logical reason. I just feel that it fits in some terrible way.'

'Did your *anam-chara*, Brother Febal, suggest this explanation to you?'

The question was sharp and direct.

Adnár blinked rapidly.

Fidelma could tell by the slight tinge of colour that rose to his cheeks that she had scored a hit with her question.

'How long have you known Brother Febal?'

'Since I returned and became *bó-aire* here.'

'What do you know of his background?'

'Once the abbey of The Salmon of the Three Wells was a mixed community, a *conhospitae* as they are called. Brother Febal was one of the monks who dwelt there. Febal and Draigen married. Under the old abbess, Abbess Marga, Brother Febal was doorkeeper of the community. Then my sister was appointed *rechtaire*, or steward, which, as you know, is a position second only to the abbess. I understand the relationship between Draigen and Febal ended abruptly. Draigen, taking advantage of the frailty and age of the old abbess, began to purge the abbey of all its male members and designed to make it a house of female religieuses only. Brother Febal was the last to be driven from his post and came to join me as my religious advisor. Not long after, the old abbess died. It did not surprise me to find that my sister Draigen was appointed in her stead.'

'You imply that Draigen is ruthless and ambitious?'

'That you may judge for yourself.'

'Well, what you are also saying is that Brother Febal has

good cause to hate Draigen; good cause to stir up enmity between you and her and good cause to create rumours over the finding of this corpse.'

'From an outsider's position this may seem true,' Adnár admitted. 'I will not try to convince you to my views. The only reason I wanted to see and speak with you before Draigen, when you arrived yesterday, was to alert you to certain things. To ask you to follow those paths I have pointed to. Whether you choose to or not is your concern. You are an advocate of the courts and is not your war-cry, *quaere verum?*'

'To seek the truth is our maxim not a war-cry,' she corrected pedantically. 'That I shall endeavour to do. But accusation is not truth. Suspicion is not a fact. I shall need to speak further with this Brother Febal.'

Adnár ran a hand through his black curly mane of hair.

'You may return with me to the fortress, though I am not sure whether Febal will be there now. As I came away, I believe he was about to conduct Torcán and his men to a place of pilgrimage across the mountain.'

'If he has done so, when will he return?'

'Later this evening, undoubtedly.'

'Then I will see him tomorrow. Tell him to come to the abbey.'

Adnár looked uncomfortable.

'He would probably not wish to, Draigen would not make him welcome.'

'My will over-rules Draigen in this matter,' Fidelma replied coldly. 'He will meet me at the guest's hostel after the breaking of the fast. I shall expect him.'

'I will convey that to him,' sighed Adnár.

Adnár suddenly raised his head in a listening attitude. A moment later Fidelma heard the crunch of shoes on the frosty ground and turned. Coming along the woodland path was figure of a religieuse, head bowed and cowled, a *sacculus* across her shoulder. She did not see Adnár and

Fidelma until she was ten yards away when Fidelma hailed her.

'Good day, sister.'

The girl halted and glanced up startled. Fidelma recognised her immediately. It was the young Sister Lerben.

'Good day,' she mumbled.

Adnár rose smiling.

'It seems a custom of the abbey religieuses to tread this path this day,' he observed ironically. 'Surely it is dangerous to be alone here, sister? It will be dark before long.'

Lerben's eyes flashed in annoyance and then she dropped them.

'I am on my way to see,' she hesitated and glanced at Fidelma, 'to see Torcán of the Uí Fidgenti.' Her hand went automatically to the *sacculus*.

Adnár continued to smile and shook his head.

'Alas, as I was just explaining to Sister Fidelma, Torcán has just left my fortress and will not return until this evening. Can I give him some message?'

Sister Lerben hesitated again and then nodded swiftly. She removed a small oblong object wrapped in a piece of cloth from her *sacculus*.

'Would you ensure that he is given this? He requested its loan from our library and I was asked to deliver it.'

'I will pass this on with pleasure, sister.'

Fidelma reached forward and effortlessly intercepted the package before Adnár could take it. She unwrapped the cloth and gazed at the vellum book.

'Why, this is a copy of the annals being kept at Clonmacnoise, the great abbey founded by the Blessed Ciarán.'

She raised her eyes to see an anxious look on Sister Lerben's face. But Adnár was smiling.

'I had not realised young Torcán was so interested in history,' he said. 'I will have to speak with him about this.'

He reached forth a hand but Fidelma was glancing through its vellum pages. She had spotted some stains on one page, a red muddy stain. She had time only to see that the page contained an entry about the High King Cormac Mac Art before Adnár had gently but firmly removed it from her hold and rewrapped it in the cloth.

'This is not the place to study books,' he observed jocularly. 'It is far too cold. Do not worry, sister,' he told Lerben. 'I will make sure the book is safely delivered to Torcán.'

Fidelma rose to her feet and began to brush the leaves, twigs and dusty, rotting wood from her dress.

'Do you know Torcán well? It is a long way from the land of the Uí Fidgenti.'

Adnár tucked the book under his arm.

'I hardly know him at all. He was a guest of Gulban at his fortress and has come down here as a guest of Olcán, to hunt and see some of the ancient sites for which our territory is renowned.'

'I did not think that the Uí Fidgenti were welcomed by the people of the Loígde.'

Adnár chuckled dryly.

'There have been battles fought between us, there is no denying that. It is time, however, that old quarrels and prejudices were overcome.'

'I agree,' Fidelma said. 'But I point out the obvious. Eoganán, the prince of the Uí Fidgenti, has conspired in many wars against the Loígde.'

'Territorial wars,' agreed Adnár. 'Were everyone to keep to their own territory and not try to interfere in the concerns of other clans then there would be no need for warfare.' He grinned crookedly. 'But, thanks be to God that there was need for warriors when I was a young man otherwise I would not have risen to my present station.'

Fidelma gazed at him a moment, head to one side.

'So you, who won your wealth in wars against the Uí Fidgenti, are now entertaining the son of the prince of that tribe?'

Adnár nodded.

'It is the way of the world. Yesterday's enemies are today's bosom friends, although, as I pointed out, to be precise, the young man is Olcán's guest and not mine.'

'And yesterday's brother and sister are today's bitterest enemies,' added Fidelma softly.

Adnár shrugged.

'Would it were otherwise, sister. But it is not otherwise but thus.'

'Very well, Adnár. I thank you for your frankness with me. I shall expect Brother Febal tomorrow.'

She turned to where Sister Lerben had been standing nervously, as if unable to make up her mind whether to depart or join in this conversation. Fidelma looked at the young girl with a warm smile. Lerben was surely no more than sixteen or seventeen years old.

'Come, sister. Let us return to the abbey and we will talk on the way.'

She turned down the path and began to retrace her steps through the wood. After a moment, Lerben fell in step with her, leaving Adnár standing by his horse, absently stroking the horse's muzzle as he watched them disappear among the trees. He took the book from under his arm and, unwrapping the cloth covering, stared moodily at it, seemed locked into his thoughts for a long time before rewrapping it, thrusting it in his saddle bag, untying the reins of his steed and clambering up. Then he nudged his horse's belly with his heels and sent it trotting along the forest track in the direction of his fortress.

Chapter Nine

Sister Fidelma was awake even before the tense voice cut through the darkness. Her sleep had been disturbed by the turning of the handle on her small chamber door and her mind, alert to possible dangers, caused her to become wide awake in an instant. A shadow stood framed in the doorway. It was still night and only the ethereal light of the moon illuminated the space beyond. The cold was intense and her breath made clouds as she struggled upwards in the pale blue light which bathed everything.

'Sister Fidelma!' The voice was almost a nervous cry from the tall figure of the religieuse.

Fidelma recognised it in spite of the unnatural tone of the voice. It was the Abbess Draigen.

Immediately Fidelma was sitting up in bed, reaching for the flint and tinder to light the tallow candle.

'Mother abbess? What is the matter?'

'You must come with me straight away.' Draigen's voice was cracking with ill-concealed emotion.

Fidelma managed to light the candle and turn to the figure.

The abbess was fully dressed and her face, even in the yellow glow of the candle light, seemed pale and her features were etched in horror.

'Has something happened?' Fidelma realised that her question was superfluous almost at once. Without waiting for a reply, she rose swiftly from her bed. She was now oblivious to the cold as she realised something terrible had taken place. 'What is it?'

The figure of the abbess stood trembling but more from some fearful emotion than from the cold night air. She appeared unable to answer coherently. She seemed to be suffering from some kind of shock.

Fidelma threw on her cloak and slipped into her shoes.

'Lead the way, Draigen,' she instructed calmly. 'I am with you.'

The abbess paused only a moment and then turned, moving towards the courtyard. It was almost as bright as day outside for there had been another snow flurry which now reflected against the light of the moon.

Fidelma glanced at the sky, noting automatically the moon's position, and judged that it was some hours beyond midnight. It was still, however, well before dawn. The stillness of the night seemed absolute. Only the sound of their leather shoes, crunching on the icy snow of the courtyard, sounded in the silence of the night.

Fidelma noticed that they were heading for the tower.

She followed behind the abbess, saying nothing, one hand holding the candle and the other shielding its flame from any wayward breath of wind. But the cold, wintry night was so still that there was hardly a flicker from the flame.

The abbess did not pause at the doorway to the tower but entered immediately. Inside, the library was dark but Draigen hurried to the foot of the steps which led up to the second floor almost without waiting for Fidelma to light the way. They moved rapidly to the third floor where the copyists worked. At the foot of the next set of steps which led on to the floor where the water-clock was situated Fidelma noticed an extinguished candle and its holder lying separately on the floor as if it had been carelessly flung aside. Draigen abruptly halted here, so that Fidelma was forced to stumble a little for fear of colliding with her. In the light of Fidelma's flickering candle, Abbess Draigen's face was ghastly. However, she appeared to be slowly composing herself.

'You should prepare yourself, sister. The sight which you

will see is not a pleasant one.' They were the first words
Draigen had uttered since rousing Fidelma from her sleep.

Without another word, she turned and mounted the
steps.

Fidelma did not say anything. She felt that there was
nothing to say until she knew the meaning of this night's
excursion.

She followed the abbess into the room of the clepsydra.
There was a soft red glow from the fire, the water was still
steaming in the great bronze bowl. There were also two
lanterns whose light made her candle superfluous.

She was but a second in the room when she saw the body
stretched on the floor. That it was female and wore the dress
of a sister of the community required no great inspection.
That much was obvious.

Abbess Draigen said nothing, merely standing to one
side.

Fidelma placed her candle carefully on a bench and
moved closer. Even though she had witnessed many violent
deaths in the violent world in which she lived, Fidelma
could not suppress the shudder of revulsion that went
through her.

The head of the corpse had been severed. It was nowhere
in sight.

The body would have been lying face down, had there
been a face. It was lying with arms outstretched. She
noticed immediately that there was a small crucifix in the
right hand and around the left arm was tied a small aspen
wand with some Ogham characters. There was a mess of
blood, still red and sticky, around the severed neck. She
saw that there was another pool of blood under the body at
chest level.

Fidelma took a deep breath and then exhaled slowly.

'Who is it?' she asked of the abbess.

'Sister Síomha.'

Fidelma blinked rapidly.

'How can you be so sure?'

The abbess uttered a strangled noise which had been intended for a short bark of cynical laughter.

'You lectured us on recognising a corpse by means other than a face only a short while ago, sister. Those are her robes. You will find a scar on the left leg where she once fell and cut herself. Also, she was on duty as keeper of the water-clock for the first *cadar* of the day. By these things I know it is Síomha.'

Fidelma pressed her lips together and bent down. She raised the hem of the skirt and saw, on the white flesh of the left leg, healed scar tissue that had once been a deep gash. Fidelma then pushed the corpse towards its left side and looked at the front of it. From the amount of blood and the slashed clothing, she presumed that Síomha had been stabbed in the heart before her head had been severed. Gently, she allowed the body to resume its original position. She peered at the hands of the corpse and was not surprised when she saw the brown red mud under the fingernails and on the fingers themselves. Then she reached forward and untied the aspen wand and read the Ogham inscription.

'The Mórrígú is awake!'

She frowned and, holding the stick in her hand, she rose to her feet and faced Draigen.

The abbess was not entirely recovered from her shock. Her eyes were red, the face pale, her lips twitching. Fidelma felt almost sorry for her.

'We must talk,' she said gently. 'Will it be here or would you prefer to go elsewhere?'

'We must rouse the abbey,' Draigen countered.

'But first the questions.'

'Then it would be better if you asked your questions here.'

'Very well.'

'Let me tell you this immediately,' Draigen went on before Fidelma could frame her first question. 'I have already caught the evil sorceress who did this deed.'

Fidelma controlled her utter surprise.

'You have?'

'It was Sister Berrach. I caught her red-handed.'

Fidelma was unable to restrain her astonishment. Abbess Draigen's announcement deprived her of speech for a space of several moments.

'I think,' Fidelma said after a lengthy pause, 'I think that you should tell me your story first.'

Abbess Draigen sat down abruptly and averted her gaze from the body, fixing it on some point beyond the far window where the moonlight was shimmering on the waters of the inlet, silhouetting the dark outline of the Gaulish merchant ship that rode at anchor.

'I have told you that Sister Síomha was taking the first *cadar*, that is the quarter day, watching the clepsydra. That is from midnight to the sounding of the morning Angelus.'

Fidelma asked no question. Sister Brónach had already explained the workings of the water-clock.

'I could not rest. I have been feeling much anxiety. What if your suggestion were true and that some evil has befallen our two sisters on their return from Ard Fhearta? I could not fall asleep. And because I could not sleep, I noticed that a lengthy time had passed since I heard the stroke of the gong, which should sound each passing time period.'

The abbess paused briefly for apparent reflection before continuing.

'I realised that the gong had not been sounded for some time. This was unlike Sister Síomha who is usually so punctilious in such matters. I rose from my bed and dressed and came to the tower to find out what was wrong.'

'Were you carrying a candle?' interposed Fidelma.

The abbess frowned uncertainly at the question and then nodded hastily.

'Yes, yes. I had lit a candle in my chambers and used it to light my way across the courtyard to the tower. I entered the tower, moving through the library and into the copyists' room. I was crossing the room when something prompted me to call to Sister Síomha. It was so quiet. I felt something was wrong and so I called.'

'Go on,' Fidelma urged after she had hesitated.

'It was a moment later that a dark shadow came charging down the stairs. It happened so suddenly that I was knocked aside, my candle went flying. The person pushed by me and out of the room.'

'What then?'

'I continued up the stairs to this room.'

'Without a candle?'

'I saw that the lamps were lit exactly as they are now. Then I saw Sister Síomha's body.'

'You saw the headless corpse on the floor?'

Abbess Draigen's face was suddenly angry.

'The person who passed me on the stair was Sister Berrach. I have no doubt of it. You know, having seen Berrach, that it would be impossible to mistake anyone else for her.'

Fidelma could concede the point but she wanted to make sure.

'That is what worries me. You say that Berrach came "charging down the stairs" – your words – but we both know that Berrach has a deformity. Are you certain that it was Berrach? Remember your candle was flung from your hand and she passed you in the darkness.'

'Perhaps I have used the wrong phrase in my agitation. The figure moved with alacrity but, even so, I know her misshapen form anywhere.'

Fidelma silently agreed that Sister Berrach was not a person one could easily mistake for another.

'And after she had run by you . . . ?'

'I came immediately to you so that you might witness this madness.'

Fidelma was grim. 'Let us go in search of Sister Berrach.'

The Abbess Draigen was now in control of her emotions since unburdening her story. She grunted cynically.

'She will have fled the abbey by now.'

'Even if she has, unless she has access to a horse and can ride, she would not have been able to go far. Nevertheless...'

Fidelma fell silent at the sound of a soft footfall on the steps below.

The abbess started forward as if to say something but Fidelma placed a finger over her lips and motioned her back. Someone was climbing the stairs towards the clepsydra room.

Fidelma found her body tensing and she felt irritated that this was so. Surely, if anything, she had been trained not to respond to outside stimuli so that she was prepared at all times. She carefully relaxed her tightening muscles. And moved to stand with the abbess so that whoever entered the room would do so with their back towards them. Someone in the robes of the community came up the stair. Fidelma saw immediately it was not the figure of a young person, she had recognised who it was before they had turned to face into the room.

'Sister Brónach! What are you doing here at this hour?'

Brónach nearly fell in her startled surprise. She then relaxed as she recognised Fidelma and then the abbess.

'Why, I have just come from the chamber of Sister Berrach. The girl is distraught. She told me that murder has been committed here.'

'You have seen her?' Draigen demanded. 'She woke you?'

'No. I was awake already. I was about to come to the tower myself,' explained Brónach. 'I had realised that some time had passed since I heard the sounding of the gong. In fact, several time periods must have elapsed since I heard it. So I had risen to come to see what ailed the time-keeper. As I was about to leave my cell, I heard the noise of someone passing hurriedly down the corridor. I realised it was Sister Berrach. I went to see her and found her sitting on her bed in a distressed state. She told me that Sister Síomha was dead and I came directly here to see if she was imagining...'

She suddenly caught sight of the crumpled heap on the floor behind Fidelma and her mouth formed a round shape. Her hand came up to cover it. The eyes widened fearfully.

'It is Sister Síomha,' Abbess Draigen confirmed solemnly.

Fidelma, watching the expression on Sister Brónach's face, was sure that she saw a momentary look of relief in her expression. But it was gone before she could be sure. The light of the lanterns helped to distort facial expressions anyway.

'Sister Brónach, I require you to see what you can do about resetting the clepsydra,' Abbess Draigen said, completely in charge again. 'For generations this community has prided itself on the accuracy of our water-clock. Do what you can to recover the accuracy of our calculations.'

Sister Brónach looked bemused but bowed her head in acquiescence.

'I will do my best, mother abbess, but...' she cast a nervous glance to the body.

'I will rouse some of the sisters to come and take our unfortunate sister to the *subterraneus*. You will not be alone long.'

It was while she was turning towards the stairs that an idea suddenly occurred to Fidelma. She turned hurriedly back to Sister Brónach.

'Didn't you show me that after each time period elapsed, and the gong was sounded, the watcher had to enter the time on a tablet of clay?'

Sister Brónach nodded affirmation.

'That is the custom in case we loose track of the time periods.'

'At what time did Sister Síomha make her last notation?'

Fidelma realised that this would at least give her an accurate knowledge of the time Sister Síomha was killed.

Sister Brónach was looking round for the clay writing tablet. She found it lying face-down by the stone-built fireplace and picked it up.

'Well?' prompted Fidelma, as she studied it.

'The second hour of the day has been marked and the first *pongc* or time period after that.'

'So? She was killed between two-fifteen and two-thirty this morning,' mused Fidelma.

'Is that important?' demanded the Abbess Draigen impatiently. 'We already know who did this terrible thing.'

'What hour do you think it is now?' Fidelma asked.

'I have no idea.'

'I have,' said Sister Brónach. She went to the window and stared up at the lightening night sky. There was a complacent expression on her face. 'It is well after the fourth hour of the day. I believe it is closer to the fifth hour.'

'Thank you, sister,' Fidelma acknowledged absently. Her mind was working rapidly. She asked the abbess, 'Can you calculate how long ago it was since you found the body?'

Abbess Draigen shrugged.

'I do not see that it matters...'

'Indulge me,' insisted Fidelma.

'Less than an hour ago, I would say. I came to you almost immediately that I discovered it.'

'Indeed. In fact it was much less than an hour ago,' agreed Fidelma. 'I would say that we have been here under half-an-hour.'

'We should go in search of Sister Berrach rather than wasting time in this manner,' Abbess Draigen insisted.

'Can't you question the poor girl in the morning?' It was Sister Brónach who spoke, surprising Draigen. 'Sister Berrach has suffered from the shock of finding the body.'

Fidelma asked: 'Did she tell you that she had found the body?'

'Not specifically. She told me that Sister Síomha was dead in the tower. So the fact that she found the body is surely obvious.'

'Perhaps,' replied Fidelma. 'I think we should see Sister Berrach now. One thing more, though, since you are here,

Sister Brónach,' she added, causing the Abbess Draigen to heave an impatient sigh. 'Does the name Mórrígú mean anything to you?'

Sister Brónach shuddered.

'Surely the name of the evil one is well known, sister? In the ancient times, before the word of the Christ was brought to this land, she was regarded as the goddess of death and battles. She embodied all that was perverse and horrible among the supernatural powers.'

'So, you have a knowledge of the old pagan ways, then?' Fidelma observed.

Sister Brónach pouted.

'Who would not know about the old gods and goddesses and the old ways? I was raised in these very forests where there are many who still cling to the old beliefs.'

Fidelma inclined her head and then, to Abbess Draigen's apparent relief, turned, took up her candle again and preceded the abbess down the stairs. They had reached the ground floor of the tower when a hollow, knocking sound caused Fidelma to halt. It was the same sound that she had heard in the *duirthech*, the chapel. The far off banging of hollow wood resonated through the building.

Fidelma turned towards a darkened corner of the room, from where the sound echoed loudest, and moved forward cautiously, holding the candle before her.

'That is only the stairs that lead to the cave below,' Draigen's voice came from behind her.

'Has no one ever traced the source of this sound?' Fidelma asked as she reached the top of the stairs.

'No, why should we?' breathed Draigen nervously. 'It certainly does not come from our *subterraneus*.'

Fidelma peered down in the gloom.

'Yet it appears to be coming from there. You said that you believed that it was caused by water filling a cave beneath the abbey?'

'So I do,' Draigen did not sound entirely convinced.

'Where are you going?' she demanded as Fidelma began to descend the stone stairs into the cave below.

'I just want to check...' Fidelma did not finish but descended the narrow stairway.

The cave below was empty and now silent. Fidelma looked around in disappointment. There was no place one could hide. A few boxes in one corner but that was all. With a stifled sigh, she turned and began to make her way back up the steps, feeling her way against the cold wall with one hand to help her in the gloom.

The substance was wet and sticky and she knew what it was before she examined her fingers by the candlelight. Then she examined the side of the wall. There was a smear of blood there. It had been made recently.

'What is it, sister?' demanded Draigen's voice from the top of the stairway.

Fidelma was about to explain when she changed her mind.

'Nothing, mother abbess. It is nothing.'

Outside, in the courtyard, they encountered the anxious figure of Sister Lerben.

'Something is wrong, mother abbess,' she greeted breathlessly. 'The simpleton, Berrach, is sobbing in her cell. I saw lights in the tower but heard no gong from the keeper of the water-clock.'

Abbess Draigen laid a hand on the young woman's shoulder.

'Prepare yourself, child. Sister Síomha has been killed. Berrach is responsible...'

'You do not know that for certain,' interrupted Fidelma. 'Let us go and question the girl before we apportion the blame.'

But Sister Lerben had already hurried away with the news, crying to rouse the sleeping community. They had hardly crossed the courtyard before the news was spreading like a wildfire. Everyone was awakening to become aware of what had happened. Abbess Draigen told a passing novice to go to the dormitories and quiet the tumult but before she could respond the courtyard began to crowd with anxious sisters. The babble of hysterical and angry voices filled the air. Candles and lamps were lit, and sisters hurriedly dressed or with draped cloaks around their shoulders, were gathering in tiny circles, speaking in fearful and angry tones.

Sister Berrach had, it seemed, barricaded herself in her cell. Sister Lerben returned to say that she could still hear Berrach's wailing cries, a curious mixture of prayers and ancient curses.

'What shall we do, mother abbess?'

'I shall go to speak with her,' Fidelma intervened decisively.

'That is not a wise idea,' the abbess advised.

'Why so?'

'You know how strong Berrach is, in spite of her deformity. She could easily attack you.'

Fidelma smiled thinly.

'I do not think that I need to fear Berrach. Where is her cell?'

The young Sister Lerben glanced at the abbess and then gestured with her arm in the direction of one of the dormitory buildings.

'She has the last cell in that building, sister. But should you not go armed?'

Fidelma shook her head with an expression of annoyance.

'Wait here and do not come until I call you.'

She raised a hand to shield her candle against the quickening morning breeze and walked across to the building which Sister Lerben had indicated. It was a long wooden building consisting of a corridor with some twelve cell-like chambers along one side. In fact, all the community dormitories seemed to be constructed in such a fashion.

She entered and examined the darkened corridor.

From the end room she could hear Sister Berrach's sobbing.

'Sister Berrach!' Fidelma called, trying to keep her voice from conveying the anxiety that she really felt. 'Sister Berrach! It is Fidelma.'

There was a pause and the crying seem to halt. There were one or two sniffs.

'Berrach, it is Sister Fidelma. Do you remember me?'

There was another pause and then Berrach's voice came defensively.

'Of course. I am no idiot.'

'I never thought you were,' Fidelma replied in a conciliative tone. 'May we talk?'

'Are you alone?'

'Quite alone, Berrach.'

'Then come forward until I see you.'

Slowly, holding her candle high, Fidelma moved down the corridor. She could hear the scraping of furniture and presumed Berrach was removing a barricade from her door. As she came towards the end of the corridor, the door opened a crack.

'Stop!' instructed Berrach's voice.

Fidelma obeyed immediately.

The door opened further and Berrach's head appeared to confirm that there was no one else there. Then the door opened wider.

'Come in, sister.'

Fidelma looked at the young girl. Her eyes were red and her cheeks tear-stained. She entered the cell and stood still while behind her Berrach pushed the door shut and heaved a table to secure it.

'Why are you barricading yourself in?' asked Fidelma. 'Whom do you fear?'

Berrach lurched towards her bed, sat down and took a grip on her thick blackthorn stick.

'Don't you know that Sister Síomha has been killed?'

'Why should this cause you to blockade the door to your chamber?'

'Because I will be accused of the crime and I do not know what to do.'

Fidelma glanced round; saw a small chair and seated herself, putting down the candle on the adjacent table.

'Why would you be accused of the deed?'

Sister Berrach looked at her scornfully.

'Because Abbess Draigen saw me in the tower when the body was found. And because most people in this community dislike me on account that I am misshapen. They will surely accuse me of killing her.'

Fidelma sat back and folded her hands in her lap, looking long and thoughtfully at Berrach.

'You seem to have lost your stutter,' she observed carefully.

The girl's face twisted in a cynical expression.

'You are quick to notice things, Sister Fidelma. Unlike the others. They only see what they want to see and have no other perception.'

'I suppose you stammered because it was expected of you?'

Sister Berrach's eyes widened a little.

'That is clever of you, sister.' She paused before continuing. 'A misshapen mind must needs be in a misshapen body. That is the philosophy of ignorance. I stammer for them because they think I am a simpleton. If I showed intelligence then they might think some evil spirit possessed me.'

'But you are honest with me, why can't you be honest with others?'

Sister Berrach's mouth twisted again.

'I will be honest with you because you see beyond the curtain of prejudice where others cannot see.'

'You flatter me.'

'Flattery is not in my nature.'

'Tell me what happened.'

'Tonight?'

'Yes. The Abbess Draigen saw you coming down from the room where the water-clock is kept. Sister Síomha, as you know, was found beheaded in that room. You were in some hurry and pushed the abbess aside causing her to drop and extinguish her candle.' Fidelma looked at Sister Berrach's clothing. 'I see a dark patch staining the front of your habit, sister. I presume that will be Sister Síomha's blood?'

The wary blue eyes stared solemnly at Fidelma.

'I did not kill Sister Síomha.'

'I believe you. Will you trust me enough to tell me exactly what happened?'

Sister Berrach spread her hands, almost in a pathetic gesture.

'They think that I am a simpleton in this place solely because I am deformed. I was born like this. Some problems with my spine, or so the physicians told my mother. Yet my body and arms are strong. Only my legs have not grown properly.'

Sister Berrach paused but Fidelma made no retort, waiting for the girl to continue.

'At first the physician said I could not live and then he said I should not live. My mother could not nurse me in her community. My father did not want to have anything to do with me. After my birth he even left my mother. So I was raised by my grandmother but she was killed when I was young. I survived and was brought to this abbey when I was three years old and here Brónach raised me. I survived and I have lived. This community has always been my home so long as I can remember.'

There was a quiet sob in the girl's voice. Fidelma now understood why Sister Brónach always seemed protective towards the girl.

'Now tell me what happened at the tower,' she pressed gently.

'Each night, before dawn, while most of the community are still sleeping, I rise and go to the library,' Berrach confided. 'That is when I devote myself to reading. I have read almost all of the great books in our library.'

Fidelma was surprised.

'Why wait until near dawn to go to the library to read?'

Berrach laughed. There was no mirth in it.

'They think I am a simpleton who can't even think let alone read. I have taught myself to read my own tongue and I can also read Latin, Greek and even some Hebrew.'

Fidelma gazed thoughtfully at her but the girl did not seem to be boasting, simply stating fact. An extraneous thought abruptly crossed Fidelma's mind.

'Did you know that this abbey has a copy of the annals of Clonmacnoise?'

Sister Berrach nodded immediately.

'It is a copy made by our librarian,' she volunteered.

'Have you read it?'

'No. But I have read many other books there.'

'Go on,' Fidelma sighed in disappointment. 'You were saying that you rise and go to the library before dawn. Are you not frightened to be alone in such a place?'

'There was always a sister on watch in the tower above. Recently,' she shivered, 'it has been Sister Síomha who took most of the night watches. Before these events there was no physical danger to fear in this place.'

Fidelma grimaced.

'I was not concerned with physical danger. What of the knocking sound under the *duirthech* which frightened the sisters the other day? I am told that it has been heard before.'

Sister Berrach thought for a moment.

'The sounds have been heard before but infrequently. Abbess Draigen says it is some underground cave which fills with water but sometimes the sisters are scared by it. It does not scare me nor should it scare anyone who cleaves to the Faith.'

'That is laudable, sister. Do you accept the abbess's explanation that it is caused by an underground cave filling with water from the inlet?'

'It is a possibility. More of a possibility than those who talk of the restless spirits of victims of pagan sacrifices which they believe were once enacted here.'

'But you are not sure? Not sure that it is only water in an underground cave?'

'Sometimes, like the other day in the *duirthech*, the abbess makes her explanation sound plausible. At other times, especially when I am in the library at night, the sound is fainter, but more like the tapping of someone hacking at rock or digging. But whatever it is, it is a sound produced by earthly agents, so why should I be afraid of it?'

'Just so. And you went, as usual, to the library this morning?'

'Yes, in the hours before dawn. I tried to be as quiet as possible for I did not wish to alarm the sister on duty at the water-clock. Especially when it was Sister Síomha who dislikes me more than most.'

'When did you enter the library this morning? Can you be fairly exact?'

'As near as I recall, I had heard the second hour strike, and perhaps the first quarter of the hour after that. I am not sure. It was not later than the third hour, of that I know, for I do not recall it being struck.'

'Go on.'

'I went into the library and found the book I wanted . . .'

'Which was?'

'Do you want the name of the book?' frowned Sister Berrach.

'Yes.'

'The *Itinerary* of Aethicus of Istria. I took the book to a small table in a corner. I usually choose this spot in case someone enters unexpectedly and then this can give me time to conceal myself. I was reading the passage of how Aethicus came to Ireland to observe and study our libraries when it occurred to me that time was passing. I had heard no gong sounded by the keeper of the clepsydra. I went to the foot of the stairs and listened. Everything was quiet. Too quiet.'

Berrach paused and rubbed her cheek absently for a moment.

'I felt that something was wrong. You know how one can suddenly get a feeling? I decided to go up to investigate...'

'Even though you did not want anyone to know you were there, least of all Sister Síomha?'

'If something was wrong, it was better not to ignore it.'

'And what did you do with the book?'

'I left it on the table where I was reading it.'

'So it will still be there? Very well. Go on.'

'I climbed the stairs as carefully as I could into the room where the clepsydra was kept. I thought I saw Sister Síomha lying on the floor.'

'You *thought*?' stressed Fidelma.

'The body had no head. But I did not see that at once. I saw only a body in the dress of a sister. I knelt down by it to feel her pulse, thinking that she must have passed out – perhaps fainted for lack of food or some other cause. My hands touched her neck, cold, not quite icy cold but a clammy coldness. Then I felt something sticky. I was feeling for her head...'

Sister Berrach's voice caught and she shuddered at the memory.

'Holy Mother of Jesus, protect me! I realised at that moment that Síomha had been slain in the same manner as the corpse found in the well. I think that I cried aloud in my horror.'

'And then you ran down the stairs?' Fidelma prompted.

'Not immediately. As I cried out, I heard a sound behind me in the room. I turned, my heart beating rapidly. I saw a shadow, a cowled head and shoulders, slipping quickly below the level of the floor down the stairway.'

Fidelma leant forward quickly.

'Was this head and shoulders male or female?'

Berrach shook her head.

'Alas, I do not know. It was so gloomy and the movement

was hurried. I was not in the mood to investigate further. I was frozen with fear. That I was alone in the dark with the monster who did this deed put the very fear of eternal damnation into me. I do not know how long I knelt there in the dark by the body. Some time must have passed, no doubt.'

'You just knelt there in the dark? You did not move or cry out?'

'Fear is a strange controller of your body, sister. Fear can make the lame run, the physically active freeze like a cripple.'

Fidelma acknowledged this with an impatient gesture.

'Then what, Berrach?'

'Finally, I rose to my feet, feeling the blood in my veins course like ice. I do not know how long this was, as I have said. I wanted to sound an alarm and was going to strike the gong. I lit the lanterns. Then I heard another noise.'

'A noise? What sort of noise?'

'I heard the thud of a door. I heard footsteps beginning to ascend the stairs. I heard them coming closer. My thought, my true thought, sister, was that the murderer was returning – returning to ensure that I would say nothing.'

She paused and seemed to have difficulty in breathing for a moment or two but then she recovered herself.

'Then my fear, instead of rooting me to the spot, as it had before, lent me strength. I turned and clambered down the stairs as fast as I could. I remember seeing a figure ascending. I thought it was the cowled figure returning. That is the truth! I used all my strength to collide violently with it, so knocking it off balance, and allowing me time to effect my escape . . .'

'Do you recall if this figure was carrying a light?'

Berrach frowned.

'A light?'

'A lamp or a candle?'

The girl gave it some thought.

'I can't remember. I think there might have been a candle.

Is it important? I heard it cry out. It was not until I was already across the courtyard that I realised that it had been the abbess.'

'Why did you not return once you realised that fact?'

'I was confused. After all, I had seen the cowled figure in the water-clock room. Perhaps it had been the abbess herself who was the killer. How was I to know?'

Fidelma did not answer.

'I came here as fast as I could. I had just reached my cell when Brónach came in and asked me why I was upset. I told her and she said that she would go and discover what had happened. I was frightened in case the murderer had followed me.'

'But the murderer did not. And surely you would have feared for Brónach's safety going alone to the tower?'

'I was confused,' repeated Berrach.

'Why then did you barricade yourself in?'

'I heard the noise of the community being awakened. There were lights in the tower and then in the dormitories. I was about to come out when I heard one of the sisters, I think it was Lerben, calling – "Sister Síomha has been killed by Berrach!" I knew then that I was doomed. What chance has someone like me to justice? I will be punished for something that I have not done.'

Fidelma regarded her thoughtfully.

'One more question, Berrach. Did you see anything peculiar about Sister Síomha's body? Apart from the decapitation, that is?'

Berrach wrenched her thoughts momentarily away from her fears and peered questioningly up at Fidelma.

'Peculiar?'

'Perhaps something similar to the way the nameless corpse in the well was left,' prompted Fidelma.

Sister Berrach thought cautiously for a moment.

'I do not think so.'

'I mean, did you notice anything tied to her left arm?'

The girl's bewilderment seemed genuine enough as she shook her head.

'Do you know anything about the old pagan customs?'

'Who does not?' replied Berrach. 'In these remote places, away from the great cathedrals and towns, you should know that people still dwell close to nature, keep to the old well-trodden paths. Scratch a Christian here and you will find the blood is pagan.'

Fidelma was about to say something further when she heard sounds which seemed to be growing in volume. It was the noise of chanting voices coming from outside the building. She stared in astonishment as she listened. The voices were chanting a name. 'Berrach! Berrach! Berrach!'

The sister gave a pitiful moan.

'You see?' she whimpered. 'You see? They have come to punish me?'

'Sister Fidelma!'

Fidelma recognised the voice of Sister Lerben as it cut through the noise. Slowly the chanting voices fell silent.

Fidelma stood up and went to the door. She glanced back at Sister Berrach and tried to smile encouragement.

'Trust me,' she reassured the girl. Then she pushed the table aside and opened the door.

Sister Lerben was standing at the far end of the corridor, some of her fellow novices were crowding behind her with lamps.

'Are you safe, sister?' demanded the young religieuse. 'We were worried when we did not hear from you.'

'What is the meaning of this unruly shouting? Disperse the sisters to their cells.'

'The members of this community have come for the murderess. The slaughter of Sister Síomha cannot go unpunished. Bring out Berrach. Her sisters have decided that death shall be her only punishment.'

Chapter Ten

The young members of the community seemed almost possessed as they crowded at the end of the passage crying out Berrach's name. Their hysteria was almost out of control and Fidelma felt anger as she realised that Draigen had done nothing to calm their fears. Lerben herself seemed to have fomented the illogical frenzy and now stood at the head of what was little more than a mob. There was no sign at all of the abbess.

'The sisters have *decided*?' Fidelma's voice rose on a dangerously icy note.

Sister Lerben was emphatic. 'The matter is now straightforward. The abbey has given refuge to a witch all these years, one who has repaid it by murder and pagan idolatry. She will receive just punishment. Your task is over.'

There was a murmur of assent from the religieuses crowding behind her. Fidelma saw that most of them were only frightened and out of their fearful state had come their hysteria. Sister Lerben had directed that overwhelming passion against Berrach. The sisters were barely controlled. They seemed about to surge forward. Fidelma planted herself firmly in the passage and held up her hand.

'In the name of God, do you realise what you are doing?' she shouted above their cries. 'I am an advocate of the courts charged by your king and bishop to investigate this matter. Will you take justice into your own hands and commit a terrible crime?'

'It is our right,' retorted Sister Lerben.

'Tell me how this can be so?' Fidelma demanded. She reasoned that any dialogue was better than blind violence. 'What is your right? You are just a novice in this abbey, without station. Where is Abbess Draigen? Perhaps she can explain your right?'

Sister Lerben's eyes flashed angrily.

'Abbess Draigen has retired to her chamber to pray. She has appointed me to act as *rechtaire* until she has recovered from this appalling shock. I am now in charge here. Hand over the murderess to us.'

Fidelma was appalled at the young girl's arrogance.

'You are young, Lerben. Too young to take the responsibility of this office. What you are suggesting is contrary to the law of the five kingdoms. Now calm yourself and instruct your sisters to disperse.'

To her surprise, Lerben stood her ground.

'Didn't Ultan, Archbishop of Armagh, and Chief Apostle of the Faith in the five kingdoms, decree that our church should follow the laws of Peter's Church in Rome? Well, we have judged our erring sister by that ecclesiastical law and found her guilty.'

'By what law?' Fidelma could hardly believe her ears. Surely someone had prompted this young novice, who now claimed to be steward of the abbey, to go against all the laws of the land. She felt that she was embroiled in an argument with someone who claimed that the colour of a day sky was black and the colour of a night sky was white. Where could she find a point of logical contact?

'By the law of the Holy Word!' replied Lerben, unperturbed by Fidelma's authority. 'Does it not say in Exodus: "thou shalt not suffer a witch to live"?'

'Has the abbess instructed you in this, Lerben?' Fidelma challenged.

'Do you argue with the Holy Word?' replied the novice stubbornly.

'Our Lord said, according to Matthew: "Judge not, that ye

be not judged. For with what judgment ye judge, ye shall be judged; and with what measure ye mete, it shall be measured to you again"' Fidelma threw back the quotation at Lerben and then turned to the suddenly subdued religieuses behind her. 'Sisters, you are being misled. Calm yourselves and return to your dormitories. Berrach is not the guilty one.'

There was some muttering among the sisters. Sister Lerben tried to restore her authority. Her face was red and angry for she had clearly hoped to win the sisters' unquestioned respect and allegiance by her knowledge.

'Do you reject the dictums of Ultan?' she demanded of Fidelma.

'Certainly, if they disagree with truth and the law of this land.'

'Draigen is abbess here, and her word is law!' replied the girl.

'That is not so,' returned Fidelma sharply, knowing that she had to defuse the situation quickly. The longer it was left festering the easier it would get out of hand. She realised that her suspicion was right. Draigen must have encouraged Lerben in this attempt to whip up fear against Berrach. The only way she could stop this dangerous situation was to attempt to exert her own authority. She repeated clearly: 'I am appointed ultimately by your High King. I have come here at the request of your king and bishop; by the authority of the abbot of Ros Ailithir, if you respect no other. If you harm Berrach in any way, you, and all who act with you, will be responsible for kin-slaying.'

There was a murmur of consternation among the sisters. They knew enough law to realise that the crime of kin-slaying was one of the most serious in the criminal code of the five kingdoms. It deprived even the High King of his honour price, it was a lawful cause for the driving out of a king from his rank and office. The crucifixion of Christ was considered by the Irish as the ultimate kin-slaying for the Jews were regarded as the maternal kin of Christ. All the laws and wisdom-texts from time immemorial stressed the horrendous nature of kin-slaying for the act struck at the very heart of the kin-based structure of society.

'You would dare...?' Sister Lerben began uncertainly. 'You would dare accuse us of that?' But already she was losing support for the argument.

'Sisters,' Fidelma now addressed those crowding uncertainly behind Lerben. Since she now held their attention, there was little point in appealing to the inexperienced and arrogant novice. 'Sisters, I have examined Sister Berrach and I believe that she is innocent of killing Síomha. She stumbled on the corpse just as, a moment later, Abbess Draigen did. She is no more guilty of the crime than Draigen. Do not let fear guide your logic. It is so easy to turn destructively on that which you fear. Disperse to your dormitories and let us forget this as a moment's madness.'

The sisters looked at each other, perhaps somewhat sheepishly in the gloom, and some began to disperse.

Sister Lerben took a step forward, her mouth thin and set firm, but Fidelma quickly decided to maintain her advantage. She caught sight of the anxious Sister Brónach newly arrived, at the rear of the group.

'Sister Brónach, I want you to escort Sister Lerben to her chamber while I go to see the abbess. That is an order by virtue of my rank,' she added when Brónach hesitated. Then she deliberately turned her back and re-entered Berrach's chamber. She stood just inside the door, her eyes closed, her heart beating fast, wondering whether she had completely defused the situation. Would Lerben make a further attempt to rally her supporters again and seize Berrach? There was a murmuring and shuffling in the corridor and then silence. Fidelma opened her eyes.

The girl was sitting on the bed shivering uncontrollably.

Fidelma glanced quickly into the corridor. It was empty. She exhaled long and deeply.

'It's all right,' she said, turning back into the chamber and seating herself on the bed next to Berrach. 'They have dispersed.'

'How can they be so evil?' shuddered the girl. 'They were going to take me out and kill me.'

Fidelma laid a hand on the girl's arm in comfort.

'They are not really evil. They are merely fearful. Of all the passions, fear weakens the judgment, especially when one is so young and inexperienced as Lerben.'

The girl was silent for a while.

'Sister Lerben has never liked me. I cannot stay here now. You heard what she said? Abbess Draigen has made her the steward of the abbey now Sister Síomha is dead.'

'An unwise, indeed, foolish choice,' conceded Fidelma. 'And I will talk about this matter with the abbess. Lerben is too young to be *rechtaire*. Wait a while, Berrach. The sisters will come to their senses and then they will feel remorse.'

'If they fear me so much then that fear will never be diminished but grow into hate. I will never be safe here.'

'Give them a chance. At least, allow me to speak with Abbess Draigen.'

Sister Berrach said nothing. Fidelma decided to take it as a sign of acceptance of her suggestion.

She rose and went to the door, glancing back briefly.

'Will you be all right here for a short while?' she asked.

Sister Berrach looked gloomy.

'*Deo favente*,' she replied. 'With God's favour.'

Fidelma left the cell and walked grimly towards the Abbess Draigen's chamber. Now that she thought about the matter, hot blood poured into her brain. She felt a rage at the conduct of the abbess. How could she have given such power to Lerben? How could she have induced the novice into encouraging her sisters to attempt nothing less than an act of murder? What hatred did the abbess feel for Berrach? Everywhere Fidelma looked a cloak of hatred hung about this place. She felt furious and then a thought came into her mind. It was easy to fly into a temper but didn't Publilius Syrus argue that one should always shun anger? Anger made people blind and foolish. She recalled the words of her mentor, the Brehon Morann of Tara: whoever experiences the white heat of anger will then experience the ice cold of regret. Better to be calm.

She had no sooner made the resolution than she found herself outside the door of Abbess Draigen's chamber.

She thrust it open and marched in without knocking.

Abbess Draigen was sitting at her chamber, upright and stiff-backed, her mouth set determinedly. Sister Lerben was standing by the fire, evidently having eluded the escort of Sister Brónach. She stared with dislike as Fidelma entered and strode firmly into the room.

'I will speak with you alone, mother abbess.'

'I am . . .' began Sister Lerben.

'You are dismissed,' snapped Fidelma.

Abbess Draigen let her eyes flicker towards the young novice and then made a dismissive motion with her hand. The young woman bit her tongue, almost bringing her teeth down painfully on her lower lip. She went, head high, from the room.

Before Fidelma could speak, Abbess Draigen's face dissolved in wrath.

'This is the second time you have interfered with the orders of someone appointed by me. Sister Lerben was appointed acting *rechtaire* in place of Sister Síomha.'

Fidelma smiled thinly against her anger.

'Fear betrays unworthy souls,' she replied as she seated herself.

Abbess Draigen grimaced.

'This is also the second time that you have quoted your Latin philosophers at me.'

'You did not allow me time to report on my interrogation of Sister Berrach before you allowed Lerben to whip up the fears of your community,' Fidelma ignored her riposte.

'What did you think she could achieve by inciting such a killing? Did you think that you, responsible for such an action as abbess, could do this without punishment?'

Abbess Draigen met her eye firmly.

'I was aware that Lerben and her fellow sisters had condemned Berrach. They acted in accordance to the law of God. I would stand by their decisions. I believe that Berrach was guilty of killing Sister Síomha. The pagan signs spoke of evil. The book of Deuteronomy says that those that practise such evil are guilty of an abomination to the Lord and must be driven out. Sister Lerben was acting in accord with the teaching of the Archbishop Ultan. I approved of her actions. My authority is Armagh.'

Fidelma decided that there was wisdom in Aristotle when he said that anyone could give way to anger but the secret was knowing when to be angry with the right person to the right extent and in the right way. It was really Abbess Draigen whom she had to deal with. Young Sister Lerben was only her voice. Clearly, Abbess Draigen had told Lerben what to do. Yet this was not the time to be angry with Abbess Draigen either for her anger would merely meet with a brick wall.

'Let us be clear that there is as much evidence to convict Berrach of the killing of Sister Síomha, at this time, as to convict you or Sister Brónach. Your incitement of Lerben to violence is based on the hidden fears that others have because of poor Berrach's deformity. It is not the way a member of the Faith should act. So I want you to guarantee that no harm will come to Berrach until I have finished my investigation.'

Abbess Draigen pursed her lips.

'I shall not swear for it is against the Scriptures.'

Fidelma smiled cynically.

'I know the passage to which you refer, mother abbess. It is the fifth chapter of Matthew. But while Christ said one should not swear by any sacred object he exhorted people to say "yes" or "no". Therefore, I shall exhort you to say "yes", that you will guarantee the safety of Berrach. The other answer is "no" and, if this is so, then I shall have to refer the matter to Abbot Brocc at Ros Ailithir and safeguard Sister Berrach myself.'

Abbess Draigen sniffed angrily.

'Then you have your "yes". I shall say no more than that I will also refer this matter, not to Brocc, but to Ultan of Armagh himself.'

Fidelma's eyes narrowed.

'Am I to understand that you prefer to accept the rule of Rome in this land?'

'I am of the Roman school,' the abbess conceded.

'So we know where we stand,' Fidelma replied softly.

Fidelma was well aware of the growing conflict between the church in the five kingdoms of Éireann and Rome. There was also a growing debate on the systems of law. The five kingdoms had long been steeped in legal tradition ever since twelve centuries before the High King Ollamh Fodhla had ordered the laws of the Brehons, the judges, to be gathered into a unified code. But with the coming of the New Faith, new ideas were entering the land. From Rome, the advocates of the New Faith had, despising the laws of the lands which they converted, devised their own ecclesiastical laws. These canon laws were based on the decisions of councils of bishops and abbots, which ostensibly dealt with the government of the churches and clergy and administration of the sacraments and were now beginning to challenge the civil laws of the land.

In a few instances, some religious foundations had tried to claim that they were above the civil laws, indeed, even above the criminal laws. But these were few and far between. However, she knew that Ultan of Armagh favoured a closer merger with Rome and encouraged ecclesiastical legislation. Ultan himself had become a figure of controversy for, since he had succeeded Commené as archbishop six years ago, he had demonstrated time and again that he wanted to centralise the church of the five kingdoms after the manner of Rome.

'I stand by the teachings of Ultan and in the evidence that he has revealed showing that we should not be governed by the laws of the Brehons,' Draigen said.

'Evidence?'

The abbess pushed forward a small manuscript book that was resting on her table.

Fidelma glanced at it: 'The bishops Patrick, Auxiliius and Isernius greet the priests and deacons and all the clerics . . .' She put down the manuscript.

'It was no secret that Ultan is circulating this document,' Fidelma told Draigen. 'I know that he claims it to be the record of a council held two hundred years ago by those who took a leading part in converting the five kingdoms to the new Faith. Archbishop Ultan claims that the thirty-five ordnances of this supposed synod are the basis of ecclesiastical law and the first ordnance states that any member of the Church who appeals to the secular courts of Éireann merits excommunication.'

Abbess Draigen stared at her in surprise.

'You seem to know the work well, Sister Fidelma,' she admitted warily.

Fidelma shrugged.

'Well enough to question its authenticity. If such rulings had been made in this land two hundred years ago we should have known about them.'

Draigen leaned forward in annoyance.

'It is obvious that it was suppressed by those who reject Rome's right to lead the Church.'

'But no one has seen the original manuscript, only the copies made on the orders of Ultan.'

'Do you dare question Archbishop Ultan?'

'I have that right. This book states ordnances which, while in agreement with Rome, are against the civil and criminal laws of Éireann.'

'Exactly so,' agreed Draigen smugly. 'That is why we argue that those of the Faith should ignore the civil law and turn to the ecclesiastical law for the way of truth. As the laws of Patrick say – no one of the Faith should appeal to a secular judge on pain of excommunication.'

Fidelma was amused.

'Then that argument is of itself a riddle for is it not recorded that Patrick employed his own Brehon, Erc of Baile Shláine, to represent him in all legal proceedings in the courts of this land?'

Abbess Draigen was taken aback.

'I do not . . .'

'Even more puzzling,' pressed Fidelma, seizing the advantage, 'is Patrick's written support of the laws of this land. This book is no more than a forgery by your pro-Roman faction if for no other reason than Patrick himself, with his companions, the bishops Benignus and Cairenech, served on the commission of nine eminent persons which gathered together by request of the High King, Laoghaire, studied, and revised the laws of the Brehons before committing them to writing in the new Latin characters. That was in the year of Our Lord Four-Hundred-and-Thirty-Eight. Surely you would agree, Draigen, that it would have been inconceivable for Patrick and his fellow churchman to advise on the civil and criminal laws of Éireann, lending their public support to them, while drawing up a set of rules contrary to them and demanding that no member of the church appeal to them on pain of excommunication?'

There was a silence. Abbess Draigen's face worked in anger as she tried to summon up a logical refutation. Fidelma smiled gently at her reddening face and leaned forward, tapping the manuscript book of Ultan with a forefinger.

'You will read in the opening lines of this forgery a piece of wise advice – it is better to dispute than to be angry.'

The abbess sat in outraged silence and Fidelma continued her attack.

'One thing that does intrigue me, mother abbess. If you believe in what you claim, why did you ask Abbot Brocc to send a Brehon to investigate this matter in the first place? You have no respect for secular law and would deny it.'

'We are still governed by secular law,' the abbess's voice was waspish. 'Adnár claims magisterial jurisdiction as *bó-aire*. I would recognise the authority of the Devil himself in order to check the power of my brother and prevent his interference in the affairs of this abbey.'

Fidelma's mouth drooped.

'So you accept the law of the Brehons only when it is for your benefit. That is no example to set for your community.'

Draigen took a moment to recover herself.

'You will not convince me. I stand by Ultan's declaration in the validity of this book.'

Fidelma inclined her head.

'That is your privilege, mother abbess. If so, then I should point out to you that the ecclesiastical laws of Rome which Lerben quoted to me this morning are not justifiable.'

'Which are?' demanded Draigen.

'Those she claimed gave her authority to seize and kill Sister Berrach, had she even been guilty of the crime that you accused her of. Doubtless, because of her youth, you instructed Lerben in these matters. The book of Exodus, chapter twenty-two, verse eighteen, was quoted.'

Draigen nodded swiftly.

'You know your scripture. Yes; that is the law. Thou shalt not suffer a witch to live. On that basis, Berrach, when demonstrated to be a witch using pagan practices, could be killed.'

'But, if you stand by Ultan's declaration, and seek justification in that text which purports to be the laws of Patrick's first synod in this land, pick it up and read to me the sixteenth law.'

An uncertainty crept into Abbess Draigen's eyes as she

returned the calm gaze of the younger woman. After a moment's hesitation, she reached forward and picked up the book and began to read.

'Would you read this law aloud?' pressed Fidelma.

'You know what it says,' countered the abbess in annoyance.

Fidelma reached over and took the book gently from her and began reading the law aloud.

'A Christian who believes that there is such a thing in the world as an enchantress, which is to say a witch, and who accuses anyone of this, is to be excommunicated, and may not be received into the church again until – by their own statement – they have revoked their criminal accusation and have accordingly done penance with full rigour.'

With deliberateness, Fidelma closed the book and replaced it, then sat back and regarded the abbess thoughtfully.

'Do you still stand by the edicts of Ultan, for if you do, you must accept that this is the ecclesiastical law which you must obey?'

Abbess Draigen did not reply. She was clearly confused.

'The penalties are clear,' Fidelma's voice was soft but contemptuous. 'Excommunication or a recantation of such accusations and penance with full rigour.'

Abbess Draigen swallowed.

'You are as subtle as a serpent,' she breathed softly. 'You do not believe in obeying this law yet you use it to ensnare me.'

'Not so,' Fidelma replied, ignoring the insult. '*Veritas simplex oratio est* – the language of truth is simple.'

'Yet you do not believe in this law which you now try to enforce,' the abbess repeated stubbornly.

'But you claim to believe in it. If your mind is dictated by logic, you must obey it. Indeed, you were the one who referred it to me as a justification of the crime that nearly happened here.'

The bell on the tower has started to sound.

Sister Lerben entered haughtily. She cast a sneering glance at Fidelma.

'I presume that you would want to know that the bell for matins is sounding, mother abbess. The congregation will be expecting you.'

'I have ears, Lerben. When my door is closed you should knock before entering.' Abbess Draigen's voice was a querulous yap. The young novice seemed stunned, obviously not expecting the reaction. Her face reddened and she went to say something, caught the angry eye of the abbess and hastily withdrew.

'Do you wish to reject Ultan's teachings...?' pressed Fidelma. 'Perhaps you need advice from your *anam-chara*, your soul-friend?'

Abbess Draigen suddenly rose angrily to her feet.

'Sister Síomha was my *anam-chara*,' she replied shortly. She seemed about to argue further but her jaw tightened. 'Very well; I will revoke my accusation against Berrach.'

Fidelma also rose to her feet, almost casually.

'That is good. It must be done before the community, as it was before the community that these accusations were made. Rescind the accusation, apologise and do penance.'

Abbess Draigen had an ugly expression on her face.

'I have said that I will do as much.'

'Good. Then, now is the appropriate time when the community are gathered for matins. I will escort Sister Berrach to the chapel as she may be wary of going abroad since violence was offered to her person – violence,' she added softly, 'in a sanctuary of the Faith.'

Then she left the abbess's chamber.

Outside she paused a moment and breathed deeply. She was beginning to feel a sympathy with Adnár; his sister was a curious woman. She would have no course but to refer this matter to Abbot Brocc for, if Draigen was innocent of all other things, she was guilty of an incitement to kin-slaying and using another's youth and lack of knowledge and experience to attempt to perpetrate that crime. That could not be absolved. There was, indeed, something perverse in Draigen's character.

The bell was tolling and the figures of the religieuses were hurrying towards the *duirthech* – the chapel of the community. In Sister Berrach's cell, Fidelma found the handicapped young sister being comforted by Sister Brónach and told them briefly what had transpired between her and the abbess.

When Fidelma arrived with Sister Berrach, struggling along with the aid of her staff and supported by the solicitous Sister Brónach, the community were gathered together. The abbess was standing behind the altar, almost directly behind the large ornate gold altar cross, while a chanter was leading the congregation in a Latin canticle.

Munther Beara beata
fide fundatacerta,
spe salutis ornata,
caritate perfecta.

Fidelma wondered whether the Abbess Draigen had purposefully chosen the chant. The words were simple. 'The blessed community of Beara, founded on certain Faith, adorned with Hope of salvation, perfected by Charity.' The sisters sang with an unquestioned conviction in their message.

As Fidelma led Berrach forward the voices lost their unison and raggedly died away. Heads raised and there was a nervous tension which swept along the rows of the congregation.

Fidelma squeezed gentle encouragement on Berrach's arm.

The chant died away and Abbess Draigen moved majestically from her position and came to stand before the altar.

'My children, I come before you to ask your forgiveness, for I have been guilty of a grievous fault. And allowing someone young and inexperienced to act wrongly on my advice.'

The opening words caused a sudden silence to descend; so silent that even the rasping winter breath of some of the congregation could be heard.

'Moreover, I am guilty of a terrible injury to one of this community.'

The congregation began to understand now and were casting ashamed glances towards Berrach and at Fidelma. Berrach stood leaning on her staff, eyes downcast. Sister Brónach stood with head held high as if she was the one accepting the apology. Fidelma, on the other side of Berrach, also kept her head erect, her eyes fastened to those of the abbess.

'Things have happened in this abbey which are the cause of alarm among our community; alarm and fear. This morning, as you will know, our *rechtaire*, Sister Síomha, was cruelly slain. Acting in partial knowledge, I accused one of this community. In impetuous enthusiasm to punish the person I deemed to be the culprit, I forgot the teachings of Our Lord, for is it not said in the book of John – "he that is without sin among you, let him first cast a stone at her"? I was with sin and I cast a stone. For my unjust actions, I crave forgiveness and will do a daily penance for a year from this day. That penance may be prescribed by you, my sisters, meeting in this congregation.'

She turned to look at Sister Lerben. The young novice stood with head held high and defiant. Fidelma glanced at her and was troubled by the depth of suppressed rage on her features. There would be problems with Sister Lerben before long, she thought.

'Furthermore, I advised our young Sister Lerben erroneously and, having appointed her as my new *rechtaire*, asked her to go forth and act on my advice. For this I accept full responsibility. Lerben had not sufficient experience to know that I was in error. I apologise on her behalf.'

Before the astonished eyes of the gathered sisters, Sister Lerben suddenly made her way noisily from the chapel, like a petulant child.

Abbess Draigen stared somewhat sadly after her. There was a silence before she turned her attention to Sister Berrach.

'Sister Berrach, before God and this congregation, I ask your forgiveness. It was fear and abomination of the dreadful death suffered by Sister Síomha and by the unnamed soul found in our well which caused me to lapse and cry "witch" at you and incite this congregation to do harm to you. Mine is the guilt and to you I turn asking for absolution.'

All eyes now turned on to Sister Berrach.

She shuffled forward a pace. There was a tense silence as she stood, as if hesitating in giving a decision. Fidelma saw that the abbess's facial muscles were twitching as if she were trying to control her emotions. Fidelma wondered whether Berrach was going to reject Abbess Draigen's apology. Then the girl spoke.

'Mother abbess, you have quoted the words of the Gospel of John. John said that we deceive ourselves if we claim that we are all innocent of sin. The acceptance of our sins and confession is the first step to salvation. I forgive you your sin . . . yet I cannot absolve you from it. Only the Ever Living God can do that.'

Abbess Draigen looked as if she had been slapped in the face. It was clearly not the form of words that she had been expecting. And a murmur of surprise went up among the congregation. They had suddenly realised that Sister Berrach was no longer stuttering but speaking in a cold, clear and well-articulated tone.

The girl, using her staff as a fulcrum, pulled herself round and slowly lurched and swayed down the aisle to let herself out of the door.

There was a silence until the doors thudded shut behind her.

'It is truly said, only God can absolve our transgressions. We can only forgive.'

Heads were turned as Sister Brónach took a pace forward, her tone was without rancour.

'Amen!' added Fidelma loudly when she saw the community stood hesitant as to their response.

There was a slow murmur of approval and Abbess Draigen bowed her head in acceptance of the verdict of the congregation and returned to her place.

The chanter rose and began to intone:

> *Maria de tribu Iuda,*
> *summi mater Domini,*
> *opportunam dedit curam*
> *aegrotanti homini . . .*

'Mary of the tribe of Judah, mother of the mighty Lord, has provided a timely cure for sick humanity.'

Fidelma swiftly genuflected to the altar, turned and made her way rapidly out of the chapel after Sister Berrach.

A timely cure for sick humanity? Fidelma pursed her lips cynically. There seemed no cure for the sickness which was permeating this abbey. She was not even certain what that sickness was except that hatred was at the heart of it. There was something here which she could not understand. This was no simple problem; no simple riddle of who killed who and why.

Two women had been found, each stabbed through the heart, each decapitated and each placed with crucifixes in the right hand and aspen wands written in Ogham in the left. How were these two women connected? Perhaps if she knew that she would be able to discover a motive. So far, the sum total of her investigation had revealed hardly anything of value in pointing a path towards a motive let alone a culprit.

All she had been able to gather was that the community of
The Salmon of the Three Wells was governed by a woman of
powerful personality and whose attitudes were, at least,
questionable.

The matins had given way to the singing of the lauds, the
psalms which marked the first of the daylight hours of the
Church. The voices of the sisters were raised in a curious
vehemence:

> 'Let the high praises of God be in their mouth, and a
> two-edged sword in their hand.
> 'To execute vengeance upon the heaven, and punish-
> ments upon the people;
> 'To bind their kings with chains, and their nobles
> with fetters of iron;
> 'To execute upon them the judgment written: this
> honour have all his saints. Praise ye the Lord.'

Fidelma shivered slightly.

Did these words take on some new meaning which she was
not privy to?'

Yet the lauds always consisted of Psalms 148 to 150, always
sung together as one long psalm each morning at the first
hour of daylight.

The words did not change. Why did she see in them some
vague threat?

She knew that there was someone who was taking her for a
fool. But she was unsure of what she was being made a fool
over.

Chapter Eleven

Sister Fidelma was about to continue crossing the courtyard in the wake of Sister Berrach when a hollow cough halted her.

'I am told that you requested my presence here this morning, sister.'

She turned to find herself gazing into the blue, humorous eyes of Brother Febal. He still wore the traditional black eyelid colouring which highlighted them. He was wrapped from head to foot in a thick woollen, fur-edged cloak which also provided a cowled hood, and he carried a stout *cambutta* or walking stick in his hand.

She stared at him blankly for a moment. So much had happened since she had talked with Adnár yesterday afternoon. She tried to recollect her thoughts.

'I did so,' she acknowledged hastily. She glanced round and then indicated the path down to the inlet and the abbey's landing stage. She realised that Brother Febal would not be welcome at the abbey if he were seen by Abbess Draigen or any of her acolytes. 'Come, walk with me a while and let us talk.'

Brother Febal examined her curiously with his large blue eyes and then he nodded and fell in step beside her. The sun was now climbing into the sky but it was still fairly chill.

'What do you wish to talk about?' he began, almost in a bantering tone.

'There are some questions I wish to ask you, Febal,' Fidelma replied.

'*Adsum*! he answered pretentiously in Latin. 'Then I am here!'

'Have you heard that there has been another death here at the abbey?' Fidelma asked.

'News travels fast in this land, Sister Fidelma. It has been spoken of at Dún Boí.'

'By whom?'

'I think the news was brought by a servant,' he replied vaguely and then seemed to change the subject. 'I have been asked to pass on a message to you, sister. It is from Adnár and the lord Olcán. They ask you to attend this evening's feasting at Dún Boí. My lord Torcán adds his voice especially to this request. He wishes to compensate you for the fright that you received in the forest yesterday. Adnár has offered to send his personal boatman to bring you from the abbey and return you safely again.'

He grinned and reached into the small leather bag which was strung at his belt.

'Oh yes, and see here!' He brought out a small purse. 'On Torcán's behalf I am also the bearer of the fine which you imposed on him. I understand that it is to be given for the good works of the abbey.'

Fidelma took the purse of coins and, without bothering to check it, absently placed it in her own *crumena*.

'I will see that this is delivered.' She was considering the invitation. It did so happen that she wanted to know more about the attitudes in Dún Boí to the situation in the abbey and she finally accepted the proposal. 'You may tell Adnár that I shall await his boatman.'

They walked on for a short time before Fidelma asked: 'Did you know Sister Síomha?'

'Who did not?' The answer was blandly given.

'You will have to explain that.'

'As *rechtaire* of this abbey, Sister Síomha was second only to the abbess. She often came to my lord's fortress.'

'For what purpose?' asked Fidelma, somewhat surprised.

'You must know that Adnár was not on the best terms with Abbess Draigen. It was better, therefore, that Sister Síomha conducted any business between the abbey and my lord.'

'And was there much business to be conducted?' pressed Fidelma.

'As chieftain along this coast, Adnár controlled much of the trading and the abbey required goods and trade which had to be reported to Adnár. Therefore, as *rechtaire* of the abbey, Sister Síomha visited Adnár very often.'

'And was Sister Síomha on friendly terms with Adnár?'

'Very friendly.'

Fidelma glanced quickly at Brother Febal but his face was inexpressive. She was not sure whether she had heard a slight inflection in his voice.

'How well did you know Sister Síomha?' she was prompted to ask.

'I knew her but not well.' The reply came back firmly.

They had reached the abbey quay and Fidelma led the way down some steps along the shoreline of the inlet. She walked towards a section of rocks by the water which seemed to provide a good, sheltered place to sit away from the northerly wind. The sun was now high in the blue, cloudless sky, and its rays were mild but warming, provided one kept out of the shadows. Only the plaintive cry of the swooping gulls together with the soft whispering of the water along the pebbled shore cut through the still air.

Fidelma seated herself on a comfortable rock on which the sun was casting its warmth and waited while Brother Febal also seated himself.

'When you were talking about Abbess Draigen yesterday, you failed to mention that you were married to her.'

'Does that matter?'

'I think it does. In view of what you had to say about her, I think it matters a great deal. I understand from Adnár that it was you who suggested that she might have been responsible for the death of the corpse in the well. Whether true or not, it indicates that there is no love lost between you.'

Febal flushed and glanced down at his sandals as if suddenly feeling the necessity to examine them in detail.

'It is obvious that you do not like your former wife,' Fidelma observed. 'Perhaps it would help if you could tell me how you first came to know her?'

Febal kept his eyes on his feet for a few moments, frowning, as if trying to make up his mind.

'Very well. I was seventeen when I entered this very abbey of The Salmon of the Three Wells. Oh, it was a mixed house at that time, a *conhospitae*. The abbess at this time was Abbess Marga. She was an enlightened lady and it was she who first encouraged scribes to come to copy the books in the library in order to sell or exchange them with other libraries.'

'Why did you join the abbey? Were you interested in books?'

Febal shook his head.

'I am no scribe. My father was a fisherman. He died drowning. I did not want to end my life like that and so I entered the religious life as soon as I reached the age of choice.'

'So you were here before Draigen arrived?'

'Oh yes. She entered the abbey when she was fifteen. She was already at the age of choice. Her parents had both died so she entered the religious life. At least that is the story as I remember it. Draigen was educated and trained by the members of the community.'

'And what was your position here when she joined the abbey?'

Febal's chest rose a moment in pride.

'I was already the *doirseór*, the doorkeeper of the abbey.'

'A position of trust,' agreed Fidelma. 'How did Draigen become your wife?'

'As you know, in some houses the brethren are encouraged to marry to raise their children in the service of the Christ. I admit that I was attracted by Draigen. She was a handsome and intelligent woman. I do not know what she saw in me, except that I was already in a position of responsibility here.'

'Are you trying to tell me that you believe that she only married you because you were the *doirseór* of the abbey?'

'It is a reason that I find as good as any.'

'How did things change? How did Draigen work her way into her present position? And how did you separate from her?'

Febal's face was a momentary mask of bitterness.

'She did it as subtly as a serpent,' he said. Fidelma almost smiled at the echo of the phrase which Draigen herself had used only a few hours before. 'The old abbess, Abbess Marga, was a kindly, trusting soul. The years passed and Draigen grew up. Oh, I am not denying that Draigen was clever. She responded to the education she received so that from a poor farmer's daughter she became fluent in Greek, Latin, Hebrew as well as our own tongue, and could read and write easily in all of those languages. She knew her scripture and could quote chapter and verse. She had a clever mind but that concealed an evil temper. I have cause to know.'

Febal paused to make ugly grimace.

'But you had married her,' prompted Fidelma.

Febal glanced at her.

'I did so. But that was not to say that I liked her ambition. She overstepped the bounds of womanhood.'

Fidelma's mouth turned down.

'What are those bounds?' she asked with asperity.

'You should know, being of the Christian Faith,' Febal sounded complacent.

'Then remind me.' A more sensitive person might have noticed the irritability in her tone.

'Did the Blessed Paul not write, "Let your women keep silence in the churches; for it is not permitted unto them to speak; but they are commanded to be under obedience . . . And if they will learn anything, let them ask their husbands at home, for it is a shame for a woman to speak in the church." It is his epistle to Corinthians.'

'So you believe that women have no place in the abbeys and church?' Fidelma had heard the argument many times before.

'Women should obey men in the Church,' declared Brother Febal. 'Paul, also in Corinthians says, "the lord of the woman is the man ... God created man not for the woman, but created the woman for the man." And, in his epistle to Timothy, he says, "women must not teach, nor usurp authority over man, but should be silent." What is more clear than that?'

'These are the words of one man, Paul of Tarsus,' observed Fidelma dryly. 'They are not the words of the Christ. Yet I would go further and observe that these words did not stop you from joining a *conhospitae* and further from marrying a religieuse.'

Febal's eyes burned with resentment.

'I was younger then. But it seems to me, in your answer, that you deny the right of Paul, divinely inspired by the Christ, to teach these things?'

'Paul was not Christ,' replied Fidelma quietly. 'In this land, men and women are coequal before God.'

Brother Febal's tone was sneering.

'The Blessed John Chrysostom once observed that woman taught once and ruined all by her teachings. The Faith has changed that. Augustine of Hippo points out that women are not made in the image of God, whereas man is fully and completely the image of God.'

Fidelma looked sadly at Brother Febal whose face was full of vehemence. She had met with many who advanced such arguments. It was true that there were religious houses in the five kingdoms where the advocates of the new Faith were even challenging the ancient laws, even as Draigen had done.

'Do I take it, Brother Febal,' she said sharply, 'that you do not accept the Law of the Fénechus?'

Febal's eyes narrowed.

'Only when it contracts the articles of Faith.'

'And on what article do you base yourself?'

'On the Penitentials of Finian of Clonard and of Cuimmíne Fata of Clonfert.'

Fidelma smiled wryly. It was strange that a few hours before Abbess Draigen had been quoting these same Penitentials, a series of ecclesiastical laws for the rule of religious communities, in support of her case. Curious how both estranged wife and husband seemed to agree. At least Fidelma knew the thoughts that motivated some of Brother Febal's attitudes.

'Then as a man who believed that woman had no place in the church, you must have resented being in a *conhospitae*, a mixed house? I still wonder that you joined such an institution. Furthermore, I wonder that you even contemplated marriage to Draigen.'

'I have said that I was young when I joined the abbey. I had not read the scriptures in their entirety. I had not come across the works of Finian nor of Cuimmíne. And at first Draigen was a quiet girl, willing and ready to obey. I did not know that she was merely biding her time, learning what she could as she awaited her opportunity.'

'Draigen's opportunity being her appointment to *rechtaire*? Was that when you sought to annul the marriage?'

'We ceased to be husband and wife within a year or so of our marriage. We went our own separate ways within the abbey. I loathed her. I will not deny it. I was doorkeeper and when the old *rechtaire* died I should have been promoted to the office. But old Abbess Marga had taken a liking to Draigen...'

'How old was Draigen at this time?'

Febal frowned, trying to recall.

'She was in her mid-twenties, I believe. Yes, that is the age that she would be.'

'And Abbess Marga made Draigen her house-steward?'

'Yes. The second most powerful office in the abbey. And Draigen certainly liked to exercise all that power.'

'In what way?'

'She began to make life difficult for the male community and introduce more and more women into the abbey. She became strident against any man who showed talent. She would send men off on missions or give them penances which necessitated them going on pilgrimages abroad. Soon there were hardly any men left in the abbey.'

'Are you saying that Draigen disliked men?'

'She hated all men!' snapped Brother Febal.

Fidelma prompted him gently.

'And is your own attitude to women governed by how she treated you, or had you come to your dislike of women in the church before that time?'

'My attitude is based on logic,' reproved Febal without rancour. 'I do not like nor dislike all women. But the Blessed Columbanus wrote a poem:

Let everyone who is dutiful in mind avoid the deadly poison
That the proud tongue of an evil woman has.
Woman destroyed life's gathered crown . . .

'In that poem, he points out that the downfall of our kind was due to Eve,' added Febal smugly.

'I see that you left out the last line of that verse,' replied Fidelma quietly. 'The line is—

But woman gave long lasting joys of life.

'In that line he refers to Mary as the mother of our saviour.'

Brother Febal flushed in annoyance at being corrected.

'She knew her place,' he said. 'Draigen did not. She was an evil woman who used her power to promote her own welfare.'

'Ah yes. According to Adnár, Draigen began to prefer the company of young women.'

'She had many young female lovers,' Febal assured her without hesitation. 'Probably, she had affairs with older women which made her rise in rank through the abbey so quickly.'

Fidelma leant forward towards Brother Febal and looked at him coldly in the eyes.

'It is now my duty, as a *dálaigh* of the courts, to caution you, brother. If you wish to have this mentioned as a matter of record, then you must be prepared to stand by your accusation. If that accusation is false, then you are liable under the law...'

'I know the law in that respect. I stand by what I have to say. Abbess Draigen is known to take many young novices to her bed.'

Under the law, homosexuality was not a punishable offence unless it be that Draigen used a position of power to coerce unwilling young girls into her bed. Usually, homosexuality was only a ground for divorce by either party under the *Cáin Lanamna*. In Fidelma's own abbey of Kildare, it was known that Brigid, the founder of the community, had a lover named Darlughdaca, a young novice, who shared her bed. Once, when Darlughdaca looked appraisingly at a young warrior staying at Kildare, Brigid flew into a jealous rage, and, according to the accounts, made Darlughdaca walk on hot coals as a penance. But when Brigid died, it was Darlughdaca who became abbess.

'Known by whom?' pressed Fidelma.

'It is common knowledge.'

'Usually, that means that it is simply rumour. I would want a more specific witness before I accepted that. Now tell me, how did Draigen became abbess?'

Brother Febal raised a hand to scratch the tip of his nose reflectively with his finger.

'The Devil's will, I suppose. Marga was old, as I have said. She had an ailing chest. In the end, Draigen insisted that she, and she alone, would nurse the old abbess. She prepared the medicines and attended in the abbess's chamber. I was not surprised when it was announced that Marga was dead.'

'When was this . . . ?'

'Five summers ago now.'

'And so Draigen became abbess?'

'Oh, there was a meeting of the community, for, like all the houses in the five kingdoms, the community met and argued the rival merits of candidates.'

'But Draigen was the only candidate?'

'I made a protest and demanded my name go forward to be considered as abbot.'

'And?'

'By that time there was only myself and two elderly brothers in the abbey. We were laughed at. Draigen did, indeed, become abbess. At that very meeting she announced that the abbey would cease to be a *conhospitae*. I was also stripped of my position as *doirseór*. Together with my brothers I was told to leave.'

'You left and joined Adnár?'

'Yes. My two companions decided to go north and join the community of Emly. I stayed here for Adnár, the chieftain, sought a brother who would be a soul-friend and celebrate the mass for him.'

'When did you know that Adnár was Draigen's brother?'

'A long time ago.'

'Can you be more specific?'

'Adnár returned from serving the armies of Gulban the Hawk-Eyed a few years before Draigen was appointed as *rechtaire* of the abbey. There was a lot of talk at the time. He even made a legal claim against her for his share of the land. It was rejected.'

'Rejected?' Fidelma frowned. 'Yet it sounds as if Adnár had a good case.'

'Yet it was rejected. Everyone knew that I had been married to Draigen and Adnár obviously felt sympathy with me.'

'And have you used that relationship?'

'Why should I use it and in what manner?'

'You had come to feel bitter about Draigen. Did that reflect on your service to her brother?'

Febal smiled. There was no warmth or humour in it.

'I did not have to use it. Brother and sister hated one another from the start. Adnár blamed Draigen for the loss of his land. Draigen blamed Adnár for the death of her father and of her mother.'

'It could be argued that you sought a position in the house of Adnár in order to play the one off against the other. To stir up more trouble between them. It could be argued that you have spread lies about Draigen. The matter of her preference for young novices, for example?'

'It is untrue. There was enough trouble between them. Adnár offered me the hospitality of Dún Boí. I accepted. It satisfied me that Draigen had not succeeded in driving me entirely from the land that is my home.'

'But you must also hate and resent Draigen?'

'No one knows the hatred that lives in my heart for that woman. But if you say that I lie about her, then seek out Sister Brónach and ask her if the abbess ever shares her bed with Sister Lerben.'

Fidelma was slightly surprised that Brother Febal was suddenly specific in his accusation.

'I will do so. But let me remind you, brother, that hatred is not a tenet of our Faith. Does John not quote our Saviour as saying: "A new commandment I give unto you, That ye love one another; as I have loved you, that ye also love one another."'

Brother Febal laughed bitterly.

'The Christ was talking of loving our fellows. Draigen is a serpent, a devil ... the Devil. Does Peter not call upon us to hate the Devil and be vigilant? I obey Peter and hate the serpent that presides over this place.'

Fidelma could feel that such was the intensity of Febal's

anger against the abbess there was no chance of logic healing
the rift.

'Is it merely your anger, then, that prompted you to
tell Adnár that it was probably his sister who murdered the
headless corpse? Otherwise what grounds have you for
such an accusation? Do not tell me that it is common
knowledge.'

Febal glanced at her quickly.

'You don't know then that Draigen has killed before?'

Fidelma was not expecting this reply.

'You must substantiate this accusation. Whom did she
kill?'

'Some old woman who dwelt in the forests not far from
here.'

'When was this?'

'Just before she joined the community, when she was
fifteen.'

'So? Then you do not give first-hand testimony?'

'No. But the story is known.'

'Ah. It is known,' she repeated sarcastically. 'Know by
whom?'

'It was rumoured ...'

'Rumour is not evidence ...'

'Then ask Sister Brónach.'

'Why Sister Brónach?'

'It was her mother that Draigen killed.'

For a moment or two Sister Fidelma stared at Febal in
quiet astonishment.

'Let me get this right,' she said slowly, after a while. 'Are
you telling me that Abbess Draigen killed Sister Brónach's
mother? The same Brónach who is now her *doirseór*?'

'The same,' grunted Febal indifferently.

'And are you telling me that Brónach knows about this?'

'Of course. Ask her, if you do not believe me. And she will
also confirm that Lerben shares the bed of the abbess.'

Fidelma was silent.

'I believe that you believe this,' she said after a moment or two. 'So curious a tale can only be the truth for if it were a lie it could be uncovered easily. However, you have not said whether this was an unlawful killing.'

'Is any killing lawful?' sneered Febal.

'That is true, but some killings can be judged worse than others. Cold, premeditated killings. Do you know the facts of the case?'

The handsome religieux shrugged.

'I would rather you took your facts from Brónach, for then it will not be said that I misled you.'

'Very well. But it is a long path from a killing twenty years ago to your suspicion that Draigen killed the person whose body was found in the well of this monastery. And if she was responsible for that death then logic would have it that she was responsible for the death of Sister Síomha.'

Brother Febal gave a disdainful gesture.

'It is not beyond the realms of possibility, Sister Fidelma.'

'Granted. If all your allegations have substance,' conceded Fidelma.

At once Brother Febal bristled with indignation.

'Do you call me liar?'

Fidelma shook her head.

'Let us examine what you have told me. You say that you have heard that Draigen killed someone before she came to this abbey. You say that rumour had it that Draigen was encouraging young novices to her bed. Even if you witnessed such matters it is not an unlawful act.'

'Unlawful in the eyes of God!' growled Febal.

'So, you also speak for God?' Fidelma's voice was soft. Then she said more sharply, 'You have told me nothing that can be used as evidence in a court of law against Draigen in order to prove that she is responsible for the deaths which have occurred at this abbey. But you have made allegations which could well convict you of spreading malicious stories and putting a blemish on the reputation of Draigen. A good advocate could destroy your story in a court by the very fact that you were once married to Draigen and were dismissed from your office in her abbey before being thrown out of the abbey itself. You are not in a strong position at all, Febal, to argue evidence and law.'

Brother Febal rose to his feet.

'I would have expected as much from you.'

Fidelma calmly returned his angry look.

'You should explain that,' she invited in a voice that was ice.

'You are a woman! "Let everyone who is dutiful avoid the proud tongue of a woman!" You merely stick together, protecting each other.'

'You misquote the poem,' pointed out Fidelma.

'It matters nòt. The sense is the same. I have heard that you like to quote from Greek and Latin sages. Then here is a quote for you, Fidelma of Kildare. It is from Euripides – "woman is woman's natural ally". I should have expected that you would do your best to protect Draigen, she being woman as are you.'

Fidelma carefully folded her arms and forced a gentle smile.

'I will not take offence, Febal. I think it is your hate of Draigen talking. Go back to Dún Boí and calm yourself. There is much anger in you.'

Brother Febal stood, swaying a little as if he had no balance, he appeared to be making up his mind as to whether he would say anything further. Then he turned and strode away, anger showing in the demeanour of his walk and the hunching of his shoulders.

Fidelma watched him until he had disappeared around the shoreline.

She suddenly felt a terrible sadness. A sense of loneliness.

She always felt sad when she came across someone whose views of life were so embittered. And she realised immediately why she was feeling a sense of loneliness. She was

thinking of Brother Eadulf. There was a man who liked life
and people. There was no malice in him. Malice. Why had
she picked that word? Malice was what she felt in Febal. His
hostility was imbued with a malevolence.

It is true that a man can find many justifications for his
emotions after the event which were not there when the seed
of those emotions was planted. Misognynism could certainly
be found in the Penitentials of Finian which Febal might
have found as justification of his hatreds. But perhaps his
hatred had other roots. And a man capable of hatred, capable
of strong emotions, could certainly be capable of expressing
those emotions in other channels. Even murder.

She stood up and stretched, feeling abruptly uncomfortable. She had a feeling of distaste; distaste not for the
individual misogynism of Febal but for a movement in the
Faith which he represented. Fidelma was a person born of
her culture but the Faith was now changing that very culture
as the new ideas from Greece, Rome and other cultures,
which helped shape the Faith, were changing the philosophies propounded by the churches of the five kingdoms. It
had been women, as well as men, who had converted the five
kingdoms to the new Faith – their names were legend; the
five sisters of Patrick, Chief Apostle of the five kingdoms,
and women like Darerca, Brigid, Ita, Etáin and countless
others. Fidelma could reel their names off like a litany . . .

But two hundred years of the spread of the Faith had
produced men, and even a few women too, who sought to
reject the rule of civil law and, led by Finian of Clonard, they
had devised ecclesiastical laws which sought to replace the
Law of the Fénechus by which the five kingdoms were
governed.

Febal had mentioned the Penitentials of Cuimmíne, which
had been inspired by Finian's laws. These were now being
taken from religious foundation to religious foundation, with
the approval of Ultan of Armagh. Cuimmíne had died only
four years ago and already his ecclesiastical laws were finding

converts among the male religious for they, like Febal's views, were based on the precepts of Paul of Tarsus.

Fidelma had good reason to resent the Penitentials of Cuimmíne. Cuimmíne had been responsible for the tragic death of her childhood friend, Liadin, who had been educated with her at Cashel. Liadin had become a religieuse and a poet of remarkable talent. She met a fellow poet from the kingdom of Connacht named Cuirithir and they had fallen in love. Cuimmíne was the abbot of the community in which Cuirithir served and he sent him away, forbidding him ever to see Liadin again and using the arguments of Paul of Tarsus to forbid the relationship. He was an abbot of ascetic extremism. Cuirithir had left the shores of the five kingdoms and was never seen again. Liadin eventually sickened and died, broken and unhappy. Her grief had been extreme.

Fidelma had little respect for laws which made people unhappy for no accountable reason, that denied human beings their greatest asset – love. Liadin and Cuirithir should have ignored the ascetic extremism of Cuimmíne and been strong enough to have gone away together. As she had lain dying, young Liadin had written her last song, ending:

> Why should I hide
> That he is still my heart's desire
> More than all the world.
>
> A furnace blast
> Of love has melted my heart
> Without his love, it can beat no more.

A few days later she had indeed stopped her heart from beating.

Fidelma suddenly exhaled and shook her head. This was not what she should be thinking of. She should not be making moral judgments but looking for the evidence which would identify the person responsible for two horrendous killings.

At least her next step was clear. She must have a longer talk with Sister Brónach.

She rose and began to walk along the seashore and up to the wooden jetty.

As she ascended the steps on to the quay she suddenly noticed a sail, white against the green and brown of the far hills which marked the opening to the inlet. She could hear a horn sounding across the little bay from the fortress of Adnár, obviously warning the occupants of the entrance of a ship into the inlet.

Fidelma raised her hand to shield the sun from her eyes and peered across the stretch of sparkling water.

Suddenly her heart began to beat more rapidly.

It was the *Foracha*, Ross's *barc*, sailing swiftly and surely into the harbour.

All thoughts of Febal and even Draigen were gone from her mind. Now her thoughts were concentrated on what news Ross was bearing. Her mind was wholly concerned with the mystery of the Gaulish merchant ship and, more importantly, the beat of her heart was more for fear, fear of what news he might have about the fate of Brother Eadulf.

Chapter Twelve

Fidelma had almost reached the side of the *barc* before Ross's crews had finished hauling down the sails. The boat that she had taken from the abbey's quay had positively skimmed the waters as she had bent into the oars with a will. The bow of the boat was bumping into the side of the *Foracha* before she realised it and she was being helped over the side of the craft while a sailor made her boat fast with a rope.

Ross came forward with a smile of greeting.

'What news?' demanded Fidelma breathlessly even before greetings could be exchanged.

Ross motioned towards his cabin at the stern of the ship.

'Let's go and talk a while,' he said, his facial expression changing to one of seriousness.

Fidelma had to contain her curiosity until they were seated in the cabin and Ross had offered her an earthenware vessel of *cuirm*, which she declined. He poured himself a measure and sipped slowly.

'What news?' she prompted again.

'I have found the place where the Gaulish merchant ship was moored three nights ago.'

'Is there any sign of Ead ... the crew or the passengers?' Fidelma demanded.

'I must tell the story in order, sister. But there was no sign of anyone.'

Fidelma compressed her lips for a moment at the disappointment which she felt.

'Tell me the story then, Ross. How did you discover what you did?'

'As I said, before I left here, judging by the tides and winds, there were two likely places from where the Gaulish ship might have been blown. The first was over to the south-eastern headland called the Sheep's Head. That is where I sailed first. We sailed around but could find nothing out of the ordinary. We encountered some fishermen who said that they had been casting their nets in those waters all week and had seen nothing. So then I decided that we should go on to the second likely spot.'

'Which was where?'

'A place at the end of this very peninsula.'

'Go on.'

'At the end of the peninsula lies a long island, it is called Dóirse, which as you will know, means "The Gates", because, in a way, it stands as the south-western gate to this land. We sailed around the island but could not see anything unusual. I have traded with the islanders several times and so I thought that I would put into the harbour there and see what gossip I could pick up. We landed and I asked my men to keep their ears open for any news about the Gaulish ship. We did not have to seek far.'

He paused and took a sip of his drink.

'What did you learn?' urged Fidelma.

'The Gaulish ship had been moored in the harbour. But therein lay a curious story. Some strange warriors had sailed it in to the island's harbour well after dusk on the evening before we encountered the ship on the high seas.'

'Strange warriors? Gauls?'

Ross shook his head.

'No. Warriors from the clan of the Uí Fidgenti.'

Fidelma hid her surprise.

'They had with them a Gaulish prisoner, however.'

'A single Gaulish prisoner? There was no sign of a Saxon monk?' Fidelma felt a pang of disappointment.

199

'No. The prisoner was apparently a Gaulish seaman. Being hospitable, the islanders invited the warriors ashore as it appeared they had no provisions on board. A single guard was left on board with the prisoner. The next morning, the people found that the ship had gone. It had sailed while the warriors were in a drunken slumber due to the islanders' hospitality. The warrior who had been left on board the vessel was discovered floating in the harbour – dead.'

'What did they discern from that?'

'That the Gaulish prisoner had somehow escaped, overpowered the guard, thrown him overboard, and sailed the ship out of the harbour.'

'A single man? Sail a big ship like that? Is that possible?' Ross shrugged.

'It is, if the man was knowledgeable and determined enough.'

'What then?'

'The warriors were angry and requisitioned some island ships to take them back across the sound to the mainland.'

Fidelma thought over the matter.

'It is a strange story. The Gaulish merchant ship is sailed into the harbour of Dóirse by a band of warriors of the Uí Fidgenti with a single Gaulish sailor as their prisoner. The ship ties up. In the morning, it has disappeared with the Gaulish sailor. The warriors then cross back to this peninsula. Later that morning, towards midday, we encounter the ship under full sail and deserted.'

'That is the story, strange or not.'

'Can the information you picked up on the island – Dóirse, you called it – be trusted?'

'The people can,' confirmed Ross. 'I have traded with them for years now. They are an independent people who do not regard themselves as under the rule of Gulban the Hawk-Eyed, though technically it is his territory. They hold allegiance to their own *bó-aire*. So they are not concerned with keeping the secrets of those on the mainland.'

'Do you know whether the warriors of Uí Fidgenti gave any explanations to the local *bó-aire* about what they were doing with the Gaulish ship?'

'There was some talk that it was trading with the mines on the mainland.'

Fidelma raised her head sharply.

'Mines? Would those be copper mines?'

Ross glanced searchingly at her before nodding agreement.

'Across from Dóirse, on the mainland, and in the next bay, there are several copper mines which are worked. They do a trade not only along the coast but with Gaul.'

Fidelma drummed her fingers on the table, frowning as she considered matters.

'Remember the red clay-like mud in the hold of the Gaulish ship?' she asked.

Ross inclined his head in an affirmative gesture.

'I think that they were deposits from a copper mine or somewhere where copper is stored. I think the answer to this mystery might lie at the site of those copper mines. Yet I cannot understand why men of the Uí Fidgenti would be sailing the ship. Their clan territory is a long way to the north of here. Where were the men of Beara, of Gulban's sept?'

'I could sail back and make further efforts to gain information,' offered Ross. 'Or I could sail to the mines, pretending to trade, and see what can be found.'

Fidelma shook her head.

'Too dangerous. There is some mystery here which is compounded by the fact that Torcán, the son of the prince of the Uí Fidgenti, is a guest at Adnár's fortress.'

Ross's eyes widened.

'There is surely a connection?'

'But a connection with what? I believe that this mystery may be fraught with dangers. If you sail back again then you might arouse suspicion. There is no need to put people on guard if we can avoid it. We must know what we are dealing with first. How far are these copper mines from here?'

'About two or three hours' sailing if you keep close to the coastline.'

'What if you simply crossed the peninsula? How many miles?'

'As the crow flies? Five miles. By a navigable route across the mountains, perhaps ten miles or less.'

Fidelma was silent as she considered the matter.

'What should we do?' prompted Ross.

Fidelma raised her head, having come to the conclusion that she must investigate the matter herself.

'Tonight, under cover of darkness, we shall ride across this peninsula to the spot where these copper mines are situated. I have a feeling that we might find an answer there.'

'Why not ride now? I could easily buy horses from one of the farmsteads further down the coast.'

'No, we will wait until midnight and for two reasons. Firstly, because we do not want anyone to know we have gone to these mines. If Torcán, or Adnár are involved in some illegal matter then we do not want to warn them of our intentions. Secondly, this evening, I have accepted to attend a feast at Dún Boí with Adnár and his guests, Torcán and Olcán. Perhaps this will turn out to our advantage for I may be able to pick up some news.'

Ross was far from happy.

'The matter of the Uí Fidgenti worries me, sister. For some weeks now there have been many rumours along the coast. It is said that the Eoganán of the Uí Fidgenti has his eyes on Cashel.'

Fidelma smiled wanly.

'Is that all? The Uí Fidgenti have always aspired to the kingship of Cashel. Did they not rise up against Cashel twenty-five years ago when Aed Slane was High King?'

The Uí Fidgenti were a large clan in the west of the kingdom of Mumam whose princes and chieftains preferred to call themselves kings and claimed that they were the true descendants of the first kings of Cashel. They argued that they had a prior claim to Cashel over that of Fidelma's own family. Fidelma's father had been king at Cashel at the time of her birth and now her brother, Colgú, had succeeded his cousin to occupy the seat of the provincial kings of Mumam. Fidelma's brother was answerable to no man except the High King. Fidelma had grown up with tales about the claims of the Uí Fidgenti who sought to depose her family's right to the kingship of Cashel. None had been more vociferous in such claims than the current prince, Eoganán.

Ross was frowning in disapproval.

'What you say is so, sister. But your brother, Colgú, has only sat on the throne these last few months. He is young and untried. It is obvious that, if Eoganán of the Uí Fidgenti wanted to make a move to overthrow Colgú, he would make his move now, while Colgú was still unsure of himself.'

'What sort of move? My brother's right to office has been endorsed by the great assembly at Cashel. The High King has approved of the decision from Tara.'

'Who knows what Eoganán is planning? But the gossip along the coast is that some evil is being concocted.'

Fidelma considered the matter carefully.

'All the more reason why I should attend the feast this evening for perhaps Torcán may reveal something of his father's plans.'

'You could only put yourself in danger,' Ross pointed out. 'Torcán will doubtless find out who you are ...'

'That I am sister to Colgú? We met in the forest yesterday. He already knows that.'

She paused and frowned a moment thinking about the arrow that nearly ended her life. Could Torcán have fired that arrow deliberately knowing her to be Colgú's sister? But then why would he attempt her life? She was nothing to do with the succession at Cashel. No. That would not be logical. Besides, Torcán and his men were equally surprised to discover her identity and sought to cover their mistake. If the arrow had been aimed deliberately by Torcán, it was not at her. They could have easily killed her in the forest.

Ross was watching her expression carefully.

'Has something happened already?' he guessed.

'No,' she lied quickly. 'At least,' she corrected herself after a pang of guilt, 'nothing to change our plan. At midnight, after the feasting at Dún Boí I will meet you and one of your men in the woods behind the abbey. Secure three horses but do so without arousing any suspicion.'

'Very well. I will take Odar, for he is a good man to have with us. But if Torcán is at this feast, I would rather that you were not attending.'

'No harm will come to an official of the law courts of the five kingdoms. It would be more than king or citizen would dare,' declared Fidelma. She wished, as she uttered the words, that she truly believed them.

She rose to her feet and Ross followed her from his cabin to the side of the *barc*. It was clear that she did not have his full approval for her plan. But, in the light of nothing better, he accepted it.

She was about to descend down the ship's side when he asked: 'How is the matter that brought you here?' He gestured with a jerk of his thumb towards the abbey. He had almost forgotten the original reason why he had brought Fidelma to this spot. 'Has the problem been resolved?'

Fidelma felt a little guilty that the mystery of the headless corpse and the matter of Sister Síomha's death had almost been driven out of her thoughts by the arrival of Ross and his news.

'Not yet. In fact,' she grimaced awkwardly, 'there has been another death in the abbey. The *rechtaire*, Sister Síomha, has been found slain in the same manner as the unknown corpse. However, I believe that the clouds of mystery have begun to clear. But there is much that I find evil in the abbey.'

'If there is danger...' Ross hesitated awkwardly. 'You have but to call on me and on any of my men. It might be best to have a bodyguard from now on.'

'And alert my quarry that I feel the hunt is nearing its lair?' She shook her head.

Sister Fidelma reached forward and laid a hand on the worried sailor's arm and smiled.

'Just be in the woods at midnight with Odar and the three horses and ensure that you are not seen.'

Fidelma was told that Sister Brónach was to be found in Sister Berrach's cell. She was walking across the courtyard to the building when the mournful-faced Brónach emerged from the doorway. She hesitated and seemed as if she wanted to avoid Fidelma but Fidelma stopped her with a greeting.

'How is Sister Berrach, sister?'

Sister Brónach hesitated.

'She sleeps at the moment, sister. She has had a trying night and an unpleasant morning.'

'That she has,' agreed Fidelma. 'She is lucky to have a friend in you. Will you walk a way with me, sister?'

Reluctantly, Sister Brónach fell in step with Fidelma, moving slowly across the flagged courtyard towards the guests' hostel.

'What do you wish of me, sister?'

'The answers to a few questions.'

'I am always at your service. I did not have the chance to thank you for what you have done for Sister Berrach.'

'Why should you thank me?'

Sister Brónach grimaced defensively.

'Is it wrong to thank someone for saving the life of a friend?'

'I only did what was right and what all members of the Faith should do. Though some sisters here appear to be easily swayed by emotion.'

'By Abbess Draigen, you mean?'

'I did not say that.'

'Nevertheless,' went on Sister Brónach confidently, 'that is what you meant. You may have noticed that all the sisters here are young? Sister Comnat, our librarian, and I are the oldest among them. There is no one else, except the abbess, over the age of twenty-one.'

'Yes, I have noticed the youth of the acolytes of this abbey,' Fidelma acknowledged. 'That I have found most strange for the idea of a community is that the young may learn from the experience and knowledge of the old.'

Sister Brónach's voice held a bitter tone.

'There is a reason for it. The abbess dislikes to be with anyone who does not accept her total authority. She can manipulate young people but often older people can see her errors and are frequently more knowledgeable than she is. She can never forget that she was a poor farmer's daughter with no education before she came here.'

'Do you censure the abbess, then?'

Sister Brónach halted outside the hostel door and anxiously looked round as if to check that they were unobserved. Then she pointed inside.

'It will be easier to talk in here.'

She led the way in and along a corridor to a small cell which she used in the manner of an office, where she conducted the business of doorkeeper and attendant of the hostel.

'Be seated, sister,' she said, seating herself in one of the two wooden chairs that were in the tiny room. 'Now what was it that you were asking?'

Fidelma seated herself.

'I was asking whether you censured Abbess Draigen in gathering such a young, inexperienced community around her? It was obvious that she used the youth and inexperience of Sister Lerben to threaten Sister Berrach. Do you censure her attitude towards Berrach?'

Sister Brónach pulled a face to demonstrate her disgust.

'Any rational person would censure such action as proposed by the abbess, although I am willing to concede that it was not entirely Draigen's fault.'

'Not her fault?'

'I would imagine that Sister Lerben has something to do with the matter.'

Fidelma was perplexed.

'My understanding is that Sister Lerben was entirely under the influence of Draigen. She is too young to be anything but a pawn in this game. Someone has told me that there is a close relationship between the abbess and Lerben and that, you'll forgive my candour, sister, Lerben sometimes shares the bed of the abbess. That same person told me that you could vouch for this.'

The doleful religieuse started to chuckle. It was an expression of genuine mirth. Fidelma had never seen mirth on Brónach's solemn features before.

'Of course Sister Lerben has been known to share the bed of the abbess! You have been in this abbey for two days and yet you do not know that Lerben is the daughter of the abbess?'

Fidelma was thunderstruck.

'I thought that Lerben...' Fidelma blurted in surprise and then snapped her mouth shut.

Sister Brónach continued to smile with amusement. It transformed the usually sad face of the *doirseór* so that she became almost youthful.

'You thought that Lerben was her lover? Ah, you have been listening to evil stories.'

Fidelma leant towards the elder woman, trying to work out the new information.

'Was Sister Síomha never the lover of Draigen?'

'Not to my knowledge. And to my knowledge Draigen is not the sort of woman who would choose such carnal relationships. Draigen is a moody woman. Capricious, is a better word. She is a misanthrope, one who distrusts men and avoids them. She surrounds herself with young women, in order to intellectually dominate them, but that does not mean there is any sexual connotation to it.'

Fidelma was thinking rapidly. If this were so, then the motive put forward by Adnár and Brother Febal, which had seemed so plausible, was now invalid. It changed her thoughts about the situation entirely.

'I have heard much gossip and speculation about Draigen. Are you saying that all those stories are untrue?'

'I have no cause to love the abbess. But I would have to say that I have no experience or knowledge in this field. Abbess Draigen simply likes to surround herself with young girls because they will not question her knowledge or her authority. There is no other reason.'

'You say that she distrusts and hates all men and yet she was married to Brother Febal.'

'Febal? A marriage that lasted less than a year. I think that they deserved one another. If the truth were known he was a misogynist balanced against Draigen's misanthropy. They both hated each other.'

'You knew Febal when he was at the abbey?'

'Oh yes,' Brónach's face was grim. 'I knew Febal well.' For a moment or two her eyes glinted. 'I knew Febal before Draigen came to this abbey.'

'Why did they marry if they hated each other?'

Sister Brónach shrugged.

'You will have to ask them that question.'

'Did the old abbess, Abbess Marga, approve of this relationship?'

'This was then a mixed house at that time with several married couples rearing their children in the service of the Christ. Marga was old-fashioned in her ideas. She encouraged marriages between the members of the community. Perhaps this was the main reason why Draigen married, in order to curry favour with her. Draigen was a calculating woman.'

'You disapprove of her and yet you remain in this abbey. Why?'

Fidelma was watching Sister Brónach's expression carefully. The religieuse blinked and there seemed a momentary expression of pain and alienation on her features.

'I remain here because I need to remain here,' she said resentfully.

'But you dislike Draigen?'

'She is my abbess.'

'That is not an answer.'

'I cannot answer in any other way.'

'Then let me help you. Did you know Draigen when she was young?'

Sister Brónach glanced furtively at Fidelma. A quick glance of assessment.

'I knew her,' she admitted cautiously.

'And did your mother know her?'

Sister Brónach breathed deeply, slowly and suddenly painfully.

'So? You have heard that story? There are so many chattering mouths in this land.'

'I would like to hear the story from your own lips, Sister Brónach.'

There was a pause before she answered.

'I dislike Draigen with an intensity which you would never understand,' the doorkeeper began. Then she paused and was silent again; this time for so long that Fidelma was about to prompt her when Brónach turned troubled eyes to her. 'Each day I spend in prayers asking the good God to ease my pain, to stop my hatred. He does not. Is that the will of God that I should retain these feelings?'

'Why do you stay here?' Fidelma pressed again.

The woman sounded bitter.

'That is like asking the ocean why it stays in the same place. There is nowhere else I can go. Perhaps this is the penance for my sins; to serve the person who took the life of my mother. But do not misunderstand me. I would do no harm to Draigen. I would not have her dead. I would prefer that she lived and suffered each minute of her life.'

'Tell me the story.'

'Draigen was fifteen years old at the time. I was in my mid-thirties. I was already a religieuse here, serving the Abbess Marga in this abbey of The Salmon of the Three Wells. My mother, Suanech, was not of the Faith. She preferred to hold her allegiance to the old gods and goddesses of this land. She was a wise woman. She knew every flower and herb. She knew their names and curative values. She was at one with the forests in which she continued to dwell.'

'And your father?' interposed Fidelma.

'I never knew him. I knew only my mother and her love for me.'

'Go on.'

'Near the forest where my mother was dwelling was an *ócaire*, a man with a small patch of land which was not enough to keep him and his wife and children. The man was Adnár Mhór, the father of Draigen.'

'Also the father of Adnár who dwells in the fort across the bay?'

'The same. My mother sometimes helped young Draigen. When Adnár the son had left to join the army of Gulban the Hawk-Eyed, Adnár the father began to grow ill. My mother felt sorrow for the young girl. When Adnár the father died, my mother offered to foster her. Soon after Draigen's mother also died. Draigen went to live with my mother.'

'By this time you were already serving in this abbey?'

Brónach nodded absently.

'This happened when Draigen was about fourteen, as you may have been told. A year of sorrow that was.'

There were suddenly tears around Sister Brónach's eyes and somehow Fidelma had the feeling that they were not tears being shed just for her mother.

'What exactly happened?'

'Draigen is a self-willed person. She is prone to rages. One day she fell into a rage, took a knife used for skinning rabbits and stabbed my mother, Suanech.'

Fidelma waited for a further explanation and when there was none asked for one.

'Since the death of her father and mother and what she saw as her abandonment by her brother, Draigen had become very possessive. She was quick to temper and very jealous. She was jealous of me as Suanech's blood daughter. It was, perhaps, a good thing that I visited my mother infrequently for the duties at the abbey allowed little time for such visits. I am sure that we would have clashed more often and more violently.'

'But clash you did?'

'Invariably; every time I went to see my mother. If my mother paid me attention, Draigen was there demanding double that attention be shown to her.'

'So, at the time of Draigen's attack on your mother...? What then?'

'My mother...' Sister Brónach hesitated, as if trying to find the right words. 'My mother had taken into care a young baby. It was the child of, of a relative.'

Fidelma noted the awkward pauses.

'My mother thought that Draigen would help her with the child as it grew. But Draigen felt the same jealousy towards that child as she had shown towards anyone or anything that took my mother's affections from her.'

'She attacked your mother because she was paying too much attention to the baby?' Fidelma felt a surge of cold repulsion.

'She did. It was an insane attack. She was then fifteen years old. The child my mother was looking after was only three years old. The Brehon who sat in judgment on the matter decreed that Draigen was not responsible in the highest degree of homicide. He ordered that compensation be paid in that the tiny plot of land which Draigen's parents had owned should be sold off and the proceeds then given to Suanech's heir. That was me, of course. And being a member of this community, the money went to the abbey. Now Draigen is abbess here, it seems ironic.' Brónach laughed dryly. 'It makes you wonder whether there is a god of justice, doesn't it?'

'Was the three-year-old child harmed by Draigen?'

Sister Brónach shook her head.

'It was returned ... to its own mother.'

'The Brehon must have placed some restraints on Draigen,' Fidelma observed.

'Yes. Draigen was ordered to enter a religious community where she would be looked after and devote her life to service of the people. That again is ironic, for she was placed in this abbey. The very abbey where I was.'

'Ah!' Fidelma interrupted. 'I now see the reason why Adnár failed in his claim for part of the land. As it was sold to fulfil a legal fine, Adnár, as Draigen's brother, had to forfeit his share for the kin must pay the fine of the culprit if that culprit cannot pay it all.'

'Yes, that is so.'

'But in law, Sister Brónach, Draigen has made reparation and atoned for this crime.'

'Yes. I know that the Abbess Marga gave her complete absolution long ago. And now she has grown up. And every day since the day she slaughtered my mother, I have borne her presence as a penance for my sins.'

Fidelma was bewildered.

'I still do not understand why you have stayed here. Why not depart to some other community where your wound could heal? Or why didn't you demand that Draigen be sent to some other abbey?'

Sister Brónach gave a long, low sigh.

'I have given you the reason. I stay here as a penance for my sins.'

'What are these sins that you are guilty of?' asked Fidelma. 'What would cause you to spend your life in the company of one who killed your own flesh and blood?'

Sister Brónach hesitated again and then seemed to straighten herself up a little.

'I was not there at the time to prevent Draigen's attack on my mother. It is the sin of absence when I was needed.'

'That is no cause for self-blame. There is no sin that has been committed.'

'Yet I feel responsible.'

Fidelma was sceptical. There was something false about Sister Brónach's explanation.

'There I cannot help you. Though if you have a soul-friend, perhaps . . .'

'I have struggled for twenty years with this problem, Sister Fidelma. It cannot be solved in twenty minutes.'

'You blame yourself too much, sister,' Fidelma rebuked. 'Also, let us try to look on things with some charity. Twenty years ago Draigen was a young girl, an immature young girl, by all that you say. What she did then, is past. The person she is now is probably not the person that she was then.'

'You are charitable, sister.'

'You do not agree?'

'Draigen is still the same character; jealous, unremitting in her ambition and a person who holds grudges.' The middle-aged religieuse suddenly held up a hand, palm upwards as if to quell any protest. 'Do not mistake me, sister. I have borne this burden for twenty years and will continue to bear it. I have nowhere in this world to go. At least, when I look up on the mountainside I can see my mother's grave and sometimes I am able to go up there and sit awhile.'

'Have you never felt that you would like to take retribution on Draigen?'

Sister Brónach genuflected as an answer.

'You mean do her physical injury? *Quod avertat Deus!* What a thing to suggest!'

'It has been known,' Fidelma pointed out.

'I cannot take life, sister. I cannot harm another human being no matter what they do to me. That was what I learnt from my mother, not from the Faith. I have already told you that I would prefer Draigen to live and suffer in her living.'

There was a dignified expression of sincerity on Sister Brónach's features. Fidelma could understand everything Brónach told her except the fact that she had remained in the abbey all these years in close proximity to Draigen, especially after Draigen had become abbess.

'It does not seem that Draigen suffers much,' Fidelma observed.

'Maybe you are right. Perhaps she has forgotten and probably believes that I have forgotten. But one night an hour will come when she awakens in fear and remembers.'

'Brother Febal has not forgotten,' Fidelma pointed out.

Brónach reddened slightly.

'Febal? What has he said?'

'Very little. Does anyone else know of the story?'

'Only myself . . . and Febal. Though Febal is selective with his memories.'

'Surely Draigen's brother, Adnár, knows of the story?'

'He learned it when he made his claim for the land and found he had forfeited it.'

'Are you telling me that no one else here knows of Draigen's past?'

'No one.'

It was only then that Fidelma realised the one thing she was overlooking. If Lerben was Draigen's daughter then surely Febal was Lerben's father? Yet he had accused his former wife and his own daughter of having a sexual relationship! What kind of man was Febal?

'Does Febal know that Lerben is his daughter?' was Fidelma's next question.

Sister Brónach looked surprised.

'Of course. At least, I think so.'

214

Fidelma was quiet for a while.

'You said that your mother followed the old pagan faith of this land. Do you know much of the old faith?'

Sister Brónach seemed puzzled for a moment at Fidelma's change of subject.

'I am my mother's daughter. She taught the old ways.'

'So you know of the old gods and goddesses, the symbol of the trees, and the meaning of Ogham?'

'I know a little. I know enough to recognise Ogham but I lack the knowledge of the old language in which it is inscribed.'

Inscriptions in Ogham were given in an ancient form of Irish, not the common language of the people, but an archaic form known as the *Bérla Féini*, the language of the land tillers. In these days, only those aspiring to be Brehons, or lawyers, studied the old language.

'Tell me, sister, what is the meaning of an aspen wand clasped in the left hand.'

Sister Brónach smiled knowledgeably.

'That is easy. The aspen is a sacred tree from which the *fé*, the rod for measuring a grave, is always cut. And always a line of Ogham is scored on it. It is a custom still used throughout the land.'

'Indeed, that is well known. But the attachment of the *fé* to the left arm – why not the right arm? What does that mean? You mentioned that you pointed this out to Draigen when the first body was found.'

'Whenever a murderer or a suicide is buried, a *fé* is placed at their left hand...' She broke off, a hand came to her mouth in surprise. 'The Ogham words are usually an invocation to a goddess of death.'

'Such as the Mórrígú? The goddess of death and battles?'

'Yes.' The reply was sharp.

'Go on,' said Fidelma quietly.

'I do not know the formula of words but it would be an acknowledgement of such a goddess. The headless corpse ...

the one in the well ... she had a rod of aspen carved with Ogham attached to her left arm.'

'So did Sister Síomha,' Fidelma agreed.

'What does it mean? Do you suggest ... ?'

'I suggest nothing,' Fidelma interrupted quickly. 'I merely asked you whether you knew what the symbolism meant.'

'Of course, I do.' Sister Brónach appeared to be thinking carefully now. 'But does this mean that the headless corpse was a murderess?'

'If that were so, surely it would follow that the same conclusion must be drawn with Sister Síomha.'

'That does not make sense.'

'It may make sense to the killer. Tell me, Sister Brónach, apart from yourself, who else would know about this symbolism here, in the abbey?'

The doorkeeper of the abbey shrugged.

'Times move on. The old ways are being forgotten. I doubt whether any of the young ones would know the meaning of such things.' Her eyes widened suddenly. 'Are you implying that I might be the culprit?'

Fidelma did not make an attempt at reassurance.

'You might be. It is my task to discover as much. Had we been talking of the murder of the Abbess Draigen, I would say that you had a very good motive and would be my choice of a prime suspect. But, at the moment, there appears to be no motive for the killing of the first corpse or of Sister Síomha.'

Sister Brónach regarded the younger woman with a resentful stare.

'You have an unfortunate sense of humour, sister,' she reproved. 'There might be some others here that are equally knowledgeable about the old ways as I am.'

'You have already said that this abbey consists mainly of young sisters and that they would not have such knowledge. Who else, then, would know about the symbolism?'

Sister Brónach thought a moment.

'Sister Comnat, our librarian. But there is no one else except...'

She paused and her eyes suddenly became hard and bright. Fidelma was watching her closely.

'Except...?' she prompted.

'No one.'

'Oh, I know the thought that has come into your head,' replied Fidelma easily. 'You were proud of the old knowledge that your mother passed on to you. Who else could your mother have passed on such knowledge to? Someone she fostered? Come, the name is on the tip of your tongue.'

Sister Brónach looked down at her feet.

'You know already. The Abbess Draigen, of course. She would know all about such symbolism and...'

'And?'

'She has been shown to be capable of killing.'

Sister Fidelma rose and nodded gravely.

'You are the second person who has pointed that out to me within the last few hours.'

Chapter Thirteen

Sister Lerben was in the chapel polishing the great ornate gold cross which stood on the altar. She was bent industriously to her task, a frown of concentration on her pretty features. It was the thud of the door closing behind Fidelma which made her glance up. She paused and straightened as Fidelma walked up the aisle between the deserted rows of benches to halt before her. Her expression was not one of welcome. Fidelma could see the glow of belligerent dislike in her eyes.

'Well?'

Lerben spoke in her clear, ice-cold soprano voice. Fidelma felt sorrow for her instead of anger. She appeared like a little girl, petulant and angry, in need of protection. A little girl, resenting that she had been caught by an adult doing something forbidden. Her mask of arrogance had given place to sullen pugnacity.

'There are a few questions that I need to ask,' Fidelma answered her pleasantly.

The girl methodically replaced the cross on its stand and carefully folded the strip of linen with which she was polishing it. Fidelma had already noticed that the girl's actions were precise and unhurriedly deliberate. She finally turned to face Fidelma, her arms folded into her robe. Her eyes focused on a point just behind Fidelma's shoulder.

Fidelma wearily indicated one of the benches.

'Let us sit a while and talk, Sister Lerben.'

'Is this an official talk?' Lerben demanded.

Fidelma was indifferent.

'Official? If you mean, do I wish to speak with you in my capacity as a *dálaigh* of the courts, then so far it is official. But such matters as we may discuss will not be placed on record.'

Sister Lerben reluctantly appeared to accept the situation and seated herself. She kept her eyes away from Fidelma's examining gaze.

'You may be assured that anything you say will not be reported to your abbess,' Fidelma said, trying to put the girl at her ease and wondering how best to approach the subject. She seated herself next to the girl who remained silent. 'Let us forget the conflict that arose between us, Lerben. I was also proud when I was your age. I, too, thought I knew many things. But you were misinformed about ecclesiastical law. I am, after all, an advocate of the courts and when you attempt to pit your knowledge against mine, it can only result in my knowledge being greater. I do not make this as a boast but simply a statement of fact.'

The girl still made no reply.

'I know you were advised by Abbess Draigen,' Fidelma continued to verbally prod her.

'Abbess Draigen has great knowledge,' snapped Lerben. 'Why should I doubt her?'

'You admire Abbess Draigen. I understand that. But her knowledge of the law is lacking.'

'She stands up for our rights. The rights of women,' countered Sister Lerben.

'Is there a need to stand up for the rights of women? Surely the laws of the five kingdoms are precise enough for the protection of women? Women are protected from rape, from sexual harassment and even from verbal assault. And they are equal under the law.'

'Sometimes that is not enough,' replied the girl seriously. 'Abbess Draigen sees the weaknesses in our society and campaigns for greater rights.'

'That I do not understand. Perhaps you might be good

enough to explain it. You see, if the abbess wants increased rights for women, why does she argue that the Laws of the Fenechas should be rejected and that we should accept the new ecclesiastical laws? Why does she stand in favour of the Penitentials which originate in their philosophies from Roman law? These laws place women in a subservient role.'

Sister Lerben was eager to explain.

'The canon laws, which Draigen wishes to support, would make it a more serious offence to kill a woman than a man. A life for a life. At the moment all the laws of the five kingdoms say is that compensation must be paid and the killer must be rehabilitated. The laws which the Roman church suggest is that the attacker should pay with his life and be made to suffer physical pain. The abbess has shown me some of the Penitentials which say that if a man kills a woman then his hand and foot should be cut off and he is made to suffer pain before being put to death.'

Fidelma stared in distaste at the bloodthirsty eagerness of the young girl.

'And a woman can be burned to death for the same offence,' Fidelma pointed out. 'Isn't it better to seek compensation for the victim than exact vengeance on the perpetrator? Isn't it better to attempt to rehabilitate the wrong doer and help the victim than exact painful revenge that gains nothing but a brief moment of satisfaction?'

Sister Lerben shook her head. Her tone was vehement.

'Draigen says that it is written in the scripture: "life for life, eye for eye, tooth for tooth, hand for hand, foot for foot . . ."'

'The words of Exodus are often quoted,' interrupted Fidelma tiredly. 'Surely it would be better looking at the words of the Christ who gave a new dispensation. Look at the Gospel of the Blessed Matthew and you will find these words of the Christ: "Ye have heard that it hath been said, an eye for an eye, and a tooth for a tooth: But I say unto you, That ye resist not evil; but, whosoever shall smite thee on thy right

cheek, turn to him the other also." That is the word of the
God we follow.'

'But Abbess Draigen said . . .'

Fidelma held up her hand to quiet the girl.

'No set of laws are perfect but there is little use rejecting
good laws for bad ones. Here women have rights and
protections. There is equality before the law. The foreign
laws that are creeping into this land by way of the Penitentials
mean that only the wealthy and people of rank can afford the
law.'

'But Abbess Draigen . . .'

'Is not an expert on law,' interrupted Fidelma firmly.
She really did not want to get waylaid into a debate on the
merits of rival law systems, especially with a young girl
who really did not know more than she had been told by a
biased authority. She knew clearly where Draigen stood in
support of the new Penitentials which, in Fidelma's estima-
tion, were threatening to undermine the laws of the five
kingdoms.

Sister Lerben lapsed into a sullen silence.

'I know that you admire the abbess,' Fidelma began again.
'That is a right and proper attitude to adopt towards one's
mother.'

'So you know that?' Sister Lerben's chin came up defensively.

'Surely an abbey is not a place wherein to keep a secret?'
Fidelma asked mildly. 'Besides, there is no law in either the
church of Ireland or Rome that forbids love and marriage
between men and women of the religious.' She could not help
adding, 'But those who support the new ecclesiastical rules
would deny that love.'

Fidelma knew that in Europe, during the last two
centuries, there had been a small but vociferous group who
had expressed doubts on the compatibility of marriage and
the religious life. Jerome and Ambrose had led those who
thought that celibacy was a higher spiritual condition than
marriage and Jerome's friend Pope Damascus had been the

first to express a favourable attitude towards the idea. So far, even in Rome, however, those favouring celibacy were still only a small but nonetheless influential group. Those who believed that celibacy should be mandatory and were therefore affecting the writing of Penitentials. Though, so far, they had not the backing of Rome's ecclesiastical laws.

Sister Lerben sat without expression.

'How long have you been in this community, Lerben? I presume that it has been since your birth?'

'No. When I was seven I was sent for fosterage.'

It was an ancient custom in the five kingdoms among those of wealth to send their children away at the age of seven to be fostered or educated, with a teacher. For boys the fosterage ended at the age of seventeen, for girls the fosterage ended at the age of fourteen.

'And you returned here when you were fourteen?' asked Fidelma.

'Three years ago,' agreed the girl.

'You had no thought of going elsewhere than to your mother's abbey?'

'No, why should I? Since I had been away many things had changed here. My mother had excluded all men.'

'Do you dislike men so much?' asked Fidelma in surprise.

'Yes!' The word was immediate and vehement.

'Why so?'

'Men are dirty, disgusting animals.'

Fidelma heard the intensity in her voice and wondered what experience had prejudiced the girl.

'Without them the human race would die out,' she pointed out softly. 'Your father was a man.'

'Then let it die out!' returned the girl uncompromisingly. 'My father was a pig.'

The hatred on the girl's features was something which amazed even Fidelma.

'I presume that you speak of Febal?'

'I do.'

222

An idea began to form in Fidelma's mind.

'So it was your father who has coloured your attitude to men?'

'My father ... a red hot stone in his throat! May he die choking!'

The curses were venomous.

'What did your father do to you to make you hate him so?'

'It is what he did to my mother. I do not wish to talk about my father.'

Sister Lerben's face was white and Fidelma noticed that a shiver passed through her slender frame as if of distaste. Fidelma began to realise that there was some deep conflict in the girl.

'So have you found solace here?' she passed on hurriedly. 'And have you found friendship with any of the other sisters?'

The girl shrugged indifferently.

'Some of them.'

'Not Sister Berrach, though?'

Lerben shuddered.

'That cripple! She should have died at birth.'

'And Sister Brónach?'

'A stupid old woman. She is always hanging round that feeble Berrach! She has had her time.'

'Then what of Sister Síomha, the steward? Were you friendly with her?'

Sister Lerben made an ugly face.

'She fancied herself, that one. She was dirty and disgusting!'

'Why? Why dirty and disgusting, Lerben?' demanded Fidelma, watching the young woman's flushed face.

'She liked men. She had a lover.'

'A lover. Do you know whom?'

'I think it is obvious. These last few weeks, on those nights she has not been attending the watch at the clepsydra, I have seen her returning before dawn from Adnár's fort. Síomha would not descend to liaisons with common warriors or servants. So you do not have to hunt far to know with whom she has defiled herself.'

'Do you mean your uncle? Adnár?'

'I do not call him such. Síomha was so full of her own importance. Attempting to tell everyone what to do.'

'She was the *rechtaire* of the abbey, after all,' Fidelma pointed out mildly. 'Did you speak of this matter with your mother?'

Sister Lerben raised her head defiantly.

'No. And now I am *rechtaire*.'

'At seventeen?' Fidelma smiled indulgently. 'You still have much to learn about the religious life before you could truly aspire to such office.'

'Draigen has made me *rechtaire*. That is an end to it.'

Fidelma decided not to pursue the matter. There were other things she wanted to follow up first.

'How well do you know Sisters Comnat and Almu?'

Lerben blinked. Fidelma's leap from one topic to another seemed to disconcert her.

'I knew them, yes.'

'*Knew* them? Isn't Comnat still the librarian and Almu her assistant?'

'They are gone to Ard Fhearta and have been away for several weeks now. It is natural to think of them as being away.'

'How well did you know them?' Fidelma corrected.

'I saw Comnat only during the services. An old woman. Older than Brónach.'

'You didn't have much to do with her?'

'She spent most of her time in the library and the rest in isolated prayer in her cell.'

'You were not interested in books?'

'I have not learned to read or write well. Draigen still teaches me.'

Fidelma was shocked.

'I thought you were sent away for an education?'

'My father arranged it. I was sent to a drunken farmer. There is a township not far away called Eadar Ghabhal. It is ten miles east of here. I was sent there to work as a servant. I became no more than a slave.'

'And you were not taught reading or writing?'

'No.'

'Did your father or your mother know what kind of place it was that you had been sent to?'

'My father knew well. That was why he arranged it. It was the last time my mother ever allowed him to interfere in our lives. He often visited the farmer.' Lerben's voice was full of pent-up passion. 'That is where I learned what pigs men are. The farmer ... he violated me. I finally managed to escape from that vile place. My mother found out only after I managed to return to the abbey. My father had kept the truth from her. It was his revenge against her. The farmer arrived here drunk, he had my father with him. They tried to get me to return, pretending that I had robbed the farmer and broken the contract my father had made. Draigen protected me, giving me sanctuary here, and driving them away.'

'What happened to the farmer?'

'He was killed when his farm burned down.'

Fidelma examined the girl's features carefully but there was no expression on them. They were almost vacuous as if she had chased any emotion out of them.

'Have you seen your father, since?'

'Only from a distance. My mother had warned him that he would not be long on this earth if he ever tried to harm me again.'

Fidelma sat quietly for a moment, turning the information over in her mind.

'You say that Draigen has been teaching you to read and write since your return to the abbey?'

'When she has time.'

'What about Sister Almu? She was young, wasn't she?'

Surely she was not much older than you? She was a good scholar and could have taught you to read and write?'

Was there some hesitation now.

'I was not friendly with her. She was a year or so older than I was. It was Sister Síomha who was Almu's friend.'

'Was Almu a pretty girl?'

'It depends on what you believe to be pretty.'

Fidelma conceded that it was a good riposte.

'Did you like her?'

'I did not really know her. She, too, worked in the library, copying those musty old books. Why are you asking me these questions?'

'Oh, just to get some background,' Fidelma rose from her seat. 'I have finished now.'

'Then, by your leave, I shall return to my duties.'

Fidelma gave a vague affirmative gesture and began to walk down the aisle towards the door. Then she halted there and glanced back as if in an afterthought.

'Why did you say that Sister Brónach has had her time?' she asked sharply. 'What did you mean by that?'

Sister Lerben looked up from where she had resumed her polishing of the gold icons of the chapel. For a moment it seemed that she had not understood Fidelma, then her expression lightened.

'Because she is old. Draigen says that she has had her man, her child, and there is nothing else in life for her. Draigen says...'

Fidelma had already passed on thoughtfully.

She was still deep in thought when Adnár's boatman reported to the abbey guest hostel that he had come to row her across to the *bó-aire*'s fortress. It was already dark but the boat had lanterns set fore and aft and there were two men who bent their backs into the oars so that the craft cleaved through the dark waters and made the crossing, so it seemed, within moments. Fidelma was handed up on to the dark quay and the boatman, bearing one of the lamps, lighted her way up the steps into the fortress.

Once through the granite walls the fortress was brightly lit with burning torches and the sounds of music came drifting from the main buildings. Warriors patrolled here and there but otherwise it seemed a peaceful enough citadel.

Adnár was coming down the stairs, hands held out in greeting.

'Welcome, Sister Fidelma. Welcome. I am glad that you have come.'

He led the way back up the wooden stairs and into the large feasting room where she had breakfasted on the previous morning. The furnishings had not changed but the great table was piled with mountains of food and a fire roared in the hearth sending out a tremendous heat. A musician sat in the corner, playing unobtrusively on a stringed instrument.

Adnár himself helped her to remove her cloak and conducted her to the circular table. Here an attendant bent to remove her shoes. It was the custom, both in secular communities as well as ecclesiastical life, to remove the shoes and sandals before sitting down to an evening feast.

Olcán was there; so was Torcán. Both young men greeted her with such an effusion of spirit that they seemed to be trying to outdo each other in manners. Only Brother Febal stood quietly, his eyes lowered, his manner almost surly. Fidelma tried not to show her distaste for him. She must keep an open mind. Yet if the claims of Sister Lerben were true then he was a bitter and evil man.

It was Olcán who opened up the conversation.

'How goes your investigation? I was given to understand that you have interrogated Brother Febal here? Is he the dread killer and decapitator of women?'

Brother Febal did not join in their humour.

Fidelma answered them gravely.

'We shall have to wait until the investigation is complete in order to make a judgment.'

Adnár raised his eyebrows in mock surprise.

'May the sky fall on us! I do believe that she does suspect you, Febal.'

Brother Febal shrugged. His handsome face was bland.

'I have nothing to fear from the truth.'

Olcán's sallow features were split by a grin and he pointed to the table.

'Well, I fear starvation unless this meal begins. Sister Fidelma, will you do us the honour of saying the *Gratias* as is the custom?'

Fidelma bowed her head.

'*Benedic nobis, Domine Deus, et omnibus donis Tuis quae ex lorgia* . . .'

She intoned the ritual and they set to the meal. Servants now came forward to pour the wine and hand round the plates. Fidelma was slightly surprised to see that Adnár not only supplied a knife for each person, for one ate with a knife in the right hand and used the fingers of the left hand only, but each diner was given a clean *lámhbrat*, or hand-cloth, which was usually placed over the knees when eating and, at the end of the meal, used to clean one's hands. Generally such refinement was found only at the tables of the kings and bishops. It was clear that Adnár had social pretensions in the setting of his feasting table.

'Please begin, Fidelma. Would you prefer wine or mead?'

Silver goblets were filled with imported red wine but jugs of local mead were also placed on the table. She saw that brother Febal selected this rather than wine. There was a choice of dishes: ox-meat, mutton and venison. There were fish dishes, goose eggs and a dish even of *rón* or seal meat. It was a dish that was once popular but now few people ate it. A story told that a family in the west of the country was once metamorphosed into seals by a druid and now no one would eat seal meat in case they were eating their own relatives.

Fidelma helped herself to some venison cooked with wild garlic, some barley cakes and parsnip.

'Seriously,' Adnár was saying, 'how is your investigation? Have you discovered the identity of the headless body?'

'Not for sure,' replied Fidelma, sipping at her wine.

Torcán's glance was searching.

'That means that you have some suspicion as to who it is?'

Fidelma pretended her mouth was too full of food to answer.

'Well, I know who I believe did it,' muttered Brother Febal.

The sallow-faced Olcán waved his knife towards Febal.

'You have already made that clear to Sister Fidelma. Certainly the Abbess Draigen is not a person who has inspired your affection.'

'She inspires it in her daughter,' Fidelma observed quietly.

Brother Febal immediately caught the inflection.

'So you have been talking to Lerben?' He seemed unperturbed. 'Well, she is but hewn of the same tree as her mother. Liars, both of them!'

'Is she not also hewn of the same tree as her father?' Fidelma asked with an innocent expression.

Brother Febal was about to retort, then seemed to catch himself. He tried to interpret Fidelma's implacable expression.

'If she has been accusing me...' he began and his face flushed angrily.

'Of what would she accuse you?'

Brother Febal shook his head negatively.

'Nothing. Nothing. The girl is simply a compulsive liar. That is all.'

'And you still say that her mother prefers women to men? You stand by that accusation? And the accusation of an unnatural relationship between mother and daughter?'

'Have I not said so?'

'No one else in the abbey would agree with you. Not even Sister Brónach whose name you conjured as your witness.'

'None of those at the abbey have any guts to go against Draigen, especially Brónach. She is a self-made martyr!'

Fidelma noticed that Torcán was regarding Brother Febal with a curious expression. It was Olcán who lightened the sudden tense turn of the conversation.

'Personally, and by the sound of it, I believe the killer is some madman. They are many tales of strange mountainy men who waylay and slaughter people. What sane person would decapitate a head from the body?'

'Then you must believe our forefathers were insane.' Torcán's tone was serious but he was smiling as he spoke. 'Years and years ago it was considered essential to take the head from a slain enemy.'

'I have heard of that ancient custom,' Fidelma observed. 'Do you know much about it?'

The son of the prince of the Uí Fidgenti selected another piece of meat with his knife and gave an affirmative gesture.

'It was once a warrior code. Great warriors, in the aftermath of a battle, would remove the heads of their slain enemies to hang them from their chariots and drive triumphantly back to their fortresses. Didn't the hero Conall Cearnach vow never to sleep unless he could do so with the head of an enemy under his foot?'

'Why would they do that?' Olcán demanded. 'Remove the heads of their enemies? It was as much as one could do to survive in battle without wasting time on such a fruitless exercise.'

It was Fidelma who supplied the answer.

'In the old days, before the coming of the Faith, it was thought that the soul of a person was to be found inside the head. The head was the centre of intellect and all reason. What else could produce such thoughts other than a soul? When the body died, the soul remained until it journeyed to the Otherworld. Am I not right in this, Brother Febal?'

Brother Febal started at being addressed by her in an apparently friendly manner and then nodded reluctantly.

'That was the belief, so I understand. Until recently, a sign of showing respect and affection among us was to lay one's head on the bosom of the person to be greeted.'

'But why did warriors remove the heads of their enemies?' demanded Olcán.

'It was like this,' Torcán explained, 'among the ancient warriors they felt that if the heads of their enemies were removed, they would capture the soul. If their enemy was a great warrior, a great champion, some of that greatness would pass down to them.'

'A primitive idea,' muttered Olcán.

'Perhaps,' Torcán conceded. 'Instead of the tales of the saints and the new Faith, you should listen to the tales of our ancient heroes, like Cúchullain who rode into Dún Dealg with hundreds of heads adorning his chariot.'

Adnár admonished his guests.

'This is hardly a conversation fitting for the presence of a woman.'

'It was a practice that even our great women warriors took part in,' pointed out Torcán, oblivious to the hint which Adnár was giving him.

'You seem to know much about this,' Fidelma observed. 'Tell me, Torcán, would one even remove the head of someone who had, for example, been a murderer?'

Torcán was surprised at the question.

'What makes you ask that?'

'Indulge my curiosity.'

'In the old days it did not matter so long as the person was seen as a great warrior, champion or leader of their people.'

'So, if someone, imbued with the old ways, encountered their enemy, and saw their enemy as a murderer, they could easily remove the head as a symbol?'

Olcán's thin features broke into a smile.

'I begin to see where the good sister's questions are leading.'

Brother Febal had snorted indignantly and sunk his nose into his mug of mead.

Torcán was looking puzzled.

'It is more than I do,' he admitted. 'But, in answer to your question, it is possible. Why do you ask?'

'She asks because she suspects that the headless corpse and the decapitated Sister Síomha may well have been the victims of some ancient head-hunting ancestor of ours!' sneered Brother Febal.

Fidelma was composed and did not rise to the bait of the religieux.

'Not exactly, Febal. It is clear however that the killer, whoever they are, put some symbolism into the methods of killing.'

Adnár was leaning forward on the table with interest.

'What symbolism?'

'That is what I want to find out,' replied Fidelma. 'It is clear also that the killer wanted whoever found the corpses to know and appreciate that symbolism.'

'You mean that the killer is actually giving you clues to his means and motive?' asked young Olcán wonderingly.

'His or her motive,' corrected Fidelma gently. 'Yes. I now believe that the way the corpses were left was meant as a message to those who found them.'

Brother Febal banged down his mug.

'Nonsense! The killings are part of a sick mind. And I know who has the sickest mind on this peninsula.'

Adnár sighed unhappily.

'I cannot argue against that assessment. Perhaps these symbols, of which you speak, Sister Fidelma, are but some trick to distract you in your investigation? Some ruse to make you follow a path which does not lead anywhere?'

Fidelma bowed her head in consideration of the point.

'It may well be,' she acceded after a moment. 'But knowing the symbolism will, I believe, eventually lead to the perpetrator whether it is intentional or unintentional. And for this information on decapitation, Torcán, I am much indebted.'

'Ha!' Olcán was smirking, 'I believe, Torcán, that you have allowed yourself to become a suspect in the good sister's eyes? Isn't that so, Sister Fidelma?'

She ignored his mocking tone.

'Not so,' replied Torcán, his eyes serious. 'I think that Sister Fidelma would know that if I had devised such an atrocious way of leaving murdered corpses about the country-side, I would not have started to prattle about its symbolism and so draw attention to myself.'

Fidelma inclined her head towards him.

'On the other hand,' she smiled grimly, 'it may well be that you would do that very thing to argue this point in order to throw me off the scent.'

Olcán was chuckling now and clapped his friend, Torcán on the shoulder.

'There you are! You will now have to find a *dálaigh* to defend you.'

'Nonsense!' For a moment Torcán looked worried. 'I wasn't even here when the first murder, of which you were speaking, was committed...'

He caught himself and grinned sheepishly as he realised that he was the butt of his friend's humour.

'Olcán has an odd sense of humour,' Adnár apologised. 'I am sure Fidelma is not serious in saying that you might be a culprit.'

'I do not think I even mentioned such an idea in the first place,' she said evasively. 'I was merely responding to Torcán's hypothetical argument. The last person that I would tell if he or she was a suspect is the suspect themselves ... unless I had a purpose for it.'

'Well said,' Adnár said, ignoring the final point. 'Let us cease this morbid talk of bodies and murder.'

'I apologise,' Fidelma agreed. 'But bodies and murder are, unfortunately, part of my world. I am, nevertheless, indebted to Torcán for his knowledge. Your information on old customs is most helpful.'

Torcán was deprecating.

'I am interested in the old warrior codes and modes of battle, but that is all.'

'Ah? I thought you had a fascination with our history and ancient annals?' Fidelma asked.

'Me? No. It is Olcán here and Adnár that like to delve into ancient books. Not me. Do not be misled by my talk of ancient warrior codes. One is taught this as part of a warrior's education.'

For a moment Fidelma wondered whether to follow this up by asking Torcán why he had requested the abbey library to send him the copy of the annals of Clonmacnoise. However, before she could continue, Brother Febal said: 'I see that Ross and his ship have returned.'

Everyone had noticed Ross's ship sail into the inlet that afternoon. There was no need for comment.

Olcán was helping himself to more wine. His thin face was flushed and he seemed to be imbibing with a healthy thirst.

'I am told that his ship was seen at the island of Dóirse, further down the coast,' continued Brother Febal.

This time she could not ignore the obvious invitation to respond. She hid her annoyance at the excellence of communication among Gulban's people.

'I believe that Ross trades regularly along the coast,' she replied.

'I would have thought there was little trade to be had on Dóirse. It is a bleak, windswept island,' Adnár observed.

'I am not acquainted with the trading conditions along this coast,' Fidelma responded.

There was a movement and some servants entered to clear away the dishes and presented a variety of new dishes for dessert with apples, honey, and nuts of many varieties.

'We do a good trade in copper from our mines near here,' offered Olcán as he helped himself to more wine.

Fidelma was pretending to examine the dish of nuts but she had the impression that Torcán was gazing at her as if trying to examine her reactions.

'I have heard that there are many copper mines in this district.' It was better to stick to truth as far as it was possible. 'Do you do much foreign trade?'

'Gaulish ships sometimes come and trade wine for copper,' Adnár answered.

Fidelma raised her goblet as if in toast.

'It seems a good exchange,' she smiled. 'Especially if this wine is anything to go by.'

Adnár deflected any further questions by offering her more wine.

'How is your brother, our king?' Torcán asked the question abruptly.

At once Fidelma felt a new tension around the table. She was suddenly on her guard wondering if the stories that Ross had picked up were true. She had been wondering how to raise this topic without alerting suspicion. She must be careful.

'My brother Colgú? I have not seen him since the judgment at Ros Ailithir.'

'Ah yes; my father was there,' replied Olcán helping himself to an apple.

'As was mine,' Torcán added coldly. 'I hear that Colgú claims many grand new plans for Muman.'

Fidelma was dismissive.

'I have seen my brother only the one time since he became king at Cashel,' she said. 'My community is at Kildare, at the house of the Blessed Brigit. I have not interested myself in the affairs of Muman very much.'

'Ah,' the syllable was a soft breath from Torcán.

Olcán turned a now somewhat bleary eye towards her.

'But you were at Ros Ailithir when the Loígde assembly rejected my father's claims for chieftainship and hailed Bran Finn Mael Ochtraighe as chieftain?'

Fidelma admitted as much.

'That upset my father greatly. You know all about Bran Finn, of course?'

She detected that the others had become uneasy.

'Who has not?' she replied. 'He has a reputation as a poet and a warrior.'

'My father, Gulban, thinks he is an usurper.'

'Olcán!' Torcán turned with a warning look on the young man who was clearly the worse for his wine.

'I hope he will prove a better chieftain than Salbach,' Fidelma rejoined.

She saw Adnár cast what appeared to be a warning glance at Torcán, nodding in the direction of Olcán, before turning with a bland smile to Fidelma.

'I am sure he will,' the chieftain of Dún Boí assured her. 'He has the good wishes of the people behind him, as does your brother Colgú. Isn't that so, Torcán?'

'Not so, according to my father, Gulban,' muttered Olcán.

'Ignore him, Sister Fidelma,' Torcán said. 'The wine is in, the wit is out.'

'Of course,' Fidelma said gravely but the words of the old Roman proverb had come to mind; *in vino veritas*, in wine there is truth.

Torcán raised his head.

'Indeed, we hope to be in Cashel soon to give our allegiance to Colgú personally.'

Olcán suddenly spluttered into his goblet, spilling some of the contents over him. He began coughing fiercely.

'Something . . . something went down the wrong way,' he gasped, looking sheepishly around him.

Torcán, with a frown, handed him some water to drink.

'It is evident that you have drunk enough wine this evening,' he reproved sharply.

But Fidelma was rising, realising the lateness of the hour.

'It is near midnight. I must return to the abbey.'

Must you go?' Torcán was pleasantry personified. 'Adnár

here prides himself on his musicians and we have yet to listen to their accomplishments.'

'Thank you, but I must return.'

Adnár waved to a servant to come forward and issued whispered instructions.

'I have ordered the boat to take you back. Perhaps you will come and listen to my musicians some other time?'

'That I will,' replied Fidelma as an attendant brought her shoes and helped her fasten her cloak around her shoulders.

As the boat pulled away from the jetty of Dún Boí into the darkness of the night, Fidelma felt a relief to be out of the dark, brooding walls of the fortress. She had a feeling that she had passed along a knife edge between safety and extreme peril.

Chapter Fourteen

The echoing tones of the gong proclaiming the midnight hour reverberated clearly from the tower of the abbey. Fidelma, her woollen cloak trimmed with beaver fur wrapped tightly around her, moved silently through the white shrouded woods. The newly-laid snow crunched crisply under her feet and her breath hung like a mist before her as the cold air caught it. In spite of the hour, the night was made bright by a full, rounded moon, which had appeared between the clouds, and whose rays sparkled against the snowy carpet below.

She was sure that no one had seen her leave the guests' hostel and make her way silently out of the abbey grounds into the surrounding woods. She had paused once or twice to look back but nothing seemed to be stirring in the deathly quiet of the night. She moved rapidly now, her breath coming in pants, the cold air causing her to make more exertion than normal.

She was reassured when she heard the soft whinny of horses ahead of her and, after a minute or two, she saw the animals with Ross and Odar holding their reins.

'Excellently done, Ross!' she greeted him breathlessly.

'Is all well, sister?' the sailor asked anxiously. 'Did anyone see you leaving the abbey?'

She shook her head.

'Let us move out straight away for I believe that we have much to do this night.'

Odar came forward and assisted her into the saddle of a

dark mare. Then Ross and Odar swung on to their mounts.
Ross led the way for he apparently knew the direction to be
taken. Fidelma came next with Odar bringing up the rear.

'Where did you get the horses from?' Fidelma asked
approvingly, as they moved slowly along the forest track. She
was a good judge of horses.

'Odar traded for them.'

'A small farmer not far from here. A man named Barr,'
Odar supplied gruffly. 'His farm seems to be prospering
since the last time I had business with him. He could not
afford horses then. I have paid him for a night's use of the
animals.'

'Barr?' Fidelma frowned. 'I seem to have heard that name
before. No matter. Oh, yes,' she suddenly recalled. 'I know
now. And has Barr found his missing daughter?'

Odar looked at her in puzzlement.

'Daughter? Barr is not even married, let alone with
children.'

Fidelma pursed her lips but made no reply.

She suddenly shivered in the cold, in spite of her cloak, as a
chill wind began to whisper its way around the snow-covered
skirts of the large mountains.

Ross pointed upwards.

'Our path lies up across the mountain. There is a track that
passes the peak and crosses to the far side of the peninsula.
Then it drops down behind the settlement where they dig for
copper.'

Odar added: 'I have brought a container of *cuirm* in my
saddle bag which will keep out the winter chill, sister. Would
you like a sip?'

'A good thought to bring it, Odar,' Fidelma replied in
appreciation. 'But I think it would be best if you kept
that for later, for we have yet to leave the shelter of this
wood and climb across the icy shoulders of the mountains.
It will get even colder later and that is when we will need
it.'

'There is much wisdom in what you say, sister,' agreed Odar stolidly.

They rode on in silence now, heads bent as the wind slowly rose and blew fine dry snow against them. There were more snow clouds bunching up from the west but Fidelma was unsure whether to be thankful or dismayed. She was thankful that the clouds might obscure the bright moon which, reflecting on the snow, made the night almost as brilliant as daylight and made them visible for considerable distances against the white background. On the other hand she was dismayed that the heavy clouds were threatening more snow and promised to make their journey as uncomfortable and as perilous as possible.

It was after they had gone five miles that the wisdom of Fidelma's advice to conserve the *cuirm*, or spirit which Odar had brought, became apparent. They were freezing in spite of their warm cloaks and she halted her horse in a small clearing. It was a rocky area by an entrance to some caves. She suggested that Odar allow each of them a sip of the *cuirm* to fortify them. Thus fortified, they rode on again. After another mile or so, they descended through a series of twisting tracks out of the mountains and through the more rounded hills towards the seashore. They could see the black, brooding sea, reflecting now and then by the moon's rays as the snow clouds parted and allowed it to shine through.

Their horses became skittish and not far away wolves started to bay. Fidelma, looking up the mountain, caught sight of several dark shadows moving hurriedly across the white snow and she suppressed a shiver.

'The queen of the night is bright,' muttered Ross, apprehensively. 'Perhaps she is too radiant.'

Fidelma, for a moment, wondered what he was referring to until she realised that sailors had a taboo about referring directly to the moon or to the sun. The moon was often referred to as the 'queen of the night' or, simply, 'the brightness'. The ancient language of Éireann gave many other names for the moon, all of them euphemisms so that the sacred name of the moon would never be spoken. It was an old pagan custom from the time the moon was thought of as a goddess of whom no mortal could evoke her power by uttering her name.

'Hopefully the clouds will thicken before we reach the settlement,' Fidelma replied.

The howling of the wolf pack gradually died away across the mountains.

After what seemed an eternity, Ross halted his horse and pointed down the hill. Fidelma could just see the tiny glow of fires.

'Those are the buildings around the mines. It is an area of fields on a cliff top. Below is a strand and the harbour from where the Dóirse islanders told me the Gaulish ship sailed from.'

Fidelma peered forward. Of course, earlier it seemed so easy to simply say that they would ride across the peninsula to the mines and find out what happened to the crew of the merchant ship. Here, in the chilly moonlight, the plan's flaws presented themselves to her. When Ross interrupted her thoughts with: 'What will you do, sister?' she could have rebuked him in her irritation.

'Do you know how many people live down there?'

'There are many mine workers and their families.'

'Are they all prisoners, hostages and slaves?'

Ross shrugged.

'I do not think so. But many are. If the Gauls are among them then they should be easy to find. Or, at least, their whereabouts will be known to most people.'

'What about guards?'

'I cannot really say. There were few warriors there when I last traded at the mines. But, after what the islanders have told me about the Uí Fidgenti warriors, there might be as many as fifty warriors or even more.

'Do you know the layout of the settlement? Where would the most likely places be in which the prisoners could be kept?'

In answer, Ross swung off his horse and beckoned her to follow suit. He chose a clear patch of snow and took out his sword. With the tip of it, he made several depressions.

'Those are the entrances to the mines, there,' he jabbed with the sword point. 'And here is the path which goes down into the settlement. Here and here, are the huts. There are many shacks where I think the workers live. Apart from that, I cannot help further.'

Fidelma stared at the depressions and sighed.

'We will ride down a little further and you and Odar will wait with the horses while I go on into the village on foot.' She held up a hand to stop Ross's protests. 'I may achieve much more on my own than the three of us. We would simply attract attention.'

'But you don't know what you will find down there,' Ross protested. 'The whole place might be an armed camp in which strangers are not welcomed.'

Before he could protest further, Fidelma had remounted and was trotting off down the track towards the flickering lights. As they approached closer to the buildings, a dog started to yelp. A raucous voice cursed the animal, thinking – or so Fidelma judged by the sense of what was shouted – that the poor beast was yapping at the wolves on the mountainside. She held up her hand and motioned her companions towards the shelter of the surrounding trees and undergrowth where they dismounted out of sight of the settlement. Without a word she handed her reins to Ross and shook her head vehemently when he began to open his mouth in protest.

She drew her cloak more firmly over her shoulders and moved off, across the slushy approach to the settlement. It was not an enclosed settlement, as some were, but the buildings seemed to be placed in a haphazard fashion. She had no idea where she was actually going or what she was going to do. She just walked firmly into the shadows cast by the buildings as if she had every right to be there. Someone actually emerged between two of the cabins, carrying a lantern, and began to walk by her without a second glance. He was a thick-set warrior, with shield and spear slung on his back.

With heart beating, Fidelma turned after him.

'Warrior!' she called, her voice filled with as much authority as she could muster.

The man paused and turned. He did not seem surprised to see a stranger accosting him in the dark and she made a point of letting the light of his lantern fall on her crucifix around her neck.

'Yes, sister?' There was no suspicion in his voice only a curiosity and respect. She could not see his features and hoped that they mirrored his tone. She decided to chance everything on a bold move.

'Among the prisoners is a Saxon religieux. I need to question him. Do you know where he has been held?'

'A Saxon?' The man thought for a moment. 'Oh, yes. He is being kept with the other religieuses. Do you see that second cabin across there, by the edge of those trees? You'll find him there.'

'Thank you, warrior.'

The warrior raised a hand in salutation and swung away.

Fidelma could hardly believe that it was so easy. She found herself recalling the line from *Phormio* by Terence: *audentes fortuna juvat* – fortune favours the daring. Her mentor, the Brehon Morann of Tara had frequently repeated that and added his own maxim. Unless one entered the wolf's lair, one could not take the cubs. Fortune had certainly smiled on her and she had entered the lair easily enough.

She hurried towards the cabin which the warrior had indicated. It was a large, isolated cabin, standing at the very edge of the settlement by the border of the woods that served as protection from the mountains. The next building was about thirty yards away. The place appeared to be in darkness, although she saw a window across which a sackcloth hung. A faint glow of a lantern seemed to be flickering behind it. She moved up to the window and listened carefully. She could hear no sound at first. Then there came a strange, scratching noise, like metal on metal. Raising herself on tiptoe, she tugged gently at the sackcloth and peered cautiously in.

The cabin seemed divided into two rooms. The window gave entrance to one of these rooms. It was bare, except for a lamp hung from the rafters giving out a faint light. There were several poles supporting the roof. A figure sat at the foot of one of these poles. It was a male, clad in brown robes, sitting with his body bent towards his feet. He appeared to be working away at something. Fidelma breathed sharply. The figure wore the tonsure of Peter of Rome. She peered around, ensuring that there was no one else in the room. The window was impossible to get through as wooden bars prevented ingress. She went to the door and found a heavy bar locking it from the outside. Fidelma looked swiftly around and, ensuring no one was in sight, she heaved at the bar, managing to slide it from its iron mountings so that she could pull the door open.

She moved hurriedly inside and closed the door behind her. For a moment she stood with her back to it and gazed into the room.

The figure on the floor had stopped his attentions to his feet and was slumped against the pole as if in an attitude of repose. Eyes fast shut.

Fidelma took a step forward and smiled with satisfaction.

'It is no time to be sleeping, Brother Eadulf,' she whispered.

It was as if a cold stream of water had suddenly hit the figure. He jerked his head upwards, his body going tense and stiff. His mouth hung open as he gazed at the shadowy figure above him.

She took another step forward and the meagre light from the lamp fell across her face.

'My God! Can be it you?' came the incredulous voice of the Saxon monk.

Impulsively, Fidelma bent forward, stretching forth both hands and grasped those that Eadulf held out to her. His hands were free but she noticed that he was shackled by one ankle to the wooden pole against which he was squatting. He looked dirty and careworn and appeared as if he had not eaten or slept for a week. The Saxon monk apparently could not believe his eyes and hung on to her hands fiercely as though afraid that she was a vision which would abruptly vanish.

'Fidelma!'

For several moments neither of them were able to speak. Then it was Fidelma who finally broke the silence.

'Of all people, Eadulf,' Fidelma said, forcing a tone of rebuke, though there was a slight catch to her voice. 'Brother Eadulf, you are the last person I have been expecting to see in this land of mine.'

'If the truth be known,' replied Eadulf, the corners of his mouth twitching in a dry grimace, 'if the truth be known, I will admit that I never hoped to see anyone I knew ever again. But how have you come here? You are surely not a friend of these people . . . ?'

'There is much to explain,' Fidelma replied with a shake of her head. 'But we must hurry and get you away from this place before we are discovered. How are you bound?'

Eadulf bit back the hundred and one questions that were obviously flooding into his mind and gestured to the iron manacle on his ankle.

'I have been trying to work it loose but I do not have the right tool.'

Fidelma examined the lock, frowning slightly in concentration. It was a simple mechanism but needed something long and thin to prise it open. She reached into her *crumena* and drew out the knife she carried and attempted to insert the point into the opening of the padlock. It was too broad.

Eadulf watched her glumly as she peered around the room obviously searching for a long piece of metal to prise the lock open.

'There is nothing within my reach. I have looked.'

She did not reply but rose and examined the lantern which was hanging on the wooden pole. She reached forward, removing it and examining the iron nail on which it had been hooked. Then she put down the lamp and using her knife began to dig at the nail. It took a few moments to remove sufficient wood around it to start to loosen it and a few moments more to wiggle it up and down so that she could extract it with ease. Then she returned to her task.

'I still do not understand how you came here, Fidelma,' Eadulf said as he watched her twist the nail in the lock.

'It will take some time to explain. More important than that is the question of how you came here.'

'I was a passenger on a Gaulish merchant ship. The captain put into this port to trade and suddenly we were all captured.'

'Where are the rest of the captives?'

'Mostly held in the mines to work. There are some copper mines here . . .'

'I know. Ah! That's it.'

There was a click of the mechanism as it turned. She unloosened the fetter from his ankle.

Eadulf began to massage his bruised flesh.

'Well, I shan't be sorry to desert these people's hospitality,' he muttered. Then he glanced awkwardly to the shut door which separated this part of the cabin from the second room. 'However . . .'

'What is it?' Fidelma demanded impatiently, she was already moving for the outer door. 'We should leave now. Our luck can't hold forever.'

'There is an elderly religieuse imprisoned in the next room. She has been here for several weeks now. I would not like to leave her. Can we take her with us?'

Fidelma did not hesitate.

'Is she alone?'

Eadulf nodded.

Fidelma took the lamp and moved cautiously to the next room and opened the door.

An elderly, white-haired woman lay on a straw palliasse in a corner. She was asleep. Like Eadulf, one ankle was gripped in an iron manacle which was fastened by a chain to the wall.

Fidelma bent beside her and shook her gently

The elderly religieuse came awake, eyes wide in fear. She opened her mouth but Fidelma placed a finger to her lips and smiled reassuringly.

'I'm here to help you. I presume that you are Sister Comnat?'

The woman stared in astonishment and then gave an affirmative gesture.

Fidelma took the nail and bent to the lock.

'This should not take a moment.'

Sister Comnat looked from her to Eadulf who was standing in the doorway, stretching and massaging his leg to restore the circulation.

'Thank God!' whispered the elderly sister. 'Then Sister Almu managed to get through safely?'

Fidelma compressed her lips for a moment and then gave a quick shake of her head.

'We will talk about this later.'

The lock on Sister Comnat's fetters was not so difficult as that on Eadulf's manacle or else Fidelma had become more learned at the art of the manipulation of the mechanism. There was a click and the fetters came undone.

'What now?' demanded Eadulf. 'There are many warriors in this place.'

Fidelma helped to raise the frail religieuse to her feet.

'I have some friends with horses close by. Come.'

She took the weight of Sister Comnat, who was swaying a little with weakness, and led her to the door of the cabin.

'Take a look outside and see if it is clear,' she instructed Eadulf.

The tall monk nodded briefly and eased open the door. A moment later he turned with a grim look of satisfaction.

'No sign of anyone.'

'Then we shall go. Move around the side of the cabin and into the cover of the woods behind. Be careful, for there is at least one dog about this place.'

They moved out of the cabin and Fidelma motioned Eadulf to close the door and thrust home the wooden bar, so, to the casual glance, the cabin would still appear secure from the outside. Then they moved cautiously to the edge of the cabin. A dog started to howl close by but its cry was taken up by the distant baying of the wolves high up on the mountainside. They heard a voice cursing and then a sharp yelp. Obviously the irritated owner of the voice had thrown something at the poor beast.

With Fidelma leading the way, they continued along the side of the cabin and into the trees and undergrowth behind. Here there was a clump of round headed yews and the area was thick with a profusion of holly and strawberry trees, some female species of holly with their bright red berries and many younger trees with green bark. Ivy leaves permeated through the trees, among the elders, so that the forest welcomed them with a natural screen. Trying to avoid the prickling of the sharp spines on the lower leaves, Fidelma pushed into the shelter of the woods.

'My friends should be close by here,' she whispered, indicating the path. She led them silently in a semi-circle around the edge of the settlement, keeping under cover of the trees and bushes until they came across Ross standing impatiently with Odar and the horses. The burly sea captain examined Fidelma's companions in amazement.

'No time for explanations now,' Fidelma cut in before he could begin to ask questions. 'We must put some distance between this place and ourselves.'

Ross responded to the urgency immediately.

'We can move to the caves on the hillside a few miles back. The old ... the sister can mount behind you, Fidelma. The monk can mount behind me.'

Fidelma agreed and swung up on her horse.

'Odar, help Sister Comnat up behind me,' she urged.

Still looking somewhat dazed, the elderly religieuse was helped to clamber up behind her. Ross mounted and helped Eadulf up behind him. Then he turned to lead the way, picking the path up through the woods which hid them effectively from anyone's prying eyes from the settlement below. It was half an hour before he called a halt in a small clearing where the snow had turned to slush in front of the rocky entrance to a large cave. He signalled for them to dismount and then led the horses into the cave entrance away from any casual observers.

'Come on,' he instructed the others, 'there is plenty of room and we will be out of sight.'

Ross was right. It was a large cave and he had been able to tether the horses well back from the entrance while they gathered in a small circle where a series of dry rocks served as excellent seats.

'I think your flask of *cuirm* is appropriate now, Odar,' Fidelma said solemnly.

The tall sailor went to his saddle bag and removed the vessel, unloosening the stopper and handing it first to the elderly Sister Comnat. She coughed a little at the fiery liquid and then smiled in gratitude.

Fidelma took it next, paused then passed it silently to Eadulf.

'I think you stand in need of this more than I do.'

Eadulf did not argue but seized the flask and took a long swallow.

He grinned apologetically before handing it back to her and wiped the back of his hand across his mouth.

'It seems a long while since I have had anything so satisfying,' he confessed.

Each in turn, now warmed themselves with a draught of the fiery liquid.

'What happened, Eadulf?' asked Fidelma, when the warming effects of the drink eased them a little. 'You give us your explanation first. How came you to be a prisoner in this place? When I left you in Rome, you were to be instructor to your new archbishop of Canterbury. I thought you were to be in Rome for at least a couple of years before returning to your own country.'

'That is what I thought also,' Eadulf agreed in a rueful tone. 'But, as Virgil says – *dis aliter visum*. It seemed otherwise to the gods. There is no escaping destiny.'

Fidelma felt the old irritation rising in her at his ponderous approach and was about to make a caustic response when she suddenly chuckled at the incongruity of the thought. She had risked much to mount a rescue of Eadulf only to be irritated with him the moment he opened his mouth. Eadulf was regarding her with perplexity.

'Go on, Eadulf,' Fidelma invited, still smiling. 'You were in Rome and expecting to stay there for some time.'

'Theodore of Tarsus was preparing for his journey to Canterbury to be installed as archbishop. He had decided to send emissaries to prepare his establishment there. Since the synod at Hilda's abbey two years ago the Saxon kingdoms have each accepted Canterbury as the seat of their chief bishop and apostle just as you, in this land, have accepted Armagh as the seat of the successors of Patrick.'

'Yes, yes,' Fidelma felt a growing irritation again at Eadulf's lengthy method of reaching the point. 'But what are you doing here in Éireann?'

'I was just coming to that,' Eadulf protested in a hurt tone. 'The archbishop also wanted to send emissaries to the Irish kingdoms to make a peace after the ejection of the Irish clergy from the Saxon kingdoms. He wanted to open dialogue with the Irish churches, especially as he has had communication with many clerics in Ireland who wish to introduce the Roman laws into the ecclesiastical establishments.'

Fidelma pulled an expressive face.

'Yes; bishops like Ultan at Armagh would welcome such dialogue. But are you saying that you were sent as an emissary to Archbishop Ultan?'

'No, not to Ultan. I was sent as emissary to the new king of Muman at Cashel.'

'To Colgú?'

'Yes, to Colgú. I was to intermediate between Canterbury and Cashel.'

'How then did you land here in this remote part of the kingdom?'

'I travelled from Rome to Gaul. In Gaul I searched the coastal ports for a ship that would take me directly to Muman so that my journey would be that much faster. That was when my luck deserted me. I managed to secure passage with a Gaulish merchant ship which was going to a Muman port where there were copper mines. The ship was going there to trade, as I was told.

'The captain of the merchant ship had a cargo to deliver and swore that when he had done so then he would take me to a place called Dún Garbhán from where I could secure a horse. From there, as I recall, it would have been an easy journey to Cashel. It presented no problem to me for I have spent some years studying in this land and knew vaguely the route . . .'

Fidelma knew well that Eadulf had studied both at the great ecclesiastical college of Durrow and at the medical college of Tuaim Brecain and spoke the Irish language fluently for even now this was their common tongue.

'But you said your luck deserted you. What happened?'

'I did not know what cargo was being taken on board. But I noticed that as well as the crew there were many Franks who came aboard. I was speaking with one of them who was quite garrulous. They were, it seems, soldiers but soldiers of fortune, prepared to sell their services.'

'Soldiers?' Fidelma raised an eyebrow. 'What would a Gaulish merchant ship be doing transporting Frankish soldiers to this corner of the five kingdoms?'

'That was also my reaction,' agreed Eadulf. 'My Frankish friend was quite boastful of the amount of money he and his friends would be getting. I think he was more open with me because I was a Saxon. It turned out that they were not ordinary soldiers. They were specially trained in the use of artillery.'

Fidelma looked blank. The word, not existing in Irish, Eadulf had used the Latin word *tormenta*.

'I do not understand military terms, Eadulf. Explain what this means. Surely a *tormentum* is an instrument for twisting or winding, a windlass, for example?'

'It is also a military engine for discharging missiles,' Eadulf explained. 'The ancient Romans used them quite a lot in their wars. The *ballistae* was an engine for throwing stones and boulders, so was the *catapulta*.'

Fidelma shuddered.

'Thank God such machines of destruction have never been used in Ireland. Here, when warriors fight, at least they stand and face each other with swords and shields, and often the battle has been resolved by single combat between one champion and another. Such machines are an abomination.' She paused and then looked closely at Eadulf as the implication of what he had said suddenly dawned on her. 'Do you mean . . . ?'

'Why import men trained in the art of using such machines as the *tormenta* unless they had those engines of destruction to work?'

'Did the cargo contain these machines?' Fidelma demanded.

'After the Frankish soldier had become so garrulous, I decided to go down into the hold of the ship and see for myself. The hold was crammed with all manner of such engines of war. The main pieces were *catapultae.*'

'What are they?'

'Special machines which are drawn by horses into battle. A *catapulta* consists of a great bow mounted on a box on wheels, rather like a cart. It can fire javelins a distance of five hundred yards.'

Fidelma now recollected the large skein of gut she had found in the hold of the ship.

'Is this large bow operated by gut?'

'Yes. The bow is strung with skeins of hair or gut. The skein is winched into place by large wooden washers and secured by a wooden pin. It can be further tightened by hand spokes fitted into holes in the edge of washers. The skein is tightened and javelins placed ready. Sometimes these can be set alight for maximum damage. The skein is released by a simple mechanism.'

'How many such machines did you see in the hold?'

'Perhaps twenty, certainly no less. And there were about sixty Franks on the ship.'

'What then?'

'I was interested, naturally. But it was none of my business at that time.'

'When did it become your business?' Fidelma caught his emphasis.

'As soon as we landed on this apparently hostile shore.'

'Explain.'

'The journey to the Irish coast was uneventful enough. We came into the harbour by the settlement. Then some young chieftain came aboard. I do not know who he was but he commanded the captain to unload. The Frankish soldiers disembarked and they oversaw the removal of their weapons. Under the eye of the warriors, slaves were brought aboard to do the heavy work of lifting the machines out of the hold.

They were a dirty-looking lot, covered in mud. I later discovered that they usually worked in the copper mines.'

He paused and after a moment or two, to collect his thoughts, resumed.

'Horses were provided on shore and they drew the engines away towards the caverns from where copper is excavated. Apparently the machines were to be hidden there. They are still there.'

'How do you know this?' asked Ross.

Eadulf allowed himself a bitter laugh.

'I discovered it by being a fool. No sooner were the Frankish soldiers and their machines taken off the ship than warriors came on board and seized the entire crew and myself. We were told by this same young chieftain that we were all hostages.'

Chapter Fifteen

'That defies all the laws of hospitality,' Ross burst out
indignantly. 'It is outrageous. If merchants can't trade
without fear of being made slaves then the world has come to
a sorry state.'

'Outrageous wasn't the word which the Gaulish captain
used,' Eadulf observed bitterly.

'Wasn't a resistance put up?' asked Fidelma.

'The surprise was total. While the young chieftain told
us that we were now all his hostages, slaves would have
been a better word. The crew were put to work in the
copper mines but as I was a religieux, I was treated with
more privileges than the others. I was taken to a cabin
where I found Sister Comnat. I was outraged to find her
manacled like an animal.'

Sister Comnat broke in for the first time since they had
begun to talk.

'Brother Eadulf is right. I had been their prisoner for
nearly three weeks and more. Thanks be to God that you
came, sister. I was hoping that Sister Almu had managed to
find someone to help us.'

Fidelma held the elderly woman's shaking hand com-
fortingly.

'It was not Sister Almu who warned us.'

'Then how did you come to find that place?'

'Again, it is a long story and, at this moment, I am more
concerned to know your story for much depends on my
knowing. I understand, Sister Comnat, that you and Sister

Almu set out from the abbey of The Salmon of the Three Wells three weeks ago. What happened?'

The old librarian hesitated.

'Do you know anything of Sister Almu's whereabouts?' she insisted.

Fidelma decided that she must be blunt.

'I believe that Sister Almu is dead. I am sorry.'

The old woman was clearly shocked. She swayed a little and Brother Eadulf reached forward a hand to steady her.

'You are among friends, good sister,' Brother Eadulf reassured her. 'This is an advocate of the courts. Fidelma of Kildare. I know her well. So do not be afraid. Tell her your story as you told it to me.'

The old woman managed to pull herself together though she was obviously distressed. She rubbed her forehead with a frail hand as if trying to dredge up the memory.

'Fidelma of Kildare? The Fidelma who solved the mystery of the deaths at Ros Ailithir?'

'Yes. I am Fidelma.'

'Then you are sister to Colgú, king of Cashel. You must warn your brother. Warn him immediately.' The old woman's voice was suddenly strident and Fidelma had to place a placating hand on hers.

'I do not understand. Of what must I warn him?'

'His kingdom stands in danger. He must be warned,' repeated Sister Comnat.

'Let me understand fully; what has happened since you and Sister Almu set out from the abbey?'

Sister Comnat gathered her wits and took a deep breath.

'Just over three weeks ago I set out with Sister Almu for the abbey of Ard Fhearta with a copy of a book which we had made for them. We reached as far as Gulban's fortress. We were thinking to rest there for the night. We received hospitality there but the next morning we perceived that there were countless warriors in training around the fort. Moreover, we saw many strange warriors among them.

256

'Sister Almu recognised Torcán of the Uí Fidgenti in the company of Gulban. We know that the Uí Fidgenti are no friends to the people of Loígde so we asked ourselves what could this mean. Almu found a young woman whom she had once known before she entered the abbey. This woman told us that Gulban had formed an alliance with Eoganán of the Uí Fidgenti.'

'An alliance? For what reason?' demanded Ross anxiously.

'It seemed that Gulban was angered at the decision of the assembly of the Loígde to elect Bran Finn, son of Mael Ochtraighe, as chieftain in the place of Salbach.'

'I know that Gulban argued that he should be made chieftain since Salbach had disgraced the office,' Fidelma said. 'I was there at that assembly.'

'Since Gulban did not get sufficient support from the assembly and Bran Finn is now chieftain, it seems that he is resorting to other means,' interposed Ross.

'Does he plan to launch an attack on Bran Finn with the help of the Uí Fidgenti?'

'Worse still,' Sister Comnat replied. 'The Uí Fidgenti princes are very powerful, as you may know. They plan to march on Cashel and overthrow Colgú, the king. In the lands of the Uí Fidgenti, there is an army gathering which Eoganán plans to lead in a direct assault on Cashel. If Colgú is overthrown, then doubtless Eoganán will reward Gulban by making him ruler of the Loígde and of all southern Muman.'

'Are you sure of this?' Fidelma was surprised at the duplicity of the Uí Fidgenti even though she knew full well their prince's long cherished ambition to seize control of Cashel.

'If I did not trust the mouth of the young woman, who had thought we were supporters of Gulban, and if I did not trust the evidence of my own eyes, having seen the warriors of Gulban being trained under the direction of Torcán of the Uí Fidgenti, then my own capture, and that of Almu, was enough to confirm the story.'

'How and why were you captured?'

'Sister Almu and I discussed what we had learned and wondered what best we should do. We are loyal to Bran Finn who, in turn, is loyal to Colgú of Cashel. We realised that we should warn them of this insurrection. But we were stupid for we roused the suspicion of Gulban's men by setting off back along the road which would return us to our abbey instead of travelling forward on the road to Ard Fhearta, which we had told them was our destination.'

'So Gulban made you both prisoners?'

'Gulban doubtless ordered the deed though we were not confronted by him. We were taken by his warriors to the copper mines where you found me. We were told that we could look after the spiritual and medical needs of the hostages working the mines until such time as Gulban further decided on our fate.'

Brother Eadulf intervened at this point.

'That is where I met the sister,' he repeated. 'It was a week after Sister Comnat's companion had escaped.'

'Do you know what Eoganán's plans are against Cashel?' Fidelma asked Sister Comnat.

'Not in the specific,' she replied with regret. 'Sister Almu and I were shackled at the end of each day, just as you found me. Sister Almu, being younger and more vigorous than I, decided that she would attempt to escape. I supported her decision and urged her to take whatever opportunity presented itself for her to escape. If she could return to the abbey and alert the community, that was the most important thing. My rescue could come later.'

'And she was able to escape?'

Sister Comnat gave a long sigh.

'Not at first. She made one attempt but was recaptured and flogged to ensure we all learnt a lesson. She was beaten on the back with a birch rod! Words are not adequate to describe that sacrilege. It took her several days to recover.'

Fidelma remembered the welts on the back of the corpse. She needed no further identification now.

'Ten days ago,' continued Sister Comnat, 'at the end of the work day, she did not return to the cabin where we were shackled for the night. I later heard that while she had been tending some of the sick, she had, apparently, disappeared – she had escaped into the woods. There was a great furore. However, I believe that she had help in this escape for she told me that she had now made friends with a young man of the Uí Fidgenti who was in a position to help her.'

'That might imply that he had some authority among them,' Fidelma observed cautiously. 'You had no warning that she was going to make an attempted escape?'

'A sort of warning, I think.'

'A sort of warning?'

'Yes. As she left that morning she smiled at me and said something to the effect that she was going to hunt wild boar. I can't quite remember exactly what she said. It didn't make sense.'

'Wild boar?' Fidelma was perplexed.

'Anyway, she did not return. I was told that the guards did not even bother to send out search parties after her. Each day I prayed for the success of her escape, although a rumour was spread that she had probably perished on the mountains. Yet I hoped. I hoped for the coming of a rescue party.' The old woman paused for a moment: then continued: 'Then, alas, more prisoners arrived, Gauls, and also this Saxon monk, Eadulf, who speaks our tongue so well.'

'What Sister Comnat says makes sense of what happened to me,' Eadulf added. 'The capture of the Gaulish ship with the *tormenta* aboard, that is. I judge these were arms bought by Gulban on behalf of the Uí Fidgenti.'

'Weapons to help Eoganán overthrow Cashel?' queried Ross, wide-eyed.

'They are good siege weapons,' Eadulf confirmed.

'A score of these terrible engines of destruction, together

with warriors from Frankia trained in their use,' muttered Ross, 'would rain terror on Cashel. I see it. Such weapons have never been seen or used in the five kingdoms before. Our warriors fight face to face, sword, spear and shield. But with these weapons Eoganán or Gulban thinks to take an advantage.'

'Could the Franks and their *tormenta* really have such an advantage?' asked Eadulf. 'These weapons are well known among the Saxon kingdoms and in Frankia and elsewhere.'

'I have been a merchant for many years,' replied Ross, solemnly, 'but when the fiery cross has been sent out by the king of Cashel, I have answered. I was a young man when I fought at the battle of Carn Conaill during the feast of Pentecost. I don't suppose you recall that, Fidelma? No? It was when Guaire Aidne of Connacht tried to overthrow the High King, Dairmait Mac Aedo Sláine. Naturally, Cúan, son of Almalgaid, the king of Cashel, led the host of Muman, in support of the High King. But his namesake Cúan, son of Conall, the prince of the Uí Fidgenti, supported Guaire. The Uí Fidgenti were perverse even then, always looking for a short cut to power. That was a bloody battle. Both Cúans were slaughtered. But Guaire ran away from the battlefield and the High King was victorious. That was my first taste of bloody warfare. Thanks be to God, it was my last battle.'

Fidelma was trying to keep her patience.

'What has this to do with the *tormenta*?' she challenged.

'Easy to see,' replied Ross. 'I have seen slaughter. I know the damage that could be inflicted with such machines. Warriors could be slaughtered in their hundreds and Cashel would have no defence. The fortifications of Cashel itself could be breached. The range of such machines of destruction is, as the Saxon says, over five hundred yards. I know from what I have heard while trading in Gaul, such engines of war made the Romans almost invincible.'

Fidelma regarded them all sombrely.

'So that is why the importation of these weapons had to be

kept a secret. Gulban and Eoganán of the Uí Fidgenti plan to use them as a secret weapon, doubtless to spearhead a surprise attack on Cashel.'

'It all makes sense now,' Eadulf sighed. 'And explains why, as soon as the weapons and the Franks were landed, the men of this Gulban seized the Gaulish ship and its crew, and me, too, as the only passenger. It was a means of preventing any news of that cargo reaching outside of this place. It was a bad day that I took passage in that ship.'

'Tell me how the Gaulish captain escaped,' Fidelma suddenly invited.

'How did you know about that?' queried Eadulf. 'I was about to tell you of that.'

'Again it is part of a long story but suffice to say we discovered the Gaulish ship.'

'I spoke to some people who had seen a Gaulish prisoner on board,' Ross explained. 'They told me that he had escaped and the ship had vanished while the Uí Fidgenti warriors were ashore.'

Fidelma motioned him to be silent.

'Let Eadulf tell his story.'

'Very well,' Eadulf began. 'A few days ago the captain and two of his sailors managed to escape from the mines. They took a small boat and headed towards an island off shore . . .'

'Dóirse,' interrupted Ross.

'The Gaulish merchant ship was still in the harbour. Some of the guards set out in pursuit using the ship. They raised the sails and chased after the smaller vessel. They returned a day later without either the ship or the three Gauls.'

'Do you know what happened?'

Eadulf shrugged.

'There was some gossip among the prisoners which I picked up while attending to them . . . that is if gossip is to be credited. It was said that the warriors had chased and sunk the small boat, killing two of the Gaulish sailors. The captain was rescued and taken prisoner. It being nearly dark by that time, the warriors put in at the small island harbour. Everyone went ashore to enjoy the hospitality of the local chieftain: That is, with the exception of a warrior and the Gaulish captain. During the night, the Gaul managed to escape again. I think they said that he killed the warrior left on board to guard him. He managed, single-handed, to raise sail and make off into the night. He was a good sailor. I had hoped that he had managed to organise a rescue party for his men.' Eadulf paused as he remembered. 'But you said that you found him and his ship?'

Fidelma made a negative gesture.

'Not him, Eadulf. He didn't survive. We encountered the merchant ship under sail the next morning but with no one aboard.'

'No one? Then what happened?'

'I think I now know that mystery,' Fidelma said quietly. Ross and Odar were leaning forward with eyes straining in eagerness, awaiting her solution to the puzzle that had mystified them these last several days.

'Can you really explain?' asked Ross.

'I can hypothesise and be fairly certain that my account is accurate. This Gaulish captain was a brave man. Did you ever know his name, Eadulf?'

'Waroc was his name,' Eadulf supplied.

'Waroc was a brave man then,' Fidelma repeated. 'Well, he escaped from the island of Dóirse where the ship was moored. We know that part of the story from the information which Ross gathered there, and which fits into your tale, Eadulf. Waroc, having escaped his captors again, decided that he would attempt to sail his ship single-handed. A brave but foolhardy adventure. Perhaps he thought only to move it along the coast to a friendly port and raise assistance.'

'How did he do it?'

'He cut the mooring ropes with an axe. We saw the severed ropes when we came upon the ship.'

Odar nodded grimly as he remembered pointing out the severed ropes to Ross and Fidelma.

'Then he probably let the tide drift him out of the sound,' Ross said, knowing the waters there.

'He managed to raise his main sail,' continued Fidelma. 'The most difficult sail to raise was the tops'l. We cannot be sure whether he was hurt or not by his captors or during his escapes or even by his efforts to raise the sails single-handed. However, he went aloft and almost succeeded in raising it into place. Perhaps the ship lurched, perhaps there was a gust of wind, or he may have lost his footing. Who can say? But Waroc fell. A spar or a nail ripped his shirt and perhaps his flesh. We found a blood-stained strip of linen on the rigging. We also found blood on the rigging itself. As he fell, he made one desperate attempt to clutch at something. His hand caught the rail of the ship. A blood-stained hand print was there. Then, unable to keep his hold, he went over the side. He could not have lasted long in those winter waters. Perhaps he was dead in moments.'

There was an uneasy silence for a moment or two before Fidelma concluded.

'It was later that morning that Ross's *barc* came close to the merchant ship being blown hither and thither in the currents. Ross is an excellent sailor and was able to trace the tides and winds. I was determined to find you, Eadulf.'

Eadulf looked surprised.

'You were on this *barc*?'

'I had been asked to go to Sister Comnat's abbey to investigate the discovery of a corpse.'

'But how did you know I was on the ship? Ah!' A look of understanding came into his eyes. 'You found my book satchel in the cabin where I left it?'

'I have your Missal safely,' confirmed Fidelma. 'It is at Sister Comnat's abbey which is not far from here. And we must reach it before dawn, otherwise questions will be asked.'

Sister Comnat was examining Fidelma anxiously.

'You mentioned a corpse? You said that Sister Almu had not successfully escaped ... You said that she was dead.'

Fidelma reached forward a hand and gently pressed the arm of the elderly religieuse again in comfort.

'I do not know for sure, sister, but I am fairly convinced that the corpse discovered over a week or so ago is that of Sister Almu.'

'But someone must have recognised the corpse?'

Fidelma did not want to cause the sister further grief but it was no use keeping the truth from her.

'The corpse was decapitated. The head was missing. It was that of a young girl, barely eighteen. There were ink stains on the right hand, on thumb, index finger and along the little finger which tells me that she worked as a copyist or in a library. There were also signs that she had recently worn a manacle and had been scourged on the back.'

Sister Comnat caught her breath.

'Then it is poor Almu but ... where was the body discovered?'

'In the main well of the abbey.'

'I do not understand. If she was caught by Gulban's men or anyone of the Uí Fidgenti why would they draw attention to the matter by placing her in the abbey's well?'

Fidelma smiled tightly.

'That is a mystery that I have still to sort out.'

'We must make a plan,' interposed Ross. 'It will not be long to daylight and as soon as Sister Comnat and the Saxon are found missing there will be search parties sent out.'

'You are right, Ross,' Fidelma agreed. 'One of us must sail to Ros Ailithir and alert Bran Finn and my brother. Some warriors must be sent here so that these infernal engines – the *tormenta* as Eadulf calls them – can be destroyed before they can be used against Cashel.'

'We should all go. The abbey is no safe place now,' replied

Ross. 'If Adnár suspects something, you will not be safe. Adnár holds the fortress opposite the abbey,' he explained for Eadulf's sake, 'and, at the moment, his guests are Gulban's son Olcán, and Torcán of the Uí Fidgenti.'

Eadulf whistled softly.

'That does not augur well.'

'And Adnár, if he is involved in this conspiracy, may have accomplices in the abbey itself,' added Fidelma meditatively.

'So we should all get to my *barc* and head for Ros Ailithir. We can be there by tomorrow evening.'

'No, Ross. You will take Sister Comnat and sail immediately for Ros Ailithir to inform Abbot Brocc. Sister Comnat will be your witness. Messengers must also be sent to my brother at Cashel in order that he may prepare for any Uí Fidgenti attack. At the same time, ask Bran Finn to send warriors to the copper mines as soon as possible so that the *tormenta* may be destroyed and the Frankish mercenaries captured before they can set off for Cashel.'

'And what about us?' Eadulf asked.

'I must return to the abbey, otherwise it will be realised that the plot is uncovered and Gulban's men may act that more quickly against Cashel. Because of this, the Gaulish ship must remain where it is, otherwise its disappearance would also alert our enemies. As for you, Eadulf, you will go with Odar. Odar and a few of Ross's men have been acting as a skeletal crew on board the Gaulish ship. You will hide on board. Odar and his men will act as an escape route in case I am discovered.'

'What if they suspect you, already? They know that you are Colgú's sister,' protested Ross. 'They may take you for a hostage.'

'It is a chance that I have to take,' Fidelma replied determinedly. 'There is another mystery here as well as this plot to overthrow Cashel. I must stay and see it through. If all goes well, Ross, you could return within three days.'

'And who guarantees your safety for these three days,

Fidelma?' demanded Eadulf. 'If you stay at the abbey, I should also stay there.'

'Impossible!'

But Ross was nodding in agreement.

'The Saxon is right, sister,' he offered. 'Someone should stay and keep close to you.'

'Impossible!' repeated Fidelma. 'Once Sister Comnat and Eadulf's escape is noticed, someone will think of looking for them at the abbey. Eadulf will stand out like a sore thumb. No, Eadulf will stay on board the Gaulish ship with Odar.'

'But surely that is equally as dangerous,' Odar objected. 'Once Uí Fidgenti know where the Gaulish ship is, they will come to reclaim it.'

'They have known where it was for some days now,' Fidelma pointed out. 'The Gaulish ship was probably recognised as soon as Ross sailed it into the Dún Boí inlet. That was probably why Adnár tried to claim salvage rights on it. It was a method of recovering it without attracting attention. I think it suits our enemy's purpose to allow it to anchor off Dún Boí for the moment. The Gaulish ship will be the last place that they will think of looking for you, Eadulf. I will arrange a system of signals to let Odar and you know if there are difficulties.'

'A good idea,' Odar finally gave his slow and deliberate opinion. 'If there is any trouble, you must signal, sister, or make your way to the ship so that we may sail if danger threatens.'

'I still cannot see why you must remain at the abbey?' Eadulf objected.

'I have my oath as a *dálaigh* to fulfil,' Fidelma explained. 'There is some evil at the abbey that I must resolve. An evil which I believe is unconnected with what is happening here, something which is above the desire for political power. There have been two deaths at the abbey which need to be resolved.'

Sister Comnat let forth a soft moan.

'Another death, one apart from poor Sister Almu? Who else has perished at the abbey, sister?'

'Sister Síomha, the *rechtaire*.'

Sister Comnat's eyes widened.

'Sister Almu's friend? She is also dead?'

'And slain in the same manner. There is something that is malignant there and I must destroy it.'

'Wouldn't it better to wait until Ross returns with help?' Eadulf suggested. 'Then you can pursue your investigation without fear of an assassin or worse.'

Fidelma smiled at the Saxon monk.

'No; I must work while there is no suspicion that the plot has been discovered. For, if I am wrong, and there is some involvement, then my quarry might well flee before I can resolve these crimes.'

Sister Comnat was shaking her head.

'I have no understanding of this.'

'No need. We must now be on our way, and you must tell Abbot Brocc at Ros Ailithir and Bran Finn, chieftain of the Loígde, all that you know of the events here.'

Fidelma stood up and helped the elderly sister to her feet. She could see that Ross kept peering at the sky and was clearly in some agitation at the approaching onset of the dawn.

'Calm yourself, Ross,' she admonished with humour. 'Horace in his *Odes* adjures *aequam memento rebus in arduis servare mentem* – maintain a clear head when attempting difficult tasks. Take the good sister to your *barc*. I shall expect to see you back here within three days.' She glanced at Odar. 'When you have seen Eadulf safely aboard the Gaulish ship, make sure that you return the horses. We do not want Barr coming in search of them and alerting Adnár.'

She swung up on her own steed. They set off at a swift canter just as the eastern sky was beginning to dissolve into lighter shades along the horizon.

Chapter Sixteen

Sister Fidelma groaned as she felt herself being pulled bodily out of a warm, dark, womb-like cocoon into the harsh cold and grey of the light. Sister Brónach was bending over her and shaking her by the shoulder.

'You are oversleeping, sister. It is late,' Sister Brónach cajoled.

Fidelma blinked rapidly, her heart beating fast. It took her a few moments to remember where she was. Then she realised that she had slunk back into the abbey, into the guests' hostel, just as dawn was coming up. She had left the others in the woods behind the abbey to depart to their appointed tasks, walking the short distance in the bitterly cold, frosty pre-dawn, into the abbey complex. She had been exhausted, throwing off her clothes and tumbling into her cot. It seemed but a moment ago. It was actually barely two hours ago, or so she judged by the light at the window.

For a moment, she wondered whether she should tell Sister Brónach that she wanted to sleep on. Perhaps she could claim that she felt ill? But Sister Brónach was standing watching her with disapproval and she did not want to raise any suspicion that she had been out all night. She climbed unwillingly from the warm bed. It was very cold and she noticed there were lumps of ice in the hand bowl awaiting her morning ablutions. She was aware of Sister Brónach watching her as she began to wash.

'There is a young warrior waiting to see you,' Sister Brónach finally said with disapproval.

Fidelma felt the nape of her neck tingle.

'Oh? Do you know who he is?' she asked, swinging round from the bowl and reaching for the towel.

'Yes, I know him. It is young Olcán, the son of the chieftain of the Beara.'

Fidelma felt her jaw set automatically.

So! Had the warriors at the copper mine alerted Olcán of the escape of Comnat and Eadulf already?

'Tell him that I shall be with him shortly,' Fidelma said as she bent to continue her morning wash. Sister Brónach left. Fidelma splashed herself feeling desperately tired and wishing she could crawl back into her warm, comfortable bed. She resisted the impulse, trying to force herself to look as though she had spent the night in deep relaxing sleep.

Ten minutes later she found Olcán seated in the *duirthech*, the oak chapel of the abbey. The fire was alight in the brazier at the back of the chapel and this seemed the only place of warmth outside of the forbidden confines of the domains of the community where visitors could shelter from the elements.

'A good morning to you, sister,' Olcán rose. He seemed bright and smiling. 'I understand that you overslept?'

Fidelma wished Sister Brónach would have been more circumspect with her information.

'The feast that Adnár prepared last evening was a pleasant one,' she countered. 'The excellent wine and good food is not everyday fare for me. I fear I indulged too freely of its richness.'

'Yet you left early,' Olcán remarked.

Fidelma kept her face straight, trying to deduce whether there was any innuendo in the young man's tone.

'Early for you but not for one of the Faith,' she replied. 'It was midnight as I came to the abbey.'

'And now it is well after the eighth hour,' Olcán said, rising and stretching himself before the brazier. He strode to one of

the windows of the chapel which gave a view across the inlet.
'I see Ross's *barc* has sailed again. It must have gone on the
early morning tide.'

Was Olcán playing some subtle game with her? She could
not see where his remarks were leading.

She crossed to join him and looked out across the bay.
Only the Gaulish merchant ship, with its tall masts,
was riding at anchor on the calm blue waters. Silently,
she breathed a sigh of relief that Ross had departed
unnoticed.

'So it has,' she said, as if it were news to her.

Olcán glanced searchingly at her.

'You did not know that he was leaving?' The question was
sudden and spoken sharply.

'Ross does not confide his business in me. I know he trades
along this coast regularly. I presume he will return eventually. He has not only left some of his crew here to look after
the ship he claims as salvage,' she indicated the merchant
ship, 'but he is to transport me back to Ros Ailithir when I
have concluded my investigation.'

'And is this investigation concluded?'

'As I said, last night, there is still much to learn and much
to consider.'

'Ah? I thought that there might have been some developments.'

Fidelma managed to look at him with a bewildered
expression.

'Some developments? Since I left the feast last night? No
one has awakened me to inform me of any developments.'

'I meant . . .' Olcán hesitated and then shrugged. 'I meant
nothing. It was just an idea.'

He hesitated awkwardly.

'Sister Brónach said that you wanted to see me,' Fidelma
now pressed her advantage. 'I presume that it was something
other than to see if I had slept well and to inform me that
Ross's ship had gone?'

Olcán looked confused for a moment at the slight sarcasm in her voice.

'Oh, it was just that Torcán and I are going hunting. We wondered whether you might join us for you said, when first we met, you would like to see some of the ancient sites of this peninsula and we will be passing some fascinating spots.'

Fidelma kept her features solemn. It was obvious that this excuse had only just occurred to Olcán.

'I thank you for the idea. Today I have to continue my inquiries here.'

'Then, if you will forgive me, sister, I will rejoin Torcán and set off. Adnár's master huntsman has spotted a small herd of deer on the mountain to the west.'

Fidelma watched the young man pulling his cloak around him as he strode out of the chapel. She followed him to the door and studied his retreating figure as he walked across the courtyard and through the buildings. A moment later, she saw him mounted on a horse, riding swiftly off through the woods in the direction of Adnár's fortress.

It was clear to her what Olcán's purpose had been.

She hurried back to the guests' hostel and found Sister Brónach.

'I am sorry that I overslept, sister,' she greeted. 'I feasted with Adnár last night. Is there a possibility that there is something with which I might break my fast for I have missed the call to the refectory.'

Sister Brónach regarded her with curiosity for a moment.

'A long feast it must have been,' she observed slyly, turning into the common room of the guests' hostel. 'I have already laid a platter for you, sister, realising that you had missed the first meal of the day.'

Fidelma slid gratefully into a chair. Dishes with some hardboiled goose eggs, some leaven bread and honey were placed before her with a small jug of mead. Fidelma was helping herself when she suddenly realised the meaning of Sister Brónach's remark and she glanced at the mournful-faced sister questioningly.

Sister Brónach almost smiled as she answered the unasked question.

'I have been too long in charge of this guests' hostel not to know the comings and goings of the guests.'

'I see,' Fidelma was reflective.

'However,' continued the doorkeeper of the abbey, 'it is not my position to question the hours our guests keep so long as they do not interfere with the running of this community.'

'Sister Brónach, you know why I am here. It is essential that my absence from the abbey is not generally known. Do I have your word on this?'

The middle-aged *doirseór* of the abbey grimaced almost disdainfully.

'I have said as much.'

After breakfast, Fidelma made her way towards the library. On the way she met the Abbess Draigen who greeted her with disapproval.

'You seem no nearer to solving this mystery than when you first arrived,' the abbess opened in a sneering tone.

Fidelma did not rise to the bait.

'On the contrary, mother abbess,' she replied, brightly, 'I think much progress has been made.'

'Progress? Another murder has been committed, that of Sister Síomha, while you were investigating. Is that progress? It seems to be remarkably akin to incompetence so far as I judge.'

'Do you know much of the history of this abbey?' Fidelma asked, ignoring the thrust.

Abbess Draigen looked a little disconcerted.

'What has the history of the abbey to do with your investigation?'

'Do you know of the history?' insisted Fidelma, ignoring her counter question.

'Sister Comnat would have been able to tell you, if she were here,' replied the abbess. 'The abbey was formed a century ago by the Blessed Necht the Pure.'

'That much I have heard. How did she come to choose this spot?'

Abbess Draigen raised a hand to encompass the abbey buildings.

'Is it not as beautiful a spot as any to set up a foundation to the new Faith?'

'Indeed it is. But I have heard that the wells here were used by the pagan priests.'

'Necht blessed and purified them.'

'So this was a spot actually dedicated to the old faith before it became Christian?'

'Yes. The story is that Necht came here and debated the doctrine of Christ with Dedelchú, chieftain of the pagans who lived here in the caves.'

'Dedelchú?'

'So the story is handed down to us.'

'Do you know why Necht called this abbey that of The Salmon of the Three Wells?'

'You should know that "The Salmon of the Three Wells" is a euphemism for the Christ.'

'But there are also three wells here.'

'That is so. A pleasing coincidence.'

'In pagan times some of the ancient wells were claimed to have a salmon of knowledge dwelling at the bottom.'

Abbess Draigen merely shrugged.

'I cannot see why you are so interested in ancient beliefs. But it is well known that the "Salmon of Knowledge" was a powerful image in ancient belief. It could well be why we hail the Christ as The Salmon of the Three Wells, expressing him as part of the trinity but fountain of knowledge. Surely that is not a matter to get us any further along the road to finding the person who is culpable of the murders committed here?'

Fidelma's expression was bland.

'Perhaps. Thank you, mother abbess.'

She continued on her way to the tower library, leaving the abbess staring in bewilderment after her.

'Sister Fidelma!'

The tone of the voice was soft but urgent. For a moment Fidelma could not place it and turned to identify its owner. A slim figure was standing in the doorway of the stone-built store room next to the tower. It was Sister Lerben.

Fidelma left the path and crossed towards her.

'Good morning, sister.'

Sister Lerben motioned Fidelma to come inside as if she did not want to be seen talking with her. Fidelma frowned but obeyed the urgent gesture. Inside the store room, Sister Lerben seemed to be sorting some herbs with the aid of a lantern. While the day outside was cloudy but bright, inside it was dark and gloomy.

'What can I do for you, sister?' Fidelma prompted.

'Yesterday you asked me questions...' began Sister Lerben. She paused but Fidelma did not make any attempt to coax her further. 'Yesterday I said some things about ... about Febal, my father.'

Fidelma returned her gaze steadily.

'You wish to retract them?' she asked.

'No!'

There was a harsh vehemence in the word.

'Very well. What then?'

'Does it have to be reported anywhere? Abbess Draigen has ... has now explained about the function of a *dálaigh*. She says that ... well, I would not like it to come out that, well ... what I said about the farmer and my father.'

Clearly the girl was in some emotional turmoil over the matter. Fidelma relented.

'If the matter is of no relevance to my investigation of the deaths of Almu and Síomha, then it does not have to come out.'

'If it is of no relevance? How will you know?'

274

'When I have completed my inquiries. Speaking of which, it was surprising to find you in the wood the other day taking a book to Torcán at Adnár's fortress. Were you not afraid that you might meet your father, Febal?'

'Him?' The voice assumed its sharpness again. 'No. I am not longer afraid of him. Not any more.'

'How do you know Torcán?'

'I have never met him.'

Fidelma registered some surprise.

'How, then, were you taking this book, what was it now . . . ?'

Sister Lerben shrugged.

'Some old chronicle, I think. I do not know. I told you, I am not proficient in reading or writing.'

'Yes, you did mention that. So you were, in fact, given this book to take to Torcán?'

'Yes.'

'Who gave you the book? I thought only the librarian would be able to give permission to remove a book from the abbey library.'

Sister Lerben shook her head.

'No, the *rechtaire* has authority.'

'The *rechtaire*?'

'Yes, it was Sister Síomha who handed me the book and asked me to take it to the fortress of Adnár and hand it to Torcán.'

'Sister Síomha! And that was during the afternoon before her death?'

'I think so.'

'Did she explain why Torcán was being allowed to borrow this book instead of coming to the abbey to look at it?'

'She did not. She simply told me to take it to him and return. That is all.'

Fidelma had a feeling of tremendous frustration. Every time she thought she was about to clear up a point, then several more questions rose to confuse her mind. She thanked Sister Lerben and left the store house, entering the tower.

It was dark inside the main library room and Fidelma peered in vain for a lamp in the gloom.

She was feeling her way to the foot of the steps leading to the second floor when she heard a sound like someone dragging a sack across the floor above her head.

She paused a moment and then moved cautiously upwards one step at a time, listening.

The dragging sound came again.

Fidelma's head reached the level of the floor and peered upwards.

Someone was seated by the light of the window peering at a book.

Fidelma heaved a sigh of relief.

It was Sister Berrach. The sound that she had heard had been the disabled sister moving across the floor.

'Good morning, Sister Berrach!' Fidelma climbed into the room.

The young sister was startled and almost dropped the book she had been looking at.

'Oh, it's you, Sister Fidelma.'

'What are you doing here?'

Berrach's chin came up a little defensively.

'I told you that I enjoyed reading. With Sister Comnat and Sister Almu not returned to the abbey, and Sister Síomha not here to tell me what to do, I no longer have to sneak here at night to do my reading.'

Fidelma seated herself beside Berrach.

'I, too, have come to do some reading but I could not find a lamp below.'

'There are some candles here,' Berrach indicated a table. 'Do you want a particular book?'

'I was going to look for one of the annals that I am told are kept here. But what are you reading?' Fidelma lent across and glanced at the text.

'*Eó na dTrí dTobar* ... The Salmon of the Three Wells!'
Fidelma was somewhat taken aback by the coincidence.
'What text is that?'

'A short account of the life of the Necht the Pure who
founded this abbey,' replied Sister Berrach.

'And does it mention her discourse with Dedelchú, the
pagan priest?'

Sister Berrach started in surprise.

'You know a lot about this place. I have lived here all my
life and am only just reading this book.'

'One picks up things here and there, Berrach. Does the
book explain much about Dedelchú? It is an odd name. The
last element is simple to recognise meaning "hound of" – the
hound of Dedel. I wonder who or what the original Dedel
was? I am fascinated by the meaning of these old names,
aren't you?'

Sister Berrach shook her head.

'Not particularly. I am more interested in history, in the
lives of people. But we do have a copy of the *Glossary of
Longarad* in the library.'

'Is that so? So you have read some of the annals?'

Berrach conceded that she had.

'I have read through all the annals that have been placed in
this library.'

'Do you known the annals of Clonmacnoise?'

'Know it? yes. Sister Comnat herself made that copy. She
spent six months away at the abbey of the Blessed Ciarán and
copied the book with the full permission of the abbot. You
will find it on the shelves here.'

'It is no longer at the abbey. It was loaned, according to
Sister Lerben, to Torcán, who is a guest of Adnár.'

'Torcán, son of Eoganán of the Uí Fidgenti?' Sister
Berrach looked bewildered. 'What would he want with
it?'

'I was hoping I might find out. I think he was particularly
interested in the story of Cormac Mac Art. There was a page

which had been much consulted. It was an entry to do with the death of Cormac Mac Art. I do not suppose you would know what was written there?'

Berrach frowned reflectively.

'I have a gift for memory. My retentive mind is quite clear.' She paused and thought carefully. 'The entry spoke of how Cormac slew his enemy Fergus and became a wise and virtuous High King. It spoke of his writing his book of instructions and . . .' She paused a moment. 'Ah yes; it went on to speak of how a gold calf had been set up in Tara and a cult had developed about it, turning it into a god to be worshipped. The priests of this cult called upon Cormac to come and worship the gold image but he refused saying he would sooner worship the goldsmith who had made so beautiful an image. The entry said that the chief priest of this cult then contrived to make salmon bones stick fast in the High King's throat during a meal so that Cormac was induced to die.'

Fidelma was fascinated at the effortless ease with which Sister Berrach recalled the passage.

'Do you know anything more about that story?'

The young religieuse shook her head.

'Only that it was symbolic, I believe. I mean, the story about the pagan priest being able to kill Cormac by three salmon bones.'

'*Three* salmon bones?' asked Fidelma quickly. 'What symbolism do you read into that?'

'I think it was probably meant as an indication of the identity of the pagan priest. Cormac may have been murdered but there was no means of deliberately causing three salmon bones to stick in a person's gullet unless you accept such a thing as evil magic.' Berrach smiled ruefully. 'And I think you helped to persuade the community here that such things as witchcraft and magic did not exist.'

'What else is known of this cult of the gold calf?'

'Little enough. The entry in the annals of Clonmacnoise is,

so far as I know, the only reference to the creation and worship of this idol, this great golden calf. I have read several other annals but no one else mentions the cult of the golden calf. Why,' she added, 'if such a fabulous idol existed, it must have been worth a great fortune.'

There was a soft scuffle on the stair. It was faint but Fidelma caught it and turned sharply, motioning Sister Berrach to silence. She was about to move across to the stairway when the head and shoulders of Sister Brónach appeared. In spite of the semi-gloom, Fidelma could see that she wore a sheepish expression.

'I am sorry to disturb you. I was on my way to the clepsydra.'

Fidelma felt that it was an excuse hurriedly invented but Sister Berrach did not seem to notice anything out of place. She smiled happily at Sister Brónach who continued her way on to the next floor. Fidelma turned back to Berrach and resumed her conversation.

'If I remember correctly, King Cormac died nearly four hundred years ago, is that right?'

'That is right.'

'Can you remember anything else about Cormac and this golden calf?'

Sister Berrach shook her head.

'No, but I know that Sister Comnat recently bought a copy of Cormac's instructions from a beggar. The book called the *Teagasg Rí*, Instructions of the King. An old man who lived up in the mountains here came to the abbey one day and told Comnat that his family had kept the copy for a long while but wanted to exchange it for food. I was passing by and heard the conversation. If you are interested in Cormac then it is worthwhile reading. It is in the library.'

Fidelma did not reply that she already knew that Cormac's book of instructions was in the library and, indeed, she had glanced through the copy which, as she recalled, had been soiled with red mud.

'When did that transaction take place?'

'Not long ago. About a week before Sister Comnat and Sister Almu left on their journey to Ard Fhearta.'

Fidelma stood up, took a candle and lit it.

'Thank you, Sister Berrach. I'll go to look for that book now. You've been a great help.'

The Instructions of Cormac, *Teagasg Rí*, was hanging in its book satchel from a peg. She took it out and looked round for a seat. Placing the candle on a ledge nearby she opened it and began to turn the vellum pages. Once more she observed the strange brown red mud stains over the book. But the book was slightly different to the last time she had glanced through it. She wished she had paid more attention to it then. She realised that two vellum pages were now missing. It was clear that they had been cut recently with a sharp blade, presumably a knife, for the next page was scored where the line had been cut.

Why had these pages been removed?

She examined the text carefully.

The section was nothing to do with the main part of the book which was the actual philosophies of King Cormac. This was an addition to the book which was an essay about the life of the High King. She could decipher nothing by looking at the preceding and proceeding pages. She turned to the opening page, seeking some other information.

The book was an old one. The style was crude enough. It had not been written by a trained scribe, of that she was certain. The main work was clearly copied, which was not surprising, but the little biography of Cormac was something new to her and seemed provincial in attitude. She wished now that Sister Comnat had remained on the Gaulish ship with Brother Eadulf. She would have been able to consult with her about the missing pages.

Eadulf! She suddenly realised that she had not even thought about him since she had dragged her tired body into her bed early that morning. She felt a momentary pleasure that he was alive, safe and well. Then, as her mind turned to her escapade of the previous night, she suddenly felt exhausted. She would have to give way to sleep for a short time.

She stood up and returned the book into the leather satchel and yawned, feeling a bone in her jaw crack in protest. She rubbed the tender spot for a moment. Then she took up the candle and was about to blow it out. Then she remembered the word 'Dedal' and found Longarad's *Glossary*. She was not surprised when she saw what the definition of the word was.

Another thought struck her.

Stifling a second yawn, she took the candle, shielding it from the draught, and, leaving the library, made her way down the stairway in the corner. Pausing halfway down she saw that the blood was dried on the side of the passage. There was little doubt in her mind that it was Síomha's blood. Had the sister been killed below in the *subterraneus* and carried up into the tower or killed in the tower and her head carried...?

She descended on into the depths. She paused again. There it was, the vaulted entrance and the scratch marks over it. She reached up a hand and allowed a finger to trace the outline of the primitive animal. Then she sighed.

'Dedelchú!' she whispered to herself. 'The hound of Dedel.'

She passed through the entrance into the vaulted cave and examined it carefully in the flickering light of the lantern.

The place where the corpse had been laid no longer had the four candles around it. It was a flat, oblong rock which the sisters apparently used as some sort of table. Starting on the right side, Fidelma began to walk carefully around the walls of the cave examining everything as painstakingly as she was able in the flickering faint light. There was little to examine. The only contents of the cave were the large boxes piled on top of each other at one side of the cave and the row of *amphorae* and other containers with their odour of wines and spirits.

A close search of the cave revealed nothing more than that it was a large cave with only the two entrances: one by the stairs from the stone store house; the other by the stairs directly from the tower. She stood to one side and gazed into the gloom with frustration. She was about to turn to leave when a sudden sound caused her to start and the candle go jumping in her hand.

It was a hollow, booming sound. Like the sound of two wooden ships knocking together.

It seemed to echo from just behind her. But there was nothing behind her but solid grey stone – the stone of the cave walls. She turned, her mind working rapidly as she stared at the solid rocks seeking some clue. Then again, there came the hollow boom as if two vessels were banging together. She placed a hand against the cold, damp rock and waited. There was nothing but silence.

She was about to turn away when she noticed a dark patch on the rocky floor. She bent down and found it was earth. Still damp and cloying. It was red brown. She saw that it was in irregular patches as if someone had trodden in the muddy earth and then proceeded to walk through the cave. She followed the trail away from the direction of the entrance, as the only logical path to take, and came up against the wooden boxes stacked against a wall.

She set down her candle and began to push at the top box but she did not have the strength required to move it. It was then that the hollow, booming sound echoed again. It seemed to resonate through the boxes. Then there was silence once again.

Chapter Seventeen

It was dark when Fidelma awoke on her cot. For a while she was disorientated. Then she remembered that she had returned to the guests' hostel after her fruitless exploration of the cave beneath the abbey and, overcome with sheer fatigue, had gone to her cell, climbed on the bed and had fallen asleep immediately. She glanced through the window. While it was not night, the gloom was the dark of an early winter evening. She assessed that it was still well before the time of the evening Angelus. She splashed her face in the cold water bowl and dried herself. Having slept in her clothes she felt decidedly chilly and stretched and moved her arms to warm her body. She felt hungry. With annoyance she realised that she had now missed the midday meal.

She went out into the candle-lit passage and made her way along to the main room, hoping that no one had noticed her absence. To her surprise she saw a cloth covering some familiar objects on the table and, raising it, saw some food had been placed there.

Sister Brónach!

There was no hiding anything from the *doirseór* of the abbey, Fidelma reflected. That made her uneasy. Sister Brónach knew that she had been out all the previous night; knew, then, that she had lain in an exhausted sleep most of the daylight hours to recuperate. If Sister Brónach was an innocent party to the planned uprising against Cashel, if she was loyal to Cashel, then there was no cause for alarm. But Fidelma was unsure if anyone in this land of the Beara could be wholly trusted. After all, everyone would nominally support their chieftain Gulban.

She sat down and relieved her hunger from the dishes that Sister Brónach had left. Then, feeling better for her rest and food, she left the guests' hostel just as she heard the gong sounding the hour followed by the bell summoning the community to the evening prayers. It had not taken long for the abbey to get the clepsydra back in proper order, she reflected. That was probably due to Sister Brónach. It would now surely take a brave spirit to stand watch during the night hours in the tower after the death of Sister Síomha.

Fidelma pressed back into the shadows as groups of sisters and one or two isolated figures moved rapidly towards the *duirthech*, in answer to the summons of the bell. She made the movement to conceal herself automatically and it was only after a moment or so that the idea struck her. She would use this time to sneak away to the Gaulish ship and seek Eadulf's assistance. She was already forming an idea in her mind as to the next step in the investigation.

She waited until she heard the voices of the community raised together in the 'Confíteor', the name by which the general confession which usually preceded the evening prayers was known. It came from the first word of the confession. Then Fidelma moved through the abbey buildings down to the quay.

She could see two lanterns twinkling out in the inlet on the Gaulish ship. It was fairly dark but Fidelma was not perturbed. She found the small rowing boat and clambered in, untying the mooring rope and pushing off from the side of the wooden quay. It took a moment to unship the oars and ease herself into a steady stroke towards the ship.

The evening was soundless and the darkness made deeper by a low covering of clouds. Not even the noise of nocturnal birds or the splash of some aquatic creature came to her ears.

Only the slap of the oars and rippling water as she propelled the boat across the still waters broke the silence.

'Hóigh!'

She recognised Odar's hail as she neared the ship.

'It's me! Fidelma!' she called back, swinging the boat alongside.

Willing hands reached down to help her up and secure her boat.

Odar and Eadulf were on the deck to greet her.

'We were worried about you,' Eadulf said gruffly. 'We have had a visitor this afternoon.'

'Olcán?' Fidelma was interested.

Odar gave an affirmative gesture. 'How did you know?' he asked.

'He also came to the abbey asking questions. I think he knows that Eadulf and Comnat have escaped. He was particularly interested to know where Ross had gone.'

'I distrusted him straight away,' Odar confirmed. 'We hid Brother Eadulf below when he was aboard.'

'Did he suspect anything?'

'No,' replied Odar. 'I told him that Ross had gone to do some trading along the coast. He pretended that he was checking about Ross's right to claim this vessel as salvage.'

'Excellent,' Fidelma said approvingly. 'That fits in with what I told him. I think our conspirators are definitely worried that Eadulf or Comnat may raise an alarm before their plan is ready.'

Odar led the way to the captain's cabin with Eadulf bringing up the rear.

'In which case, is it not wise to leave here at once?' asked Odar.

Fidelma gave a negative shake of her head.

'I still have my duty to perform at the abbey. And I think that I am near solving this mystery.'

'But surely we know who is responsible for the murder of Almu?' broke in Eadulf. 'Odar here has been telling me of the events at the abbey and it seems logical that Almu was killed by the young man at the copper mines who helped her escape. That he was able to do so and then stop any search parties indicates that he was someone of rank, perhaps a chieftain. It sounds as if it is Olcán who is the culprit.'

'Did you see and recognise Olcán, then?'

'No,' admitted Eadulf. 'But it does seem to fit.'

Fidelma grinned impishly at Eadulf.

'You have been busy,' she said in amusement. 'The one problem with your theory, Eadulf, is that there is no motive. Why allow Almu to escape and then kill her? For every action there is a motive, even if the motive is madness. Olcán does not seem insane to me. Also how would you account for Sister Síomha's death?'

Eadulf shrugged.

'I confess that I had not worked that one out yet.'

Fidelma smiled briefly.

'Then perhaps I will be able to enlighten you, Eadulf. In the morning I shall need your help. There is a place of mystery under the abbey which I need to enter and I cannot do that alone. You know my methods. You have worked with me before. Your help will be invaluable.'

Eadulf studied Fidelma inquisitively. He knew her expression. It was clear that he would not get any further information out of her until she was ready. He sighed. 'Wouldn't it be better to wait for the return of Ross before we embark on this matter?'

'The longer we leave it, the easier it will be for those responsible for the deaths of Almu and Síomha to make their escape. No, before dawn tomorrow, I want you to meet me under the abbey tower. And be careful. Come before it gets light because there is always a sister in the tower who watches the water-clock there.'

'Why not do this tonight?'

'Because I am wary of the *doirseór*, Sister Brónach. She

knows that I was out all last night and I think she is suspicious
of me and watching carefully.'

'You believe that she is involved?'

'Perhaps. Though involved in what, I am not sure yet.
Involved in the conspiracy for insurrection? Or involved in
the murders? I do not know.'

'You seem sure that the two things are separate issues,'
observed Eadulf.

'I am now certain of it. I hope tomorrow that we will know
the truth.'

It was still dark when Fidelma rose, bathed her face and
hurriedly dressed, throwing on a heavy cloak to warm her
against the chill. Outside, across the abbey buildings and
courtyard, it was white and Fidelma thought another snow
had fallen. It was, however, a frost as she realised from the
sparkling glint of the covering. She could also see that high
on the mountains snow had certainly fallen and it reflected
in the pre-dawn creating a twilight landscape. She paused
to examine the sky from the window to estimate the time
by the fading stars for the snow clouds had already vanished.
Her attention was caught by a couple of dark moving
specks on the mountain. Squinting, in order to focus
better, she could see that they were two riders and horses,
ploughing through the snow at a dangerous pace. So fast
and so dangerously did the two horsemen press their steeds
that Fidelma found herself fascinated for a moment or two.
She noted they were on the road to Adnár's fortress and
wondered what took the early morning visitors there with
such urgency.

She turned to the task in hand and left the guests' hostel as
quietly as she could, setting off across the white crisp carpet
of frost which lay like slippery ice on the courtyard. The
crunch of frost beneath her feet seemed loud as she hurried
towards the tower. Eadulf was not waiting for her in its
shadows and she halted.

Almost immediately her ears caught the sound of wood striking water and a moment later the tall figure of Brother Eadulf scrambled up towards her. He, too, was wrapped in a heavy cloak.

'It's cold enough, Fidelma,' he greeted.

Fidelma placed a finger against her lips.

'Follow me and be quiet!' she hissed.

Eadulf followed Fidelma as she led the way beyond the tower doorway before quietly entering the stone store house. Here she paused and fumbled in the darkness. Eadulf heard the flint strike and the next moment, Fidelma had lit and trimmed a lantern to illuminate the room.

'What are we going to do?' inquired Eadulf softly.

'We are going to explore a cave,' replied Fidelma in a whisper.

She started down the rough-cut stone steps into the cave store room below with Eadulf following warily.

'Nothing much can be hidden in here,' he observed, peering over her shoulder. 'Where do those other steps lead to?'

'Those? Up into the watch tower. But come across here. This is where I need your help.'

She led the way to the boxes which had defied her attempts to move them on the previous day. She carefully set down her lamp.

'As quietly as you can,' she instructed as she motioned him to help her move the boxes. To her surprise, only the top two boxes were heavy. These, in fact, were very heavy and, inquisitively, Eadulf carefully wrenched one of the rotting pieces of wood aside to examine its contents. He stared at them in disgust.

'Earth? Nothing but earth and bits of rock. Who would want to store earth in a box?'

Fidelma was satisfied that she was on the right track but did not enlighten him, gesturing for him to help her lift the other boxes. They were empty and were easily shifted. As

Eadulf pushed one of the lower boxes out of the way, Fidelma smiled in grim gratification.

Behind the box was a hole in the cave wall, a dark aperture some two feet in width and three feet in height. She bent down and examined it. It was a tiny passage which, after only a few feet, seemed to open up a little. The condition of the entrance showed that it had only recently been excavated. Logic indicated that the material from the passage was the excavated earth and stones now stored in the boxes. However, it was also clear that only the immediate entrance to the passage had been filled in with the rubble and that the passage itself was older than the rubble filling. So, at some previous period, someone had filled in part of the passage and, more recently, someone had excavated it.

Fidelma stretched out the lantern as far as she could into the passage. The light did not extend far for the narrow access appeared to bend into darkness. However, she could see that after a few feet the passageway rose in height to some five feet though it did not widen to any greater breadth. She considered the matter cautiously. The air was chill and somewhat fetid. There was a smell like that of stagnant water. But the passage must lead somewhere and someone had been anxious to excavate it.

'I will have to squeeze through,' she decided.

Eadulf looked dubious.

'I doubt there is room. What if you get stuck?'

Fidelma gave him a scornful glance.

'You can wait for me here, if you will.'

It was cold, icy cold as she squeezed forward. The rocky surface was damp and sharp in places, scratching at her and tearing at her clothes. It was hardly any easier after she had progressed through the first few feet. The passage suddenly turned and then turned again and, with abruptness that was confusing, she found herself in a smaller cave, its ceiling was low, no more than six feet in height. It was also dark and almost freezing and the air was putrid, it reeked of some foul decay.

She reached forward to raise her lantern, stretching out a hand to steady herself.

The surface that she touched was curious, cold and soft. There was also a sensation of what seemed like wet fur.

She withdrew her hand immediately and held the lantern close to the spot.

She felt the nausea well inside her and struggled to prevent herself from crying out in disgust.

She had put her hand on a head. A severed head placed on a rocky shelf on the cave wall. It was a female head, the long dark hair was plastered about it in dampness. Alongside it was a second female head. One of them had reached the stage where it had begun to decay, the flesh white and rotting. The stench was intolerable.

Fidelma did not need to be a seer to know that these were the missing heads of Sister Almu and Sister Síomha. Sister Síomha's features were easily recognisable.

Fidelma felt a hand descend on her shoulder and this time the fear escaped as a terrified groan. The lantern nearly dropped from her hand. She swung round to find the puzzled features of Eadulf staring at her.

'A fox on your fishing hook!' she snapped vehemently, before giving a breath of relief.

Eadulf blinked, unused to an Irish curse on the lips of the young religieuse.

'Sorry, I thought you knew that I was following.'

He broke off as his eyes fell on the grisly discovery in the flickering light of her lantern. He swallowed hard.

'Are those ... ?'

Fidelma was still trying to regulate her pounding heart.

'Yes. One is certainly Sister Síomha. The other I presume to be Sister Almu.'

'I don't understand. Why would their heads be placed here?'

'There is much that is confusing at this time,' responded Fidelma. 'Let's explore further.'

Fidelma, with head bent, moved forward a pace into the low-ceilinged cave, holding the lantern before her.

Eadulf's hand suddenly closed round her wrist and yanked her to a halt, making her gasp for breath.

'Another step and you would have fallen in!' he explained as she cast him a startled glance.

She looked down at her feet.

Before her was a large dark area. The lamp reflected mirror-like against it. She realised that it was water. Most of the cave was an underground pool. And floating on the water were a couple of apparently empty casks. Now and again there was a ripple and the casks passed perilously close to one another. If they touched, mused Fidelma, then they would produce the hollow, knocking sound. This would undoubtedly resonate with the cave acting like a sounding chamber.

But apart from the pool and the casks there seemed nothing else in the cave. The pool seemed to be fed by some sort of underground conduit from the inlet which accounted for the ripples which appeared every now and then on its surface. But mainly the water appeared stagnant so she presumed the pool was not completely tidal. She was, however, disappointed in the barrenness of the cave for she had been expecting to find more, much more, than simply the desolate pool and empty casks. She saw that amidst the rocks and slabs which made up the floor of the cave, the earth was churned into a brown red mud.

She carried the lantern to the rocky walls and observed traces of a greenish surface film here and there marking indications of a metallic element veined into the rock.

It was Eadulf who asked: 'What's that? Shine the light this way.'

He was pointing to something just on the edge of the circle of light from the lantern, something on the cave wall at eye level. Fidelma drew closer.

The scratch marks on the wall resembled those at the foot of the steps on the arch into the storage cave behind them.

'The hound of Dedel,' Fidelma said quietly.

Eadulf was critical.

'A hound? It looks more like a cow to me,' he objected.

'Dedelchú,' Fidelma said, almost to herself. 'The sign of the hound of Dedel. A pagan priest who...'

Eadulf suddenly grunted, as if in pain.

Fidelma had barely time to turn before the Saxon monk collapsed in a heap, falling against her and sending her staggering back into the wall. For a moment she thought she would loose her grip on the precious lantern but she managed to recover her balance. She did not know what had happened to Eadulf and her first thought was to bend down to see what had made him fall. For a moment, she was bewildered to see blood on his head. Then something made her look up.

A few feet away, just inside the pale rays of the lantern, stood a figure. The light glinted wickedly on the burnished naked sword blade which he held threateningly in his hand.

Fidelma felt a chill run through her body.

'So it is you, Torcán!' She controlled her voice, hoping that he would not recognise the tremulous fear in her tone.

The young prince of the Uí Fidgenti had no expression on his face

'I have come for...' he began, his blade raised.

Then everything became blurred.

The blade was raised in the confined space on a level with her throat. Torcán, the son of Eoganán of the Uí Fidgenti, appeared to have drawn it back as if to throw his weight behind it, and then ... Then he seemed to halt and looked surprised. He staggered a pace or two. His mouth opened and something dark began to dribble from a corner of it. He stood swaying, a strange woebegone, almost comical expression, on his face. The sword dropped out of his hand, clanging on to the rocky floor of the cave.

Torcán sank slowly, so slowly it seemed, first to his knees and then he fell abruptly forward on to his face.

It was then that Fidelma saw the second shadow which had been behind him.

The lantern was clasped in her hand so tightly that it would have been impossible to prise it away from her grip at that moment.

The shadow moved forward, a sword was held in one hand. The light caught the dark stains on the blade which had been Torcán's blood.

There was a silence and then Fidelma heard Eadulf beginning to groan. The Saxon monk rose to his knees and shook his head.

'Someone hit me,' he moaned.

'That much is obvious,' muttered Fidelma with gentle irony, attempting a sparkle of her old self. Her eyes never left the newcomer.

Adnár of Dún Boí took another pace forward into the circle of light.

'Are you hurt badly?' he asked, sheathing his sword.

Eadulf, recovering his senses, scrambled to his feet in dismay. There was still blood on his head but he drew his strength from some hidden reserve. He stared down at the body of Torcán and his eyes widened as he saw the young man's features. He began to open his mouth to say something but Fidelma jerked at his arm to silence him.

'I am not hurt but my companion is in need of attention,' Fidelma replied. She had bent down to examine the body of Torcán but it did not really need a second glance to see that the sword thrust that Adnár had made was fatal. Fidelma raised her eyes to the chieftain of Dún Boí.

'You appear to have saved my life, Adnár.'

Adnár looked concerned as he stared down at the son of the prince of the Uí Fidgenti.

'I did not mean to take a life in doing so,' he confessed. 'I was hoping that I might gather some further information from Torcán.'

'Information?'

'I have just learned some grave news, Fidelma.' Adnár paused and glanced quickly at the tall Saxon. 'Doubtless this is Brother Eadulf? You are wounded, brother. Perhaps it would be best if we removed ourselves from this unhealthy place and got your wound attended to.'

Fidelma examined Eadulf's head by the lantern light.

'A superficial wound,' was her verdict. 'Nevertheless, he should have it dressed. I think Torcán must have hit you with a well-aimed rock rather than his sword. Come, we must bathe it immediately. Lead the way back into the other cave, Adnár.'

The chieftain squeezed back through the twisted aperture with Eadulf following and then Fidelma.

In the *subterraneus* of the abbey, where either Torcán or Adnár had left a second lantern, Fidelma bade Eadulf sit on one of the wooden boxes while she took a strip of cloth and indicated that Adnár should hand her one of the jugs stacked along one side of the cave whose odours announced them to contain *cuirm*. She dampened the cloth in it and began to apply the alcohol to Eadulf's wound.

'What is this grave news that have you learned, Adnár?' she demanded as she worked, ignoring Eadulf's soft moan of protest as the fiery spirit reacted on his grazed skin.

'You must send a message to your brother, Colgú. He is in danger. Torcán's father, Eoganán of the Uí Fidgenti, is organising an insurrection against your brother at Cashel. Torcán was in on the plot for I heard him speaking of it. I believe that Olcán is also involved as his father, Gulban the Hawk-Eyed, was also a conspirator. His reward would be that Eoganán would make him chieftain of the Loígde. I have placed Olcán under guard. I followed Torcán here thinking that he was coming to meet fellow conspirators. Then I saw him about to strike at you and so I struck first. I meant only to wound him so that he would be able to tell us more about this plot.'

Fidelma's surprise was not feigned. She had been certain that Adnár had been part of the Uí Fidgenti conspiracy. Adnár's statement dramatically overturned her suspicion.

'Gulban is your chieftain, Adnár,' she pointed out. 'Surely your first loyalty is to him?'

'Not when he plots against the Loígde and my rightful king. Why,' he frowned abruptly, 'do you disapprove of my loyalty to the Loígde and to Cashel?'

Fidelma shook her head.

Adnár continued: 'I cannot understand what Torcán could achieve in killing you. It would have been better for him, and his fellow conspirators, if he had taken you hostage in case some negotiations were needed if their attack on Cashel failed.'

'There is more to this matter than that,' Fidelma made the comment softly. 'In that cave yonder are the heads of Sister Almu, who escaped from the copper mines of Gulban, and who, I believe, was trying to warn the abbey of the uprising. There is another head, that of Sister Síomha.'

Adnár looked at her in astonishment.

'I did not understand. Do you suggest that Torcán killed them as well? But why? Perhaps to prevent them revealing this conspiracy?'

Fidelma had finished cleaning Eadulf's wound. It was merely an abrasion and confirmed her judgment that it had been caused by a stone. Torcán must have either thrown it or used it to crash against the side of the Saxon monk's head.

'If what you say is true, as magistrate here, I must be witness to this find.'

When she did not object, Adnár disappeared back through the opening into the next cave.

'You'd better tell me what is going on,' groaned Eadulf, one hand holding the side of his head.

'What is going on,' whispered Fidelma, 'is that the mist of confusion is beginning to clear.'

'Not for me,' Eadulf sighed in perplexity. 'But the boy who was killed just now was our captor at the copper mines.'

'Ah, I thought you were about to reveal as much,' Fidelma said. 'Stay silent awhile.'

'Who is this man, then?'

Fidelma relented a little and explained. By that time Adnár had returned. His face was grim.

'I have seen them, sister. This is a bad thing. As *dálaigh*, you have higher jurisdiction than I do. What do you mean to do about this matter?'

Fidelma did not reply directly. Instead she helped Eadulf get to his feet.

'Firstly, you may assist me in taking Brother Eadulf to the guests' hostel,' she instructed. 'He has had a bad blow. I think he needs to have some herbal dressings and some rest. Then, Adnár, we shall talk.'

Later that morning Fidelma and Eadulf headed a small group returning to the cave. Abbess Draigen, who ignored her brother with studied coldness, came with Sister Brónach. Each, in turn, identified the terrible remains of Sister Almu and of Sister Síomha. Two sisters then placed the remains in a sack and carried them away under the direction of Sister Brónach, ready to be interred with the rest of their corpses.

Draigen was gazing down disdainfully at the body of Torcán, still lying as he had fallen.

'Perhaps your companion,' the abbess motioned towards Eadulf, who was now much recovered, 'will help Adnár to remove this body. It has no place in the grounds of this abbey.'

'Of course, mother abbess,' Eadulf agreed readily, not picking up the antagonism in the abbess's voice. But Fidelma held Eadulf back a moment. She was frowning as she bent once more over the body and ran her hand to where her discerning eye had marked a bulge under the dead man's jerkin. 'Curious,' she muttered, as she reached forward and drew out some sheets of vellum. The lantern revealed that they were stained with red brown mud.

'Well?' demanded Abbess Draigen expectantly?

Fidelma silently folded the pages and put them into her *crumena*. Then she smiled at the abbess.

'Now the body can be removed. But perhaps it would be better if Adnár sent some of Torcán's retainers to dispose of the body? Such a task would be ill befitting for a *bó-aire* and a brother of the Faith.'

The abbess snorted in annoyance and turned away with an: 'As you wish, so long as it is removed.' Then she was gone without another word. Adnár waited until she had gone and then he shrugged.

'I will do as you say, Sister Fidelma, and send Torcán's retainers to retrieve his body.'

When Fidelma made no reply he, too, followed his sister from the *subterraneus*.

It was later in her cell in the guests' hostel that Fidelma, seated in front of Eadulf, flattened out the sheets of vellum she had recovered from Torcán's body.

'What are they?' demanded the Saxon monk straining forward. 'The abbess did not like it that you failed to enlighten her about them.'

Fidelma had identified them immediately she had removed them from Torcán's body.

They were the missing pages from the book *Teagasg Rí*, the Instruction of the King. The missing pages of the biographical appendix to Cormac Mac Art's philosophical instructions. She glanced through quickly. Yes; as she had suspected, there was the story of Cormac and the gold calf. The tale went on to speak of the revenge of the priest of the gold calf and how he was supposed to have murdered Cormac by causing three salmon bones to stick in the king's throat.

'After this infamy,' Fidelma read aloud, 'the ungodly

priest retired, taking with him the fabulous idol which was worth the honour price of all the kings of the five kingdoms of Éireann combined together with that of the High King himself. The priest returned to his own country in the farthest point of the kingdom, to the place of the Three Salmons, and hid the gold calf in the primal caverns to await the time when the new Faith could be overthrown. And for generations after that each priest of the golden calf, awaiting the day of atonement, took the name Dedelchú.'

Eadulf frowned.

'The hound of Dedel? You mentioned that before.'

Fidelma smiled.

'The hound of the calf. I checked with Longarad's *Glossary*, *Dedel* is an ancient word, barely used now, meaning specifically a calf of a cow.'

'Ah, didn't I say that cave drawing was more like a calf than a hound?' Eadulf observed brightly.

Fidelma suppressed a weary sigh.

It was on the next day that the sound of a trumpet from Adnár's fortress caused Fidelma to come out of the guests' hostel and look across the inlet. Two ships were entering the sheltered harbour. She had no difficulty recognising the *barc* of Ross. The sleek-looking vessel that accompanied it, trailing in its wake, was undoubtedly a warship, its streamers showing the colours of the kings of Cashel. Fidelma heaved a long sigh of relief. The waiting was over and, for the first time since Ross had departed, she felt no longer threatened.

Chapter Eighteen

They had gone down to the quay to meet the new arrivals. Fidelma and Eadulf, Abbess Draigen and Sister Lerben, whom Draigen had, in spite of Fidelma's advice, confirmed as *rechtaire* of the abbey. They stood watching as the small boat from Ross's *barc* tied up to the jetty.

Ross came forward accompanied by a tall, silver-haired man of imposing appearance. This elderly man was still handsome and energetic-looking in spite of his apparent years. He wore a golden chain of office over his cloak. Had not his physical appearance distinguished him, his chain proclaimed him as a man of rank.

Ross was beaming with relief as he saw Fidelma among the welcome party. He greeted her first, quite forgetting protocol by ignoring Abbess Draigen.

'Thanks be that you are safe and well, sister. I have spent several sleepless nights since I left you here.' He smiled a brief greeting to Brother Eadulf.

Fidelma returned his salutation.

'We have kept well and safe, Ross,' she replied.

'*Deo adjuvante!*' muttered the elderly official. '*Deo adjuvante!* Your brother would never have forgiven me had anything happened to you.'

It was Ross who answered the question which came into Fidelma's eyes.

'This is Beccan, chief Brehon and judge of the clan Loígde.'

The elderly Brehon held out both hands towards Fidelma

299

with a grave expression but there was much humour in his eyes.

'Sister Fidelma! I have heard much of you. I have been asked to stand here in place of Bran Finn, chieftain of the clan Loígde, to judge who is guilty and of what crimes connected with this treachery.'

Fidelma acknowledged the Brehon. She had surmised that Bran Finn would send his chief legal official to sit in judgment on the matter. She now introduced Eadulf.

Beccan was solemn.

'If there was no other crime, brother, apart from your being held captive, then this matter would be grave indeed. The transgression of the laws of hospitality to strangers in our kingdom is one which is regarded as reflecting on all of us from the High King down to the lowest in the land. For this I ask your pardon and promise you will be compensated accordingly.'

'The only compensation I require,' Eadulf replied, with equal solemnity, 'is to see that justice is done and truth prevails.'

'Well said, Saxon,' replied Beccan, his eyes widening a little at Eadulf's fluency in the language. 'Your tongue proclaims that you have studied in our colleges. You speak our language well.'

'I have spent some years studying at Durrow and at Tuam Brecain,' explained Eadulf.

The Abbess Draigen intervened, vexed that she was being ignored. In normal circumstances, protocol demanded that she should have been the first to greet the Brehon.

'I am glad that you have come, Beccan. There is much that needs to be sorted out here. Unfortunately, this young *dálaigh* sent by Brocc does not appear capable of resolving these mysteries.'

Beccan raised his eyebrows in interrogation.

'This is the abbess of the community,' Fidelma introduced her, 'and this is her *rechtaire*.'

The Brehon greeted them gravely, ignoring the chagrin on Draigen's face that she had to be announced to Beccan.

'Come, abbess, walk with me. Bring your youthful steward and we will discuss what is to be done.'

He inclined his head with a half smile towards Fidelma and ushered the abbess and her acolyte away.

'He is an astute man,' Ross observed. 'He knows we need some time to speak without Draigen to overhear us.' He paused and shook his head. 'Truly, I was in fear for your life, Fidelma. I thought that you might have been caught up in the insurrection.'

'What news of that? What has happened?' Fidelma asked eagerly.

'I left here to sail to Ros Ailithir with Sister Comnat. We were only half a day's sail from here when, as luck would have it, we encountered a loyal warship of the Loígde. The captain, whom I knew, took it upon himself to sail directly to the copper mines of Gulban. We went on to Ros Ailithir and sought out Abbot Brocc and Bran Finn who immediately raised his clan and sent messengers to your brother at Cashel. Bran gave me a warship as escort and together with the Brehon, here, we sailed back as fast as we could. Sister Comnat has also insisted on returning.'

'Has any attack taken place on Cashel?' Eadulf intervened, knowing how anxious Fidelma was about her brother.

'We do not know,' Ross replied. 'Beccan has been instructed to confine Adnár and any others who might support Gulban. He will protect the abbey until he hears further from Bran Finn. As soon as we hear news from Cashel then Beccan can sit in judgment on the matter of the abbey deaths.'

Fidelma considered for a moment or two.

'That is acceptable to me, Ross,' she agreed. 'In fact, the delay is a help for there are a few more points I wish to clear up before I present my case. But are we safe enough here from Gulban's men?'

Ross silently indicated the warship of Cashel in the inlet.

'A fair enough guarantee,' grunted Eadulf. Then his eyes narrowed. 'And here comes the local chieftain, Adnár, to make himself known to the Brehon.'

A boat was pulling away from the quay of Dún Boí and crossing the water. The black-haired figure of Adnár could be seen sitting in the stern.

'I think, Ross, that I would like to come out to your *barc* and have a word with Sister Comnat,' Fidelma said, not particularly wishing to confront Adnár again at that moment.

Ross immediately helped Fidelma into his boat, with Eadulf following, and they were able to leave before Adnár's boat arrived at the quay.

They found Sister Comnat in the cabin of Ross's *barc*. While her face was a little strained, she appeared in far better health than when Fidelma had last seen the elderly religieuse.

'Is everything all right?' Sister Comnat asked almost immediately as Fidelma and Eadulf entered the cabin.

'Apparently we will not know that for a day or two, sister,' replied Fidelma. 'However, Torcán of the Uí Fidgenti can be added to the list of deaths in the abbey.'

'The son of Eoganán of the Uí Fidgenti? Has he been at the abbey?' There was alarm on the face of the elderly librarian.

Fidelma seated herself on the side of the bunk and gestured to Sister Comnat to resume her seat.

'You mentioned that you saw him training Gulban's men when you were captured with Sister Almu?'

'Yes.'

'Brother Eadulf has identified him as the young chieftain in charge at the mines.'

'Yes. He was at the copper mines.'

'Tell me, Sister Comnat, as you are a good scholar, do you know the meaning of the name Torcán?'

Sister Comnat was perplexed.

'What has that to do with anything?'

'Indulge me.'

'Well, let me see ... It would derive from *torcc*, a wild boar.'

'You told me that Sister Almu said something to you before she escaped which you did not understand, didn't you?'

'Yes. She said...' Her voice trailed off as she realised the connection. 'Perhaps I heard the remark wrongly. Almu said something about a wild boar, or so I thought ... Are you saying that it was Torcán who helped Almu escape and then slew her? But why? That doesn't make sense.'

'You mentioned that Almu was a friend of Síomha, didn't you?'

Sister Comnat nodded.

'They were very good friends.'

'If Almu had reached the abbey safely, it would have been natural for her to seek out Síomha, perhaps, before speaking with, say, even the Abbess Draigen, wouldn't it?'

'Perhaps.'

'Let me take you back to the day that the old beggar came to sell you the copy of the work by the High King Cormac the work called *Teagasg Rí*. Do you remember that?'

Sister Comnat was baffled. She would have demanded to know why Fidelma was leaping from one subject to another but she caught the glint in the young advocate's eye.

'Yes,' she replied. 'It was the week before Sister Almu and I set out for Ard Fhearta.'

'Did the beggar come directly to the library?'

'No. He went to the abbess and gave her the book. The abbess then sent for me and asked me whether it was worth buying. Abbess Draigen has many talents but librarianship and the knowledge of books is not one of them. I saw that it was a good copy.'

'There were no pages cut or damaged in the copy?'

'No. It was in excellent condition for a book so old. It had an additional value. At the end of the book was added a short biography of the High King. So I agreed that the abbey could well buy it or barter food for it with the old man.'

'I see. Did the abbess keep the book?'

'No, I took charge of it and brought it straight to the library. I asked Sister Almu to examine it and catalogue it.'

'Sister Almu was a competent scholar in spite of her tender years?'

'Very competent. She wrote a good hand and knew Greek and Latin as well as Hebrew.'

'Did she know Ogham and the language of the Féine?'

'Of course. I had tutored her myself. She had a quick mind. With respect to her shade, she was not entirely devoted to the propagation of the Faith but she was particularly enthusiastic in her attitude to books and fond of ancient chronicles.'

'So Sister Almu examined the book?'

'She did.'

'If she had found anything of significance in that book, to whom would she have talked about it?'

Sister Comnat frowned slightly.

'I am the librarian.'

'But,' Fidelma chose her words carefully, 'if she did not want to bother you, might she, as a friend, confide in Sister Síomha?'

'It is possible. I do not understand why she should do so.'

Fidelma stood up abruptly and smiled.

'Do not worry, Sister Comnat. I think I am beginning to understand more completely now.'

Outside, on the deck, Fidelma asked Ross if one of his sailors could row them directly to Adnár's fortress. On the way across, Eadulf confessed his total perplexity even though Fidelma had discussed all the events that had occurred since she had arrived at the abbey of The Salmon of the Three Wells. Eadulf had seen Fidelma's bland expression before. He knew the meaning of the trite, composed features. The closer Fidelma was to her quarry, the more she was loath to reveal what was in her mind.

But she laid a hand on his arm and was reassuring.

'We will not be able to have the hearing until Beccan is prepared,' she said. 'Plenty of time for you to obtain an understanding.'

'Are you saying that Almu and Síomha shared some secret that Torcán was after? A secret that he killed them for and would have killed us?'

'You have a quick mind, Eadulf.' Fidelma smiled briefly. Then the boat had come up alongside the quay of Adnár's fortress.

A warrior barred their entrance to the fort.

'Adnár attends at the abbey, sister. He is not here.'

'It is not Adnár that I wish to see. It is Olcán.'

'Olcán is a prisoner. I do not have the authority to let you see him.'

Fidelma scowled.

'I am a *dálaigh* of the courts. You will accept my authority.'

The warrior hesitated and then, observing the gathering storm on her brow, decided on a hurried retreat.

'This way, sister,' he muttered.

Olcán was locked in a cell in the vault below the fortress. He looked dishevelled and angry.

'Sister! What is happening?' he demanded, springing up from where he had been laying on a straw palliasse. 'Why am I being held captive like this?'

Fidelma waited until the warrior had removed himself outside the cell, closing the door behind him, before replying to the young man.

'Hasn't Adnár told you?'

The son of Gulban looked from Fidelma to Eadulf and spread his hands helplessly.

'He accuses me of some conspiracy.'

'Your father Gulban has conspired with the Uí Fidgenti to overthrow Cashel.'

'My father?' Olcán was bitter. 'My father does not confide his plans in me. Am I to be blamed because I am my father's son?'

'Not for that reason but Adnár claims that you were involved in this conspiracy with Torcán. Are you denying that you know anything about this plot? Even though your friend Torcán was involved in it?'

Olcán's face was an angry mask.

'Torcán was a guest of my father's. It was my father's wish that I accompanied him to hunt and fish. I was asked to keep him company and extend every courtesy to him.'

'Why did you come to the abbey the other day and question me and then go to see Odar on the Gaulish ship and question him?'

'Because Torcán asked me to do so.'

The reply surprised Fidelma.

'Do you obey Torcán without demanding an explanation as to why you should be an errand boy for him?'

'No, it was not like that. Torcán said that he suspected that you and Ross were plotting something ... He thought that you had interfered with Adnár's right of salvage compensation for the Gaulish ship.'

'And you believed that?'

'I knew that there was something strange happening at this place. I knew that you and Ross seemed to be part of it.'

'Are you saying that you heard nothing about the insurrection until Adnár had you imprisoned?'

'Truly. I was asleep in my bed yesterday morning when Adnár had his men wake and bring me here. Then he came by later that day and told me that he had killed Torcán. He told me that my father, Torcán and Eoganán of the Uí Fidgenti had been in some plot together to overthrow Cashel. By the holy cross of Christ, sister, I am not interested in power or principalities. I knew nothing of it.'

Fidelma shook her head wonderingly.

'Your story is so weak, Olcán, that you might just be

telling the truth. A conspirator, indeed, a murderer, would tend to weave some more elaborate tale.'

Eadulf looked at Fidelma with surprise. He had been thinking just how guilty Olcán's tale had sounded.

'Fidelma,' he interrupted, 'we have heard from Sister Comnat that Gulban's capital was a military camp where Torcán was training Gulban's men. How could Olcán not have been aware of this?'

'I have not seen my father for several months. We do not mix well together. I have already explained that.'

'How long have you been a guest of Adnár?' Fidelma asked.

'I arrived here two days before you. I think I mentioned as much to you previously.'

'So you were not here when the headless corpse was found at the abbey?'

'No. I told you so.'

'Where were you before that?'

'I was a guest of the chieftain of the clan of Duibhne.'

'For how long?'

'For three months.'

'We have only to send to the chieftain of the Duibhne to verify this.'

'By all means do so. I have nothing to hide.'

'So when did you return to the Beara?'

'A few days before I came to Adnár. I came more or less straight here knowing my welcome by Adnár would be better than any welcome my father would give me. He has already adopted a cousin of mine as *tánaiste*, his heir-elect. I have no ambitions among my father's clan.'

'Then how was Gulban able to ask you to play host to Torcán?' Eadulf demanded.

'It was the morning after Fidelma arrived here that Torcán arrived bringing a written message from my father requesting me to accompany him while he was hunting in the area. My father knew my preference lay in hunting rather than any other pursuit. I probably still have the message in my baggage.'

'And you heard no talk or rumours of conspiracy or insurrection?'

'None, I swear it!'

'How did Adnár come to learn of the plot against Cashel?' pressed Eadulf.

'I presume he heard it from Torcán or one of his men. I don't know.'

'But, he said . . .' began Eadulf.

There was a sound at the cell door and Brother Febal stood in the entrance. There was anger on his handsome features.

'What is the meaning of this? What right have you to be here, sister?' he demanded, recognising Fidelma. 'This young man is a prisoner of Adnár. He is accused of plotting against Cashel.'

'I have the right to question him by reason of my rank and authority,' Fidelma replied calmly. 'You should know that, Febal.'

'I can't allow it without approval of Adnár.'

'You do not have to.' Fidelma gazed thoughtfully for a moment at Olcán. 'I have finished with you, Olcán. Soon this matter will be heard before the chief Brehon of the Loígde. Until then you will have to put up with this new accommodation.'

'But I am innocent!' protested Olcán.

'Then look on this passing misfortune as a test,' Fidelma smiled. 'Seneca, in *De Providentia*, warns us: *ignis aurum probat, miseria fortes viros*. Fire tests gold; adversity strong men. May you prove to be strong.'

She left the cell, followed by Eadulf.

Brother Febal followed them, motioning the guard to shut the door again.

'I will have to report this to Adnár.'

'Everyone in this fortress is now answerable to the Loígde warship anchored in the inlet and to Beccan, the chief judge of the Loígde, acting as the voice of Bran Finn, your chieftain. Then it will not be up to Adnár to approve or disapprove. At the hearing we will discover the truth of these tragedies.'

Brother Febal regarded her resentfully.

'There is no one more anxious than I am for that time. Then everything that I have said about Draigen will be brought into the open.'

Before he could say anything further, Fidelma had led Eadulf back in the direction of the small jetty outside the fortress. She surprised Eadulf by asking the waiting boatmen to row them back to the Gaulish merchant ship and once there asking Odar to join them.

'I want you to take me to see that farmer from whom you obtained the horses,' she told him.

'Barr?'

'Yes, that is the man. Is it far from here?'

'A moderate walk across the mountain but easily done if we take it steadily,' answered the sailor.

Barr was a stocky little man with a bushy brown beard and gave the impression of never washing. His clothes were as dirty as his face. He was hoeing a small patch of ground when they arrived. He regarded them with small dark eyes in a round face that caused Fidelma to think that a pig was handsome by comparison.

'Odar,' the farmer greeted in a gruff voice, 'if you have come to trade for horses again, I have sold them. *Cuirm* is better comfort to me than horses during this cold winter.'

'It is not for horses that we have come, Barr,' Fidelma said.

The man waited, a questioning look on his face.

'Have you found your daughter yet?'

The man gave a bark of laughter.

'I have no daughter. What . . .'

His eyes went wide and a flush of guilt spread across his cheeks. Clearly Barr was not a good liar.

'Why did you tell the abbess that your daughter was missing?'

Barr stood confused.

'You were told to go to the abbey, weren't you?'

'There was nothing wrong in it,' protested the farmer. 'The young man told me to go and ask to see a corpse, pretending that my daughter had gone missing and that I was anxious to identify whether it was her or not.'

'Of course. He offered you money?'

'Enough to buy three good horses.' The farmer pulled a face. 'You see, I bargained with him. He was most anxious for my services.'

'And exactly what were you supposed to do?'

'Just look at the corpse, very carefully, mind you, and report back to the young man with a description.'

'A description?' Fidelma pressed. 'And that is all?'

'Yes. It was easy money.'

'Achieved by lying to the abbess and her community,' pointed out Fidelma. 'Had you seen this young man before?'

'No. Only when he stayed the night waiting for the woman.'

'He stayed a night? Waiting for what woman?'

'Some woman was supposed to meet him at my farm. She didn't turn up. The next morning he went off but returned on the following morning and that is when we made our bargain.'

'Can you describe him?'

'Better still. He had servants with him, I heard one of his men call him by name. It was the lord Torcán.'

It was two days later, just as the community of the abbey of The Salmon of the Three Wells were emerging from the refectory having had the first meal of the day, that another warship came sailing into the inlet and took its station between Ross's *barc*, the Gaulish merchant ship and the

Loígde warship. It, too, bore the banners of the Loígde and of Cashel streaming from its masts.

Fidelma and Eadulf followed on the heels of Abbess Draigen, Beccan and Ross down to the quay to watch a small boat being launched from the newcomer. They could see a muscular young sailor taking the oars while a becloaked religieux sat incongruously next to a lean-looking warrior in the stern. As the boat came alongside the wooden quay, the agile warrior jumped ashore first while the religieux had to be helped out by the sailor.

The warrior came up to Beccan, whom he clearly recognised, and saluted him.

'This is Máil of the Loígde,' introduced Beccan. But he stood uncertainly while the warrior's companion, a cherub-faced young man clad as a brother of the faith, came up and saluted them with a general gesture. The young monk was pleasant looking. In spite of his ruddy cheeks, and soft baby-like features, there was something which gave him an aura of command.

'I am Brother Cillín of Mullach,' he announced.

Máil, the warrior, obviously decided that a further introduction was needed.

'Brother Cillín has recently served at Ros Ailithir. He was sent by Abbot Brocc and Bran Finn to this place after they heard of the sad state of affairs.'

Brother Cillín regarded them solemnly.

'I have effectively been given charge of all the religious on this peninsula.'

There was an audible gasp from Abbess Draigen. Cillín heard it and smiled as he let his eyes flicker in her direction.

'I am given the task by Abbot Brocc to reorganise the religious and try to return them to the ways of the Faith and obedience to their lawful rulers. I will be here but a day or so before starting north for Gulban's capital.'

Fidelma caught sight of the expression on the abbess's features. Clearly she would not greet Cillín in friendship.

'Brother Cillín,' Fidelma stepped forward and greeted the monk, performing the introductions. 'Do you bring any news from Ros Ailithir?'

'I do, indeed, sister. I do indeed. Eoganán and his rebels have made their move. Have you not heard the news of this?'

Anxiety immediately tugged at Fidelma's heart.

'You mean Eoganán has actually risen against Cashel? What news of my brother, Colgú?' She tried to keep anxiety out of her voice.

'Have no fear,' Máil, the warrior, replied quickly. 'Colgú is safe in Cashel. The insurrection is over. Indeed, it was over almost before it had begun.'

'Do you have details?' asked Beccan. Fidelma was too relieved to speak.

'It appears that Colgú ordered his warriors to strike against Eoganán and the Uí Fidgenti before they were prepared. The insurrection was planned for spring when the ground would have been harder and they could move their Frankish engines of destruction which Gulban had acquired. The Arada clan led the attack directly into the territory of the Uí Fidgenti.'

'Go on,' urged Fidelma. She knew the clan of the Arada Cliach held a territory to the west of Cashel, standing between the ancient capital and the lands of the Uí Fidgenti. They were a people renowned for their horsemanship as, in ancient times, they had been famed throughout the five kingdoms as charioteers.

Máil continued, obviously liking the role of newsbringer.

'Eoganán found that he could not wait for the help that he was expecting from Gulban and had to muster his clansmen to defend himself. The two armies met at the foot of the Hill of Áine.'

Fidelma had been to the Hill of Áine in her travels. It was a low, isolated hill where an ancient fortress stood, dominating the surrounding plains. It was said to be the throne of the goddess whose name it bore.

'The casualties were light...'

'*Deo gratias!*' interposed Beccan.

'The victory went to the Arada and to Cashel. The Uí Fidgenti fled the field leaving, among many other dead rebels, Eoganán, their prince and self-proclaimed king. Cashel is safe. Your brother is well.'

Fidelma was silent for a long time, standing with head bowed.

'And what news of Gulban and his Frankish mercenaries?' asked Eadulf.

This time it was the young monk, Cillín, who supplied the answer.

'One of our warships had already been alerted by Ross here a few days ago and sailed directly to Gulban's copper mines just in time to find Gulban in personal command of moving his accursed alien machines of destruction. What were they called? *Tormenta?* The Loígde warriors attacked before Gulban could organise a defence and all his engines of destruction were burnt and destroyed. The Franks, those who were not killed, that is, were captured. There were some Gaulish and other prisoners there, and these have now been released.'

'And when did that event happen?' asked Fidelma.

'Four days since,' replied Máil frowning. 'Why is it so important to know the exact dates? Are you engaged in writing a chronicle, sister?'

'A chronicle?' Fidelma chuckled loudly in her amusement, causing the others to stare at her as if she had taken leave of her senses. 'Ah, my friend, you are so very close to the truth. Four days?' Fidelma was satisfied. 'Then I think, Beccan,' she turned to the elderly judge, 'we need to delay no further. I shall be able to argue a case as to the identity of the person responsible for the terrible deaths in this abbey as soon as you wish.'

'What?' It was the Abbess Draigen who spoke up. 'Surely that matter is already cleared up? It was the son of Eoganán who was responsible; Torcán of the Uí Fidgenti. It is a matter of Beccan here simply concurring...'

'Is Torcán, the son of Eoganán here?' interrupted Máil, his face eager, as he turned to the abbess. 'I have orders to take him to Cashel. He is to be held for his involvement in the conspiracy with his father.'

'No, he is dead,' Fidelma explained. 'Adnár, the local chieftain, slew Torcán when he tried to kill me. Olcán the son of Gulban is also here, being held prisoner by Adnár as being a party to the insurrection.'

'I see.' Máil clearly meant that the events were beyond his comprehension.

'You *will* see,' smiled Fidelma with slight emphasis. 'At least, I hope so, when I present the case before Beccan. I am now ready to do that.'

'Very well,' the elderly judge conceded. 'We will assemble a court in the abbey buildings this afternoon. Draw up a list of all those you wish to be present, sister, and we will ensure their attendance.'

Chapter Nineteen

The *duirthech*, the wooden chapel of the abbey of The
Salmon of the Three Wells, was chosen by Beccan as the
place to hold the hearing. The abbess's ornately carved oak
chair had been placed before the altar, immediately in front
of the tall gold cross. Beccan sat here. His personal scribe
was seated on a stool to his right-hand side to take down the
evidence which Fidelma would present. Fidelma herself sat
on one of the front benches to the right of the chapel's aisle
with Eadulf alongside her. Ross sat as a spectator behind
them together with Brother Cullín of Mullach. Behind
them were seated Adnár and Brother Febal. Next to them
sat the old farmer, Barr, whom Fidelma had summoned to
the abbey. Then behind them, seated between two warriors
of the Loígde, sat the dejected young Olcán.

On the benches on the opposite side of the aisle sat the self-
assured Abbess Draigen with Sister Lerben and next to her
Sister Comnat. Behind them was Sister Brónach and diffi-
dent Sister Berrach. The back benches of the chapel were
crowded with as many of the community as had been able to
squeeze into the building. At the door stood Máil and two
more warriors.

Lanterns had been lit in the *duirthech*, their flickering light
reflecting on the gold of the altar cross and the many icons
and artifacts along the walls. They not only gave out a light
but also a heat so that there had been no need to light the
brazier in spite of the chill weather outside.

Beccan opened the proceedings by announcing that he sat

315

in judgment to hear the evidence gathered by Fidelma, as a *dálaigh* of the courts, into the causes of the death of two sisters of the community. He could, on the basis of the evidence she presented, consider whether there was a case to be answered by any she alleged to be the culprit or culprits. If so, they would be taken for trial to Cashel at a later date.

Having finished the formalities, Beccan indicated that Fidelma should begin.

She rose to her feet and uttered the ritual, '*Pace tua*' meaning 'with your permission' but then was silent several moments, hands clasped together before her, head slightly forward as if contemplating something on the floor, while she gathered her thoughts.

'I have rarely encountered such sadness housed in one place as it is in this abbey.' Fidelma's opening words echoed sharply in the confines of the building and caused a stir among the community at the back of the chapel. 'There is much hatred in this place and that is not compatible with a house dedicated to the Faith. I found among this community living proof of the words of the psalm – that their mouths were as smooth as butter but their hearts were war, their words were smoother than oil, yet they were drawn swords.'

Abbess Draigen made to speak but the Brehon Beccan silenced her with a swift gesture.

'This is now a court of law, not a chapel, and in this place I will say who shall speak,' he admonished. 'The *dálaigh* is making her opening remarks. Her words can be challenged at the proper time, as I shall indicate to you.'

Fidelma went on as if no interruption had been made.

'Abbess Draigen called upon her superior in the Faith, Abbot Brocc of Ros Ailithir, and requested the presence of a *dálaigh*. A headless corpse had been discovered in the abbey's main drinking well. There were certain things about this headless corpse that had a special significance. In the right hand was a crucifix and fastened on the left was an aspen

316

wand carved in Ogham, in other words a *fé*, a measuring stick for the grave. The Ogham referred to the pagan goddess of death and battles, the Mórrígú. The symbolism of this was, as I was informed by Sister Brónach, such as betokens someone who is a murderer or a suicide.

'Some days later, the steward of the abbey, Sister Síomha, was likewise found decapitated, with the same symbolism. From the start, I was informed that the only person that had a motive was Abbess Draigen. I was told that she had a reputation for an attraction to young novices...'

This time Draigen rose to her feet and began to protest loudly but Beccan's firm tone quelled her.

'I have said that you will have a chance to answer later. Do not interrupt again otherwise it is in my power to exact a fine for such disregard of the rules of this court.'

As Abbess Draigen sat down abruptly, Fidelma continued with a cutting motion of her hand: 'But there were many stories, mostly born out of malice or, as I have found, for other sinister purposes. Had Draigen been guilty of such misconduct she would have hardly asked Abbot Brocc to send a *dálaigh* to investigate matters. Yet the abbess has shown that she prefers the rule of Penitentials to our secular law. This was a mystery which intrigued me until I realised that the resolution was simple and one which she admits. The abbess sent to Brocc for a *dálaigh* simply because she did not want her brother, Adnár, who was local magistrate, to have any power in this abbey.'

The abbess glowered at her but made no response. Fidelma continued.

'My first task was to identify the first headless corpse. It was that of a young girl whose thumb, index and little finger were stained with blue. That is typical of someone engaged in penmanship. When I found out that two sisters of the community, Sister Comnat the librarian, and Sister Almu, her young assistant, were missing from the abbey, I suspected that it might be the body of the latter. They had set off three weeks before to the monastery of Ard Fhearta and not returned. To make a long story shorter, my suspicion eventually proved correct. This was the body of Almu.

'Having discovered the identity of the corpse, the next question had to be the motive for the murder? Why and how had Sister Almu returned to this abbey? Why had she been decapitated after being slain? And what was the meaning of the pagan symbolism? From her corpse, there were only three other clues. She had been shackled before her death and there were some signs of ill-treatment. And there was brown red mud on her feet and under her fingernails. I was told by Sister Brónach that such mud was indicative of the copper rich land in this vicinity. Is this not true, Sister Brónach?'

The glum-faced sister started to rise in her seat. Then she inclined her head in silent agreement and sat back.

'The death of Sister Síomha was even more intriguing and perplexing. Her body was found in the tower here, also decapitated and with the same symbols in her hands. This time the body had not been stripped of clothing. The murderer knew that we would know who she was or perhaps the murderer wanted us to know. Why the symbolism? Why the decapitation? But what intrigued me more than anything was the fact that the same brown red mud was under her fingernails. It had not been there the last time I had seen Sister Síomha just a few hours earlier.

'There was blood smeared on the stairway from the tower into the *subterraneus*. It was Síomha's blood. Her killer had severed the head in the tower and taken it down into the cave below. Why?

'Was there some insane person at work here? Was the motivation some hatred of the sisters, hatred of the abbey, hatred of the abbess? Brother Febal certainly felt hatred in all those respects, particularly of Abbess Draigen, who had once been his wife. He, it was, who to tried to convince me that

Draigen had unnatural liaisons with the young novices. Brother Febal had more than enough hate to motivate such murders.'

She glance over her shoulder. Brother Febal was sitting staring at her with a malignant expression on his handsome features.

'Febal's accusations against Draigen were untrue.'

For the first time Abbess Draigen looked vaguely satisfied.

'But,' Fidelma continued after a pause, 'was there some more subtle plot than the one suggested by Febal?'

Beccan cleared his throat.

'Have you come to any conclusion?'

Fidelma raised her head and answered: 'Yes. I trust you will bear with me while I tell you a story, which it is necessary to appreciate, in order to get to the truth of this matter. All that I claim, I can now prove.'

'Then proceed, sister.'

'Four hundred years ago the annals record that a fabulous gold calf was made and worshipped. But the High King Cormac Mac Art refused to indulge in this practice and condemned it. The story is that the priest of the gold calf was so angered that he killed Cormac by arranging for three salmon bones to stick in Cormac's throat and choke him to death. Now this is symbolism again. Three salmon bones. It was merely a means of identification.

'Not long before Sister Comnat and Sister Almu set out to Ard Fhearta a man came to the abbey with a copy of Cormac's *Teagasg Rí*, Instructions of the King. This man had fallen on hard times and wanted to exchange the book for food. The man probably did not know the contents of that book. He brought it to the abbess for trade and she sent for the librarian Sister Comnat. The librarian agreed that it was a worthwhile exchange especially because she had noticed that there was a short biography of Cormac at the end of the book. In turn, she asked Sister Almu, her assistant, to look at the book and catalogue it.

'Sister Almu did so. Imagine her excitement when she found an addition to the story of the gold calf. The fabulous beast, fashioned of gold, did exist, according to this text. Moreover, the priest of the cult of the gold calf was from this very area. Indeed, isn't the symbol of the goddess known as the Old Woman of Beara, a cow? Isn't Adnár's fortress called Dún Boí, the fortress of the cow goddess. A calf is the offspring of the cow.'

'We have heard this old folk story!' cried Abbess Draigen, interrupting impatiently. 'But when are we getting to the bottom of this tale?'

Beccan was exasperated by her continual interjections.

'I have warned you once, mother abbess. It is not your place to interrupt. A fine of one *sét* for interruption. However, I am inclined to believe that this story grows tedious in the telling, Sister Fidelma. What has this to do with current events?'

'The symbolism of the three salmon!' replied Fidelma. 'We know that the site of this abbey was formerly a pagan centre. And we know that it is now called the abbey of The Salmon of the Three Wells. That is not only a euphemism for the Christ but it links to the pagan past. The fabulous gold calf was hidden in the caves under this abbey. Most will have seen the crude carving of the calf on the wall of the cave used as a store room. There is a similar carving in the cave next to it.'

There was a murmuring of excitement from the community.

'Sister Almu, reading the text, was the first to realise this. The story said that the priests of the gold calf took the name Dedelchú, hound of the calf, and dwelt here in isolation. Then Necht the Pure came to convert the land to the new Faith. She was able to drive out the pagan priests. According to the text, under the abbey, for over one hundred years, ever since Necht the Pure drove out the pagans and founded this community, the gold calf had been hidden and probably forgotten about apart from this one reference in a local book.

Imagine how excited Almu must have been and, more particularly, imagine the fortune such a fabulous statue would command. It was literally worth its weight in gold for it was, according to the story, solid gold.'

'Can you prove this?' Beccan demanded.

Fidelma turned to Eadulf who handed her the two soiled pages of vellum.

'These two pages were recently cut from the book and contain this story. They were found on the body of Torcán.'

'Proceed,' Beccan grunted, glancing at the vellum sheets.

'I discovered that Sister Almu was a close friend of Sister Síomha. A very close friend. So, naturally, the first person that she went to tell of her find was Síomha. And out of that conversation came the desire to find and possess that gold calf. The one motive that has remained constant in all the sorry events of this story has been greed. Didn't the poet Lucan say that greed is a cursed vice and if enough gold is offered a person would, even if they were starving to death, part with their small hoard of food to possess it? In this story Sister Síomha was particularly starving but hers was a starvation of a moral and spiritual nature.

'Sister Síomha was so overcome with greed that she even betrayed her friend Almu. She persuaded Sister Almu to say nothing about the story, perhaps saying they would discuss the matter on her return from Ard Fhearta. As soon as Sister Almu was gone, Síomha immediately drew a third person into this story. To that third person, Síomha told all. Using the pages of the book as a guide, Síomha and her companion found the place where they thought the fabulous beast was hidden but the entrance, in the abbey's *subterraneus*, had been blocked in by rocks and earth.

'In order to gain the time and space for her companion to excavate the entrance into what they thought was a treasure cave, Síomha volunteered to take as many of the night watches as she could in the tower. There was only one person who heard the knocking as the passage was excavated and that was Sister Berrach. Sister Berrach, an intelligent young woman who through prejudice had to put on an act that she was almost half-witted, was in the habit of going to the library each morning well before dawn to read – she did not want her fellow sisters to know how intelligent she was. But even Sister Berrach thought the banging was merely an extension of the sounds often heard coming from the hidden cave under the chapel. That knocking, by the way, was due to two old wooden casks floating on an underground pool incited by the sea water from the inlet which flooded every now and again. In that presumption, the Abbess Draigen was correct.'

Fidelma paused as she saw Beccan's scribe having difficulty to keep up with her.

'Síomha's companion had only just broken through to the second cave when a complication arose. Sister Almu returned unexpectedly to the abbey. There had been a terrible twist of fate, Sister Comnat and Sister Almu had been taken prisoner because they had discovered the conspiracy by Gulban, the chieftain of the Beara to aid the Uí Fidgenti in an insurrection against Cashel. This was an entirely unrelated set of events.

'Sister Almu sought to escape. Now there was a young Fidgenti prince at the place where the sisters were confined. Almu, having made one escape attempt and been scourged for it, knew there was little chance of her escaping from the confines of the copper mines, where she was being kept a prisoner, unless she had some help. She proceeded to ingratiate herself to this young man. Almu, although I did not know her, I judged to be an astute judge of personality. She knew that greed was a prime factor in the young man's thinking. She told him the story of the gold calf and promised to share the secret of the gold calf, not realising that her friend had already betrayed her trust.'

'I presume by this prince that you mean Torcán?' intervened Beccan.

'I do,' Fidelma acknowledged. 'Torcán, for no other

motive than greed, brought Almu to the abbey. He arranged
to meet with her later at the farm of Barr. Innocently, Almu
arrived back. What were Síomha and her companion to do
when Almu returned? We know what happened to her.
Torcán was waiting at the farm. You can imagine his
annoyance when she did not return. He probably thought
that she had betrayed him. He waited there all night.

'There was no word the next day and he left. But then he
returned. He learned that a corpse had been discovered in the
abbey. Torcán paid the farmer to go to the abbey and say his
daughter was missing and asked to see the body in case it was
her. The farmer had no daughter, missing or otherwise. The
farmer returned and gave a description of the corpse. In spite
of its decapitation, Torcán recognised the description. Barr
will confirm all this, by the way.'

Heads were craning to where the farmer sat shuffling his
feet, eyes downcast.

'Torcán recognised the description of the corpse while we
did not?' sneered Abbess Draigen cynically. 'It is too much to
believe.'

'But it is the truth. You were all misled by Sister Síomha's
denial that it was her friend. Almu had undoubtedly told
Torcán that her friend Síomha was a party to the secret. When
he knew that Síomha had failed to identify Almu then he
began to suspect that Síomha was involved in obtaining the
treasure for herself.'

'Are you saying that Sister Síomha killed Almu?' Abbess
Draigen was once more on her feet, a tone of querulous
amazement in her voice, forgetting the censure of the
Brehon.

'If she did not do the actual deed, then she was a partner to
it. I began to suspect Síomha's involvement because of these
facts: firstly, she was a good friend of Almu but said that the
body was definitely not that of her friend. It is just possible
she did not recognise the corpse but so unlikely as to be
discounted. Secondly, Síomha clearly lied when she told

Sister Brónach that she had drawn water from the well shortly before they found the corpse. The body of Almu had to have been placed down the well by Síomha and her companion before daylight otherwise the risks would have been too great. A third matter made me realise Síomha's involvement and that was her miscalculations that night with the water-clock.'

'Miscalculations?' queried Draigen sharply.

'Síomha was said to be very meticulous. On the night of Almu's murder, she made several miscalculations which Sister Brónach mentioned to me in passing. In other words, at some point, Síomha had to leave the water-clock and the tower to go to the help of her companion in dealing with Almu. You see, Almu went, or was lured, down to the excavated cave for she had red mud under her fingernails. The same mud, I was told, was on her body before it was washed for burial. Sister Síomha had missed the essential time sequences and had to fudge them later. Errors that were picked up by Sister Brónach when she took over the watch early the next morning.'

'Why didn't Torcán come to the abbey to search for the gold calf immediately?' asked Beccan.

'Torcán had to return to the copper mines for a few days due to his involvement in the conspiracy. When he returned to Adnár's fortress and contacted Sister Síomha, he thought he was dealing only with her and demanded that she bring him a copy of the book which had the references he needed. He did not know which book it was. Síomha, taking advantage of this, sent him a copy of the annals of Clonmacnoise. In addition, suspecting that Torcán was likely to betray her, she decided to send the book by Sister Lerben. As a further precaution, Síomha cut the two essential pages from the real book, the *Teagasg Rí*, which was still in the library, and gave them to her companion.

'By chance I happened to be going to Adnár's fortress a short time before Torcán was expecting Síomha to travel that path through the wood bearing the copy of the book. I was mistaken for Síomha and shot at. I barely escaped the arrow meant for Síomha. When Torcán and his men realised their mistake they tried to cover it up by claiming they were hunting and had mistaken me for a deer. It was a weak story. And my suspicion was confirmed when a short while later, Sister Lerben appeared along that woodland path bearing a book to deliver to Torcán.'

Sister Lerben was sitting with her face almost the colour of snow.

'I could have been killed!' she blurted.

Fidelma ignored her and added: 'It did not take too long for Torcán to realise that he had been duped. He went to find Síomha.'

'And slew her?' Beccan demanded.

'No. Síomha's companion in this intrigue had now realised that Síomha was a liability.'

'Ah, the companion,' breathed Beccan. 'I was losing sight of this mysterious companion.'

'Síomha was now Torcán's open link to that companion. So Síomha had to be killed to prevent Torcán discovering the truth.'

'And who was this companion?' demanded Draigen. 'You have spoken much about this companion but you have not identified who the companion was.'

'The companion was Síomha's lover. The person responsible for both the murders of Almu and Síomha.'

The excitement in the chapel was full of tension.

'In both murders it had been the idea of this person to present the corpses in such a way that a two-fold purpose would be achieved. Some symbolism would be placed on the bodies in order to throw any investigator off the scent and would, at the same time, put fear into the abbey community; perhaps even in the hope that such fear would drive members of the community away from the abbey because they might believe it was under a pagan curse. So the victims were decapitated and a *fé* bound on one arm and a crucifix placed in the opposite hand.

'By now, of course, Torcán was not so much concerned with his father's insurrection against Cashel. Perhaps he never was. He was concerned with obtaining a personal fortune which would make him rich and with those riches he would have power. His greed overcame his good sense. He knew that I was on the trail of this mystery and he used young Olcán as a decoy, sending him to the abbey and to the Gaulish ship to ask certain questions which would place suspicion on Olcán.

'Torcán kept a close watch on me. I confess that I did not know how close. He followed Eadulf and me into the cave when we discovered the entrance to the so-called treasure cave. He followed us in and knocked Eadulf momentarily unconscious. I suspect that he thought that we had already discovered the gold calf and was about to attempt frightening me into revealing to him what he thought I knew.'

'Adnár says Torcán was about to kill you when he intervened to save your life,' Beccan pointed out.

'Adnár was wrong. No deaths can be laid at the feet of Torcán in this matter. Only one attempted killing when he thought I was Síomha. Torcán would not have killed me in the cave until he had obtained the information which he believed that I could give him about the gold calf.'

'You have spoken about Síomha's mysterious companion as her lover. It seems to be that you are pointing the finger at Adnár.'

'Síomha's lover!' The Abbess Draigen had half-turned angrily to regard her brother with a look of disgust. 'I might have suspected.'

'That is not so!' shouted Adnár. 'I was never Síomha's lover.'

'Yet Síomha spent enough time at your fortress, especially during these last three weeks,' replied Sister Lerben. 'I told Sister Fidelma so.'

There was a restless murmur from the community.

'You are wrong,' Fidelma said. 'Adnár was not Síomha's lover.'

A tense silence fell.

'You have lost me, Sister Fidelma,' Beccan said slowly. 'Of whom, then, are you speaking?'

'As chance would have it, Sister Berrach actually saw him just after he had killed Síomha. In fact, he was probably in the very act of carrying Síomha's mutilated head down to the *subterraneus*. Berrach saw a cowled figure. Consider. There was only one person who had fed Adnár with lies about Draigen; only one person who tried to feed me with those same lies; only one person who has been the subtle serpent whispering here and there and guiding people in this tragedy; only one person who was not of this community yet who could wear a cowl.'

Brother Febal had leapt to his feet and was pushing his way towards the window of the *duirthech*.

The warrior Máil and his men were there before him, dragging Febal back as he attempted to clamber through it.

There were gasps of astonishment and horror.

Adnár was sitting pale and shaking as he saw them binding Febal.

'Brother Febal told you that it was Torcán who was behind everything, didn't he?' Fidelma asked Adnár. 'Febal was good at spreading stories. He gave you the two pages which had been removed from the *Teagasg Rí*...'

'I thought that you said that you found the two pages on Torcán's body?' intervened Beccan.

'So I did. How did they get there? Brother Febal gave them to Adnár...'

'He said that he had found them in Torcán's saddle bags,' Adnár admitted.

'Did he suggest that you should plant them on Torcán's body?'

Adnár hung his head.

'I really did think that he was going to kill you. I believed all that Febal had told me. But it was my idea to leave the pages on Torcán. When we went into the larger cave, I thought that you might not have all the evidence you needed to lay the blame on Torcán. Febal said he found the pages in Torcán's saddle bags and so I decided to place them on his body for you to find.'

'I know. You made an excuse to return to the body while I was nursing Brother Eadulf in order to place the pages on Torcán.'

Adnár was surprised.

'How did you know?'

'It is no mystery. You remember that I bent down to examine Torcán before we removed Brother Eadulf to the other cave. When I returned with Eadulf, after you had returned there, I saw the bulky pages under Torcán's shirt. I knew that they had not been there when I checked to ensure that he was dead. It was obvious that you had placed them there.'

'So,' Beccan interrupted with a sigh, 'are you saying that Adnár is not guilty of involvement in this matter? That he was misled and manipulated by Brother Febal?'

'Adnár was not guilty of involvement with the murders of Almu and Síomha nor did he really know about the hunt for the gold calf. He is, however, guilty of complicity in the conspiracy of insurrection against Cashel.'

Adnár rose looking desperately about him.

'But I warned you about it!' he protested. 'I warned you about the insurrection before it became generally known.'

'This is so,' whispered Brother Eadulf. 'He did warn us.' Fidelma ignored him.

'Yes, Adnár,' she said. 'You warned me of it when it had already failed. Messengers arrived at your fortress in the early hours of that morning, the morning when you decided to arrest Olcán and follow Torcán to the cave. They came to inform you and Torcán that Gulban had been killed and the

Frankish mercenaries and their weapons destroyed. I actually saw them arriving while I was making my way to meet with Brother Eadulf. Perhaps that was what compelled Torcán to come into the open and come to the abbey for one last desperate search for the gold calf.'

It was clear from the expression on Adnár's face that Fidelma had scored a point.

'You knew you would soon have to clear yourself of the charge of conspiracy. To show your loyalty, you first seized Gulban's son Olcán, who, in fact, was innocent of any complicity in the plot for the insurrection. Then you followed Torcán here and were so able to warn me about the insurrection knowing that Gulban's part in it had already failed.'

Beccan had a whispered exchange with his scribe before turning to Fidelma.

'Let me get this straight, sister. Adnár is not guilty of killing Sisters Almu and Síomha. But what you are implying is that he slew Torcán believing it was justifiable?'

'It is confusing,' admitted Fidelma, 'but the fact is, while he thought Torcán was guilty of murdering Almu and Síomha, he also killed him in premeditation in order to prevent him revealing that he, Adnár, was part of the insurrection. He is, therefore, still guilty of murder.'

There was a moment of silence before Adnár started to protest.

'You can't prove that I knew about the plot and what was happening at the copper mines.'

'I think I can,' Fidelma assured him. 'You see, when you entered the cave and slew Torcán, you were able to recognise Brother Eadulf here by name. How would you know who he was if you did not know what was going on at the copper mines and that he had just escaped from them?'

Adnár made to speak but hesitated, his guilt written on his face. He sat down abruptly as if the strength had left him.

Beccan looked satisfied as he addressed Fidelma.

'This leaves Brother Febal as the murderer of Almu and Síomha?'

'That is so. He slew Almu and laid the false trail. When Torcán came close to him, he sacrificed Síomha. And Síomha was his lover.' She looked across to Sister Lerben. 'Síomha was not visiting Adnár at Dún Boí, as you thought, but Febal.'

Brother Febal had stood, hands bound, between the two warriors. He started to laugh, a slight hysterical note in his voice.

'All very clever, *dálaigh*! Didn't I tell you once that all you women stick together. Well, *dálaigh*, tell me this; where is the gold calf now? If I have done so much to find it, where is it now?'

The Brehon Beccan looked across to Fidelma.

'Though we seem to have enough evidence and confession, Febal has raised an interesting point. Where is this fabulous gold calf that has cost so much blood?'

Fidelma shrugged eloquently.

'Alas, that is a mystery that may never be solved.'

There were gasps of astonishment.

'You mean my sacrifice was for nothing?' Febal's voice rose to a high pitch.

'Your sacrifice?' thundered Beccan. 'You killed two members of this community and your scheming caused the death of Torcán.' He gestured to the warriors. 'Remove him from this place and take him aboard my vessel. Adnár also. They will be taken to Cashel.'

Adnár and Febal were hustled from the *duirthech* by Máil and his warriors.

Beccan gazed quizzically at Fidelma.

'Are you saying that this gold calf never really existed?' he asked.

Fidelma gave a wry grimace.

'I think it probably did. Who are we to doubt the words of the ancient chronicles? But it is certainly no longer in the cave. It may be that it was removed from that cave many long years ago. And perhaps that may be the reason as to why the entrance had been blocked up. Perhaps, years ago, one could enter that cave complex from the inlet and that was how people originally went in and out.'

'What makes you say this?'

'Because of the casks. The two wooden casks floating on the underground pool, knocking into each other.'

'I do not understand.'

'Simple enough. How had the casks come into the cave? How could the statue have been placed in that cave or have been removed? The entrance through which Febal and Síomha gained their access was, as I and Eadulf know, only two feet wide. The logic is that the casks came by another entrance and through that same entrance the statue had been placed or removed. One thing more; the casks were less than a century old by the look of them. They were certainly no older for they were not rotten. They were still fairly dry inside and firm enough to create the hollow knocking when they banged together. I'd hazard a guess that when those casks were taken into the cave, the gold calf was taken out.'

'So we may never know who removed the gold calf or its whereabouts now?'

Fidelma's lips twitched slightly. Before answering she let her gaze wander slowly around from the large gold altar cross and the other gold icons hanging on the walls of the *duirthech*. Then she returned her mocking blue eyes to the figure of the Brehon.

'I think, perhaps, when Necht the Pure drove the pagan Dedelchú and his people away from here and purified this place in the new Faith, the gold calf vanished with them.'

There was a pause and then the Brehon rose from his seat.

'This hearing is now ended. We have seen here today much wisdom from you, Fidelma of Kildare,' Beccan said approvingly.

Fidelma shrugged diffidently.

'*Vitam regit fortuna non sapientia,*' she responded in deprecation.

'If chance, not wisdom, governs human life,' retorted the Brehon dryly, 'then you are truly possessed of a great deal of luck.'

Epilogue

Fidelma met Brother Cillín at the door of the chapel.

'Congratulations, sister. It was a complicated case well presented.'

'Febal is not the only one here who seems to have fallen from the path of the Faith,' Fidelma said pointedly.

Brother Cillín glanced in the direction in which she had been looking and saw Abbess Draigen talking intently to Sister Lerben.

'Ah yes. The arrogance of the abbess. *Vanitas vanitatum, omnis vanitas.* I have the authority from Abbot Brocc to request that the abbess go on a pilgrimage in order that she may discover true humility again. Sister Brónach will be placed in charge of the abbey here under my direction.'

'I understood that you were going to Gulban's capital across the mountains?'

'I am. I intend to raise a new religious house there and this abbey, once cleansed of the sin of pride, will take instruction from it. Let us pray that Abbess Draigen may accept the lesson and learn from it.'

'Was it Syrus who said *vincit qui se vincit* – they conquer who conquer themselves?'

Brother Cillín chuckled.

'Who knows themselves and overcomes their problems can go on to achieve many things in life. It is a fine thought. I hope that it is not too late and that Draigen is not as arrogant as to misunderstand the sentiment.'

'Will you be able to insist that she obeys? She is not someone who meekly accepts instruction?'

'There is the matter of her incitement of Sister Lerben to commit murder which you have told me of. Murder might well have resulted if you had not interceded to protect Sister Berrach. I will make it plain that Draigen has a choice, to obey in humility or answer for her behaviour before a council of her ecclesiastical peers at Ros Ailithir.'

'In that case, I am sure that she will go. Draigen is conceited but her arrogance hides a life that was destroyed before it began. Conceit is only the armour she has put on to protect her against life.'

Brother Cillín looked at her wryly.

'Am I to have pity for her? Surely her conceit is comfort enough for her?'

'It would be sad if we did not feel pity for the wreckage of life.'

'Rather would I feel pity for her daughter, Sister Lerben. She had been doomed by her mother and has suffered from the actions of her father. What hope for her?'

'That will be up to you, Cillín,' replied Fidelma. 'Your hand must now guide the paths of these people.'

'It is a heavy responsibility,' agreed the monk. 'I would rather pilgrimage among the barbarians who have not heard the word of Christ than tried to solve the conflicts of these minds and souls. I will be sending Sister Lerben to Ard Fhearta where she must spend the time learning from her elders.'

'Poor Lerben. She was proud of being *rechtaire* here.'

'She has much to learn before she can guide or have authority over others.' Brother Cillín held out his hand. '*Vade in pace*, Fidelma of Kildare.'

'*Vale*, Cillín of Mullach.'

Fidelma rejoined Eadulf in the courtyard of the abbey.

'What now?' asked the Saxon monk anxiously.

'Now? I have no wish to stay in this sad place. I am returning to Cashel.'

'Then we will journey together,' Eadulf said brightly. 'Am I not the emissary of Theodore of Canterbury to your brother at Cashel?'

On the quay, they found Ross was waiting for them. Fidelma saw Sister Brónach standing to one side with Sister Berrach, supporting herself on her heavy staff. It was clear that Brónach and Berrach were both waiting to speak with her. Fidelma, with a muttered excuse to Eadulf and Ross, went across and greeted them.

'I did not want you to go before I could speak to you,' Sister Brónach began hesitantly. 'I wanted to thank you...'

'There is nothing to thank me for,' Fidelma protested.

'I also wanted to apologise,' the solemn-faced religieuse went on. 'I thought that somehow you had suspected me...'

'It is my profession to suspect everyone, sister, but is it not said *vincit omnia veritas* – truth eventually conquers?' she replied whimsically.

Sister Berrach snorted loudly and pointed towards the abbey buildings.

'Should your Latin tag not be that from Terence – *veritas odium parit?*'

Fidelma's eyes widened slightly in amusement.

'Truth breeds hatred?' She glanced towards the abbey buildings. The abbess was engaged in heated argument with Brother Cillín. 'Ah yes. I am afraid that is the nature of truth because so many people seek to hide the truth from one another. But the greater hatred arises when the person has hidden the truth from themselves.'

Sister Berrach bowed her head in acceptance of the wisdom.

'I would like to thank you, Fidelma. Had it not been for you, I would also have stood falsely accused. Prejudice would have convicted me.'

'Heraclitus says that dogs bark at people they do not know.

Indeed, prejudice is but a child of ignorance. People often hate others because they do not know them. I cannot blame you, but you yourself did contribute something to that ignorance by playing the role others gave you instead of standing firm for yourself. You pretended that you were something of a simpleton, pretended to stutter, pretended to be uneducated and confined your reading to the hours when no one could observe you.'

'We cannot eliminate prejudice,' replied Sister Berrach, defensively.

'Knowledge is the one thing that makes us human and not simply animal. Sister Comnat will be looking for a new assistant librarian. If she had knowledge of your ability among books, Sister Berrach, I am sure that she would offer you that role.'

Sister Berrach responded with a wide smile.

'Then I will ensure that she has that knowledge.'

Fidelma nodded and then, glancing at Brónach, said softly: 'Your mother should be proud that you are her child, Sister Berrach.'

Sister Brónach's solemn face dissolved into awe.

'You know even that?' she gasped.

'If you had not demonstrated your maternity by the way you keep close to Berrach and help her, the stories that you both told me were enough. You told me that your mother was Suanach. You told me that you were a member of this community, disagreeing with your mother's adherence to the old ways. You came to this community, met someone and had a child. You felt you could not look after your daughter here and so you took her to your mother to be raised. Why did you find it so difficult to look after a child in this community? Because the child had physical problems which needed constant attention.'

Sister Brónach was pale but she held up her head defiantly.

'It is so,' she conceded. 'Tell me no more truth.'

Berrach was clinging on to her mother's arm.

'I have known for some time. You are right, sister. My father would not help Brónach look after me. Only my grandmother helped until I was three years old. She was fostering another child then, a child who was older than I was. That child was full of malice and jealousy and in a fit of rage slew my grandmother, leaving me almost helpless. Then Brónach defied my father's wishes and brought me back to the community and raised me – deformity and all.'

Sister Brónach grimaced.

'The condition was that I would never identify her father. I have kept to that condition. The knowledge would not add pleasure for Berrach.'

'I am happy in that ignorance,' Berrach assured her. 'It is no great loss.'

'What is ironic is that the child who killed my mother would be allowed to enter the community also and eventually became our abbess.'

'She will not be here for long. Neither will Sister Lerben,' Fidelma assured them.

Sister Berrach reached forward and clasped Fidelma's hand.

'But you will tell no one of our story?'

'No one,' Fidelma reassured the girl. 'Your secret is buried and forgotten, so far as I am concerned.'

Sister Brónach paused to wipe a tear from her eye.

'Thank you, sister.'

Fidelma held out her hands, taking Brónach's and Berrach's hands in each of her own.

'Care for one another, sisters, in the future as you have in the past.'

The canvas sail came cracking down the mast to fall into place. Ross watched his sailors with critical eyes as they swarmed up to secure it in place. A stiff winter wind was blustering across the inlet and bearing within its bosom snow squalls. The sky was almost black and the air was damp and chill, yet Ross was in no way perturbed at putting out to sea, in spite of the fact that even in this inlet the waters were choppy and the *barc* was bobbing to and fro alarmingly. Now the sails were finally in place, with Odar at the helm, the ship began to move forward at a cracking rate.

Sister Fidelma and Brother Eadulf stood on the stern deck with Ross. The two religious gripped the side rails to steady themselves, both jealous of the easy manner with which Ross stood by the helm, feet apart, balancing against the pitch of the deck. The burly seaman turned half apologetically to them.

'It will be rough for a while,' he called above the blustering wind, 'but it will ease when we have stood out to sea.'

Fidelma grinned at Eadulf's anxious face.

'I'd rather be at sea than confined further in the grim atmosphere of that abbey,' she replied as Ross turned to his other tasks

'I shall not be sorry to leave here either,' Eadulf confessed. 'It has not been the best of times.'

Fidelma glanced sympathetically up at him. Then her eye caught the sight of the tall Gaulish merchant ship, still bobbing at anchor, vanishing behind them in the inlet.

'I thought it was a mark of a fine man that Ross forwent his salvage on that ship and returned it to its Gaulish crew for their safe return home.'

'A pity Waroc was not with them. As I said, he was a brave man.'

'How long do you think that you will remain at Cashel?' Fidelma changed the subject abruptly.

'I am not sure. Until I hear from Theodore of Canterbury, I suppose.'

'I plan to spend some time at Cashel myself,' Fidelma remarked lightly. 'It is so long since my brother and I have had any time together.'

'You will want some rest after this,' agreed Eadulf. 'Plots and insurrections apart, the abbey of The Salmon of the

Three Wells seemed filled with vain, greedy and twisted people. It will be pleasant to be among friends.'

'You are too hard on them. Sister Comnat was an upright and sensible lady. And as for Brónach and Berrach ... they, at least, knew love and caring.'

'Yes. I felt sorry for them, especially.'

'Sorrow? No, I would have said envy was what one should feel for them. It is not given to many to give and receive an unselfish mother's love.'

Fidelma suddenly frowned and turned looking seaward, leaning on the ship's rail.

'I wonder if Brónach will ever tell her daughter the name of her father?' She had seen the pleading eyes of Brónach and obeyed that silent prayer not to utter the name of Febal. Perhaps it was as well.

Eadulf had not caught her words.

'What was that?'

Fidelma looked up at the tall Saxon monk and her face relaxed into a look of contentment.

'I am glad that you are coming to Cashel, Eadulf,' she said.

If you enjoyed this book here is a selection of other bestselling titles from Headline